ANIMAL STORIES

Other books for children by Walter de la Mare

ANIMAL STORIES

*chosen, arranged,
and in some part rewritten*

by

WALTER DE LA MARE

FABER AND FABER LIMITED

*3 Queen Square
London*

First published in 1939
by Faber & Faber Limited
3 Queen Square, London, W.C. 1

Second Impression 1945
Third Impression 1954
Fourth Impression 1959
Fifth Impression 1965
Sixth Impression 1972
Printed in Great Britain
at the University Press, Oxford

ISBN 0 571 06312 8

To

RICHARD II

CONTENTS

STORIES

CONTENTS

CONTENTS

CONTENTS

x

CONTENTS

xi

INTRODUCTION

The briefest, and certainly the most hopeful Introduction to any book I know is this old rhyme:

> Friend, if thou dost buy this book,
> Be sure that thou do on it look,
> And read it o'er, then thou wilt say
> Thy money is not thrown away.

No more *need* be said. What is good (and this volume is as full of good things as a plum pudding) requires little recommendation. What is bad deserves none. And any reader of the rhymes and stories in this Collection who has no wish or even dislikes to be told anything about them—facts, dates, origins and so forth—is entreated not to trouble himself any further with what

xiii

I have to say. He may much prefer to judge for himself what he reads, and that purely and solely on its own merits and graces. Indeed, he will probably have not stayed to consider my ardent invitation, but will at once have gone on to the fountain head—page 2.

Nevertheless, there are many extremely interesting questions in connection with many of the stories here. Some of them still lie beyond a complete and definite answer, others do not. I am venturing then to pass on a few crumbs of information which have come my way concerning them, and which perhaps will not have grown stale in the meantime. A little knowledge is, as we all know, a dangerous thing. My only hope is that the very little on this thorny subject that I possess myself is not already familiar to the reader, and is neither inaccurate nor indigestible.

There are scores of books and treatises on tales such as these. There are hundreds on folklore in general. The first translation of Grimm's "Household Tales" into English was made and published in 1823. This volume —*Popular Tales*—which contains notes, was reissued in 1925. Much later, a complete collection of the tales was translated and edited by Miss Margaret Hunt. It contains a Preface, packed tight with information, by Andrew Lang, and notes by Jacob Grimm himself. Last, there is a selection, also containing notes, entitled *English Fairy Tales*, made by Joseph Jacobs; and thoroughly, richly, and spicily English they are. These three volumes are mentioned merely as suggestions for further reading. Space would not permit the inclusion of many similar tales from all parts of the world—France, Italy, Russia,

Arabia; bushman's and Red Indian's. There is nothing, for example, from that gold-mine, the *Arabian Nights*. What I have to say now, then, in the hope that it will be of interest to the reader and neither too dull nor too dry, is no more than a directing fingerpost. The high road itself and its many byways await the adventurous.

EARLY LOVES

To begin with, then, many of these old tales, rhymes and jingles were either said or told to me, or read to me, for the first time when I was a small child. It was then I fell in love with them. Naturally, it never entered my mind in those far-off days that I should ever attempt to make my own versions of any of them. Few things have given me more pleasure; but if I have failed in the attempt, there is very little to be said in excuse.

A few tales towards the end of the book were written in recent years—"The Seal Man", for example, "Running Wolf" and "How the Manx Cat Lost Its Tail". Apart from the excellence of these tales in themselves, it is interesting, if one enjoys doing so, to compare them— their point of view, and the way in which they are told —with the rest. Old or new, both rhymes and stories have one chief and particular feature in common. In one way or another, they are about animals; but we shall come to *them* later.

I have included nothing that, for various reasons, would not, I am sure, have engrossed and delighted me when I was young, and nothing that does not continue to delight me now that I am old. So I hope it may be with every reader of them. It may be childish, or should

I say second-childish, to find myself as happy as ever in the company of Dick Whittington, the Three Bears, and the Man of Double Deed; laughing at the god-kittens' names in "ALL GONE", or sighing a sigh for the hundredth time over the death of poor Cock Robin. But there it is. For one thing, being of "advanced years" need not imply that one has forgotten what being young is like or means, or that one's thoughts and fancies and feelings resemble one's looks. That would be a gloomy thought indeed. After all, an infant only twelve hours old may *look* more ancient than an animated Egyptian mummy—as well as indescribably more beautiful. The acorn *is* the oak. There are old and elderly young people, there are remarkably young *old* people. And ours is a question that concerns the mind rather than the body.

My private impression, for what it is worth, is that in mind and in spirit we are most of us born (as it were) the age at which for the rest of our lives we are likely to remain. We have each of us been given our senses—sight hearing, taste, and the rest. These may be sure and keen, or not so. We have certain mental faculties and a certain amount of intelligence, which by experience, and by acquiring knowledge, we can practise and try to perfect to our heart's content. But there is a limit even to that, and it is doubtful if we can originate or acquire any more *intelligence,* or at any rate much more, than we were given to begin with. In that case, everything depends not only on the mind we may possess, but on the self that uses (or misuses) that mind.

Good nature, at any rate, need not wear out, nor good sense wear thin; and bad nature may wear *in*. Small

xvi

minds may become conceited, and that is a calamity;
sharp ones may become blunted; minds none too bright
already may be dimmed and dulled, or—with the help
of those who can "find out a way" with them—they
may be quickened and enlightened. In any case, a child
may be as new to the world as snowdrops in January, and
yet already have a good and keen and deep understanding, a full mind, and a hospitable heart. He (or she) may
be able to think hard, imagine richly, face trouble, take
good care of himself, and of others, keep well and live
abundantly. Men, great and small, were all once children. Horses were once foals, sheep lambs, and cats
kittens. That is certain. And although knowledge and
experience are of the greatest value, you cannot, except
in a folk-tale, spin gold out of straw; and good honest
straw is better than sham gold.

By God's grace, moreover, and here one may speak
with assurance for both young and old, there are many
things in life which, however familiar they may become
to us, however much accustomed we may be to them,
need never fail to interest, satisfy and give us pleasure—
things of the senses and the body, things of the mind and
the spirit. Not only is "a thing of beauty" a joy for ever,
but mere necessities may be so also—bread-and-butter
when we are hungry; water (and especially well or
brook water) when we are thirsty; apples and honey,
hawthorn and wild violets, Painted Lady and goldfinch,
pond and stream, the sea and its sand-dunes, snow and
ice, sunshine, moonshine, starlight, smells and colours,
games and talk, bed, sleep and dreams. Our pleasure and
interest in things like these need never grow stale, fail us,

cheat us or wear out. That will depend upon ourselves.
And so with these old tales and rhymes—with songs,
pictures, music, old buildings and so forth.

MERRY OR SAD

As with loved and valued old friends, we need never
weary of sharing them again, and of enjoying all they
are and mean to us. They come—like dew; they go—
like hoarfrost; and they come again—like the nightingale. Unless, as it very well may be at times, we are
tired out or in low spirits or in a bad or sullen temper,
they and all that resembles them have a curious power to
revive us, to set the heart beating, the wits working, the
fancy day-dreaming, the tongue wagging, the feet
dancing. Even a few words can achieve this, a few mere
broken scraps of rhyme. They sound like a cockcrow—
away out there in the mind. "Hey diddle diddle", for
example; "A dis, a dis, a green grass"; "Here we come
a-piping"; "Gay go Up and Gay go Down"; "Boys and
Girls come out to play". And, in another vein, "Spring,
the sweet Spring, is the year's pleasant king"; "My heart
leaps up when I behold A rainbow in the sky"; "To sea,
to sea! The calm is o'er".

Not that all good stories are gay stories. Mamillius,
the small boy in "The Winter's Tale", is asked, you will
remember, to tell the court ladies a story. "Merry or sad
shall't be?" he enquires, and then at once decides on a
sad one, as being best for winter; and he begins, "There
was a man dwelt by a churchyard." He knew that a
story need not consist solely of sugar and spice, jollity
and merriment. A headless doll, a broken toy—the mere

sight of which may have brought floods of tears to our eyes in early childhood—is not for that reason the less beloved in memory. So with a sorrowful, a tragic, even a terrifying tale, picture or poem. That too may feed the imagination, enlighten the mind, strengthen the heart, show us *ourselves*. It may grieve, alarm or even shock us, and still remain intensely interesting. Of its own grace and truth and value it will also comfort and console us— with what it recalls to memory of life itself, with what it creates in our minds, with the things, the scenes, the people in it; by the manner in which it reveals itself and its deeper meanings, by its very beauty and verbal music. A scrap of rhyme or of a poem, again, may affect us instantly in this fashion. "Poor Jinnie is a-weeping"; "Now the day is over"; "Ah! County Guy"; "Fear no more the heat o' the Sun"; "A widow bird sat mourning for her love Upon a wintry Tree"; "It was many and many a year ago".

So even things by no means sad or grievous in themselves may yet affect us sadly. We resemble looking-glasses in this world, reflecting all we see; but we are by no means always flattering glasses. We also reflect what we do *not* actually see. Most living things we welcome as bright and enlivening; but not all—not even all trees or birds or flowers: the deadly nightshade, the hemlock, the yew, the weeping-willow, the shriek-owl, the vulture. There are fresh green woods, and there are forests dark and menacing with their own night. There are merry, sunny, chattering brooks, and there are pools cold and stagnant under a waning moon. There are jolly little gigs and there are hearses; red cheeks and bones.

Watch then what sounds and words like those above and all that follows them do to you. They may make you sigh, even weep, but such sighs waste never a drop of blood, and some tears are refreshing. There are tales and jingles in this book fairly bubbling over with liveliness and high spirits, cram-full of nonsense and magic and heart's ease. They are no less closely packed with good sense, good nature and mother wit than a blue tit's nest is packed with eggs, and they with titlings. A few others—however "happy" the ending may be—are touched with the sorrowful and the forlorn, and tinged with dread and horror. But all this, too, is part of life. There are wagtail's eggs in a wagtail's nest, but one egg there may prove to be a cuckoo's. And in this world there are always owls and rats, weasels and small robbers about. "There was a man of *double* deed". If you feel you cannot endure to read a story that begins to make you either unhappy or afraid—turn over the pages and begin another.

I know of a little girl who would stop up her ears with her fingers and weep bucketsfull when she heard her father begin to sing-song "Dillie, dillie"—and yet would go on listening through the cracks! A very small boy may go shivering to bed after listening to the teeny tiny tale of the teeny tiny little woman who found a teeny tiny little bone in the churchyard. The very marrow in his bones may tremble at that final "TAKE IT!" Mine used to; and yet I delighted to have it told me again and again by my mother. Some stories, on the other hand, are a little too much for me even at my age. Much depends on how they have been told, and with what reason and intention. Still, even in my youngest days, I could easily manage to stare into Bluebeard's silent and dreadful cupboard, could watch the nail-pierced barrel containing the wicked queen go rolling down a steep place into the sea, and Great Claus's execution with his club. I could dance with Morgiana from oil-jar on to oil-jar as she dispatched the Forty Thieves; listen entranced to Falada's head, nailed up on the arch over the gateway, lamenting the misfortunes of his beloved mistress; gasp at the preparation of the ghastly soup in "The Juniper Tree"— and read on. I *enjoyed* these stories, knowing them to be stories, and I am as certain as can be that they did me not the least harm. On the other hand, I can recall one or two tales, of a different kind from these, which I detested, and still detest—anything concerned with deliberate cruelty, for instance. So far as I can remember, not one of these was a folk-tale.

Not that we are all of the same mind in this respect. Skins differ in thickness, and some hearts are more sensitive than others. There are people, too, who consider that sad stories, and any story that is in the least alarming, are bad for the young; and would even refuse them all fairy tales. They maintain that even fairy tales, one of the joys of my young life, only mislead us about the world of the actual, and that we should not be misled. I cannot believe that they do, and have not found it to be so. And speaking merely for myself, I am convinced that, after reading the stories I have mentioned, I was even less inclined as a child to approve of little-boy soup, to grow a blue beard, to help to burn a witch, or to turn to a jelly at thought of a ghost. Many young and imaginative children are afraid of being alone in the dark—a cupboard door ajar, a creaking staircase, an owl or a bat at the window, hobgoblins, nightmares. A small boy with tears rolling down his cheeks as he sat up on his pillow confessed to me once that he couldn't sleep for terror because there was a bear under his bed. To console him I assured him on my honour that there wasn't a real bear and certainly not an uncaged bear for miles and miles around.

"But you see, Daddie," he replied, "this isn't a 'real' bear!"

Where was I then! One method of losing one's fear of the dark, that may be worth passing on, is to become accustomed to playing games in it—the noble game of pretending to be Nelson, for example. I am speaking only of young children, of course; and this book is not intended for *them*. If you make-believe you are a hero, you cannot be less likely to become one. The bravest man is brave in spite of being afraid. Nor need the experience of fear (and certainly not of fear in the imagination) or the experience of feeling pain, be solely waste. Jam is good, and so is the powder that may be in it. Any such experience if it is not extreme stirs us up, adds to the joy of being bold or *out* of pain, helps us to understand and to sympathise with the fears and pains of others, and it may be an extremely vital and useful experience to recall in memory.

A FEW FACTS

But this is running far away from this book. And it is with the old tales and rhymes in it that we are now concerned. A few of these can be given dates. "The Three

Bears" for example (the wicked old woman in which is for some odd reason nowadays so often transformed into a nice little girl), is by Robert Southey, who was the author of "The Battle of Blenheim", "The Inchcape Rock", "The Life of Nelson", and many other books. He died nearly a century ago. His Bears live on.

"Puss in Boots", which with "The Sleeping Beauty", "Tom Thumb", "Cinderella" and other tales first appeared in France in 1697, is said to have been made up by "the little boy" of a poet named Charles Perrault—although papa must, surely, have had a busy finger in every one of that little boy's delicious pies, and although most of the fruit inside them (as with some of Hans Andersen's[1] stories) came from an apple-tree as thickly

[1] This famous prince of tale-tellers was the son of a shoemaker of Odense in Denmark; he died in 1875. Here is a glimpse of him, recorded by a young Englishman, Edmund Gosse, who met him about a year before his death. "Suddenly . . . as we were seated in the living room, there appeared in the doorway a very tall, elderly gentleman, dressed in a complete suit of brown, and in a curly wig of the same shade of snuff-colour. I was almost painfully struck, at the first moment, by the grotesque ugliness of his face and hands, and by his enormously long and swinging arms. . . . He immediately took my hand in his two big ones, patting and pressing it. . . . He had but to speak, almost but to smile, and the man of genius stood revealed. . . . All sense of shyness and reserve fell away. . . . He proposed to read to me a new fairy-tale he had just written. He read in a low voice, which presently sank almost to a hoarse whisper; he read slowly, out of mercy to my imperfect apprehension, and as he read he sat beside me, with his amazingly long and bony hand—a great brown hand, almost like that of a man of the woods—grasping my shoulder." This was the man who, like Lewis Carroll, is famous and beloved by children all over the world.

encrusted with moss and lichen as an old derelict ship is with barnacles.

The ripe and sober old *story* of Dick Whittington (the real Richard Whittington who was Lord Mayor of London town in 1396, 1397, 1406 and 1419, died in 1423) was not put into print until 1605, and the version of it to be found in this book was "cobbled up" by Joseph Jacobs out of "three chap-book versions". It is said that Dick's Cat was by no means the kind of cat that may look at a king, that has nine lives, and is killed not "by kindness" but by care. It was either a ship, like a Norwegian brig, which was called a cat, or the word itself came from *achat* meaning barter. It is certain that Charles Perrault's Cinderella's slippers were not made of glass—brittle stuff indeed to run down marble stairs in at midnight—but of fur. The word *vair* in the French having been mistaken for *verre*. Either way, cats in stories long before Dick Whittington made fortunes for their masters; and a story called "Ashputtel" also in this volume, and in many respects resembling that of Cinderella, was in being long before any fairy god-mother turned a pumpkin into a coach.

Of the rest of the older stories we do not know when they were first told, or by whom, or even their place of origin.

It is known, however, when practised writers and other people of culture and learning began to take an interest in them and to make use of them. Apart from still older chapbooks and broadsides, about the middle of the sixteenth century some of these tales, with others from Arabia, were collected by Margaret, Queen of

Navarre, in France; and by Giovanni Straparola in Italy. But their versions of them are not told barely and simply. The water from the folk wellspring is enriched and flavoured with so many rare meats, sauces, and condiments that the result more closely resembles a soup than anything out of a well. You may take a child's plain frock and trim it up with ribbons and laces and flounces and finery until it would be hard to tell where the frock itself leaves off and the frills begin. So with these Frenchified and Italianized versions. Mere ornament solely for its own sake, whether in a frock or a room or building, or in poetry and music, may be pretty enough and even beautiful in itself; but it may also be too ornate as well as unnecessary, or merely common and vulgar— in the usual meaning of these two words.

Later, there came a change in this point of view. A century or two ago certain learned philologists, lovers of language, who were keenly interested in the ways of thinking, the customs and habits of bygone times and peoples, realising that the genuine old tales were not only brimming over with life and beauty and imagination, but were also packed with evidence of ancient beliefs and superstitions, began to collect them, and having collected them, to arrange, classify, and compare them one with another. It was discovered that variants of the same story might be found in almost every language under the sun—Greek, Norse, Gaelic, Scottish, Egyptian, Finnish—and in almost every country in the world, from Zululand to Malay, from China to Peru.

How they had thus become "diffused", whether travellers in old times passed them on in their wanderings over the world, or they were made up and invented independently in the places in which they were found, is a question not even yet finally decided. It was thus, at any rate, that these folk tales in their truest and purest form first came into print.

Chief among these recorders and enquirers were two noble scholars, the brothers Grimm. They were born— Jacob in 1785, Wilhelm a year afterwards—at Hanau, near Frankfurt, in Prussia. And they went about from house to house, village to village, not duck-hunting or fox-hunting or collecting old furniture, but just tale-hunting. They listened patiently to any version of any old tale which they could persuade the country people to tell them. Word for word as the tales were told to them they wrote them down, just as more recently old folk songs have been taken down in England and Ireland.

Not of course that the tales so acquired were equally old, admirable, or well-told. There was one woman in particular, for example, the wife of a cowherd, to whose excellent memory and neat and artless tongue the Grimms owed some of the best of their finds. She was about fifty; she had "agreeable but somewhat resolute features" and bright penetrating eyes. Best of all, she had a vivid and delighted genius for sheer story-telling. First she would tell the whole story without a break, and exactly as the impulsive or chosen words might come. Then it was slowly repeated, and Jacob Grimm, then a young man in his later twenties, as slowly and steadily took it down. One or two stories in this book were so taken down in Scots or dialect. Given a little trouble by the reader, they are among the very best. So the "House-

hold Tales" came into the world, and the name of
Grimm to be blessed in every English nursery.

MÄRCHEN

The tales are of more than one kind. A good many are
known as Märchen—nursery tales. The most simple are
"penny plain" or "twopence coloured". Some of them
lead up to some scrap of worldly wisdom, a minute
lesson, even to a moral. In this they resemble the fables
of old Aesop (said to have been a hunchback) who lived
2,500 years ago. Some, like the absurd and charming
little tale of the Mouse, the Bird and the Sausage (called
Roundabout), or "The Three Little Pigs" leave what
small lessons they contain only hinted at. None is more
fantastical than "No-Beard". It is no more than a pack of
thumping taradiddles. But how quick and lively it all is.
With what clearness one sees the utterly absurd and impossible taking place before our very eyes—the small
bold widow-woman's son sleeping peacefully hung up
in space beside his fire of needle splinters; or even busily
knocking a hole in the ice with his snatched-off head. To
have a fancy as free and inventive as that! The Walrus
and the Carpenter met in this region of Nonsense:

> The sun was shining on the sea,
>   Shining with all his might:
> He did his very best to make
>   The billows smooth and bright—
> And this was odd because it was
>   The middle of the night . . .

The briefest tale of this kind I have ever seen is this:

INTRODUCTION

"Once upon a time there was a naked man, a blind man, and a lame man. The blind man saw a hare, the lame man ran and caught it, and the naked man put it in his pocket."

Many others, and only a hint or two of this appears in this book, are *fairy*-tales. Fairies: those exquisite, ageless un-human beings—Puck, Ariel, Queen Titania, the Silent Ones. Their many kinds are scattered all over the world, and haunted Salisbury Plain ages before the gigantic grey-wether or sarsen stones of Stonehenge were set up in circles with a vast monolith in their midst —the slaughter-stone—to mark where the first beams of the risen sun strike across the Plain on Midsummer Day. Frolic elves and sprites, pixie, bogle, nixie, changeling, fairies of the daybreak, of secret places, of subterranean caverns and the wild; their voices thin and sweet on the air; beings outlandish, strange and dangerous to miscreant or enemy—their name is Legion.

Even to taste of their food (as with that of the shades of the underworld) entails banishment from the life of man. How useless a question it seems, then, to ask anyone who is completely town-bred *and* slow of daydreaming, who can see only what is under his nose, who must touch to make certain of anything, who is contemptuous of what are called old wives' tales, who has never in the open been out alone with the dying, star-clustered moon, or been lost in a wood towards dusk, or listened among the rocks when the Atlantic breakers are pounding in at Spring tide, or ever even looked out of his window in the small hours across orchard and meadow, and away to hill and valley, when the last night lights are beginning to pale in the sky and the mists of daybreak still hide the voiceless birds—how useless it would be to ask *him* (or her) if he *believes* in fairies—as if they were cabbages or suet pudding, motor-cars or home-work. What is real need not be actual. We may believe in Angels, but we cannot incarcerate an Angel even in a Church.

MYTH AND SAGA

Quite another kind of story is of the "Saga" kind—a story of heroic trial and adventure, of deeds wild and strange and marvellous achieved by some renowned human in the mists of the distant past who, because of this wild and magic wonder, not only secured a niche in history but came to be thought of and told about as if he were half divine, or an actual deity. A deity who had come to earth to reveal himself and his divine grace and power in the affairs of men. A few of the constellations and of the brighter stars in the heavens are still named after these legendary or mythical heroes—Gemini, the heavenly twins; Perseus and Andromeda and Cassiopeia. And for company, they have English "Jack-by-the-middle-horse" in the northerly Plough.

Yet other stories, myths, as they are called, tell of similar mysteries, or of events beyond nature. By giving fancy names to the Sun and the Moon, to the Dew and the Spring, and to Time itself; or to the Spirits of the mountains, or the forests, or of well-springs and water-ways, they may put into the form of a tale thoughts, fancies, imaginations, legends concerning what happens around us every radiant day and every silent night of our lives. All primitive people appear to have invented or divined such myths—much as Perrault's little boy may have made up his "Tom Thumb"; much as many famous writers who, even when they were children, or at school, would invent stories to amuse their brothers and sisters or their schoolfellows after lights had gone out in the dormitories; and who went on telling stories to the very end of their days. It is a queer unaccountable habit when one comes to think of it, but how rich a blessing it has been for the rest of us. Walter Scott was one such boy. Late in life, in memory of the folk tales which he himself used to read to his children, he called his family cat Hinze. "I can perfectly remember," he says in a letter, "the nursery stories of my childhood, some of them distinctly, and others like the memory of a dream." But he took little pleasure in mere goody-goody stories. "Truth is," he said, "I would not give one tear shed over Little Red Riding Hood for all the benefit to be derived from a hundred histories of Jemmy Goodchild." He believed that these old wild tales, "like our own simple music," quite apart even from the delight they give, are of "wonderful good to the mind and the imagination".

After all, whatever we love dearly, whatever image in the mind sheds a deep and constant and inexhaustible blessing upon us, is touched with the divine in the same way as every saint or martyr is for those who believe in and treasure his goodness, his selflessness and sanctity.

We most of us refer to the Sun as He and to the Moon as She, just as we give names to dolls and objects and even to quite imaginary creatures (which we should delight to see with the naked eye as well as with the eye of fancy)—the Dryad sitting under her oak, or the Naiad asleep in her loveliness on the green banks of her stream. It is not only the small child who, for punishment, slaps the table against which it has bumped its head. To human ears the wintry wind sighs and laments; a brook chatters over its stones; the ebbing tide at twilight moans on the sea-shore; the meadows rejoice in Spring; the thunder raves; the morning stars sing together. I know (only too well) indeed of one particular grown-up who will kick the dumb and patient stool he has blindly stumbled over in the dark, and who, less stupidly, perhaps, believes—when he has bidden good-night to the room he has been sitting in, has put out the light and gone to bed—that he has left it to other and unseen company who, in their peace and gentleness, are as different from himself as a shadow is from that which casts it, and as light is from what it dwells on and gives beauty to. What is called Animism is simply this natural and instinctive inclination in human minds and hearts to give life and consciousness and feeling to that which may perhaps have none; a life which in respect to all animated Nature at least remotely resembles our own.

Everything, indeed, however much our senses can tell us about it, or we can read and learn about it, remains in the end a mystery—a pebble, for example, sea-rounded and millions of years old, an apple pip, a fly, a lock of hair; or, for that matter, a button or a penny whistle. The button, when we begin thinking about it, may lead us on into the complete theme of man and his astonishing clothes; the whistle into his music and into all the other arts. Ponder, meditate on any such thing, think of it and about it and into it as long and as hard as you like and can, you will never get to the final secret of it. No man even of the widest knowledge or science has yet. And even if at last you fancy you can fully explain it, you will not be able to explain it away; and even if you did, you would still have yourself to explain away too.

What we make up in our minds, then, can be as supreme a delight to us, can busy all our wits, all our learning and any wisdom we may have, and is just as much a mystery as everything that we have found "made up" for us already in the world around us. Life within us, life outside us, life beyond us—there is no end to any of them until the life, that is within us for earthly purposes, itself comes to an end: only to begin again, as it is believed.

ORIGINS

Now, going back to the nursery tales and the myths and sagas once more, even the most learned persons in languages, in folk-lore, in knowledge of primitive and savage customs and beliefs, have found it extremely difficult to decide which came first. Whether, that is, what had been passed down as ancient legend and adorned with glory and fantasy became in the course of time changed by the people into the Märchen and folk tales as we know them now, or whether on the contrary, tales told by the people came at last to be magnified and glorified into the myths and sagas. So long as we now have both safely in print, it does not to most of us greatly matter. But enquiring minds are made like that. They are as anxious and greedy for knowledge as a bee is for pollen and nectar. They ask questions and take infinite pains to find sufficing answers to them. They pine to get to the heart of things; with the ardent hope that it will be found still beating.

Possibly, and this is little more than guesswork, some myths became tales, and some old tales became myths. In either case, both are immeasurably ancient. Nine hundred and ninety-nine Methuselahs in a row would fail to recover the beginnings of them. For centuries on centuries—whether any such tale or rhyme was made up only for the delight of children (as mothers and fathers and nurses do still), or to amuse and interest other grown-ups—they were passed on from mouth to mouth by the common people, and even by primitive and pre-historic people.

Not that the word "common" is intended to suggest, as it so often does, what is of little value or account, or what is even worse than valueless. Far from it. It refers to those men and women who, in their natures, ways, and habits, and in their day's work—whether that was the keeping of flocks and herds, or hunting, or the growing of crops—were always by far the most numerous kind of people, and who even nowadays, although profound changes are taking place, are still the most numerous kind of people. Even the word *savage* is derived from a word meaning the woods or the woodland and the wild, and so was applied to the humans who lived in the wild, and who, in the eyes of the "civilised"—the book-learned, the city-bred and taught and mannered—are what wild flowers are by comparison with garden or cultivated flowers. Many of the wild flowers have been wooed by man's patience and ingenuity into other shapes and forms and tints and hues; and many of them have been enlarged. Not always to their own advantage —cup-and-saucer Canterbury bells, for example. It is a matter of taste. But leave them alone and they'll go home—back, that is, to the wild again and to their original nature. Nor were there any flowers even in the Hanging Gardens of Babylon or among the roses of Damascus, that, quite apart from the energy and mystery of life, can have been lovelier or more delicate or full of the energy of life than are many weeds.

It may help us to fancy ourselves no more than we need, to keep our heads and to refrain our hearts from excessive vanity over human triumphs in recent years, if we remember that, centuries hence, we ourselves may be considered as primitive people; and that we may then seem in much (if at any rate bad things in our own days are to be made better), little different from "savages" also. *Not* because we live wild and free in the green woodlands, but, on the contrary, are pent up among bricks and mortar, multitudes of us in the vilest slums, more or less in the service of the machines we have invented rather than being their masters, and by no means necessarily more intelligent or even more knowledgeable than the folk, the "common people", of by-gone times. There is book-learning, an excellent thing if we take advantage of it; there is also self-teaching. There is the knowledge that comes by watching and practice and doing things—a countryman's, say, who can neither read nor write. The ability to think and do and make things for ourselves, to rely on our own gifts and faculties is better than most things borrowed at second hand.

INTRODUCTION

If any one no further back than, say, our great grand-fathers could revisit this earth, and you could "take him round", he would of course be lost in wonder for a while at our cars and telephones, aeroplanes, submarines and radio—and human marvels they are indeed. All of them were novelties in my lifetime, and neither of the remote and frozen Poles had been "discovered" when I was a boy. But as soon as great-grandpapa had been told how they worked, and had become a little accustomed to them, there is much else that he would begin to wonder at—but on the other side of his face! The servitude, for example, in which so many "common" people in this world exist; the evil, monstrous, Satanic horrors of modern War.

That these stories continue to delight every imagina-tive child to whom they are told or read is proof of how little radical change—change down to the very *roots*—has taken place in the human mind (and body) over the centuries. Not long ago a small carved ivory head was dug up out of the earth—in Moravia, I think. It was computed to be between 20,000 and 30,000 years old. And what did the photograph I saw of it remind me of? Of a nightmare? Of a savage mask? Of a monkey? No, lovely and smiling, it reminded me of a charming niece!

Not long ago a great fish was hauled up alive out of the sea off the coast of Africa. It weighed about 120 lbs. In all its chief features it precisely resembled the fossil remains of one of its own species, and that species had been assumed until then to have been extinct for ten million years! This creature of the sea, then, had changed as little from its fossilised predecessor as, in essentials, we ourselves seem to have changed from the craftsman who cut out of ivory that small smiling face 20,000 years ago.

TALES ABOUT WHAT?

As has been said already, tales that have been told again and again through the centuries are apt at length to be worn down to their bare bones, so to speak. Very few words in them are wasted; nothing is mentioned that isn't positively part and parcel of the tale itself. And although we may feel sure that the teller of some particular tale must have known much else in relation to it, he has none the less refrained from saying it. Now and then it is clear that something has been left out or forgotten. In the tale called "Ashputtel", for example, we hear no more of the half-mad old king who was the cause of his lovely daughter's adventures. In general, the little that is said, gives us enough—and not another syllable—to tell the story *through*; whereas many of the stories of our own times often give a good deal more than we need. That is why it is difficult and dangerous to attempt to tell the old tales again in our own words.

It will be found, for example, in the very simplest and plainest of them, that few things—even the strangest or rarest or most beautiful—are *described*. Not with any fullness at any rate. In "The Ass, the Table and the Stick"—a tale, by the way, which is said by some to be a sun-myth—the magic table ("Table, be covered!" —and lo, a feast) is just a table. We are not told how big it is, what wood it is made of, what it looks like, or whether it is a plain deal table or a carved mahogany table. What I see myself is a *very* plain table. So, usually, with the houses, the palaces, the castles, the villages and woods and forests; and so with the kings and queens, the princes and the princesses. And in folk-tales these are as common as birds' nests in April. The castles, indeed, appear to be only a few miles apart. The kings are old or young, wise or foolish; they differ in what they do and how they do it. But that, again, is generally pretty nearly all that we are told about them.

If any king has three sons—his usual allowance—then the youngest, however unpromising he may be when the tale opens, is almost certain to have been proved the most adventurous and courageous and the luckiest of them when it ends. Sons or daughters, of blue blood or otherwise—it is almost invariably the youngest that comes off best. Craft and cunning may help to win him his reward; good-nature and truth and faithfulness of heart are more certain of it. But there are many degrees in this.

Things, again, generally go by extremes. A beautiful queen or princess is usually the most beautiful in the world—just that; no more, no less. And she is usually as good as her hair is golden. A wicked queen may also be beautiful, but she is wicked through and through; black—without tinge of grey or patch of white. And where do such things happen? The ass, the dog, the cock and the cat in "The Travelling Musicians", still brave and venturesome, however old and weary, are on their way to the old city of Bremen. The strange virgin with her host of mares, in the gipsy-story called "Tropsyn", dwells at the bottom of the Danube. These are exceptional. Actual places on the map are very seldom mentioned.

Then again, these tales are always of a "Once upon a time", of "Ages and ages ago". No dates are available. Time itself in them may go its usual pace, or very rapidly. The Poor Miller's Boy works for seven years for his Cat Mistress in her enchanted castle; and nothing alive in it but cats to be seen—no mice. But when his seven years are over they resemble a moment in a dream. Many of the tales themselves indeed resemble dreams. As for that completely mysterious thing called Magic, you can never tell in these stories where its wizardry and enchantments will begin, or end. But magic even in things of the mind seems nowadays to have gone out of fashion. Nevertheless it is a *kind* of magic of the mind to be able to delight in it in a story.

Above all, it must be remembered that, however real and actual the characters, scenes and events may seem to us as we read, these are tales of the *imagination*. Up to a point and within their own framework they are reasonable enough; but it is a wild reasonableness, like the beauty of flowers in a hedgerow, like the wigwam of a Red Indian, the ice-hut of an Eskimo. Whether we can accept what they tell us, whether we delight in them or not, depends, then, on how much imagination we have ourselves. It would be merely ridiculous to say that such and such a thing in them cannot have *happened*. It cannot have happened, perhaps, in our world of the actual. But theirs is not a world of the actual. It is a world imagined, and it is made to happen there.

INTRODUCTION

This is certainly true in regard to some of the animals in them. And ours are Animal Stories. In the times when they were first told, there must have been as many birds, beasts, fishes and creeping things in the world as there are at present. Roughly there are about 200,000 different kinds of animals now named and classified by man, not to mention about a million varieties of insects—creatures with no more than six legs. In the tales, very few indeed of these are mentioned; and there would still be very few even if all the old folk-tales with animals in them from every country in the wide world had been included in this book.

On the other hand, and again in view of the age of these stories, it is remarkable that in most respects the animals in them differ scarcely at all from our own ideas of them—except when by a secret enchantment some unfortunate prince or princess, as in "The Queen Bee", or Cherry in "The Frog-Bride", has been changed into one. The fox in "The Golden Bird" is crafty enough in his dealings with the two kings, one of whom owns the Golden Bird, and the other the Golden Horse; but good sense and kindness are his chief characteristics. With certain sharp exceptions, the other animals do as they would be done by. They come, as every decent creature should, to the rescue of any human friend in need.

None the less, nowadays we seem in some ways, and expecially in fellowship, to be a little *less* close to the living creatures around us than were these old tale-tellers. As with the cat and white mice and canaries which I have seen living together in peace (it seemed) in the same cage, man, animal and bird seem with them to have been more of a "happy family". One might have expected the contrary. Just as men did of old, we keep, of course, many animals and birds almost solely for our own use and service—the hen for her eggs, the gentle cow for her milk, the sheep for her wool, the turkey for Christmas. We also store them alive, so to speak, for food. Some we "break in". Animals have not as yet so treated man.

What about our wild animals? Well, it is said that if the fox, the otter and the badger were hunted no more in England, she would soon have no foxes, otters[1] and badgers left. Still, it would be Man who would be responsible for "killing them off". His destruction has been enormous, either for the purpose of trade, or for mere amusement. Many strange and lovely living creatures are no longer to be found in freedom, only in captivity—the European bison, the white rhinoceros, the kiwi, the platypus, the giant tortoise. Even the gorilla, and that old Man of the Woods, the orang-outang, are in danger. Others are gone for ever—the dodo, the quagga, the auroch, the moa, the passenger pigeon and the great auk, among them. No fewer than seven kinds of birds, including the exquisite spoonbill, osprey and ruff, have abandoned this "emerald isle" of ours—and the last century has been the most destructive. "The stories of the pioneers"—in lands then strange to civilized man—"read like fairy tales or accounts of the

---

[1] A fascinating account of the *life* of the otter will be found in Mr. Henry Williamson's *Tarka*—and of that of the salmon, the otter's prey, in his *Salar*.

Garden of Eden." Man "is the greatest of all hunters";
he is also one of the very few animals that hunts solely
for pleasure. We must try not to be sentimental or
hypocritical. I confess that I devour my leg of mutton,
wear wool, loathe flies, not merely look askance at a
mosquito, and can sit for hours watching a float gently
bobbing about in a pond, so long as there may be a fish
in it, and there is the least chance of a "bite".

But whatever our feelings towards our fellow creatures may be, and whether or not we take continual
pleasure in them, we can ask ourselves two small questions. First, what difference to our life on earth would it
make if nothing were left alive on it but the "vegetable
kingdom" and ourselves? Is it even imaginable? Next,
and contrariwise, how much difference would it make
for us if we were "friends with" every living thing that
meant us no harm, and were no longer distrusted, feared
or dreaded by any? An entrancing difference, surely?

> He prayeth best, who loveth best
> All things both great and small;
> For the dear God, who loveth us,
> He made and loveth all.

That, as we all know, is the simple "moral" of one of the
loveliest and most magical poems in the language—
about a sailor, and his remorse:

> God save thee, ancient Mariner,
> From the fiends, that plague thee thus!—
> Why look'st thou so? "With my crossbow
> I shot the Albatross."

INTRODUCTION

Like the animals, we all of us have instincts of many kinds: the instinct to preserve our own lives, to love, to have children, to care for them, to make ourselves shelters, houses for refuge, to flock and live together, and to take pleasure in solitude. Like the animals, we keep more or less true to kind—but hardly by our own efforts. Apart from the apes and the monkeys, their outward appearance is very different from our own, and it is often enchantingly beautiful—Solomon in all his glory was not arrayed like one of these. But there is little difference inside. They have hearts and lungs and brains. They have a nervous system which is infinitely complex in its workings but which serves (as does ours) the simple purpose of being of sovereign use to its owner. They share our senses—a sight, exquisite for its own purpose (imagine an owl's or an eagle's or a mackerel's or a dragon fly's), a hearing quick and alert for the faintest *Cave* of danger. Their noses—a dog's, for example—defy our competition. For the most part, and of their own will, all creatures of Nature fend for themselves, keep fit and well, and spotlessly clean into the bargain. At certain seasons one would expect them to become hopelessly "dull boys". Watch, indeed, any small bird in the nesting season—a chaffinch or a long-tailed tit, collecting her host of tiny feathers; a swallow hawking the air from dawn to dusk for her young; a robin steadily hunting for and devouring daily many times his own weight in food to keep himself alive; a bat fluttering swiftly at dead of dark through the twigs of an apple tree. The spider's web, the bees' hive, the badger's earth, the mole's run, the beaver's dam, the bower-bird's mansion, the stickleback's nursery, and a host of similar devices among the insects fill us with admiration. And in much most of them resemble many of our own. And what of the mysteries of migration—the swift, the cuckoo, the eel and the salmon? Such activities as these, it is said, are the outcome of instinct.

In consciousness, on the other hand, and in the working of our minds, we differ widely, it is generally supposed, from other living creatures. We grieve and fret over our losses and troubles, it seems, far more than they do—though a cow deprived, as it usually is, of its calf, can keep us awake at night for hours with her lowings; and a swallow robbed of her nestlings *appears* to be less happy than usual. We seldom cease to take thought for the morrow. We are continually, that is, thinking of and imagining the "future"; and often distress ourselves with difficulties and troubles that never come. Not so, it is supposed, with the animals—although sheep grow restive when they come within scent of a slaughterhouse, and a dog uneasily eyes his master when he has done amiss. We, above all, have our souls to save. They, it is thought, have none.

INTELLIGENCE

Apart from instinct, there is the problem of intelligence—an abstruse one. In general we test any other intelligence than our own *by* our own. What other method is practicable? But the tests vary. We teach, or "learn" animals "tricks"—and, if they have intelligence, silly tricks many of them must seem—a dog to beg, (cocker spaniels, it seems, beg by instinct); a horse, noble and beautiful creature, to stand up in the shafts of a cart on his hind legs to "drink beer like a man"; a seal to play at ball; an elephant, gentle and sagacious monster, to perform on the drum and the cymbals. And we reward this one with a lump of sugar and that with a bottle of hay. An old rhyme in this book, "The World Turned Upside Down", has a word or two to say on this.

But much that they know or teach themselves is beyond our comprehension—especially the insects, as Miss Eleanor Doorly's book on the work of Henri Fabre vividly shows. But for a fairly common example, how does a thoroughly domesticated cat, after it has been carried off, shut up in a basket, a great distance over country completely strange to it, contrive to return home again, perhaps as sprightly as ever, or emaciated and all but dead. In this it shows a homing instinct, which is shared by nearly every small boy at a boarding-school. But what was the creature's method? A cat, a few years ago, was so taken from Exmouth many miles north. In a few days, back she safely came again, having crossed two moors, and either passed through or round the great city of Exeter on her way. *Can* she have asked that way of her fellow cats?[1]

[1] Every cat that has consented to live with me I have easily persuaded to leap on to my shoulder and then walk along my arm for a tit-bit of meat or cheese held in my fingers. Any lively house cat can be taught little tricks and feats by its "owner". The contrary is unusual. Here are a few sentences from a story called "Broomsticks" about a cat called Sam.

"Like most cats who live under the same roof with but one or two humans he had always appeared to be a little more sagacious than cats of a larger household. He had learned Miss Chauncey's

There are innumerable accounts of animals such as these to be found in print, which are intended to prove

ways. He acted, that is, as nearly like a small mortal dressed up in a hairy coat as one could expect a cat to act. He was what is called an intelligent cat. But although Sam had learned much from Miss Chauncey, I am bound to say that Miss Chauncey had learned very little from Sam. She was a kind, indulgent mistress; she could sew, and cook, and crochet, and make a bed, and read and write and cipher a little. And when she was a girl she used to sing 'Kathleen Mavourneen' to the piano. Sam, of course, could do nothing of this kind. But then, Miss Chauncey could no more have caught and killed a mouse or a blackbird with her five naked fingers than she could have been Pope of Rome. Nor could she run up a six-foot brick wall, or leap clean from the hearth-mat in her parlour on to the shelf of her chimney-piece without disturbing a single ornament, or even tinkling one crystal-drop of her lustres against another. Unlike Sam, too, she could not find her way in the dark, or by her sense of smell; or keep in good health by merely nibbling grass in the garden. If, moreover, she had been carefully held up by her feet and hands about a yard above the ground and then dropped, she would have at once fallen plump on her back, whereas when Sam was only three months old he could have managed to twist clean about in the air and come down on his four feet, as firm as a table. . . . Quite early in life he had learned to know his meal-times—though how he told them was known only to himself, for he never appeared even to glance at the face of the grandfather's clock on the stair-case. He was punctual, particular in his toilet, and a prodigious sleeper. He had learned to pull down the latch of the back door. He never slept on Miss Chauncey's patchwork quilt unless his own had been placed over it. He was fastidious almost to a foppish degree in his habits, and he was no thief. He had many kinds of mew, with different meanings. Not, of course, that the creature talked *English*."

One morning, in my garden, many years ago, I stood watching an exquisite spider's web, and in curiosity put a tiny scrap of paper into it. Its owner rushed out, stayed, examined it, and cut it out of its web. So with a second scrap. The third—or fourth—it merely examined and then retired. I then scattered about half a how active and ready an intelligence they appear to possess. But caution is always needed—to make sure.

dozen scraps of paper on to the web and went in to lunch. When I returned, every scrap had been cut out and the web had been repaired. I have often wondered whether, if some prodigious monster began throwing stones through my window, I should act (given the courage) any differently—but with the help of a glazier! "Dr. Moschkau fed a spider several times a day with flies held in a forceps. At first the spider took the fly timidly and hurriedly. Latterly it seized it boldly and with confidence. On one occasion the doctor in sport took away and returned the fly which the spider had seized. The spider was annoyed and sulked. On another occasion he completely removed the fly. This broke up the friendship. On the following day the spider refused to accept a fly from him, and on the third day it disappeared.*" As for the ants: "Ants clean and groom each other; they ventilate their dwellings and remove from them everything which is calculated to make them unsanitary. Thus they carry off their dead, and whatever is likely to decay, to a distance. In collecting seeds for food they not only pick them off the ground, but they ascend plants, shrubs, and trees, and harvest them. In these operations they sometimes throw them down to be picked up by others in preference to ascending and descending themselves, and so save time and tissue. If certain of the seeds become damp they take them out of the nest and dry them. It is even stated that they sow seeds, and raise near their nests a plant known as 'ant rice', of which they are very fond. Ants make pets of small beetles and crickets." They keep and milk green fly, and carry them in their mandibles to new shoots in plants to pasture. "They cross small rivers by the aid of tiny pieces of wood, which they employ as rafts.*" Would that some kindly visitor from Mars would come and tell us of our own little intelligent ways and habits. "What a piece of work is a Man! How noble in reason! how infinite in faculty . . . in apprehension how like a god! the beauty of the world! the paragon of"—"animals! . . ."

*This comes from a book welling over with fascinating knowledge, entitled *Design in Nature*.

For this reason, methodical, patient and precise experiments and tests have been made—like those of the king in "Cherry", with his three sons. In a book entitled *Animal Intelligence*, Professor Edward Lee Thorndike tells us of his own. The difficulty, he declares, of studying the workings of the minds of animals "exists only in the case of their consciousness". We *cannot*, alas, share that. "Their *behaviour*", on the other hand, is often far easier to study than that "not only of children but of adults". He devised ingenious boxes with a variety of contrivances—loops of string or of wire, wooden movable buttons, latches, loose bars and so forth—by which any live creature shut up in them, cat or dog or monkey, might at length manage to set itself free. He steadily observed his animals, thus engaged, and, watch in hand, took notes. After studying the careful, laborious and exact records which he made of these tests, I began to ponder. Supposing, I thought, I were myself shut up (by one of the larger apes, let us say) in a room containing, as the only means of getting out of it, contrivances *utterly strange* to me—whether clockwork, magnetic or electrical, perhaps—how long should *I* remain in captivity? I wonder.

"Never," says Professor Thorndike, "will you get a better psychological subject than a hungry cat." And he concludes his intensely interesting book as follows:

"Nowhere more truly than in his mental capacities is man a part of nature. His instincts, that is, his inborn tendencies to feel and act in certain ways, show throughout marks of kinship with the lower animals, especially with our nearest relatives physically, the monkeys. His sense-powers show no new creation. His intellect we have seen to be a simple though extended variation from the general animal sort. This again is presaged by the similar variation in the case of the monkeys. Amongst the minds of animals that of man leads, not as a demi-god from another planet, but as a king from the same race."

That being so, it is a thousand pities, surely, that this "king" is not on far better and friendlier terms with his subjects. For the most part they give him little trouble, and if they do give trouble, it is usually because they are intent, as a bee-keeper with his hives, on sharing the good things which he wishes to keep for himself. Not that a fox is always satisfied with but one pullet for supper! How seldom they revolt and rebel. Indeed, if ever even some of the most minute creatures around us had the power to plot man's overthrow—then woe be-tide him! Mr. H. G. Wells's *The Food of the Gods* has a good deal to say about this.

Watch a "wild" animal, as far as you can, following its own ways and habits. Imagine what a joy it would be if, in wood or field or garden, a rich and genuine friend-liness were the rule between yourself and it; and if it could, as far as nature allows, share your mind to the extent to which, as far as nature and a generous heart allows you, you *might* learn to share *its*. Imagine a traveller who, from infancy had never lifted his eyes on any living creature except man, and who, on ascending a little hill, suddenly discovered himself looking down upon—well, let us say, the Garden of Eden: with its multitudes sharing that little universe of beauty together, and at peace. It was a celestial spectacle reserved for two innocents—Adam and Eve. Of one thing, at any rate, we can be positively certain: namely, that, with very few exceptions—a tiger in the kitchen, say, a boa constrictor in one's bed, or a scorpion in one's shoe (unusual little experiences all three)—we shall never regret having spared the life of the least of living creatures, or be sorry for having shown kindness to one in need. Two old men, great in heart, and of a rare genius, once confided in me —and I feel sure that neither would mind my passing this on—that on one thing in their lives in particular each looked back with unchanging sorrow and regret. One of them as a small boy had been cruel to a cat; the other had been unkind to a younger child. Well, turn home: the heart knoweth its own secrets.

And now, once more, to come back to this book. Whatever our own "views" concerning God's living, mysterious and wonderful creatures may be, there is no doubt what the folk, the tellers of these old tales, thought and felt about them. The animals in them, the birds, even the bees and ants, each in its own kind, act very much as humans would if they were in their skins. They are each of them given *man's* intelligence in a certain degree—his common sense, wisdom, courage and enterprise, his heart and feelings; or his stupidity, greed, guile and craft. The wolf is a wolf with, as it were, a wolfish man inside him. Tropsyn, the colt, adorable creature, is a horse like a young hero. *And* practically every animal is endowed with the gift of human speech.

INTRODUCTION

That many, if not all, creatures of any particular kind by some means contrive to communicate *one with another* is at any rate probable, and this not only by means of their voices. Indeed, our own faces and gestures often reveal even more than do the words that go with them; as also does the intonation or the spoken tune in which we say anything. Nevertheless, no ape, no dog, no cat, no horse, no elephant, no eagle, no wren, no frog, no bee has ever learned or been taught to talk a human language. Not that I am aware of. Certain birds, it is true—parrots, magpies, jackdaws and budgerigars—may learn to mimic a few words, even a small sentence. A hoary old parrot or cockatoo may even appear to know what the words it mimics mean. It may repeat, not wholly "parrot-fashion", its bits of sentences at appropriate moments—*"Poor Robin Crusoe!"* But this is leagues away from their being able to converse with us freely in our own vulgar tongue.

On the other hand, apart from *Gee—Whoa;* Good *dog; Sook, Sook; Gag gag; Dill dill; Puss, Puss,Puss,* and many other calls and biddings shared between animals and those in charge of them; and apart perhaps from rudiments of a monkey-language, man, so far as I know, has never been able to master any code of communication, noises, touchings, signs, odours, telepathy and so forth that animals *may* use among themselves. Although we might perhaps do a little better if we could observe them with more affection, patience, intelligence and modesty. How often we hear it said of a beloved dog or cat: "He understands everything I say." Now in these tales, as we

1

know, nearly *all* the animals have this priceless gift of human speech. And uncommonly good use they make of it.[1]

Not only do they talk—and, if need be, insects, birds and even trees also—but each animal, whatever its own kind and species may be, talks to some extent in his or her own particular fashion. Just as we do ourselves. Each is what we call in a book a "character". Take the cats. And I could never weary of them. Nine cats at least flourish in the following pages. But what subtle and delicious differences there are between them.

Dick Whittington's cat, for example, is simply a cat, no more and no less; a house or kitchen cat, made use of by Dick as a garret cat; but also a cat born lucky and one that brings good—amazingly good luck to its owner. This cat, the most famous in English history, utters never a word. The cat in "The Three Children of Fortune" merely wails "Miaow, miaow, miaow, miaow!" as most cats will, at need. As for the perpetual feud

---

[1] It is curiously interesting to observe that in the Bible only two creatures reveal this faculty—of speech with humans. One of them is a—is *the*—Serpent: a creature "more subtil than any beast of the field which the Lord God had made". The other is a beast that is usually and falsely regarded as the most stupid, and the most stubborn—the ass. And Balaam's ass began to speak because neither his master nor the two servants who were with him had the eyes to see, as she could, that an angel was standing in their way—"in a path of the vineyards, a wall being on this side, and a wall on that side". "What have I done unto thee," said she, "that thou hast smitten me these three times?" Alas, how many a jackass and jenny since then, if they too had the ability to address *their* Balaams, would have had to change the "three" to "three-thousand".

between cats and mice, it is at least as old as the Ark. "All gone" and a few rhymes deal with that. False, treacherous Sly-boots has a tongue like a Siren's—so long as it suits her purpose.

The cat in "Puss in Boots" is a sort of fine relation of these other cats; just as the worn-out yet fiery old mouser in "The Travelling Musicians" is their poor relation. Miss Young's Manx cat actually goes back to the Ark— and where would all the cat-tribe ever since have been without her? But the two very queer cats in "Knurre-Murre" are of quite another kin. One is a fairy off to her sister's funeral; and the other a sweetheart avoiding his own. Still, all in their measure and degree, these cats keep true to kind. True, that is, to the cat that drowses half the day away on our footstool in front of the fire, and who, on waking, would, we may be certain, indulge in a real secret talk with any human worthy of her if only that human had the sense and skill to follow her private language. Alas and alas, none has.

Next to the cats come the foxes; and these too keep true to our usual notions of them and to kind. One (like the mouse in "All gone") is not quite crafty enough to have avoided accepting as a fine friend a wolf that turns out to be a stupid and pitiless glutton and at last comes to a bad end. One—of Cocky-locky and others—makes a more than usually hearty meal; and another is still left waiting for one—for a *Michaelmas* feast. There is a none too "happy pair" of foxes in a very short story called "Mrs. Fox", but it leaves us with a perfectly happy married-again widow; and there is a certain "Mr. Fox", who is both Fox by name and (since he is human and should know better) a murderously crafty fox by nature. Most enchanting of all, there is the fox in "The Queen Bee", gentle, sagacious, steadfast and kind. But *he* is waiting to die in order that he may rise again and reveal himself for what he is. And so with the rest—horse, ass, dog, hare, hedgehog, duck and ant. Most of them have been old friends of mine since I was seven. In the same tones as then the spectral voice of Falada echoes under the gateway in "The Goose Girl"; and precisely the same rousing *Hee Haw* in "The Four Musicians" still deafens my ears as I listen, just as it did of old.

How very pleasant it would be if we could borrow one of the many old castles and palaces in these tales and there feast and fête these enchanting, enchanted creatures one and all, not excluding even the venomous dragon in "The Bad Mother" or "that" whose hidden name was Tom Tit Tot. The kings and queens and all the royal families should be of the party; and even the wicked queens, returned from their ashes, might give a little salt to such a feast! It is astonishing, indeed, how, one by one in the later stories, these heartless, soul-less She's, queenly or common, come to the same appalling end—the stake. Only one He shares a *similar* fate—he is boiled in milk. And yet—such is the way of the imagination—however evil they may be, and cruel and pitiless, they come to life again in our minds whenever we read again what is told about them.

THE CUTS

And last, the pictures, the wood-cuts. These are from Edward Topsell's *Historie of Foure-footed Beastes,* which was published in 1658. I have chosen them not merely for their own sake, but also because it is interesting and amusing to see what the craftsman responsible for them fancied certain animals looked like—animals which he surely can never have actually seen. Also because some of them are as pure inventions of his fancy and imagination as are the animals that talk in the tales.

Such horrors, for example, as the Hydra, destroyed by Hercules, of which Topsell, after a lengthy description of it, sagely remarks: "that there should be such a serpent with seven heads, I think it un-possible". Or, again, the dragon (beloved by the Chinese), of which Topsell says, "there were great plenty of these in Egypt in the time of King Ptolemy, which were taught to leap, play, and dance, at the hearing of musicke, and in many poore mens houses they served instead of servants for diversions". And, again, the unicorn; of which he says, "By the Unicorne wee do understand a peculiar beast, which hath naturally but one horne, and that a very real one." The unicorn, indeed, needs a complete book to itself, and that book has been supplied by Mr. Odell Shepard, who knows no less about these fabulous and mythical creatures than the Pied Piper knew about rats. And last, the salamander. "Some do affirme that it is cold Ise . . . and that it walketh in the fire and extinguisheth it not." Well, even so recently as the sixteenth century, the exquisite artist, Benvenuto Cellini, was given in his childhood a sound thrashing by his father in order that he should remember to the end of his days having seen this little animal disporting itself in the flames.

These creatures may be of man's invention. There is yet

another kind of animal, *not* pictured in these cuts, concerning which only its bones or its fossil or frozen remains give us any information; animals that flourished untold ages ago, and are now extinct. The Mammoth, for example, a gigantic elephant, one-third again greater in stature than the largest elephant, Asian or African, alive, and about twice its weight; its tusks twelve feet long. It was shagged with long black hair and reddish wool. There was the Dinotherium, also trunked like an elephant, but with tusks drooping downwards, and resembling a hippopotamus, a tapir and a dugong, all three. Once upon a time, again, a "time" even beyond the very furthest "Once upon a time" of these tales, there flourished a monster reptile whose mere thigh-bone was over twelve feet in length; and the Pterodactyl, a winged and fingered lizard, from thirty to forty yards long from tip of snout or beak to tip of tail.

Iced carcases of some of these ancient creatures have been found in Siberia, still fresh—a dainty coveted and devoured by their discoverers. Chiefly, as we know, we learn of them solely from their bones. In the same manner, if you yourself chanced on a human skull on the shingled beach at Dunwich in Suffolk, whose seven or more churches, it is said, now lie—their bells numbly tolling in a storm—under the sea; or that of a rabbit, bleaching on the turf of a cliff in Cornwall or Pembrokeshire among the sea pinks and the harebells, you might at glimpse of each put together, as it were, in fancy, the whole skeleton of a man or of a rabbit. But you could no more than guess at the colour of that man's eyes, the skill of his hands, how quick his brains were, and

lv

whether he loved his children or hadn't any children to love. All his bones, that is, and the rest of him would be purely imaginary. And so we ourselves are, to *them*, when we are absent from our friends.

So much for the mammoths that have gone, have died out for ever; including even perhaps that enormous fowl, the Roc, to whose claws Sindbad, in the *Arabian Nights*, tied himself with his scarf in order to escape from the sand-dry Valley of Diamonds. Marvellous, indeed, is man's Imagination. It ranges this way and that in Time, and to the very ends of the universe. With love and faith to aid him, it would save him from most of his miseries. With it, and with his own desire for goodness, he could, by the mercy of God, build his world anew. In their own primitive, queer, various, exquisitely simple, or rich and fascinating fashion, these ancient tales build *their* world anew. But not a syllable of their magic will be audible unless the right kind of ear is bent to attend to their spell.

ANIMAL STORIES

"UNDERNEATH"

Underneath this hazelin mote,
There's a braggoty worm with a speckled throat;
   Nine double is he:
Now from nine double to eight double,
And from eight double to seven double,
And from seven double to six double,
And from six double to five double,
And from five double to four double,
And from four double to three double,
And from three double to two double,
And from two double to one double,
And from one double to no double,
    No double hath he!

THE HARE AND THE HEDGEHOG

Early one Sunday morning, when the cowslips or paigles were showing their first honey-sweet buds in the meadows and the broom was in bloom, a hedgehog came to his little door to have a look at the weather. He stood with arms akimbo, whistling a tune to himself—a tune no better and no worse than the tunes hedgehogs usually whistle to themselves on fine Sunday mornings. And as he whistled, the notion came into his head that, before turning in, and while his wife was washing and tidying up the children, he might take a little walk into the fields and see how the young nettles were getting on. For there was a tasty beetle that lived among the nettles; and no nettles—no beetles.

Off he went, following his own little private path into the fields. And as he came stepping along around a bush of blackthorn, its blossoming now over and its leaves showing green, he met a hare; and the hare by the same chance had come out early to have a look at his spring cabbages.

The hedgehog bowed and bade him a polite "Good-morning". But the hare, who felt himself a particularly

3

fine sleek gentleman in this Sunday sunshine, merely sneered at his greeting.

"And how comes it", he said, "that *you* happen to be out so early? I always supposed you were one of these night-creepers."

"I am taking a walk, sir," said the hedgehog.

"A walk!" sniffed the hare. "I should have thought you would use those bandy little legs of yours to far better purpose."

This angered the hedgehog, for as his legs were crooked not by choice but by nature, he couldn't bear to have bad made worse by any talk about them.

"You seem to suppose, sir," he said, bristling all over, "that you can do more with your legs than I can with mine. We both have four."

"Well, perhaps," said the hare, airily.

"See here, then," said the hedgehog, his beady eyes fixed on the hare, "I say you *can't*. Start fair, and I'd beat you in any race—nought to ninepence. Ay, every time."

"A race, my dear Master Hedgehog!" said the hare, laying back his whiskers. "You must be beside yourself. It's crack-brained. It's *childish*. But still, what will you wager?"

"I'll lay a Golden Guinea to a Bottle of Brandy," said the hedgehog.

"Done!" said the hare. "Shake hands on it, and we'll start at once."

"Ay, but not quite so fast," said the hedgehog. "I have had no breakfast yet. But if you will be here in half an hour's time, so will I."

The hare agreed, and at once indulged in a little frisky

4

practice along the dewy green border of the field, while the hedgehog went shuffling home.

"He thinks a mighty deal of himself," thought the hedgehog on his way. "But we shall see what we *shall* see." When he reached home he bustled in and, casting a solemn look at his wife, said:

"My dear, I have need of you. In all haste. Leave everything and follow me at once into the fields."

"Why, what's going on?" says she.

"Well," said her husband, "I have bet the hare a Golden Guinea to a Bottle of Brandy that I'll beat him in a race, and you must come and see it."

"Heavens, husband!" Mrs. Hedgehog cried. "Are you daft? Are you gone crazy? You! Run a race with a hare! And where's the guinea coming from?"

"Hold your tongue, woman," said the hedgehog. "There are things simple brains cannot understand. Leave all this fussing and titivating. The children can dry themselves; and you come along at once with me." So away they went together.

"Now," said the hedgehog, when they had reached the ploughland beyond the field which was sprouting with young green wheat, "listen to me, my dear. This is where the race is going to be. The hare is over there at the other end of the field. I am going to arrange that he shall start in that deep furrow, and that I shall start up there beside him in this one. But as soon as I have scrambled along a yard or two and he can't see me, I shall turn back. And what *you*, my dear, must do is this: When he comes out of his furrow *there*, you must be sitting puffing like a porpoise *here*. And when you see

5

him, you will say, 'Ahah! so you've come at last?' Do you follow me, my dear?"

At first Mrs. Hedgehog was a little dense because she was so nervous, but she was amused at her husband's cunning, and gladly agreed at last to do what he said.

The hedgehog then went back to where he had promised to meet the hare, and he said, "Here I am, you see; and very much the better, sir, for a good breakfast."

"Indeed," simpered the hare scornfully. "How shall we run? Down or over; sideways, longways; two, three or four legs? It's all one to me."

"Well, to be quite candid with you," said the hedgehog, "let me say this. I have now and then watched you taking a gambol and disporting yourself with your friends in the evening, and a very dainty and pretty runner you are. But you never keep *straight*. You all go round and round, and round and round, scampering now this way, now that and chasing each other's scuts as if you were crazy. And as often as not you run uphill! But you can't run *races* like that. You must keep straight, you must begin in one place, go steadily on, and end in another."

"I could have told you that," said the hare angrily.

"Very well, then," said the hedgehog. "You shall keep to that furrow, and I'll keep to this."

And the hare, being a good deal quicker on his feet than he was in his wits, agreed.

"*One! Two! Three!—and AWAY!*" he shouted, and off he went like a little whirlwind up the field. But the hedgehog, after scuffling along a few yards, turned back and stayed quietly where he was.

6

THE HARE AND THE HEDGEHOG

When the hare came out of his furrow at the upper end of the field, the hedgehog's wife sat panting there as if she would never be able to recover her breath, and at sight of him she sighed out, "Ahah! sir, so you've come at last?"

The hare was shocked by her words. His ears trembled. His eyes bulged out of his head. "You've run it? You've *run* it!" he cried in astonishment. For she being so exactly like her husband, he never for a moment doubted that her husband she actually was.

"Ay," said she, "but I began to be afraid you must have gone lame."

"Lame!" said the hare, "lame! But there, what's *one* furrow? 'Every time,' was what you said. We'll try again."

Away once more he went, and he had never run faster. Yet when he came out of his furrow at the top of the field, there was the hedgehog! And the hedgehog laughed, and said: "Ahah! So here you are again! At last!" At this the hare could hardly contain himself for rage.

"Not enough! not enough!" he said "Three for luck! Again, again!"

"As often as you please, my dear friend," said the hedgehog. "It's the long run that really counts."

Again, and again, and yet again the hare raced up and down the long furrow of the field, and every time he reached the top, and every time he reached the bottom, there was the hedgehog, as he thought, with his mocking, "Ahah! So here you are again! At last!"

But at length the hare could run no more. He lay

panting and speechless; he was dead beat. Stretched out there, limp on the grass, his fur bedraggled, his eyes dim, his legs quaking, it looked as if he might fetch his last breath at any moment.

So Mrs. Hedgehog went off to the hare's house to fetch the Bottle of Brandy; and if it had not been the best brandy, the hare might never have run again.

News of the contest spread far and wide. From that day to this, never has there been a race to compare with it. And lucky it was for the hedgehog that he had the good sense to marry a wife like himself, and not a weasel, or a wombat, or a whale!

THE MARRIAGE OF THE FROG
AND THE MOUSE

It was the frog in the well,
    Humbledum, humbledum,
And the merry mouse in the mill,
    Tweedle, tweedle, twino.

The frog would a-wooing ride
Sword and buckler by his side.

When he upon his high horse set,
His boots they shone as black as jet.

When he came to the merry mill-pin,—
"Lady Mouse, been you within?"

Then came out the dusty mouse:
"I am Lady of this house:

"Hast thou any mind of me?"
"I have e'en great mind of thee?"

"Who shall this marriage make?"
"Our Lord which is the rat."

"What shall we have to our supper?"
"Three beans in a pound of butter?"

When supper they were at,
The frog, the mouse, and e'en the rat;

Then came in Gib our cat,
And catched the mouse e'en by the back.

9

MARRIAGE OF THE FROG AND THE MOUSE

Then did they separate,
And the frog leaped on the floor so flat.

Then came in Dick our drake,
And drew the frog e'en to the lake.

The rat ran up the wall,
 Humbledum, humbledum;
A goodly company, the Devil go with all!
 Tweedle, tweedle, twino.

T. RAVENSCROFT

THE MOUSE, THE BIRD, AND
THE SAUSAGE

Long, long ago, when somewhere was scarcely anywhere, a mouse, a bird, and a sausage took it into their heads to keep house together. And, for some little time, to be sure, they managed it prettily enough, and lived in peace. By this means, too, they added to their possessions and became rich. As for the housework, they shared it between them. The bird would fly away every morning into the forest and bring in sticks; the mouse had to carry in water from the well, to look after the fire, and lay the table for meals; and the sausage, who was called Roundabout, was cook.

Now it happened one day that the bird on its rambles met an old friend of his in the forest, and began to boast of his good fortune. After listening a while, his friend merely laughed and mocked at him for being nothing but a poor stupid overworked dolt whilst the mouse and the sausage had far too easy a time of it at home. And the bird began to believe it. After all, he thought to himself, when the mouse has lit the kitchen fire and brought in a bucket or two of water, she always goes to lie down for a nap in her own little room until it is time to lay the cloth; while that old lazy sausage sits watching the pot, and has nothing to do after making the soup for supper than to add butter, salt and pepper, and get it ready for dishing up. And that can be done in a few minutes.

So thinking, as he had never thought before, he flew away home. But that night he said nothing. After he had stacked up his bundle of sticks in the kitchen, they all three sat down to table, and, the meal over, they went up to bed and slept as sound as usual until the morning. Could any life be pleasanter than this?

Next day, however, the bird, who had been advised what to do by his friend, refused to fly off into the forest. "No more of that," he said. He had done nothing, he kept repeating, but slave and wait on the others morning, noon and night, and had been made a fool and drudge of long enough. He would stand it no longer. In future, they should all three change and change about, and take turns at the housework. Although the mouse and the sausage begged hard that things might go on as they were, the bird carried the day. So the three of them cast lots, and the lot fell upon the sausage to fetch kindling wood, while the mouse was to do the cooking, and the bird was to bring in the water from the well.

What happened? Slow-footed Roundabout next morning set off into the woods, the bird laid and lit the fire, the mouse put on the pot, and then instead of taking her usual nap in her own little room, sat anxiously waiting for the sausage to come home and bring in firewood for the next day. But the sausage was so long gone that the two poor creatures left at home began to dread what might have happened to him. As the moments crept slowly by, they pined for his company as they had never pined before. At last they could bear themselves no longer; and the bird went out in search of him. He had not flown far when he encountered a mangy dog on the road, who told him that he had hours ago met the sausage in the forest, and, at sight of so tasty a mouthful, had knocked him down and gobbled him up.

The bird accused the dog of open robbery and murder. But words were of no avail, since the dog said that he had found the sausage where it had no business to be, and that, stooping and stumbling, it could not be doing its proper work, that it must therefore have been a spy, and had deserved even a worse end than it got. The little bird in great sorrow took up the sticks which poor Roundabout had left behind him, went home, and told the mouse what he had seen and heard. The mouse was grieved to the heart that their friend was no more, but they decided to do their best and keep together.

So the bird undertook to lay the table, and the mouse

got ready the soup for their supper. Alas, when that evening she crept down the handle of the pot to add salt and pepper, she overbalanced, fell in, and was drowned. When the bird came into the kitchen to serve up the soup, no cook was to be seen. Wildly searching for her, he scattered the dry sticks that were stacked up in the hearth. He called her again and again, high and low, and sought her everywhere, house and garden, but all in vain. When he came back into the kitchen, he found that a burning ember out of the grate had fallen on to the firewood and set it blazing He winged away as fast as he could fly to fetch water, but the bucket fell into the well, and he after it.

So that was the sad end of that.

WHAT?

A flock of white sheep
  On a red hill;
Here they go, there they go,
  Now they stand still!

"THERE WAS"

There was an old man,
And he had a calf,
      And that's half;
He took him out of the stall,
And put him on the wall,
      And that's all.

THE STORY OF THE THREE LITTLE PIGS

Once upon a time when pigs spoke rhyme
And monkeys chewed tobacco,
The hens took snuff to make them tough,
And ducks went quack, quack, quack, O!

There was an old sow with three little pigs, and as she had not enough to keep them, she sent them out to seek their fortune. The first that went off met a man with a bundle of straw, and said to him:

"Please, man, give me that straw to build me a house."

Which the man did, and the little pig built a house with it. Presently came along a wolf, and knocked at the door, and said:

"Little pig, little pig, let me come in."

To which the pig answered:

"No, no, by the hair of my chiny chin chin."

The wolf then answered to that:

"Then I'll huff, and I'll puff, and I'll blow your house in."

So he huffed, and he puffed, and he blew his house in, and ate up the little pig.

The second little pig met a man with a bundle of furze, and said:

"Please, man, give me that furze to build a house."

Which the man did, and the pig built his house. Then along came the wolf, and said:

"Little pig, little pig, let me come in."

"No, no, by the hair of my chiny chin chin."

"Then I'll puff, and I'll huff, and I'll blow your house in."

So he huffed, and he puffed, and he puffed, and he huffed, and at last he blew the house down, and he ate up the little pig.

The third little pig met a man with a load of bricks, and said:

"Please, man, give me those bricks to build a house with."

So the man gave him the bricks, and he built his house with them. So the wolf came, as he did to the other little pigs, and said:

"Little pig, little pig, let me come in."

"No, no, by the hair of my chiny chin chin."

"Then I'll huff, and I'll puff, and I'll blow your house in."

Well, he huffed, and he puffed, and he huffed and he puffed, and he puffed and huffed; but he could *not* get the house down. When he found that he could not, with all his puffing and huffing, blow the house down, he said:

"Little pig, I know where there is a nice field of turnips."

"Where ?" said the little pig.

"Oh, in Mr. Smith's Home-field, and if you will be ready to-morrow morning I will call for you, and we will go together, and get some for dinner."

"Very well," said the little pig, "I will be ready. What time do you mean to go?"

"Oh, at six o'clock."

Well, the little pig got up at five, and got the turnips before the wolf came (which he did about six) and who said:

"Little pig, are you ready?"

The little pig said: "Ready! I have been and come back again, and got a nice potful for dinner."

The wolf felt very angry at this, but thought that he would be up to the little pig somehow or other, so he said:

"Little pig, I know where there is a nice apple-tree."

"Where?" said the pig.

"Down at Merry-garden," replied the wolf, "and if you will not deceive me I will come for you, at five o'clock to-morrow and get some apples.

Well, the little pig bustled up the next morning at four o'clock, and went off for the apples, hoping to get back before the wolf came; but he had further to go, and had to climb the tree, so that just as he was coming down from it, he saw the wolf coming, which, as you may suppose, frightened him very much. When the wolf came up he said:

"Little pig, what! are you here before me? Are they nice apples?"

"Yes, very," said the little pig. "I will throw you down one."

And he threw it so far, that, while the wolf was gone to pick it up, the little pig jumped down and ran home. The next day the wolf came again, and said to the little pig:

"Little pig, there is a fair at Shanklin this afternoon, will you go?"

"Oh yes," said the pig, "I will go; what time shall you be ready?"

"At three," said the wolf. So the little pig went off before the time as usual, and got to the fair, and bought a butter-churn, which he was going home with, when he saw the wolf coming. Then he could not tell what to do. So he got into the churn to hide, and by so doing turned it round, and it rolled down the hill with the pig in it, which frightened the wolf so much, that he ran home without going to the fair. He went to the little pig's house, and told him how frightened he had been by a great round thing which came down the hill past him. Then the little pig said:

"Hah, I frightened you, then. I had been to the fair and bought a butter-churn, and when I saw you, I got into it, and rolled down the hill."

Then the wolf was very angry indeed, and declared he *would* eat up the little pig, and that he would get down the chimney after him. When the little pig saw what he was about, he hung on the pot full of water, and made up a blazing fire, and, just as the wolf was coming down, took off the cover, and in fell the wolf; so the little pig put on the cover again in an instant, boiled him up, and ate him for supper, and lived happy ever afterwards.

THE WORLD TURNED UPSIDE DOWN

[From a little old "penny book", with cuts to illustrate the rhymes.]

To see a butcher kill a hog,
>   is no news;
But to see a hare run after a dog,
>   is strange indeed!

To see a cat catching a mouse,
>   is no news;
But to see a rat building a house,
>   is strange indeed!

To see a bird picking at fruit,
>   is no news;
But to see a dog playing the flute,
>   is strange indeed!

To see a greyhound catch a hare,
>   is no news;
But to see a lamb hunting a bear,
>   is strange indeed!

To see a gardener gather a sallad,
>   is no news;
But to see an ass singing a ballad,
>   is strange indeed!

To see a dog baiting a bull,
>   is no news;
But to see a ram spinning of wool,
>   is strange indeed!

20

THE WORLD TURNED UPSIDE DOWN

To see a tailor making a coat,
                         is no news;
But to see a hog rowing a boat,
                         is strange indeed!

To see a man fish in a moat,
                         is no news;
But to see a monkey shaving a goat,
                         is strange indeed!

To see a miller grinding corn,
                         is no news;
But to see an ox blowing a horn,
                         is strange indeed!

To see a shoemaker hammer his leather,
                         is no news;
But to see a hound and a buck drinking together,
                         is strange indeed!

To see a good boy read his book,
                         is no news;
But to see a goose roasting a cook,
                         is strange indeed!

To see a beau at his toilet dress,
                         is no news;
But to see two horses playing at chess,
                         is strange indeed!

To see a high-bred horse when prancing,
                         is no news;

THE WORLD TURNED UPSIDE DOWN

But to see a cat fiddling and mice all dancing,
       is strange indeed!

To see a lady drinking of tea,
       is no news;
But to see a bird shoot a man in a tree,
       is strange indeed!

To see a boy swim in a brook,
       is no news;
But to see a fish catch a man with a hook,
       is strange indeed!

To see a cobbler mending a shoe,
       is no news;
But to see a goat cry old clothes like a jew,
       is strange indeed!

To see a haymaker using of rakes,
       is no news;
But to see a bear making plum cakes,
       is strange indeed!

To see wrestlers kicking shins,
       is no news;
But to see cats playing at nine pins,
       is strange indeed!

To hear a parrot say, pretty Poll,
       is no news;
But to see a sow with a parasol,
       is strange indeed!

THE STORY OF THE THREE BEARS

Once upon a time there were Three Bears, who lived together in a house of their own, in a wood. One of them was a Little, Small, Wee Bear; and one was a Middle-sized Bear, and the other was a Great, Huge Bear. They had each a pot for their porridge, a little pot for the Little, Small, Wee Bear; and a middle-sized pot for the Middle Bear, and a great pot for the Great, Huge Bear. And they had each a chair to sit in; a little chair for the Little, Small, Wee Bear; and a middle-sized chair for the Middle Bear; and a great chair for the Great, Huge Bear. And they had each a bed to sleep in; a little bed for the Little, Small, Wee Bear; and a middle-sized bed for the Middle Bear; and a great bed for the Great, Huge Bear.

One day, after they had made the porridge for their breakfast, and poured it into their porridge-pots, they walked out into the wood while the porridge was cooling, that they might not burn their mouths, by beginning too soon to eat it. And while they were walking, a little old Woman came to the house. She could not have been a good, honest old Woman; for first she looked in at the window, and then she peeped in at the keyhole; and seeing nobody in the house, she lifted the latch. The door was not fastened, because the Bears were good Bears, who did nobody any harm, and never suspected that anybody would harm them. So the little old Woman opened the door, and went in; and well pleased she was when she saw the porridge on the table. If she had been a good little old Woman, she would have waited till the Bears came home, and then, perhaps, they would have asked her to breakfast; for they were good Bears—a little rough or so, as the manner of Bears is, but for all that very good-natured and hospitable. But she was an impudent, bad old Woman, and set about helping herself.

So first she tasted the porridge of the Great, Huge Bear, and that was too hot for her; and she said a bad word about that. And then she tasted the porridge of the Middle Bear, and that was too cold for her; and she said a bad word about that too, And then she went to the porridge of the Little, Small, Wee Bear, and tasted that; and that was neither too hot, nor too cold, but just right; and she liked it so well, that she ate it all up: but the naughty old Woman said a bad word about the little porridge-pot, because it did not hold enough for her.

Then the little old Woman sate down in the chair of the Great, Huge Bear, and that was too hard for her. And then she sate down in the chair of the Middle Bear, and that was too soft for her. And then she sate down in the chair of the Little, Small, Wee Bear, and that was neither too hard, nor too soft, but just right. So she seated herself in it, and there she sate till the bottom of the chair came out, and down she came, plump upon the ground. And the naughty old Woman said a wicked word about that too.

Then the little old Woman went upstairs into the bed-chamber in which the three Bears slept. And first she lay down upon the bed for the Great, Huge Bear; but that was too high at the head for her. And next she lay down upon the bed of the Middle Bear; and that was too high at the foot for her. And then she lay down upon the bed of the Little, Small, Wee Bear; and that was neither too high at the head, nor at the foot, but just right. So she covered herself up comfortably, and lay there till she fell fast asleep.

By this time the Three Bears thought their porridge would be cool enough; so they came home to breakfast. Now the little old Woman had left the spoon of the Great, Huge Bear, standing in his porridge.

"Somebody has been at my porridge!"

said the Great, Huge Bear, in his great, rough, gruff voice. And when the Middle Bear looked at his, he saw that the spoon was standing in it too. They were wooden spoons; if they had been silver ones, the naughty old Woman would have put them in her pocket.

"Somebody has been at my porridge!"

said the Middle Bear in his middle voice.

Then the Little, Small, Wee Bear looked at his, and

there was the spoon in the porridge-pot, but the porridge was all gone.

"Somebody has been at my porridge and has eaten it all up!"

said the Little, Small, Wee Bear, in his little, small, wee
voice.

Upon this the Three Bears, seeing that some one had
entered their house, and eaten up the Little, Small, Wee
Bear's breakfast, began to look about them. Now the
little old Woman had not put the hard cushion straight
when she rose from the chair of the Great, Huge Bear.

"Somebody has been sitting in my chair!"

said the Great, Huge Bear, in his great, rough, gruff
voice.

And the little old Woman had squatted down the soft
cushion of the Middle Bear.

"Somebody has been sitting in my chair!"

said the Middle Bear, in his middle voice.

And you know what the little old Woman had done to
the third chair.

**"Somebody has been sitting in my chair
and has sate the bottom out of it!"**

said the Little, Small, Wee Bear, in his little small, wee
voice.

Then the Three Bears thought it necessary that they
should make farther search; so they went upstairs into
their bedchamber. Now the little old Woman had
pulled the pillow of the Great, Huge Bear, out of its
place.

26

"Somebody has been lying in my bed!"

said the Great, Huge Bear, in his great, rough, gruff voice.

And the little old Woman had pulled the bolster of the Middle Bear out of its place.

"Somebody has been lying in my bed!"

said the Middle Bear, in his middle voice.

And when the Little, Small, Wee Bear came to look at his bed, there was the bolster in its place; and the pillow in its place upon the bolster; and upon the pillow was the little old Woman's ugly, dirty head,—which was not in its place, for she had no business there.

"Somebody has been lying in my bed,—and here she is!"

said the Little, Small, Wee Bear, in his little, small, wee voice

The little old Woman had heard in her sleep the great, rough, gruff voice of the Great, Huge Bear; but she was so fast asleep that it was no more to her than the roaring of wind, or the rumbling of thunder. And she had heard the middle voice, of the Middle Bear, but it was only as if she had heard some one speaking in a dream. But when she heard the little, small, wee voice of the Little, Small, Wee Bear, it was so sharp, and so shrill, that it awakened her at once. Up she started; and when she saw the Three Bears on one side of the bed, she tumbled herself out at the other, and ran to the window. Now the window was open, because the Bears, like good, tidy Bears, as they were, always opened their bedchamber window when they got up in the morning. Out the little old Woman jumped; and whether she broke her neck in the fall; or ran into the wood and was lost there; or found her way out of the wood, and was taken up by the constable and sent to the House of Correction for a vagrant as she was, I cannot tell. But the Three Bears never saw anything more of her.

ROBERT SOUTHEY

THE DERBY RAM

As I was going to Derby, all on a sunshine day,
I met the finest ram, Sir, that ever was fed on hay;
And indeed, Sir, 'tis true, Sir, I never was given to lie,
And if you'd been to Derby, Sir, you'd have seen him as
well as I.

It had four feet to gang on, Sir, it had four feet to stand,
And every foot it had, Sir, did cover an acre of land.
And indeed, Sir, 'tis true, Sir, I never was given to lie,
And if you'd been to Derby, Sir, you'd have seen him as
well as I.

The backbone of this ram, Sir, made the mainmast of a
ship;
And that did carry the finest sail in all the British fleet.
And indeed, Sir, 'tis true, Sir, I never was given to lie,
And if you'd been to Derby, Sir, you'd have seen him as
well as I.

The wool that grew on his sides, Sir, made fifty packs
complete,
And that was sent to Flanders to clothe the British fleet.
And indeed, Sir, 'tis true, Sir, I never was given to lie,
And if you'd been to Derby, Sir, you'd have seen him as
well as I.

The horns that grew on his head, Sir, they grew up to
the sky;
And the eagles did build their nests there, for I heard the
young ones cry.

THE DERBY RAM

And indeed, Sir, 'tis true, Sir, I never was given to lie,
And if you'd been to Derby, Sir, you'd have seen him as
well as I.

The tail was fifty yards, Sir, as near as I can tell,
And it was sent to Rome, Sir, to ring Saint Peter's Bell.
And indeed, Sir, 'tis true, Sir, I never was given to lie,
And if you'd been to Derby, Sir, you'd have seen him as
well as I.

THE WOLF AND THE FOX

A foolish fox once made friends with a wolf. With his silky brush and pointed nose he fancied himself a fine smart fellow, and hardly knew at first which way to look he was so vain of his new company. But he soon found out that his new friend was not in love with him for his own sweet sake only, and that *being* a wolf, a wolf he *was*. For one thing, he was a greedy glutton and could never eat enough; and next, he had no manners.

"And what's for supper to-night?" he would say, his white teeth glinting in the moon. "Bones! Bones! Again! Lor', friend Fox, if you can't get me anything really worth eating, I shall soon have to eat *you*." This was an old joke now; and though he grinned as he said it, his sharp fangs and bloodshot eyes looked none too pleasant.

As for the fox he smiled on one side of his face but not on the other. "Well, friend Wolf," he said, " keep up your spirits. There's a farmyard over the hill where some plump young lambs are fattening. Softly now, and away we go!"

So off they went together. When they reached the farmyard the fox sneaked in through the gate, snatched up one of the lambs, leapt over the stone wall and carried it off to the wolf. After which, he trotted round to the henhouse to get his own supper in peace. But when the wolf had finished off his lamb—leaving not so much as a bone for his friend to pick—he felt hungrier than ever, and determined to slip away himself and get the other.

But he was so clumsy in scrabbling over the stone wall of the farmyard that the old mother sheep heard him, and began bleating aloud in the darkness. At this the farmer, who was sitting in his kitchen, ran out with his dog and a cudgel, and managed to give the wolf such a drubbing as he climbed back over the wall, that he came creeping back to the fox as wild with pain as he was with rage.

"A nice thing *you've* done," he said to the fox. "I went to fetch another lamb, and I'm beaten to a jelly."

"Well," said the fox, "one's one and two's two; but enough is as good as a feast;" and he thought of the tasty young pullet he had stolen for his own supper.

Next day they decided to be getting off into country where they were less well-known. After a pleasant afternoon's journey, they found themselves on the edge of a small green coppice basking in the sun. The wolf stretched himself out and soon fell asleep. He woke up as surly as a bear with a sore head.

"Come, rouse, friend Fox! Supper!" he bawled.

"What's for supper? No more lamb to-night. I'd sooner eat *you*!"

The fox trembled with rage, but he answered him civilly and said: "I seem to smell pancakes—rich pancakes. Squat here awhile, friend Wolf, and I'll see what I can do."

He slipped off and away to the other side of the wood, and came to a house from whose brick chimneys a faint smoke was wreathing up into the evening air laden with so sweet and savoury an odour of pancakes that the fox lifted his nose into the air and snuffed and snuffed again. Then first he crept this way; and then he crept that way; and at last he stole in through an open window, and so into the pantry, and leaping up on to a shelf, carried off at least six of the pancakes.

The wolf swallowed them down without so much as a thank'ee, and champed for more. The glutton then asked the fox which way he had gone. The fox told him.

"You'll know the house by the smoke," he said, "and the window is by the water-butt. But step quiet, my friend, if go you must, for I heard voices." The greedy wolf, thinking that if the fox came with him to the house he would expect a share of the pancakes that were left, at once scuffled off alone into the night to finish the dish.

But he made such a hullabaloo in the pantry as he went sprawling along the shelf, upsetting a great cooking crock as he did so, that the farmer and his wife, and the friends who had been supping with them, heard the noise and came rushing in, and gave him such a basting that he hardly escaped with his life.

When he had licked his bruises and got some breath into his body again, he came snarling back to the fox, and blamed *him* for his beating. The fox coughed and turned his head aside; he could hardly speak for rage and contempt. However, the duck he himself had supped off was still sweet in memory; so he answered the wolf smoothly, reminding him that he had been given a fair warning. "Besides," said he, "as I've said before, enough is as good as a feast, friend Wolf; and with *some* sauces, much better."

Yet, even now, the wolf had not learnt his lesson. For, a very few evenings afterwards, though he could only limp along on three legs, and every bone in his body ached, he turned sullenly on his friend the fox, and said: "Friend Fox, I'm sick and tired of you. You've no more wits than a rabbit. 'Sly,' indeed! Now, see here; if before that moon up there has climbed an inch in the sky you don't get me a meat meal, a tasty meal, and plenty of it— a supper worth a gentleman's eating, I'm saying—then it will surely be the last of you, for I'm *done* with your shilly-shallying."

The fox trembled and said, "Softly, softly, friend Wolf; why lose your temper? I do my best. This very morning I heard that the human that lives by the stream on the other side of the hill yonder has been killing a pig. A fat pig—a very fat pig; a pig *stuffed* with fatness. And the salt pork of that pig is packed in a barrel in the human's cellar. Ah, I see your mouth watering. Come, we will go together."

"Why, yes," said the wolf, "and you shall keep watch while I eat."

So the fox led him off by a green ride through the woods and over the crest of the hill, and by a cart-track, till at last they came down to a mill. It was a clear moonlight night, with a sparkle of frost in the air. And as it chanced, there was a small, round-topped outside little door under the wall of the house that led into the cellar. The fox pushed up its latch; paused; sniffed; listened; sniffed again.

His green eyes glistened like fireballs, as he turned his sharp muzzle and looked back at the wolf. "Follow," he said, "and do not so much as grin or gruff. The human of this house has a gun."

The wolf, being overfed and overfat, only just managed to scramble through the doorway. But at last he followed the fox into the cellar, and was soon guzzling away at the barrel of salted pork.

"Tell me, friend Fox," he said, glancing over his shoulder, his jaws dripping, "why do you keep sniffing and snuffing about like that? Restrain yourself. It vexes me, it annoys me. How can I feed in comfort with you fidgeting and fretting? Keep still; and you shall, perhaps, have a gobbet or two for yourself by and by. All depends on what I leave!"

"Gobble on, gobble on," said the fox meekly. "There's plenty of time for me. But I warn you: don't make a noise, and don't eat too hearty!"

"Ah," said the wolf, "you thought this fat luscious feast of pork was for you, did you? And after all my pains in finding it! Have no fear, greedy-guts, there won't be much left when *I've* finished with it."

At this, with a stroke of his paw and a heave of his

shoulder, he turned the great salty tub clean over on the stones of the cellar; and a fine clatter it made.

Indeed, the miller, who was at that moment shaving himself in a looking-glass, hearing this noise in his cellar, supposed for a moment there was an earthquake. Then he snatched up his blunderbuss, and with the soapsuds still foaming on his cheek, came clumping down the steep stone steps into the cellar.

At first sound and whiff of him, the fox was out through the hole at a bound, and in a moment or two his friend the wolf, stricken with terror, was struggling hard to follow him. But the greedy guzzler had so puffed and swilled himself out with his feast of pork that, wriggle and wrench as he might, he could not squeeze through the hole. So there he stuck. And the miller, although he had lost a good half of his pickled pork, at least gained a thick warm wolf's skin in exchange.

Meanwhile, the fox on the crest of the hill, hearing the roar of the blunderbuss, shivered a little, then danced a little dance all to himself in the moonlight. There and then he made up his mind that his next friend should be neither wolf nor glutton, but of his own size and liking; and one with a brush.

WHO KILL'D COCK ROBIN?

[*Old Version*]

Who kill'd Cock Robin?
 I, said the sparrow,
  With my bow and arrow,
I kill'd Cock Robin.

Who see him die?
 I, said the fly,
  With my little eye,
And I see him die.

Who catch'd his blood?
 I, said the fish,
  With my little dish,
And I catch'd his blood.

Who made his shroud?
 I, said the beadle,
  With my little needle,
And I made his shroud.

Who shall dig his grave?
 I, said the owl,
  With my spade and showl,
And I'll dig his grave.

Who'll be the parson?
 I, said the rook,
  With my little book,
And I'll be the parson.

WHO KILL'D COCK ROBIN?

Who'll be the clerk?
　　I, said the lark,
　　　If 'tis not in the dark,
And I'll be the clerk.

Who'll carry him to the grave?
　　I, said the kite,
　　　If 'tis not in the night,
And I'll carry him to his grave.

Who'll carry the link?
　　I, said the linnet,
　　　I'll fetch it in a minute,
And I'll carry the link.

Who'll be chief mourner?
　　I, said the dove,
　　　I mourn for my love,
And I'll be chief mourner.

Who'll bear the pall?
　　We, said the wren,
　　　Both the cock and the hen,
And we'll bear the pall.

Who'll sing a psalm?
　　I, said the thrush,
　　　As she sat in a bush,
And I'll sing a psalm.

WHO KILL'D COCK ROBIN?

And who'll toll the bell?
    I, said the bull,
    Because I can pull;
And so, Cock Robin, farewell!

All the birds in the air
    Fell to sighing and sobbing,
When they heard the bell toll
    For poor Cock Robin!

THE CAT AND THE MOUSE

The cat and the mouse
Play'd in the malt-house:

The cat bit the mouse's tail off. Pray puss, give me my tail. No, says the cat, I'll not give you your tail, till you go to the cow, and fetch me some milk:

First she leapt, and then she ran,
Till she came to the cow, and thus began,—

Pray, Cow, give me milk, that I may give cat milk, that cat may give me my own tail again. No, said the cow, I will give you no milk, till you go to the farmer and get me some hay.

First she leapt, and then she ran,
Till she came to the farmer, and thus began,—

Pray, Farmer, give me hay, that I may give cow hay, that cow may give me milk, that I may give cat milk, that cat may give me my own tail again. No, says the farmer,

I'll give you no hay, till you go to the butcher and fetch me some meat.

> First she leapt, and then she ran,
> Till she came to the butcher, and thus began,—

Pray, Butcher, give me meat, that I may give farmer meat, that farmer may give me hay, that I may give cow hay, that cow may give me milk, that I may give cat milk, that cat may give me my own tail again. No, says the butcher, I'll give you no meat, till you go to the baker and fetch me some bread.

> First she leapt, and then she ran,
> Till she came to the baker, and thus began,—

Pray, Baker, give me bread, that I may give butcher bread, that butcher may give me meat, that I may give farmer meat, that farmer may give me hay, that I may give cow hay, that cow may give me milk, that I may give cat milk, that cat may give me my own tail again.

> Yes, says the baker, I'll give you some bread,
> But if you eat my meal, I'll cut off your head.

Then the baker gave mouse bread, and mouse gave butcher bread, and butcher gave mouse meat, and mouse gave farmer meat, and farmer gave mouse hay, and mouse gave cow hay, and cow gave mouse milk, and mouse gave cat milk, and cat gave mouse her own tail again!

"COCK-COCK-COO"

I had a cock, and a cock lov'd me,
And I fed my cock under a hollow tree;
  My cock cried—cock-cock-coo—
Every body loves their cock, and I love my cock too!

I had a hen, and a hen lov'd me,
And I fed my hen under a hollow tree;
  My hen went—chickle-chackle, chickle-chackle—
   My cock cried—cock-cock-coo—
Every body loves their cock, and I love my cock too!

I had a goose, and a goose lov'd me,
And I fed my goose under a hollow tree;
  My goose went—qua'k, qua'k—
  My hen went—chickle-chackle, chickle-chackle—
   My cock cried—cock-cock-coo—
Every body loves their cock, and I love my cock too!

I had a duck, and a duck lov'd me,
And I fed my duck under a hollow tree;
  My duck went—quack, quack, quack—
  My goose went—qua'k, qua'k—
  My hen went—chickle-chackle, chickle-chackle—
   My cock cried—cock-cock-coo—
Every body loves their cock, and I love my cock too!

I had a drake, and a drake lov'd me,
And I fed my drake under a hollow tree;
  My drake went—ca-qua, ca-qua, ca-qua—
  My duck went—quack, quack, quack—

"COCK-COCK-COO"

My goose went—qua'k, qua'k, qua'k—
My hen went—chickle-chackle, chickle-chackle—
    My cock cried—cock-cock-coo—
Every body loves their cock, and I love my cock too!

I had a cat, and a cat lov'd me,
And I fed my cat under a hollow tree;
    My cat went—miow, miow, miow—
    My drake went—ca-qua, ca-qua, ca-qua—
    My duck went—quack, quack, quack—
    My goose went—qua'k, qua'k, qua'k—
    My hen went—chickle-chackle, chickle-chackle—
    My cock cried—cock-cock-coo—
Every body loves their cock, and I love my cock too!

I had a dog, and a dog lov'd me,
And I fed my dog under a hollow tree;
    My dog went—bow, wow, wow—
    My cat went—miow, miow, miow—
    My drake went—ca-qua, ca-qua, ca-qua—
    My duck went—quack, quack, quack—
    My goose went—qua'k, qua'k, qua'k—
    My hen went—chickle-chackle, chickle-chackle—
    My cock cried—cock-cock-coo—
Every body loves their cock, and I love my cock too!

I had a cow, and a cow lov'd me,
And I fed my cow under a hollow tree;
    My cow went—moo, moo, moo—
    My dog went—bow, wow, wow—
    My cat went—miow, miow, miow—

"COCK-COCK-COO"

My drake went—ca-qua, ca-qua, ca-qua—
My duck went—quack, quack, quack—
My goose went—qua'k, qua'k, qua'k—
My hen went—chickle-chackle, chickle-chackle—
My cock cried—cock-cock-coo—
Every body loves their cock, and I love my cock too!

I had a sheep, and a sheep lov'd me,
And I fed my sheep under a hollow tree;
My sheep went—baa, baa, baa—
My cow went—moo, moo, moo—
My dog went—bow, wow, wow—
My cat went—miow, miow, miow—
My drake went—ca-qua, ca-qua, ca-qua—
My duck went—quack, quack, quack—
My goose went—qua'k, qua'k, qua'k—
My hen went—chickle-chackle, chickle-chackle—
My cock cried—cock-cock-coo—
Every body loves their cock, and I love my cock too!

I had a donkey, and a donkey lov'd me,
And I fed my donkey under a hollow tree;
My donkey went—hi-haugh, hi-haugh—
My sheep went—baa, baa, baa—
My cow went—moo, moo, moo—
My dog went—bow, wow, wow—
My cat went—miow, miow, miow—
My drake went—ca-qua, ca-qua, ca-qua—
My duck went—quack, quack, quack—
My goose went—qua'k, qua'k, qua'k—

"COCK-COCK-COO"

My hen went—chickle-chackle, chickle-chackle—
My cock cried—cock-cock-coo—
Every body loves their cock, and I love my cock too!

I had a horse, and a horse lov'd me,
And I fed my horse under a hollow tree;
    My horse went—whin-neigh-h-h-h-h—
    My donkey went—hi-haugh, hi-haugh—
    My sheep went—baa, baa, baa—
    My cow went—moo, moo, moo—
    My dog went—bow, wow, wow—
    My cat went—miow, miow, miow—
    My drake went—ca-qua, ca-qua, ca-qua—
    My duck went—quack, quack, quack—
    My goose went—qua'k, qua'k, qua'k—
    My hen went—chickle-chackle, chickle-chackle—
        My cock cried—cock-cock-coo—
Every body loves their cock, and I love my cock too!

I had a pig, and a pig lov'd me,
And I fed my pig under a hollow tree;
    And my pig went—hoogh, hoogh, hoogh—
    My horse went—whin-neigh-h-h-h-h—
    My donkey went—hi-haugh, hi-haugh—
    My sheep went—baa, baa, baa—
    My cow went—moo, moo, moo—
    My dog went—bow, wow, wow—
    My cat went—miow, miow, miow—
    My drake went—ca-qua, ca-qua, ca-qua—
    My duck went—quack, quack, quack—
    My goose went—qua'k, qua'k, qua'k—

"COCK-COCK-COO"

My hen went—chickle-chackle, chickle-chackle—
My cock cried—cock-cock-coo—
Every body loves their cock, and I love my cock too!

And so the pig—grunted,
The horse—neigh'd,
The donkey—bray'd,
The sheep—bleated,
The cow—low'd,
The dog—bark'd,
The cat—mew'd,
The drake—quackled,
The duck—cackled,
The goose—gobbled,
The hen—chuckled,
The cock—crow'd—
And my cock cried—cock-cock-coo—
Every body loves their cock, and I love my cock too!

HENNY-PENNY

*[As it was told to Joseph Jacobs
in Australia in 1860]*

One day Henny-penny was picking up corn in the cornyard when—whack!—something hit her upon the head. "Goodness gracious me!" said Henny-penny; "the sky's a-going to fall; I must go and tell the king."

So she went along, and she went along, and she went along till she met Cocky-locky. "Where are you going, Henny-penny?" says Cocky-locky. "Oh! I'm going to tell the king the sky's a-falling," says Henny-penny. "May I come with you?" says Cocky-locky. "Certainly," says Henny-penny. So Henny-penny and Cocky-locky went to tell the king the sky was falling.

47

They went along, and they went along, and they went along till they met Ducky-daddles. "Where are you going to, Henny-penny and Cocky-locky?" says Ducky-daddles. "Oh! we're going to tell the king the sky's a-falling," said Henny-penny and Cocky-locky. "May I come with you?" says Ducky-daddles. "Certainly," said Henny-penny and Cocky-locky. So Henny-penny, Cocky-locky and Ducky-daddles went to tell the king the sky was a-falling.

So they went along, and they went along, and they went along, till they met Goosey-poosey. "Where are you going to, Henny-penny, Cocky-locky and Ducky-daddles?" said Goosey-poosey. "Oh! we're going to tell the king the sky's a-falling," said Henny-penny and Cocky-locky and Ducky-daddles. "May I come with you?" said Goosey-poosey. "Certainly," said Henny-penny, Cocky-locky and Ducky-daddles. So Henny-penny, Cocky-locky, Ducky-daddles and Goosey-poosey went to tell the king the sky was a-falling.

So they went along, and they went along, and they went along, till they met Turkey-lurkey. "Where are you going, Henny-penny, Cocky-locky, Ducky-daddles and Goosey-poosey?" said Turkey-lurkey. "Oh! we're going to tell the king the sky's a-falling," said Henny-penny, Cocky-locky, Ducky-daddles and Goosey-poosey. "May I come with you, Henny-penny, Cocky-locky, Ducky-daddles and Goosey-poosey?" said Turkey-lurkey. "Why, certainly, Turkey-lurkey," said Henny-penny, Cocky-locky, Ducky-daddles, and Goosey-poosey. So Henny-penny, Cocky-locky,

Ducky-daddles, Goosey-poosey and Turkey-lurkey all went to tell the king the sky was a-falling.

So they went along, and they went along, and they went along, till they met Foxy-woxy; and Foxy-woxy said to Henny-penny, Cocky-locky, Ducky-daddles, Goosey-poosey and Turkey-lurkey: "Where are you going, Henny-penny, Cocky-locky, Ducky-daddles, Goosey-poosey, and Turkey-lurkey?" And Henny-penny, Cocky-locky, Ducky-daddles, Goosey-poosey, and Turkey-lurkey said to Foxy-woxy: "We're going to tell the king the sky's a-falling." "Oh! but this is not the way to the king, Henny-penny, Cocky-locky, Ducky-daddles, Goosey-poosey and Turkey-lurkey," says Foxy-woxy; "I know the proper way; shall I show it you?" "Why certainly, Foxy-woxy," said Henny-penny, Cocky-locky, Ducky-daddles, Goosey-poosey and Turkey-lurky. So Henny-penny, Cocky-locky, Ducky-daddles, Goosey-poosey, Turkey-lurky and Foxy-woxy all went to tell the king the sky was a-falling.

So they went along, and they went along, and they went along, till they came to a narrow and dark hole. Now this was the door of Foxy-woxy's cave. But Foxy-woxy said to Henny-penny, Cocky-locky, Ducky-daddles, Goosey-poosey, and Turkey-lurky: "This is the short way to the king's palace: you'll soon get there if you follow me. I will go first and you come after, Henny-penny, Cocky-locky, Ducky-daddles, Goosey-poosey and Turkey-lurky." "Why of course, certainly, without doubt, why not?" said Henny-penny, Cocky-locky, Ducky-daddles, Goosey-poosey and Turkey-lurkey.

So Foxy-woxy went into his cave, and he didn't go

very far but turned round to wait for Henny-penny, Cocky-locky, Ducky-daddles, Goosey-poosey and Turkey-lurkey. So at last, first Turkey-lurkey went through the dark hole into the cave. He hadn't got very far when "Hrumph," Foxy-woxy snapped off Turkey-lurkey's head and threw his body over his left shoulder. Then Goosey-poosey went in, and "Hrumph," off went her head and Goosey-poosey was thrown beside Turkey-lurkey. Then Ducky-daddles waddled down, and "Hrumph," snapped Foxy-woxy, and Ducky-daddles' head was off and Ducky-daddles was thrown alongside Turkey-lurkey and Goosey-poosey. Then Cocky-locky strutted down into the cave and he hadn't gone far when "Snap, Hrumph!" went Foxy-woxy and Cocky-locky was thrown alongside of Turkey-lurkey, Goosey-poosey and Ducky-daddles.

But Foxy-woxy had made two bites at Cocky-locky, and when the first snap only hurt Cocky-locky, but didn't kill him, he called out to Henny-penny. So she turned tail and ran back home. So she never told the king the sky was a-falling.

"CHITTERABOB"

There was a man, and his name was Dob,
And he had a wife, and her name was Mob,
And he had a dog, and he called it Cob,
And she had a cat called Chitterabob.

       Cob, says Dob,
       Chitterabob, says Mob.
       Cob was Dob's dog.
       Chitterabob Mob's cat.

PUSS IN BOOTS

A miller once had nothing else to leave to his three children but his mill, his donkey, and his cat. The sharing was easily arranged—no solicitor or attorney had to be called in. Their fees would soon have eaten up all the little patrimony. The eldest took the mill, the second took the donkey, and the third had to be content with the cat. The last of the three was quite disconsolate over having got so poor a share. "My brothers", said he, "can join forces and make a decent livelihood; but as for me, when I have eaten my cat, and made a muff of the skin, I shall just have to die of hunger." The Cat, who had heard him talking, though all unbeknown, said to him with a sedate and serious air, "Don't worry, master! You have only to give me a sack, and make me a pair of top-boots so that I can walk through the brushwood, and you will see that I am not such a bad bargain as you think."

Although the Cat's young master did not lay great stock by the notion, he had seen his comrade achieve such feats of suppleness and cunning in catching rats and mice—as when he would hang by his feet, or hide amongst the flour to give his final spring—that he was

not altogether without hope of turning it to some purpose in his trouble.

When the cat had got what he asked for, he pulled on
the boots himself, and, to be sure, he made a brave show
in them! He then put his sack over his shoulder, and,
taking the strings between his two front paws, went to
a warren where he knew there were any number of
rabbits. He put some bran and some sow-thistles in his
sack, and, stretching himself out as if he were dead, he
waited until some young rabbit, less experienced than
the others in the wiles of the world, should nose his way
into the sack to eat what had been put there.

Hardly had he lain down, when his design was
fulfilled. A silly young rabbit crept into the sack, and
Master Puss pulled the strings as quickly as might be,
caught him, and killed him without mercy.

In the full pride of his achievement, the Cat went to
the palace of the King, and asked to see him. He was
shown into his Majesty's room. As he came in, the Cat
made a deep bow to the King, and said, "Sire, here is a
rabbit which the Marquis of Carabas (this was the name
he chose to give his master) has given me to present to
you on his behalf." "Tell your master," replied the King,
"that I thank him, and accept his gift with pleasure."

Another time he lay in the corn, keeping his sack open,
and when two partridges had gone into it, he pulled the
strings and caught them both. Then he went to present
them to the King, as he had done the rabbit. The King
received the partridges with still greater pleasure, and
gave the cat a little present in return.

The Cat continued doing this for two or three months,

taking all sorts of game to the King on his master's behalf. One day he found out that the King would be going to take the air by the riverside with his daughter, the
most beautiful princess in the world. So he said to his
master, "If you take my advice, your fortune is made.
You have only to bathe in the river, at a place that I will
show you, and then leave the rest to me."

The Marquis of Carabas did as his Cat advised, without knowing what it was all for. While he was bathing,
· the King came along, and the Cat began to cry with all
his might, "Help! help! the Marquis of Carabas is drown-
ing!" On hearing this cry, the King put his head out of
the carriage-window, and recognised the Cat who had
brought him game so often. He ordered that his guards
should go to the help of the Marquis of Carabas.

"While they were dragging the poor Marquis out of
the water, the Cat came up to the carriage, and told the
King that, while his master was bathing, some thieves
had come and carried off his clothes, although he had
cried "Stop thief!" as loud as he could. The artful puss
had hidden them under a large stone!

The King thereupon ordered the officers of his ward-
robe to go and find out some fine clothes for the Marquis of Carabas. The King himself showed him all
possible courtesy, and as the fine clothes which had just
been given him showed off his figure to advantage (for
he was a handsome, well-built young fellow), the King's
daughter took quite a fancy to him. Indeed, the Marquis
of Carabas had but thrown a few glances, half-respectful,
half-tender, in her direction, before she was over head
and ears in love with him.

The King asked him to come into his carriage, and join them in their drive. The Cat, delighted to find his plans succeeding so well, went on before, and meeting some peasants, who were mowing a meadow, said to them, "Look here, my fine mowers, if you don't tell the King that the meadow that you mow belongs to the Marquis of Carabas, you will be chopped into little bits like mincemeat."

Sure enough, the King asked the mowers whose meadow it was that they mowed. "It belongs to the Marquis of Carabas," they answered with one accord, for the Cat's threat had frightened them.

"You have a fine estate here," said the King to the Marquis of Carabas. "As you see, sire," replied the Marquis, "this particular meadow always yields me a rich hay-crop."

Master Puss, who kept on in front, met some reapers, and said to them, "Look here, my fine reapers, if you don't say that all this corn belongs to the Marquis ot Carabas, you will be chopped into little pieces like mincemeat." The King passed by a moment after, and asked who was the owner of all this corn that he saw. "It belongs to the Marquis of Carabas," replied the reapers; and the King again complimented the Marquis. The Cat, going still in front of the carriage, told everyone he met in the same way to say the same thing, and the King was amazed at the Marquis of Carabas' wealth.

Master Puss arrived at last at a beautiful castle, whose owner was an Ogre, the richest ever known, for all the country that the King had passed through was really the castle's domain. The Cat, who had taken pains to find

who this Ogre was, and what he could do, asked to speak
with him, saying that he could not think of passing so
near the castle without giving himself the honour of paying his respects.

The Ogre received him as civilly as an Ogre can, and
asked him to sit down. "They tell me," said the Cat,
"that you have the power of changing into all sorts of
animals—that you could, for example, turn yourself into
a lion, or an elephant." "That is true," replied the Ogre,
gruffly; "and to prove it, you shall see me change into
a lion." The Cat was so frightened to see a lion in front of
him, that he scrambled on to the roof as quickly as he
could, and not without difficulty, by reason of his boots,
which were not of much use for walking on the tiles.

Some time after, the Cat, seeing that the Ogre had
quitted his first shape, came down, and confessed that he
had had a terrible fright. "They have told me, too," said
the Cat, "but I can hardly bring myself to believe it yet,
that you have also the power to take the form of the very
smallest animals—that you could, for example, change
yourself into a rat or a mouse. I must say it seems to me
quite impossible." "Impossible!" retorted the Ogre;
"you shall see!" At the same time he changed himself
into a mouse, which ran about the floor. The Cat no
sooner saw this than he pounced upon the mouse, and
ate it.

Meanwhile the King, who had seen in the distance the
Ogre's castle, wished to go inside. The Cat, who heard
the rumbling of the carriage going over the drawbridge,
ran to the front of the castle, and said to the King, "Your
Majesty is welcome to the Marquis of Carabas' castle!"

"How now, my dear Marquis!" exclaimed the King; "is this castle yours too? Certainly nothing could be more beautiful than this courtyard and these buildings all around. I should very much like to go in."

The Marquis gave his hand to the young Princess, and following the King, who went up first, they entered a great hall, where they found a magnificent feast. This the Ogre had prepared for some friends who were coming to see him that very day, but who had not dared to venture in, knowing that the King was there. The King, charmed with the personality of the Marquis of Carabas, as also with his daughter—who was, as we have seen, already madly in love with him—and noticing the vast wealth that he appeared to possess, said to him after having drunk a glass or two, "Would you care to be my son-in-law, Marquis? It only rests with you!" The Marquis, with a profound bow, accepted the honour that the King had offered him, and that very day he married the Princess. The Cat became a great lord, and he never chased mice afterwards except in the way of sport.

THE MOUSIKIE

There was a wee bit mousikie,
    That lived in Gilberaty, O,
It couldna get a bite o' cheese,
    For cheetie-poussie-cattie, O.

It said unto the cheesikie,
    'Oh fain wad I be at ye, O,
If 't were na for the cruel paws
    O' cheetie-poussie-cattie, O'.

ALL GONE

There was once a cat called Slyboots, who, after
having lived most of her life with a rich widow
in a very comfortable house, suddenly found
herself without a home. She had seen a good deal of the
world, and knew how hard it might prove for a creature
like herself no longer young and in this sad state of
affairs to live easy. Besides, she was indolent by nature,
had been brought up in luxury, and could only hope for
the best. With this in mind, she struck up an acquaintance
with a mouse. At first they merely exchanged the time
of day; and if they met by chance in one of the rooms
of the empty mansion, it was the mouse who was

59

quickly gone. And when, later, it came to a little talk
and gossiping between them, the mouse much preferred
to be on the other side of her hole in the wainscot. But
she was a simple and good-natured little creature, if vain
and fond of flattery, and was so proud of her fine new
acquaintance that she at length put aside all doubts,
qualms and misgivings, and agreed to keep house with
the cat.

A very good bargain this was for Slyboots. The mouse
had not only agreed to do all the housework—sweep,
dust, tidy and keep things neat and trim; but she it was
who at night went scampering off in the dark from house
to house, snuffing out wheresoever good food and
dainties were to be found—meat and marrow, bones
and scraps, cheese and butter. She knew every cranny
and crevice and hole; and if any larder door had been
left ajar, the cat soon heard of it. All Slyboots had to do
was to steal out and fetch in what they needed (and the
mouse needed very little), and to idle away the rest of
the day in daydreaming and drowsing at home in ease
and idleness. It was a hot and thundery summer when
first they met, no weather for exercise; so this way of life
suited her very well; and she never ceased whispering sly
pleasant little speeches in the mouse's small round ear
whenever she appeared in sight or they sat together at
meals. And so the time went by until it drew on towards
autumn.

"There is one little matter that is troubling me," said
the cat one evening, after a private look round the house
when the mouse had been out marketing. "A trifle as
yet, my dear, but yet worth your pondering over. We

have *no* provision for the winter. Not a morsel. And, since we are now living alone, we have none of these clumsy, selfish humans to help us. Winter will be *our* hungry time. I am strong and lusty and can, of course, fend for myself. It's little you I am thinking of. It troubles me. The cold will come—frost and snow and bitter winds. Doors and windows will be shut. You musn't risk your precious life too often. There are traps, and I know what a temptation toasted cheese may be; there are—er—hungry enemies always in wait. Now what shall we do about the winter?"

At this, the simple mouse could scarcely contain herself for pride. "Ah, my dear friend, I long ago thought of that. When I was living alone. Before I had your precious, precious company. Come with me, and you shall share a little secret."

Without another word she went into the back parts of a dusty old closet and showed the cat where, by hook and by crook, she had stowed away a fine, large, earthenware gallipot brim-full of fat. "That jar, my dear, contains all my hard-won savings; and I would rather starve than waste it."

" 'Starve,' " said the cat, and stared, her tail-tip twitching softly from side to side. She sniffed. She purred. "Excellent," she cried again and again. "How clever! how ingenious! How thoughtful and how wise! There is but one little doubt in my mind, my dear. Is this cupboard safe? Surely the rats or—other creatures—might get in here *any* fine moonlight night."

At this the mouse was much alarmed. At length, after long and anxious discussion, the cat said, "Wainscots are good, cupboards are good, cellars are good; so are holes in the ground, hollows in trees, empty houses, caves, chasms and grottoes. But there is no place in the wide world, my dear, where a treasure like ours can be more safely stowed away than in a church. A church. Not even the wickedest thieves and robbers would dare to steal anything out of a church. St. Thomas's is the very place. It's cold. Most days it's empty, and there is a broken pane of glass under the belfry. I know the very place where we can hide the pot—behind a stone tomb, my dear—where no-one would look for it. It shall be done to-morrow; and we will not so much as touch, taste or even think of it until we are really and truly in *need* of it. No, my dear."

So towards evening next day they set out together to the church. The pot was hidden in its niche behind the tomb, not a soul being by to see them there. And as darkness came on, they stole out of the church and returned home. The days passed in peace and quiet; and they seemed to be closer friends than ever.

But it was not very long before the cat began to grow a little weary of the mouse's company, looks, and ways; and to pine on and on even for but just one secret sniff of the great gallipot of fat. As time went on she could think of little else; and, paws tucked in, would sit brooding all day in a corner, sulky and silent.

"I hope, dear friend," said the mouse at last, "you are not in any trouble, not indisposed, not ill?"

"Dear me, no!" the cat replied. "*Me*, ill! Never. Still, there is a little something on my mind. It is this. My favourite cousin who lives nine streets away has just brought a small, handsome son into the world. A beautiful little creature, creamy-white with cinnamon-brown patches, and I have been asked to be his godmother. They live in a fine house, and on the fat of the land; and it is, of course, a great honour. No need to tell *you* that, my dear! But I have been unable to decide whether or not to go to this christening only because I felt that, well, you *might* be a little hurt—a *little* hurt perhaps, at not having been asked to come too."

"Hurt!" said the mouse, stifling a gasp and a shiver at the very thought of being a guest in such a company. "Certainly not, my dear. I'll take every care of the house while you are gone, and shall be almost as happy alone thinking of you in the feasting and merrymaking as if I were with you. And if there *should* be any morsel very much to my taste at the christening, I am sure you will remember me. There's nothing like a sip and a suppet of sweet red christening wine! Please not to forget me!"

But the cat had no such cousin, not she. Nor had she been invited to be a godmother. By no means. Without another word, she slipped out of doors, and first this turning, then that, stole on and made her way straight to the church, looked, listened, then crawled in through the hole in the belfry window which was easily wide enough to admit her without brushing her whiskers. Once safe inside, in the cool great empty place, she had soon pushed off the lid of the pot. Crouched up in the niche behind the stone image, she at once set to at her feast.

Nor did she desist until she had licked off the complete upper layer of the rich ripe fat. After which, well fed, she replaced the pot in its hiding-place, stole out of the

63

church, and took a walk upon the roofs of the town, on the lookout for other little opportunities. She then stretched herself out in the sun, sleeked herself with her long well-oiled tongue from chin to tail-tip, licking her chops whenever she thought of her feast; composed herself for a nap, and it was far on in the evening before she returned home.

"So here you are," said the mouse, "safe and sound. I've waited supper, my dear. But I was beginning to get anxious. I hope you've had a happy day."

"Happy enough," said the cat.

"And what name did they give the infant?"

"'Name?' 'Name'?" repeated the cat. "Why Top-off!"

"Topoff!" murmured the mouse. "*Topoff*! That is an odd, uncommon name—a very odd name."

"Usual or not, what does it signify?" said the cat. "It's no worse than *Crumbstealer* or *Cheesepicker*, I suppose, as so many of *your* godchildren seem or ought to be called." And at that the mouse fell silent.

Before long Mistress Slyboots was seized with yet another fit of longing for the fat. The savour and sweetness of the pot haunted her very dreams. And at last she said to the mouse, "You must do me yet another favour, my dear, and once more for an hour or two manage the house in my absence. I am again asked to be godmother, —friends at a little distance too—and, as this time the infant is jet-black with a milk-white ring round its neck, a rare thing indeed if you knew anything about it, I simply cannot refuse."

The good kind mouse consented, and, waving Slyboots farewell from the porch, returned humbly into the house. And she—the cat—sly, gluttonous creature—she crept out once more by her short cuts and along the town walls to the church, and in at St. Thomas's window. And this time she half emptied the delicious pot of fat.

"It's a strange thing," she thought to herself, licking her chops, now this side, now that, "but nothing in this world ever tastes so good as the dainties one keeps to oneself." And she was well satisfied with her day's work.

The stars were already shining bright by the time she came back home. And a glossy, comfortable creature she looked as she stepped delicately into the house.

"And what is the name of your god-child this time?" enquired the mouse.

" 'Name'? 'This time'? What a nose, my dear, you have for trifles! Why Half-gone," answered the cat, with an inward grin.

"*Halfgone!* do you say? Well! Halfgone! I never heard so strange a name in the whole of my life! I'll wager *that* name's not in the Calendar!"

"The Calendar," cried the cat, "what's the Calendar to me? *Half-gone* was the name I said; and a plump, needle-clawed, silky-whiskered little creature it is." The mouse trembled a little at sight of her speaking these words, and presently crept off to bed.

For a time matters went much as usual; and all was friendly once more. But not many days had gone by before the cat's mouth began to water again. She would actually wake up in the middle of the morning, licking her chops at rich flavours which although they were but memories seemed to be on her very tongue. She paced about, restless and yawning, stared at nothing, and became so contrary and morose that her house-mate the mouse would hide herself away in her room for hours together merely to be out of reach of her sullen stare.

And then one fine October afternoon, the cat delayed no longer, but cried out in a loud voice to the mouse: "All good things go in threes, my dear. You will scarcely credit it; but I am asked to stand godmother yet again. This time the child is rarest tortoiseshell—of a pattern and colouring never seen outside a Queen's palace. It has opened its eyes, and it mews, my dear, a complete octave—an infant seven days old! Think of it! Why, it can happen but once in a century—if that. But it's blood that tells. I hate, I grieve, I can't endure to leave you lonely, beds unmade, rooms unswept. But how can I help myself? How can I resist? And you so much amused at my family names! Ah, well; I bear no grudge. Jeer if it pleases you. *I* shall not be hurt."

"*Topoff! Halfgone!*" murmured the mouse. "They were certainly odd names. They made me a little thoughtful. Perhaps you are growing a little tired of me. And now another to come!"

"Ah, but you sit at home," said the cat, "in your demure dark-grey fur coat and that long dainty tail, and you are filled with fancies. That's because you so seldom venture out in the day-time. You are *too* dainty, you don't eat enough. No variety: nothing rich. You think too much. We must keep up with the times. We must turn over a new leaf." With that she pricked up her whiskers, and off she went.

During the cat's absence the mouse cleaned the house from top to bottom, putting everything in spotless trim.

And while she scrubbed and polished, there was no time for sad, perplexing thoughts.

Meanwhile Slyboots was cowering greedily over the pot in the church; and this time she licked it as clean as a whistle. There wasn't a speck, not a vestige or flavour of fat left.

"When everything is finished, one may have a little peace," she said to herself. And thoroughly satisfied, she enjoyed a long dreamless sleep in the sunshine, took a jaunt through the town, gossiped with friends, saw the sights, and did not return home till well after midnight. At the first whisper of her at the door, the mouse looked out and at once enquired what name had been chosen for the third child.

"It will give you no more pleasure than the others," said the cat, with a surly glare. "We called him *Allgone*."

" '*Allgone*'!" cried the mouse. " '*Allgone*'! Oh, but how strange, how outlandish a name! Never in all my born days could I believe there was such a name. *Allgone!* Never. Nowhere."

"Well," said the cat, "you have heard it *now*. And that's the end of that." Whereupon she yawned as if her head would split in two, and went off to bed.

From that night on, Slyboots received no further invitation to stand godmother, and was so short with the mouse when she enquired after her three god-children that little more was said about the matter. Summer gone, she grew more and more sulky and ill-natured as the days of autumn drew in, and hardly ceased complaining of the food, professing that she was an invalid, had a dainty stomach, and needed constant care and every nourishment.

At last, one cold frosty morning the mouse crept up to her bedside and said, "My dear, it is nearly winter now. There is scarcely anything but rinds of vegetables to be found outside. Do you not agree it would be a very pleasant thing if we started off together and enjoyed just a taste or two of our pot of fat?"

Her face twinkled all over at the thought of it; and indeed, poor thing, having been so long skimped even of her crumbs, she was by now little but a packet of bones.

The cat opened her mouth as she lay in bed: "By all means," said she, "by all means. And you will enjoy your taste as you call it exactly as much as you would enjoy putting out that dainty tongue of yours at the window to flout the full moon!"

"What can *that* mean?" thought the mouse to herself. But she was too much excited to put her question into words. Off she scampered to make ready for the journey.

They set out, and as soon as the sexton's back was turned among the gravestones, they crept in at the belfry window. So cold and stony and gloomy was it inside the great church that a shiver ran down the mouse's spine, while her mouth watered the more. And at last they came to the hiding-place. And there was the pot, its parchment top tied down, and as neat as a new pin.

And the cat said, grinning, "My dear, *you* shall open it; *you* shall have first nibble; *you* shall first enjoy what we have so long been looking forward to. But leave a morsel for me!"

Whereupon Mistress Mouse nibbled through the

string, pushed off the cover, paused, and stared. The pot was empty. Bare.

"Oh! Ah! Alas! Alackaday!" broke out Slyboots in a wild shrill caterwauling. "Robbers, robbers! Thieves, thieves!" Her voice echoed dreadful and hollow in the cold church, and died away. The mouse turned slowly, and out of her little round bright jet-black eyes gazed at her friend.

"Aha!" she cried bitterly, "I see; oh, I see. Now I begin to understand. Now I know. Friend that you professed yourself; true, faithful friend that you *are*! First it was '*Topoff*'. Next it was '*Halfgone*'. And last it was . . . ."

"Hold your tongue this instant," yelled the cat, bristling all over. "Another syllable, and —"

' " '*Allgone*'," squeaked the mouse with her last breath.

For scarcely were the words out of her mouth, when Slyboots, claws extended, and with a yell of rage, had pounced upon her and swallowed her down.

"Truly," said she, as she turned away from the empty pot, and sallied out of the church, "that was a sad end to an old friendship. But such is the way of the world."

"TILLYVALLY"

Tillyvally, lady!
There dwelt a man in Babylon, lady, lady,
Farewell, ancient lady; farewell,
Lady, lady, lady.

WILLIAM SHAKESPEARE

KNURRE-MURRE

A farmer of Staindrop, in Durham, was one night crossing a bridge, when a cat jumped out, stood before him, and looking him full in the face, said:

> Johnny Reed! Johnny Reed!
> Tell Madam Momfort
> That Mally Dixon's dead.

The farmer returned home, and in mickle wonder recited this awfu' stanza to his wife, when up started their black cat, saying, "Is she?" and disappeared for ever. It was supposed she was a fairy in disguise, who thus went to attend a sister's funeral, for in the North fairies do die, and green shady spots are pointed out by the country folks as the graveyards of the silent people. Then again, near a town called Lyng is the hill of Brondhoë, inhabited by the trold-folk, or imps. Amongst these trolds was an old sickly devil, peevish and ill-tempered, because he was married to a young wife. This quarrelsome, querulous trold often set the rest by the ears, so they nicknamed him Knurre-Murre, or Rumble-Grumble. Now it came to pass, that Rumble-Grumble discovered that his young wife—sick and weary of his sullen temper and mean ways—still loved an old sweetheart of hers. And the old trold was green with jealousy. This sweetheart, to avoid his vengeance, was compelled to fly for his life from the great cavern in the mountain of Brondhoë, and take refuge, in the shape of a tortoise-shell cat, in the house of Goodman Platt, who harboured him with much hospitality, let him lie on the great wicker chair, and fed him twice a day with bread and milk out of a red earthenware pipkin. One evening the goodman came home, at a late hour, full of wonderment. "Goody," exclaimed he to his wife, "as I was passing by Brondhoë, there came out a trold, who spake to me, saying,

Hear thou, Platt,
Say to thy cat
That Knurre-Murre is dead."

The tortoise-shell cat was lying on the great wicker chair, and eating his supper of bread and milk out of the red earthenware pipkin, when the goodman came in; but as soon as the message was delivered, he jumped bolt up-

right upon his two hind legs, for all the world like a
Christian, and kicking the red earthenware pipkin and
the rest of the bread and milk before him, he whisked
through the cottage door, mewing, "What! Knurre-
Murre dead! Then I may go home again!"

THE HARE

In the black furrow of a field
 I saw an old witch hare this night;
And she cocked a lissom ear,
 And she eyed the moon so bright,
And she nibbled of the green;
 And I whispered "Wh-s-st! witch hare,"
Away like a ghostie o'er the field
 She fled, and left the moonlight there.

THE WITCH HARE

I was out thracking hares meself, and I seen a fine puss of a thing hopping, hopping in the moonlight, and whacking her ears about, now up, now down, and winking her great eyes, and—"Here goes," says I, and the thing was so close to me that she turned round and looked at me, and then bounced back, as well as to say, do your worst! So I had the least grain in life of *blessed powder* left, and I put it in the gun—and bang at her! My jewel, the scritch she gave would frighten a ridgment, and a mist, like, came betwixt me and her, and I seen her no more; but when the mist wint off I saw blood on the spot where she had been, and I followed its track, and at last it led me—whist, whisper—right up to Katey MacShane's door; and when I was at the thrashold, I heerd a murnin' within, a great murnin', and a groan-

75

in', and I opened the door, and there she was herself, sittin' quite content in the shape of a woman, and the black cat that was sittin' by her rose up its back and spit at me; but I went on never heedin', and asked the ould— how she was and what ailed her.

"Nothing," sis she.

"What's that on the floor?" sis I.

"Oh," she says, "I was cuttin' a billet of wood," she says, "wid the reaping hook," she says, "an' I've wounded meself in the leg," she says, "and that's drops of my precious blood," she says.

"GO AND TELL"

Go and tell Aunt Nancy,
Go and tell Aunt Nancy,
Go and tell Aunt Nancy
The old grey goose is dead.

The one that she'd been saving
For to make her feather-bed.

She died last Friday
With a pain all in her head.

Old gander is weeping
Because his wife is dead.

The goslings are mourning
Because their mother's dead.

Go and tell Aunt Nancy,
Go and tell Aunt Nancy,
Go and tell Aunt Nancy
The old grey goose is dead.

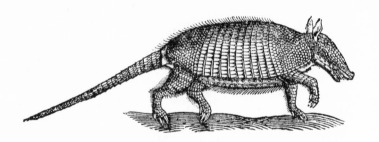

THE FOX AND THE GEESE

An old fox happened to come idling one fine morning into a meadow in which sat sunning and preening themselves a flock of fine fat geese.

He smiled on them and said, "My, now! Lorramussy! I come in the very nick of time! There you all are, sitting together so happy and comfortable there won't be the least little bit of trouble for any of us. I can just gobble you up one after the other. And I promise you it will be a very merry little party."

The geese began cackling with rage and terror, sprang up, hissing and wailing, and begged piteously for their lives. But the old fox refused to listen.

" 'Mercy' do you say?" he said; " 'mercy,' my dear friends! What, I pray you, is the meaning of the word? No, I am hungry; you are fat. Alas, you must die."

At sight of his sly conceited grin, the craftiest and eldest of the birds, an old gander, began to take heart of grace, and said, "Well, Sir, if there is no help for it, if every single one of us poor innocent creatures must yield up our lives in what you think is so good a cause, so it must be. But first grant us, Sir, I entreat you, but one small favour. Give us leave to say one more prayer, lest

we should die in our sins. That done, we will stand in
a row, and you can pick us out, one by one, fattest to
leanest, for your breakfast, just as you please."

The old fox eyed the gander. "That seems to sound
reasonable enough," he said at last. "Once one's head is
off, there is not much left to ask. Pray away, then, all of
you, and I will promise to wait until you have done."

At this, the old gander at once began a long, long
prayer, saying over and over, "*Ga! Ga! Ga! Ga!—Ga!
Ga! Ga! Ga! Ga!*"

When, in sheer weariness, he began to make an end,
the plump young goose next to him, who had been
hardly able to await her turn, began also, "*Ga! Ga! Ga!
Ga!—Ga! Ga! Ga! Ga! Ga!*"

And so with the third and the fourth and the fifth and
all the rest of them. There they all stood, cackling and
cackling and cackling together, turn and turn about;
now one, now two, now a quartette, and anon a complete chorus, "*Ga! Ga! Ga! Ga!—Ga! Ga! Ga! Ga! Ga!
Ga! Ga!*" On and on and on.

When they have all finished praying, then this story
shall be continued. At present, there is no sign of it. Ask
the old fox.

"LITTLE SHON"

Little Shon a Morgan,
    Shentleman of Wales,
Came riding on a nanny-goat,
    Selling of pigs' tails.

MRS. FOX

There was once an old fox, well on in years, who had nine tails. As his days grew on him, he became even more wily and suspicious, and what he particularly pined to discover was whether his vain, handsome young wife still loved him. And one fine day he took it into his head to try a trick on her. He stretched himself out stiff and stark under an old bench, and pretended to be as dead as a doornail. Nose-tip to tail-tip there was no sign but that he had breathed his last.

When Mrs. Fox discovered that her husband was dead, she hastened up into her bedroom, shut and bolted the door, and burst out a-weeping; leaving only her faithful maid, Mrs. Cat, downstairs at the kitchen fire, busy over her cooking.

Long before to-morrow-come-never it was known

all over the country round that old Mr. Fox was dead and gone. The very next evening indeed, there was a footstep in his backyard, someone came softly knocking at the kitchen door, and a voice murmured:

> "Is that Mistress Pussie? How *are* you to-day?—
> Asleep, or just watching the hours slip away?"

Mrs. Cat stepped over and opened the door; and there, in the entry, stood a spruce and handsome young Fox.

> "Nay, nay Master Fox—Me sleep in the *day!*
> I am making some capital white-wine-whey.
> Would your honour be pleased to dinner to stay?"

"I thank you kindly," replied Master Fox; "but not perhaps to-day. And how is poor, poor *Mrs.* Fox?" And the Cat answered:

> "She sits all alone in her chamber upstairs,
> Bewailing her sorrow with floods of tears.
> She has wept till her beautiful eyes are red.
> Alas, Master Fox, her husband is dead."

"Indeed and indeed," said Master Fox, his green eyes fixed on her. "That is very sad and doleful news. Pray go to her at once. Tell her that a cousin of hers, young Mr. Fox, has called, and that he beseeches her to marry him."

> Upstairs stepped the Pussycat, *trippety trap;*
> And knocked on the door—*tip-tippety tap:*
> "Is that my dear Mistress within?" cried she.

> "Alas! What want you, my dear, with me?"

MRS. FOX

"A suitor is waiting below at the gate."

"A suitor, my dear! Is he tall and straight?
Has he nine bushy tails? There must be nine,
Not a single tail less shall have suitor of mine!"

" 'Tails'?" repeated the Cat. "No, mistress. He has but one."

"Then," said Mrs. Fox, "I can't have him."

So the Cat tippeted downstairs again, and sent Master Fox about his business. Not long after, there came another knock at the door. The sprightly Fox, now on the other side of it, was one tail better off than the first; but he was no more welcome. After him came several others. But none of them had nine tails, and every one was sent away with a flea in his ear. At last, towards nightfall, there knocked on the door as sprightly and handsome a Fox as anyone could wish to see; and, one—two—three —four—five—six—seven—eight. . . . There could be no doubt of it. He had nine tails!

Up went the Cat, then, *trippety trap;*
And knock on the door she did, *tippety tap.*
"News, news!" she whispered, "sweet Mistress mine,
Here's another one come; and his tails are nine!"

When the widow heard this, she at once dried her eyes, jumped out of her chair, and called:

"Then, Pussy, my dear, open windows and doors,
And bid all our friends at our wedding to meet;
And as for that jealous old master of yours,
Just bundle his body out into the street."

Not a moment was wasted; the guests came, the feast was ready; the new nine-tailed bridegroom stood at the top of the table, bowing and smirking and smiling all over his face, when, all of a sudden, up sprang the old gentleman, and with a great cudgel at once set about him, and drove every single one of them out of the house—Mrs. Fox, the bridegroom, and all.

There came a day at length, however, when old Mr. Fox really and truly did breathe his last. Having this time made perfectly sure that dead he was and dead indeed, Mrs. Fox again retired to her room. But not to weep. She had been there less than an hour when an old grey wolf came to pay his respects. He knocked at the kitchen door, lifted the latch, looked in, opened his mouth and muttered gruffly, "Good day, Mrs. Cat.

> How sleek we are looking, and slim and trim;
> But why are you sitting alone—so prim?
> I seem to smell cooking too; what, I pray?"

> "It's a giblet pudding for dinner to-day.
> Would your Worship be pleased to stay and dine?
> Be seated; I'll fetch you a glass of wine."

"No, no; I thank you," replied the Wolf. "*Mrs.* Fox is not at home, I suppose?"

> "She sits all alone, her griefs to bemoan;
> Alas, and alas! *He's*—dead and gone."

> "Ah! sweet Mistress Puss; that's sad tidings indeed! . . .
> D'ye think she'd take *me* for a husband instead?"

"Why, that, Mr. Wolf, I can't say. It *might* be.
Excuse me a moment; I'll step up and see."

She gave him a chair, and pricking her ears,
She very obligingly tripped it upstairs.
And tapped at the door, her rings on her toes,
"It's me, ma'am," she said. "You're alone, I suppose?"

"Alone," sighed the widow; "pray enter, my dear;
And whose is that voice in the kitchen I hear?"

"Mr. Wolf's," said the Cat; "he has brushed up his
    skin!
He was passing this way, and has just stepped in
To enquire—as he's heard Mr. Fox is now dead—
If you'd care to take him for a husband instead."

"Tell me," said Mrs. Fox, "has he neat red feet and a
lean sharp snout?"

"No," said the Cat.

"Then," said Mrs. Fox, "he won't do for *me*."

Soon after Mr. Wolf had been sent about his business,
there came first a Mr. Dog, then a Mr. Goat, and after
that a Mr. Bear, a Mr. Lion, and many another beast,
great and small, one after another. In every single one of
them something was missing that old Mr. Fox could
boast of, or was not to Mrs. Fox's liking, and, each in
turn, the Cat was told to send them away.

Last of all, there came knocking at the door a Mr. Fox
as slim and sleek as he was young and handsome.

"Tell me," said Mrs. Fox to Mrs. Cat, "has he four red
feet and a long sharp snout?"

"That he has," said the Cat.

MRS. FOX

"Then, Puss, make the parlour look tidy and neat.
Throw that nine-tailed old gentleman into the street;
A numskull old rascal! I'm thankful he's dead,
Now I have such a charming young suitor instead."

So the wedding was held, and the merry bells rang,
And the friends and relations, they danced and they
     sang,
Never seen in those parts was so canty a throng;
They feasted and drank—I can't tell you how long.

THE MAGICIANS

O She looked out of the window,
    As white as any milk;
But He looked into the window,
    As black as any silk.

Hulloa, hulloa, hulloa, hulloa, you coal black smith!
    O what is your silly song?
You never shall change my maiden name
    That I have kept so long;
I'd rather die a maid,   yes, but then she said,
And be buried all in my grave,
Than I'd have such a nasty, husky, dusky, musty, fusky
    Coal black smith:
                A maiden I will die.

Then She became a duck,
    A duck all on the stream;
And He became a water dog,
    And fetched her back again.
      Hulloa, etc.

Then She became a hare,
    A hare all on the plain;
And He became a greyhound dog,
    And fetched her back again.
      Hulloa, etc.

Then She became a fly,
    A fly all in the air;
And He became a spider,
    And fetched her to his lair.

THE MAGICIANS

Hulloa, hulloa, hulloa, hulloa, you coal black smith!
    O what is your silly song?
You never shall change my maiden name
    That I have kept so long;
I'd rather die a maid,   yes, but then she said,
And be buried all in my grave,
Than I'd have such a nasty, husky, dusky, musty, fusky
    Coal black smith:
          A maiden I will die.

TOM TIT TOT

Once upon a time there was a woman, and she baked five pies. And when they came out of the oven, they were that overbaked the crusts were too hard to eat. So she says to her daughter:

"Darter," says she, "put you them there pies on the shelf, and leave 'em there a little, and they'll come again." She meant, you know, the crust would get soft.

But the girl, she says to herself: "Well, if they'll come again, I'll eat 'em now." And she set to work and ate 'em all, first and last.

Well, come supper-time the woman said: "Go you, and get one o' them there pies. I dare say they've come again now."

The girl went and she looked, and there was nothing but the dishes. So back she came and says she: "Noo, they ain't come again."

"Not one of 'em?" says the mother.

"Not one of 'em," says she.

"Well, come again, or not come again," said the woman, "I'll have one for supper."

"But you can't, if they ain't come," said the girl.

"But I can," says she. "Go you, and bring the best of 'em."

"Best or worst," says the girl, "I've ate 'em all, and you can't have one till that's come again."

Well, the woman she was done, and she took her spinning to the door to spin, and as she span she sang:

> "My darter ha' ate five, five pies to-day.
> My darter ha' ate five, five pies to-day."

The king was coming down the street, and he heard her sing, but what she sang he couldn't hear, so he stopped and said:

"What was that you were singing, my good woman?"

The woman was ashamed to let him hear what her daughter had been doing, so she sang, instead of that:

> "My darter ha' spun five, five skeins to-day.
> My darter ha' spun five, five skeins to-day."

"Stars o' mine!" said the king, "I never heard tell of any one that could do that."

Then he said: "Look you here, I want a wife, and I'll marry your daughter. But look you here," says he, "eleven months out of the year she shall have all she likes to eat, and all the gowns she likes to get, and all the company she likes to keep; but the last month of the year she'll have to spin five skeins every day, and if she don't I shall kill her."

"All right," says the woman; for she thought what a grand marriage that was. And as for the five skeins, when the time came, there'd be plenty of ways of getting out of it, and likeliest, he'd have forgotten all about it.

Well, so they were married. And for eleven months the girl had all she liked to eat, and all the gowns she liked to get, and all the company she liked to keep.

But when the time was getting over, she began to think about the skeins and to wonder if he had 'em in mind. But not one word did he say about 'em, and she thought he's wholly forgotten 'em.

However, the last day of the last month he takes her to a room she'd never set eyes on before. There was nothing in it but a spinning-wheel and a stool. And says he: "Now, my dear, here you'll be shut in to-morrow with some victuals and some flax, and if you haven't spun five skeins by the night, your head'll go off."

And away he went about his business.

Well, she was that frightened, she'd always been such a gatless girl, that she didn't so much as know how to spin, and what was she to do to-morrow with no one to come nigh her to help her? She sat down on a stool in kitchen, and law! how she did cry!

However, all of a sudden she heard a sort of a knocking low down on the door. She upped and oped it, and what should she see but a small little black thing with a long tail. That looked up at her right curious, and that said:

"What are you a-crying for?"

"What's that to you?" says she.

"Never you mind," that said, "but tell me what you're a-crying for."

"That won't do me no good if I do," says she.

"You don't know that," that said, and twirled that's tail round.

"Well," says she, "that won't do no harm, if that don't do no good," and she upped and told about the pies, and the skeins, and everything.

"This is what I'll do," says the little black thing, "I'll come to your window every morning and take the flax and bring it spun at night."

"What's your pay?" says she.

That looked out of the corner of that's eyes, and that said: "I'll give you three guesses every night to guess my name, and if you haven't guessed it before the month's up you shall be mine."

Well, she thought she'd be sure to guess that's name before the month was up. "All right," says she, "I agree."

"All right," that says, and law! how that twirled that's tail.

Well, the next day, her husband took her into the room, and there was the flax and the day's food.

"Now there's the flax," says he, "and if that ain't spun up this night, off goes your head." And then he went out and locked the door.

He'd hardly gone, when there was a knocking against the window.

She upped and oped it, and there sure enough was the little old thing sitting on the ledge.

"Where's the flax?" says he.

"Here it be," says she. And she gave it to him.

Well, come the evening a knocking came again to the window. She upped and she oped it, and there was the little old thing with five skeins of flax on his arm.

"Here it be," says he, and he gave it to her.

"Now, what's my name?" says he.

"What, is that Bill?" says she.

"Noo, that ain't," says he, and he twirled his tail.

"Is that Ned?" says she.

"Noo, that ain't," says he, and he twirled his tail.

"Well, is that Mark?" says she.

"Noo, that ain't," says he, and he twirled his tail harder, and away he flew.

Well, when her husband came in, there were the five skeins ready for him. "I see I shan't have to kill you to-night, my dear," says he; "you'll have your food and your flax in the morning," says he, and away he goes.

Well, every day the flax and the food were brought, and every day that there little black impet used to come mornings and evenings. And all the day the girl sate trying to think of names to say to it when it came at night. But she never hit on the right one. And as it got towards the end of the month, the impet began to look so maliceful, and that twirled that's tail faster and faster each time she gave a guess.

At last it came to the last day but one. The impet came at night along with the five skeins, and that said:

"Wat, ain't you got my name yet?"

"Is that Nicodemus?" says she.

"Noo, 'tain't," that says.

"Is that Sammle?" says she.

"Noo, 'tain't," that says.

"A-well, is that Methusalem?" says she.

"Noo, 'tain't that neither," that says.

Then that looks at her with that's eyes like a coal o' fire, and that says: "Woman, there's only to-morrow night, and then you'll be mine!" And away it flew.

Well, she felt that horrid. However, she heard the king coming along the passage. In he came, and when he sees the five skeins, he says, says he:

"Well, my dear," says he. "I don't see but what you'll have your skeins ready for to-morrow night as well, and as I reckon I shan't have to kill you, I'll have supper in here to-night." So they brought supper, and another stool for him, and down the two sate.

Well, he hadn't eaten but a mouthful or so, when he stops and begins to laugh.

"What is it?" says she.

"A-why," says he, "I was out a-hunting to-day, and I got away to a place in the wood I'd never seen before. And there was an old chalk-pit. And I heard a kind of a sort of humming. So I got off my hobby, and I went right quiet to the pit, and I looked down. Well, what should there be but the funniest little black thing you ever set eyes on. And what was that doing, but that had a little spinning-wheel, and that was spinning wonderful fast, and twirling that's tail. And as that span that sang:

> "Nimmy nimmy not
> My name's Tom Tit Tot."

Well, when the girl heard this, she felt as if she could have jumped out of her skin for joy, but she didn't say a word.

Next day that there little thing looked so maliceful when he came for the flax. And when night came, she heard that knocking against the window panes. She oped the window, and that come right in on the ledge. That was grinning from ear to ear, and Oo! that's tail was twirling round so fast.

"What's my name?" that says, as that gave her the skeins.

"Is that Solomon?" she says, pretending to be afeard.

"Noo, 'tain't," that says, and that came further into the room.

"Well, is that Zebedee?" says she again.

"Noo, 'tain't," says the impet. And then that laughed and twirled that's tail till you could hardly see it.

"Take time, woman," that says; "next guess, and you're mine." And that stretched out that's black hands at her.

Well, she backed a step or to, and she looked at it,

and then she laughed out, and says she, pointing her finger at it:

> "Nimmy nimmy not
> Your name's TOM TIT TOT."

Well, when that heard her, that gave an awful shriek and away that flew into the dark, and she never saw it any more.

"THERE WAS A MAN"

There was a man of double deed
Who sowed his garden full of seed;
And when the seed began to grow,
'Twas like a garden full of snow;
And when the snow began to fall,
Like birds it was upon the wall;
And when the birds began to fly,
'Twas like a shipwreck in the sky;
And when the sky began to crack,
'Twas like a stick upon my back;
And when my back began to smart,
'Twas like a pen-knife in my heart;
And when my heart began to bleed,
Then I was dead—and dead indeed.

THE FALSE KNIGHT UPON
THE ROAD

"O whare are ye gaun?"
  Quo' the fause knicht upon the road:
"I'm gaun to the scule."
  Quo' the wee boy, and still he stude.

"What is that upon your back?"
  Quo' the fause knicht upon the road:
"Atweel[1] it is my bukes."
  Quo' the wee boy, and still he stude.

[1] Why, sure.

"What's that ye've got in your arm?"
Quo' the fause knicht upon the road:
"Atweel it is my peit." [1]
Quo' the wee boy, and still he stude.

"Wha's aucht[2] they sheep?"
Quo' the fause knicht upon the road:
"They're mine and my mither's."
Quo' the wee boy, and still he stude.

"How monie o' them are mine?"
Quo' the fause knicht upon the road:
"A'[3] they that hae blue tails."
Quo' the wee boy, and still he stude.

"I wiss ye were on yon tree:"
Quo' the fause knicht upon the road:
"And a gude ladder under me."
Quo' the wee boy, and still he stude.

"And the ladder for to break:"
Quo' the fause knicht upon the road:
"And *you* for to fa' down."
Quo' the wee boy, and still he stude.

"I wiss ye were on yon sie:"[4]
Quo' the fause knicht upon the road:
"And a gude bottom[5] under me."
Quo' the wee boy, and still he stude.

---

[1] Peat for the school fire.   [2] Who owns.
[3] All.   [4] Sea.   [5] Vessel, ship.

THE FALSE KNIGHT UPON THE ROAD

"And the bottom for to break:"
   Quo' the fause knicht upon the road:
"And *ye* to be drowned."
   Quo' the wee boy, and still he stude.

NO-BEARD

There was once a widow-woman, and one fine morning she sent her son with a bag of corn to be ground at the mill. "Go quick," she said, "and come back soon. And if," she said, "when you come to the mill, you look and see that cunning old wizard No-beard there, run away, and go on to the next mill. He's a rare old deceiver." She gave him a kiss, he slung the bag over his shoulder, and off he went.

Sure enough, when he came to the mill and peeped and peered he spied old No-beard inside grinding his corn. So he tiptoed away again and went on to the next mill. He peeped and he peered, and sure enough inside was old No-beard again—as if he had never stirred foot —still grinding his corn. And so it was with the third mill.

This time, however, he decided to go no further. In

he went, and there was No-beard, wizen and humpty-backed, stooping over the hopper.

"Good morrow," says No-beard, scarcely squinting round at him.

"Good morrow," said the small boy, and waited until the old cheat's sack was empty.

When he had poured out his own small bag of corn into the hopper and the meal had begun to trickle into the bin below, No-beard says to him, "Odds-sake, son, it's a fine loaf we'll be baking, you and me, out of *that* meal. Run along and fetch some water in the hollow of your hands and put it into the tub, and I'll be bolting it."

The boy ran to and fro fetching water in the cup of his hands until there was enough for the dough, and all his flour had been bolted. Nevertheless, No-beard kneaded up only one great lump out of all that dough. This, after sweeping out the wood ashes, he put into the brick oven to bake.

When the loaf was baked and ready and had come out of the oven smoking hot, No-beard says to the small boy, "Now, hearken unto me, my pretty little boy; whichever one of us can tell the best lie shall have the whole loaf. And I'll begin."

And so he did; and gabbled off a dozen lies or more—one or two of them right-down flaming crams and whoppers—as fast as his tongue could wag; and he wound up with, "So the old fox said to the little fox, folding its paws for grace, 'that there loaf there smoking hot out of the oven is for No-beard and for nobody else, man, woman or child.' " For truly he could lie the hands off an old clock, and a cat out of her whiskers. "Now what," says No-beard, "what d'ye say to that, my pretty little boy?" And he made to put the whole loaf into his sack."

But, "Stay a while," says the small boy.

Now it happened that at this moment the two of them, No-beard and the widow-woman's son, were standing beside an old brick pig-sty not far from the mill, where cosy and comfortable in the sun a great black sow was stretched out, and all her little pigs around her.

"That was a fine pack of lies you told," began the boy. "At least one or two. But I know better. In *my* young days, when I was an old old man, I used to count all my father's bees every morning. It was easier to count the bees than the beehives because there were so many. Once when I was counting, what should I find but that my father's best bee was missing, the very best bee that ever was. So I saddled a fine red cock out of the yard, set out after the bee, and a little before sunset as soon as morning was come I came on his track. Over the valleys and under the mountains I followed him, never letting my nine eyes off him as long as he was out of sight, until we came to the sea. And a mighty fine wooden bridge over the sea *that* was, all made of shiny stone and all. And on the other side, there was my bee, harnessed to a plough; and he was ploughing a parcel of land, twelve miles there and back, for millet. So I yelled out to the ploughman, 'That bee of yours is my bee!' The ploughman gave him back to me; and filled a bag twice full into the bargain with the millet he had just been reaping. I hung the bag of millet on the bee's back, took the saddle off the cock, buckled it on to the bee, and as the cock

was tired out with long travel, I took hold of his hand
and led him along beside me.

"Me coming back on the bridge over the sea, the string
broke, and all the millet came spilling out of the bag until
there was no more than twice times of it left. Night
came down on me while I was on the wide sea shore, so
I tethered the cock to the bee, and lay me down to sleep.
When in the middle of the dark I woke in the morning,
I found that a pack of wolves had come and devoured
my bee, and all the honey had run out of his body. So
deep was the honey in that valley that it came up thick
as treacle over the knees of the mountains. I seized a
hatchet and ran off with it into the forest. There I saw
two fine fat dappled roes leaping about on one leg. I
dashed them in pieces with my hatchet, skinned them,
and out of the two skins I made a little leather bottle
which I filled with the honey and lashed to the cock's
back. With this I went home to my father who, a moment before, had just been born. Says I to my grand-
mother, who had been twenty years dead, I must skip
along off to heaven, grandma, and fetch some holy
water for the christening. And how was I to get there?
thinks I to myself. And I thought of my millet. Damp
had set it sprouting, and when I came to it, it had grown
up and up and up and down and down and down again
until it reached the blue sky and back. I climbed and I
climbed and I climbed and I climbed; and when I came
to Paradise, what if the reapers hadn't mown down my
millet, made meal of it, and had baked a loaf of it which
they had broken into small pieces over a skillet of stone-
cold boiling milk, and were eating their breakfast. They

gave me a half-empty bottle full of holy water; and I was just about to climb down out of Paradise on my way back to earth again when I found that a great storm of wind and thunder had swept away my millet. I lay down on the edge, and looked over; and found that my hair, which, when I stood up came down as far as my ears, now dangled down low enough to reach the earth. I pulled a strand of it out; knotted one hair fast to another; and began to slide down. When darkness came on, I tied a knot in the hair, and stayed where I was. But it was cold as hot potatoes up there in the night. So I took a needle out of my coat, split it into chips, made a fire of them, and lay down by it until I had fallen asleep.

"While I was wide awake and dreaming, a spark out of the fire fell on to the hair I was hanging by, and burnt it through. The hair broke; down I fell for three days and half a night; and sank into the earth up to my very breastbone. I couldn't stir; so I ran along home as fast as I could to fetch a mallet, and I dug myself up out of the ground.

"On my way home, I crossed a field where three hundred reapers were cutting the corn. But the sun beat down so hot on their heads that their toes were all frostbitten. Off I ran and fetched our mare, which was two weeks long and as broad as midnight, with willows growing on her back; and in the shadow of our old mare, the reapers were able to go on with their reaping. But whiles and whiles they got very dry, and I went to a well to fetch water. When I came to the well it was a river and covered with ice twenty foot thick from shore to shore. So I took off my head, broke a hole in the ice with it, and took the reapers the water. They says, says they, just as you might:

"'But where, my pretty little boy, have you left your head?'

"Then I saw that I had forgotten it, and as fast as my heels could carry me, I ran back to the river. And what should I find but an old grey fox just licking the last of the brains out of my skull; so I stole up behind him and, might and main, gave him a kick. The fox was scared stiff, he was; he was so frightened, that fox, that he swallowed his tongue, squealed out '*Ohé, Ohé, Ohé*', and took out of his empty pocket a piece of paper, on which was written:—'That smoking hot loaf of bread is for the widow-woman's son every slice of it; and that wicked wily wizen-faced old No-beard can have the pigs'-wash!'"

So saying, the boy with a thumping shove tumbled the old wizard hind foremost into the sty; seized the loaf; and, as fast as his legs could carry him, ran off home to his mother.

"A PIE"

A pie sat on a pear tree,
A pie sat on a pear tree,
A pie sat on a pear tree,
Heigh ho! heigh ho! heigh ho!

THE LITTLE BIRD

There was once upon a time a shepherd boy whose renown spread far and wide by reason of the wise answers he made when he was asked questions. He spent his days alone with his sheep, in solitary places, hill and stream and valley; and would sometimes watch all through the starry night, summer or winter—the bells of his wandering sheep sweet on the quiet air. Now it happened that the king of that country came to hear of this shepherd boy; but he did not believe all that was told of him, and at last sent for the boy.

When he had been brought before the king, the king said to him, "I am told that thou hast wisdom far beyond thy years, and hast pondered within thyself on many things. If that be so and thou can'st answer me three questions which I am about to put to thee, thou shalt henceforth dwell with me in my royal palace, and I will look on thee as my own child."

The shepherd boy answered and said, "What are the three questions, my Lord King?"

"The first," said the king, "is this: How many drops of water are there in the ocean?"

The shepherd boy considered within himself, then answered and said, "If the king would give command that all the rivers on the earth shall be dammed up so that not a single drop shall run down from any one of them into the sea until I have counted it, then I will tell the king how many drops there are in the ocean. "

"Good," said the king. "And how many stars are there in the heavens?"

The shepherd boy asked the king for a large sheet of paper. When this was brought to him, he took a fine needle and pricked in the paper a multitude of holes so infinitesimally minute that although a sunbeam or a ray of moonlight might find its magic way through every one, they were so small as to be scarcely visible to the naked eye. He then gave the king the sheet of paper and said, "If this, my Lord King, be held up to yonder window, it will be seen that there are a myriad times as many stars in the sky as there are pricks in the paper; they need only be counted."

But even to attempt to count them was to risk blindness; and not one of his counsellors, wise men, or astrologers was able to give the king the sum.

The king looked long at the boy. "Good," he said again at last. "Very good. My third and last question is this, and think well: how many seconds are there in Eternity?"

The shepherd boy meditated within himself like one a moment lost in dream. Then he answered and said, "In Pomerania my Lord King, there is a solitary mountain made wholly of adamant. It is a league and half a league high; a league and half a league wide; and a league and half a league of it goes down in under the earth. At the last second of the last minute of the last hour of the last day of every hundred years a little bird comes flying from afar, perches upon the mountain, and whets his bill on it: one stroke this way, one stroke that. When, with its rubbings the little bird shall have worn away the whole mountain of adamant down to its deepest roots, *then,* my Lord King, will the first second of eternity be at an end."

"Good indeed! Nay, better than best," said the king. And added, smiling fondly at the shepherd boy, "Thou has answered the three questions I put to thee with the wit, sagacity and wisdom of the wise. From henceforth thou shalt dwell with me in my royal palace, and thou shalt be to me as a son."

"THE DOGGIES"

The doggies gaed to the mill,
   This way and that way;
They took a lick out o' *this* wife's poke
And they took a lick out o' *that* wife's poke,
And a loup in the lead, and a dip in the dam,
   And gaed walloping, walloping, walloping, *hame.*

THE KNIGHT AND THE GREY-HOUND

There was a certain valiant knight which had only one son, the which he loved so much, that he ordained for his keepers three nourishers or nurses. The first should give him suck, and feed him; the second should wash him, and keep him clean; and the third should bring him to his sleep and rest. The knight had also a greyhound and a falcon, which he also loved right well. The greyhound was so good that he never ran at any game, but he took it and held it till his master came. And if his master disposed him to go into any battel, if he should not speed therein, anone as he should mount upon his horse, the greyhound would take the horse-tail in his mouth, and draw backward, and would also howl and cry marvellouslie loud. By these signs, and the due observation thereof, the knight did always understand that his journey should have very ill success. The falcon was so gentle and hardy, that he was never cast off to his prey but he took it. The same knight had much pleasure in justing and tourney, so that upon a time under his castle he proclaimed a tournament, to the which came many great lords and knights. The knight entered into the tourney, and his ladie went with her maidens to see it: and as they went out, after went the nourishers, and left the child lying alone there in the cradle in the hall, where the greyhound lay near the wall, and the hawk or falcon standing upon a perch. In this hall there was a serpent lurking, or hid in a hole, to all of them in the castle unknown, the which when he perceived that they were all absent, he put his head out of the hole, and when he saw none but the child lying in the cradle, he went out of his hole towards the cradle, for to have slain the child. The noble falcon perceiving that, made such a noise and rustling with her wings presently, that the greyhound awoke and rose up: and when he saw the serpent nigh the child, anone against him he leapt, and they both fought so long together, until that the serpent had grievously hurt and wounded the greyhound, that he bled so sore, that the earth about the cradle was all bloody. The greyhound, when that he felt himself grievously hurt and wounded, starts fiercely upon the serpent, and fought so sore together, and so eagerly, that between them the cradle was overcast with the child, the bottome upward. And because that the cradle had four pomels like feet falling towards the earth, they saved the child's life and his visage from any hurt. What can be more exprest to make good the wonder in the preservation of the child? Incontinently thereafter, with great pain the greyhound overcame and slew the serpent, and laid him down again in his place and licked his wounds. And anon after the just and turney was done, the nourishers came first into the castle, and as they saw the cradle turned upside down upon the earth, compassed round about with blood, and that the greyhound was also bloody, they thought and said among themselves that the greyhound had slain the child, and were not so wise as to turn up the cradle again with the child, for to have seen what was thereof befallen; but they said, Let us run away, lest our master should put or lay any blame upon us, and so slay us. As they were thus running away, they met the knight's wife, and she said unto them, Wherefore make ye this sorrow, and whither will ye run? Then said they, O lady, wo and sorrow be to us, and to you. Why, said she, what is there happened? show me. The greyhound, they said, that our lord and master loved so well, hath devoured and slain your son, and lyeth by the wall all full of blood. As the lady heard this she presently fell to the earth, and began to weep and cry piteouslie, and said, Alace, O my dear son, are ye slain and dead? What shall I now do, that I have mine only son thus lost? Wherewithal came in the knight from the tourney, and beholding this lady thus crying and making sorrow, he demanded of her wherefore she made so great sorrow and lamentation. She answered him, O my lord, that greyhound that you have loved so much hath slain your only son, and lyeth by the wall, satiated with the blood of the child. The knight, very exceeding angry, went into the hall, and the greyhound went to meet him, and did fawn upon him, as he was wont to do, and the knight drew out his sword, and with one stroke smote off the greyhound's head, and then went to the cradle where the child lay and found his son all whole, and by the cradle the serpent slain; and then by diverse signs he perceived that the greyhound had killed the serpent for the defence of the child. Then with great sorrow and weeping he tare his hair, and said, Wo be to me, that for the words of my wife I have slain my good and best greyhound, the which hath saved my child's life, and hath slain the serpent, therefore I will put myself to penance. And so he brake his sword in three pieces, and went towards the Holy Land, and abode all the days of his life.

"WHAT'S THERE?"

What's there?
Cheese and bread, and a mouldy halfpenny.
Where's my share?
I put it on the shelf, and the cat got it.
Where's the cat?
She's run nine miles through the wood.
Where's the wood?
The fire burnt it.
Where's the fire?
The water sleckt it.
Where's the water?
The oxen drunk it.
Where's the oxen?
The butcher kill'd 'em.
Where's the butcher?

Up on the church-top cracking nuts, and you may go and eat the shells; and *them as* speak first shall have nine nips, nine scratches, and nine boxes over the lug!

WHITTINGTON AND HIS CAT

In the reign of the famous King Edward III. there was a little boy called Dick Whittington, whose father and mother died when he was very young. As poor Dick was not old enough to work, he was very badly off; he got but little for his dinner, and sometimes nothing at all for his breakfast; for the people who lived in the village were very poor indeed, and could not spare him more than the parings of potatoes, and now and then a hard crust of bread.

Now Dick had heard a great many very strange things about the great city called London; for the country people at that time thought that folks in London were all fine gentlemen and ladies; and that there was singing and music there all day long; and that the streets were all paved with gold.

One day a large waggon and eight horses, all with bells at their heads, drove through the village while Dick was standing by the sign-post. He thought that this waggon must be going to the fine town of London; so he took courage, and asked the waggoner to let him walk with him by the side of the waggon. As soon as the waggoner heard that poor Dick had no father or mother, and saw by his ragged clothes that he could not be worse off than he was, he told him he might go if he would, so off they set together.

So Dick got safe to London, and was in such a hurry to see the fine streets paved all over with gold, that he did not even stay to thank the kind waggoner; but ran off as fast as his legs would carry him, through many of the streets, thinking every moment to come to those that were paved with gold; for Dick had seen a guinea three times in his own little village, and remembered what a deal of money it brought in change; so he thought he had nothing to do but to take up some little bits of the pavement, and should then have as much money as he could wish for.

Poor Dick ran till he was tired, and had quite forgot his friend the waggoner; but at last, finding it grow dark, and that every way he turned he saw nothing but dirt instead of gold, he sat down in a dark corner and cried himself to sleep.

Little Dick was all night in the streets; and next morning, being very hungry, he got up and walked about, and asked everybody he met to give him a halfpenny to keep him from starving; but nobody stayed to answer him, and only two or three gave him a halfpenny; so that the poor boy was soon quite weak and faint for the want of victuals.

In this distress he asked charity of several people, and one of them said crossly: "Go to work for an idle rogue." "That I will," says Dick, "I will go to work for you, if you will let me." But the man only cursed at him and went on.

At last a good-natured looking gentleman saw how

hungry he looked. "Why don't you go to work my lad?" said he to Dick. "That I would, but I do not know how to get any," answered Dick. "If you are willing, come along with me," said the gentleman, and took him to a hay-field, where Dick worked briskly, and lived merrily till the hay was made.

After this he found himself as badly off as before; and being almost starved again, he laid himself down at the door of Mr. Fitzwarren, a rich merchant. Here he was soon seen by the cook-maid, who was an ill-tempered creature, and happened just then to be very busy dressing dinner for her master and mistress; so she called out to poor Dick: "What business have you there, you lazy rogue? There is nothing else but beggars; if you do not take yourself away, we will see how you will like a sousing of some dish-water; I have some here hot enough to make you jump."

Just at that time Mr. Fitzwarren himself came home to dinner; and when he saw a dirty ragged boy lying at the door, he said to him: "Why do you lie there, my boy? You seem old enough to work; I am afraid you are inclined to be lazy."

"No, indeed, sir," said Dick to him, "that is not the case, for I would work with all my heart, but I do not know anybody, and I believe I am very sick for the want of food."

"Poor fellow, get up; let me see what ails you."

Dick now tried to rise, but he was obliged to lie down again, being too weak to stand, for he had not eaten any food for three days, and was no longer able to run about and beg a halfpenny of people in the street. So the kind merchant ordered him to be taken into the house, and have a good dinner given him, and be kept to do what work he was able to do for the cook.

Little Dick would have lived very happy in this good family if it had not been for the ill-natured cook. She used to say: "You are under me, so look sharp; clean the spit and the dripping-pan, make the fires, wind up the jack, and do all the scullery work nimbly, or—" and she would shake the ladle at him. Besides, she was so fond of basting, that when she had no meat to baste, she would baste poor Dick's head and shoulders with a broom, or anything else that happened to fall in her way. At last her ill-usage of him was told to Alice, Mr. Fitzwarren's daughter, who told the cook she should be turned away if she did not treat him kinder.

The behaviour of the cook was now a little better; but besides this Dick had another hardship to get over. His bed stood in a garret, where there were so many holes in the floor and the walls that every night he was tormented with rats and mice. A gentleman having given Dick a penny for cleaning his shoes, he thought he would buy a cat with it. The next day he saw a girl with a cat, and asked her, "Will you let me have that cat for a penny?" The girl said: "Yes, that I will, master, though she is an excellent mouser."

Dick hid his cat in the garret, and always took care to carry a part of his dinner to her; and in a short time he had no more trouble with the rats and mice, but slept quite sound every night.

Soon after this, his master had a ship ready to sail; and as it was the custom that all his servants should have some chance of good fortune as well as himself, he called them all into the parlour and asked them what they would send out.

They all had something that they were willing to venture except poor Dick, who had neither money nor goods, and therefore could send nothing. For this reason he did not come into the parlour with the rest; but Miss Alice guessed what was the matter, and ordered him to be called in. She then said: "I will lay down some money for him, from my own purse;" but her father told her: "This will not do, for it must be something of his own."

When poor Dick heard this, he said: "I have nothing but a cat which I bought for a penny some time since of a little girl."

"Fetch your cat then, my lad," said Mr. Fitzwarren, "and let her go."

Dick went upstairs and brought down poor puss, with tears in his eyes, and gave her to the captain. "For," he said, "I shall now be kept awake all night by the rats and mice." All the company laughed at Dick's odd venture; and Miss Alice, who felt pity for him, gave him some money to buy another cat.

This, and many other marks of kindness shown him by Miss Alice, made the ill-tempered cook jealous of poor Dick, and she began to use him more cruelly than ever, and always made game of him for sending his cat to sea. She asked him: "Do you think your cat will sell for as much money as would buy a stick to beat you?"

At last poor Dick could not bear this usage any longer, and he thought he would run away from his place; so he packed up his few things, and started very early in the morning, on All-hallows Day, the first of November. He walked as far as Holloway; and there sat down on a stone, which to this day is called "Whittington's Stone", and began to think to himself which road he should take.

While he was thinking what he should do, the Bells of Bow Church, which at that time were only six, began to ring, and their sound seemed to say to him:

"Turn again, Whittington,
  Thrice Lord Mayor of London."

"Lord Mayor of London!" said he to himself. "Why, to be sure, I would put up with almost anything now, to be Lord Mayor of London, and ride in a fine coach, when I grow to be a man! Well, I will go back, and think nothing of the cuffing and scolding of the old cook, if I am to be Lord Mayor of London at last."

Dick went back, and was lucky enough to get into the house, and set about his work, before the old cook came downstairs.

We must now follow Miss Puss to the coast of Africa. The ship, with the cat on board, was a long time at sea; and was at last driven by the winds on a part of the coast of Barbary, where the only people were the Moors, unknown to the English. The people came in great numbers to see the sailors, because they were of different colour to themselves, and treated them civilly; and, when they became better acquainted, were very eager to buy the fine things that the ship was loaded with.

When the captain saw this, he sent patterns of the best things he had to the king of the country; who was so much pleased with them, that he sent for the captain to the palace. Here they were placed, as it is the custom of the country, on rich carpets flowered with gold and silver. The king and queen were seated at the upper end of the room; and a number of dishes were brought in for dinner. They had not sat long, when a vast number of rats and mice rushed in, and devoured all the meat in an instant. The captain wondered at this, and asked if these vermin were not unpleasant.

"Oh yes," said they, "very offensive; and the king would give half his treasure to be freed of them, for they not only destroy his dinner, as you see, but they assault him in his chamber, and even in bed, so that he is obliged to be watched while he is sleeping, for fear of them."

The captain jumped for joy; he remembered poor Whittington and his cat, and told the king he had a creature on board the ship that would despatch all these vermin immediately. The king jumped so high at the joy which the news gave *him*, that his turban dropped off his head. "Bring this creature to me," says he. "Vermin are dreadful in a court, and if she will perform what you say, I will load your ship with gold and jewels in exchange for her."

The captain, who knew his business, took this opportunity to set forth the merits of Miss Puss. He told his majesty: "It is not very convenient to part with her, as, when she is gone, the rats and mice may destroy the goods in the ship—but to oblige your majesty, I will fetch her."

"Run, run!" said the queen; "I am impatient to see the dear creature."

Away went the captain to the ship, while another dinner was got ready. He put Puss under his arm, and arrived at the palace just in time to see the table full of rats. When the cat saw them, she did not wait for bidding, but jumped out of the captain's arms, and in a few minutes laid almost all the rats and mice dead at her feet. The rest of them in their fright scampered away to their holes.

The king was quite charmed to get rid so easily of such plagues, and the queen desired that the creature who had done them so great a kindness might be brought to her, that she might look at her. Upon which the captain called: "Pussy, pussy, pussy!" and she came to him. He then presented her to the queen, who started back, and was afraid to touch a creature who had made such a havoc among the rats and mice. However, when the captain stroked the cat and called: "Pussy, pussy," the queen also touched her and cried: "Putty, putty," for she had not learned English. He then put her down on the queen's lap, where she purred and played with her majesty's hand, and then purred herself to sleep.

The king, having seen the exploits of Miss Puss, and being informed that her kittens would stock the whole country, and keep it free from rats, bargained with the captain for the whole ship's cargo, and then gave him ten times as much for the cat as all the rest amounted to.

The captain then took leave of the royal party, and set sail with a fair wind for England, and after a happy voyage arrived safe in London.

One morning, early, Mr. Fitzwarren had just come to his counting-house and seated himself at the desk, to count over the cash, and settle the business for the day, when somebody came tap, tap, at the door. "Who's there?" said Mr. Fitzwarren. "A friend," answered the other; "I come to bring you good news of your ship *Unicorn*." The merchant, bustling up in such a hurry that he forgot his gout, opened the door, and who should he see waiting but the captain and factor, with a cabinet of jewels, and a bill of lading; when he looked at this the merchant lifted up his eyes and thanked Heaven for sending him such a prosperous voyage.

They then told him the story of the cat, and showed the rich present that the king and queen had sent for her to poor Dick. As soon as the merchant heard this, he said,

> "Go send him in, and tell him of his fame;
> Pray call him Mr. Whittington by name."

Mr. Fitzwarren now showed himself to be a good man; for when some of his servants said so great a treasure was too much for him, he answered: "God forbid I should deprive him of the value of a single penny, it is his own, and he shall have it to a farthing."

He then sent for Dick who at that time was scouring pots for the cook, and was quite dirty. He would have excused himself from coming into the counting-house, saying, "The room is swept, and my shoes are dirty and full of hob-nails." But the merchant ordered him to come in.

Mr. Fitzwarren ordered a chair to be set for him, and so he began to think they were making a game of him, at the same time he said to them: "Do not play tricks with a poor simple boy, but let me go down again, if you please, to my work."

"Indeed, Mr. Whittington," said the merchant, "we are all quite in earnest with you, and I most heartily rejoice in the news that these gentlemen have brought you; for the captain has sold your cat to the King of Barbary, and brought you in return for her more riches than I possess in the whole world; and I wish you may long enjoy them!"

Mr. Fitzwarren then told the men to open the great treasure they had brought with them; and said: "Mr. Whittington has nothing to do but put it in some place of safety."

Poor Dick hardly knew how to behave himself for joy. He begged his master to take what part of it he pleased, since he owed it all to his kindness. "No, no," answered Mr. Fitzwarren, "this is all your own; and I have no doubt but you will use it well."

Dick next asked his mistress, and then Miss Alice, to accept a part of his good fortune; but they would not, and at the same time told him they felt great joy at his good success. But this poor fellow was too kind-hearted to keep it all to himself; so he made a present to the captain, the mate, and the rest of Mr. Fitzwarren's servants; and even to the ill-natured old cook.

After this Mr. Fitzwarren advised him to send for a proper tailor and get himself dressed like a gentleman; and he told him he was welcome to live in his house till he could provide himself with a better.

When Whittington's face was washed, his hair curled, his hat cocked, and he was dressed in a nice suit of clothes, he was as handsome and genteel as any young man who visited at Mr. Fitzwarren's; so that Miss Alice, who had once been so kind to him, and thought of him with pity, now looked upon him as fit to be her sweetheart; and the more so, no doubt, because Whittington was now always thinking what he could do to oblige her, and making her the prettiest presents that could be.

Mr. Fitzwarren soon saw their love for each other, and proposed to join them in marriage; and to this they both readily agreed. A day for the wedding was soon fixed; and they were attended to church by the Lord Mayor, the court of aldermen, the sheriffs, and a great number of the richest merchants in London, whom they afterwards treated with a very rich feast.

History tells us that Mr. Whittington and his lady lived in great splendour, and were very happy. They had several children. He was Sheriff of London, thrice Lord Mayor, and received the honour of knighthood by Henry V.

He entertained this king and his queen at dinner after his conquest of France so grandly, that the king said: "Never had prince such a subject;" when Sir Richard heard this, he said: "Never had subject such a prince."

"HINTY MINTY"

Hinty, minty, cuty, corn,
Apple seed, and apple thorn,
Wire, briar, limber lock,
Three geese in a flock.
One flew east, and one flew west,
One flew over the cuckoo's nest.
      Up on yonder hill.
That is where my father dwells;
He has jewels, he has rings,
He has many pretty things.
He has a hammer with two nails,
He has a cat with twenty tails.
Strike Jack, lick Tom!
      Blow the bellows, old man!

THE THREE CHILDREN OF FORTUNE

Once upon a time a father sent for his three sons, and gave the eldest a cock, the second a scythe, and the youngest a cat.

"I am old," said he, "my end is approaching, and I would fain provide for you all before I die. Money I have none, and what little else I have to leave you may seem of little value; it rests with yourselves alone to turn my gifts to good account. Seek out, then, a land where what each of you possesses is as yet unknown, and your fortunes are made."

After the death of their father, and he was in his grave, the eldest son at once set out with his cock. But in whatever direction he went, town or village, he always saw from afar a bird exactly like his own sitting up aloft on a church steeple, shimmering in the sunshine, turning and turning with the wind. Midnight and daybreak, far and near, he always heard cocks crowing. His bird, then, was nothing new; and he despaired of making his fortune.

It happened however one fine day that he came to an island whose people had not only never seen or heard of a cock, but had never even been told how to reckon the time. They knew by the looks of the sky when it was morning or evening; but at night, if they lay awake, they had no means at all of telling how the time went. Clocks—water-clocks, candle-clocks, or cog-clocks— they had none.

"Behold," said he to them, "what a noble creature I have here! How like a valiant knight he is. How gay! how gallant! Look at the bright-red splendid crest upon his head, the sharp spurs at his heels. Every night of his life he crows for me, thrice, and at his third crow proclaims that the sun is about to rise. Nor is this all. He may be heard screaming in broad daylight, and then you must take warning, for without the least doubt the weather's going to change."

This mightily pleased the people of the island. They kept awake the whole night long, and heard, to their joy, how gloriously the cock called the hours—*Cockadiddle-doo*—at two, at four, and at six o'clock in the morning. They asked him if his bird was for sale, and, if so, how much he would take for it.

"How much," he repeated, eyeing them. "Well, about as much gold as an ass can carry."

"A fair and moderate price indeed for such a wonder of a bird," they cried with one voice; and agreed to give him what he asked.

When he returned home with his wealth, his brothers wondered greatly; and the second of them said, "I will now set out myself, and see if I can turn my scythe to as good account."

There seemed, however, little likelihood of this. Go where he would, he was met by peasants who had as sharp-set scythes over their shoulders as he had himself. At last, as good luck would have it, he too came to an island where the people had never so much as seen or heard of a scythe or even a sickle. As soon as their corn was ripe for harvest, they went into the fields and pulled it up by the roots. But this was hard, slow work, and a great deal of the corn was lost. The man at once set to it with his scythe; and mowed the whole field so quickly and so clean that the people of the island stood staring open-mouthed with wonder. They would have given him anything in the world for so marvellous an invention: but he asked of them only a horse laden with as much gold as it could carry.

What wonder, when he came back, that the third brother had a great longing to set out and see what he could make of his cat. So off he went. At first, it happened to him as it had to the others. So long as he kept to the mainland, he met with no success; there were plenty of cats of every size and colour everywhere, black, white, snuff and tabby—so many, indeed, that their kittens for the most part, as soon as, poor blindlings, they came into the world, were drowned in a bucket of water.

At last he too took ship, sailed away over the sea, and came to an island where, as it chanced, nobody had ever so much as seen or heard of a cat. No wonder this island was over-run with such multitudes of mice that the little wretches skipped about and danced on the tables and chairs whether the master of the house were at home or not. Bed or board, there was no peace for them. The people were continually complaining of this pest and abomination of mice, but even the king hadn't a notion how to rid himself of them in his own palace. In every corner of it mice were squeaking and scampering; they nibbled the bread beside him on the table, jumped into his porridge and gnawed his shoes where he sat. Here, then, was plenty of company for Puss.

In a trice she set to work and had cleared two rooms of the little creatures in little more than the twinkling of an eye. The people at once besought the king to buy this wonderful animal, for his own good, for theirs, and at any price. With joy the king gave everything that was asked for it—a mule laden with gold and precious stones, rubies, emeralds, pearls and diamonds. So the third and youngest brother came home with a prize even richer than either of the others.

Meanwhile, the cat was as happy as the king. It feasted away on the mice in the royal palace, and devoured so many that you could tell by their noise that a mort of them had gone for good, never to come back. At length, after a week or two of this sport, she became so utterly spent and weary, dry and thirsty, that she was like to die for a drop of water to drink.

"*Miaow, miaow, miaow, miaow!*" she wailed.

131

At this strange cry, repeated again and again, the king was dumb with dismay. He summoned his people to come and listen to it, and many of them ran shrieking in fright, pell-mell out of the palace.

Whereupon the king held a council to consider what had best be done; and it was at length decided that a herald should be sent to the cat, warning her to leave the king's palace without delay, and that if she failed to do so, she would be *driven* out.

This the king did since his counsellors had decided that they would far more willingly put up with the mice, which they had long been accustomed to, than attempt to get rid of them at the risk of their lives. The herald was accordingly sent to the cat. He asked her whether she was willing to quit the king's palace. But poor Puss, whose thirst was now so extreme that her long thin tongue was dangling out of her mouth between her sharp teeth, could say nothing but *"Miaow, miaow, miaow, miaow!"*

The herald took this to mean, "No, no, no, no!" and at once went off to the king.

"In that case," cried the counsellors, "we must try what force will do."

So the king bade his soldiers bring up their guns. They fired upon the palace from every side. When the cannon-balls began to drop into the room where the cat was sitting, hissing and spitting, she sprang up out of her corner, leapt out of the window, and ran away. But the king's soldiers in the noise and flames and smoke had failed to see her go, and continued to bombard the palace until it caught fire and was burnt to the ground.

CAT AND MOUSE

The cat sits at the mill door, spinnin', spinnin'.

Up comes a wee moose, rinnin', rinnin'.

"What are ye doin' there, my lady, my lady?"

"Spinnin' a sark for my son," quo' Batty, quo' Batty.

"I'll tell ye a story, my lady, my lady."

"We'll hae the mair company," quo' Batty, quo' Batty.

"There was once a wee woman, my lady, my lady."

"She tuk the less room," quo' Batty, quo' Batty.

"She was sweepin' her hoose one day, my lady, my
lady."

"She had it the cleaner," quo' Batty, quo' Batty.

"She found a penny, my lady, my lady."

"She had the mair money," quo' Batty, quo' Batty.

"She went to the market, my lady, my lady."

"She didna stay at hame," quo' Batty, quo' Batty.

"She bocht a wee bit o' beef, my lady, my lady."

"She had the mair flesh meat," quo' Batty, quo' Batty.

"She cam' home, my lady, my lady."

"She didna stay awa'," quo' Batty, quo' Batty.

"She put her beef on the coals to roast, my lady, my
lady."

"She didna eat it raw," quo' Batty, quo' Batty.

"She put it on the window to cool, my lady, my lady."

"She didna scaud her lips," quo' Batty, quo' Batty.

"Up comes a wee moose an' ate it all up, my lady, my
lady."

"Ay, and that's the way I'll eat *you* up too," quo' Batty,
quo' Batty,

> Quo' *Batty*, quo' BATTY,
> Quo' BATTY.

THE POOR MILLER'S BOY AND THE CAT

In an old mill, once upon a time, there lived a solitary miller. He had neither wife nor children, only three apprentices, who had worked for him for many years. There came a day at length when he called his three apprentices to him, and said, "I am old, too old to toil and labour as I have done in the past. For the rest of my days, I wish to sit in peace in my chimney corner. You are young; the wide world lies before you with all its adventurings. Fare away, then, the three of you, and seek your fortune; and whichever one of you, after his travels, brings me back the finest horse, he shall have this old mill and everything in it as a reward. But in return, he shall have the care of me until I die."

Now the third and the youngest of the three apprentices, whose name was Hans, had always been the dupe
and drudge of the other two. They despised him,
took him for a noodle and a fool; and on hearing this at
once made up their minds that whatever might happen
to them, the mill at any rate should never be Hans's.

The three of them forthwith set out together. When
they came to a village not far distant, they said to Hans,
"Now see here, dolt that you are, it's no use your coming
any further. Do you stay here, then, and tend the geese.
In a few days, they won't know you from one of themselves. It is certain sure *you* will never manage to get a
horse."

Nevertheless, Hans refused to leave them, and on they
went. When night came down, they found a dry and
sandy cave in which to sleep. The two other apprentices
lay down together and waited quietly until Hans was fast
asleep and snoring. Then they stole out of the cave into
the moonlight, and continued their journey. And a
clever pair they fancied themselves.

When the rays of the morning sun stole into the cavern, Hans woke up, gazed round him, and found himself alone. At first he thought he must be dreaming, and
then that his dream had come true; and he sat for a while,
his head in his hands, lost in despair. But at last a spark of
courage began to twinkle in his heart. He got up, went
out of the cavern, quenched his thirst at a little brook
near by, and journeyed on till he came to a forest. There
he sat down to think.

"Well, Hans, here you are," he said to himself; "alone
in the wide, wide world, and no one to help you. Ass

you may be; but how will *you* ever manage to get any horse, let alone the finest horse in the world?" At this moment, who should he see come stepping along the path through the forest but a small and solitary Cat. She seemed to have sprung out of nowhere, was as black as ebony, sleek as satin, and a gold collar encircled her neck. When she came near, she stayed, looked long and earnestly at him, and at last addressed him.

"Very well met, Hans," says she. "And where are you off to this fine morning?"

"Alas," said Hans, "that I cannot tell. My friends have forsaken me, and I have no one to help me."

"Come," said the Cat; "have courage, Hans. I know your secrets. Mine are my own. You are off to seek your fortune—and a horse. Come with me, then. If for seven years you serve me faithfully, a finer and nobler horse shall be yours than any which in your whole life long you have ever seen or dreamed of; and much else besides."

"Well," thought Hans to himself; "this seems to be a strange and marvellous Cat. What harm can there be in doing what she says?" Besides, there was something in the Cat's demeanour, in the look in her clear dark eyes and in her manner of speech that persuaded him to trust in her.

So the two of them went along together, Hans and the Cat, until at last they came to a castle, an enchanted castle. In this great castle, the Cat had none but other cats to wait on her, to work for her, and to do her bidding. These creatures were for ever leaping nimbly upstairs and down. They were as merry as the day is long. In the evening, when Hans and his Mistress and the other cats sat down to sup, three of them made music until their turn came to share in the meat and drink. One played the bassoon, one the fiddle, and a third the trumpet, blowing out his cheeks as he did so as round as a China orange.

When supper was over, the long table was removed and carried away, and the Mistress of the cats said to Hans, "Up now, Hans, and come and dance with me."

At this, poor Hans was shy and troubled. "Alas," he said, "I cannot dance. But even if I did, how could I with you, Mistress? I have never done such a thing in my life."

The Cat looked at Hans and smiled to herself, her eyes shining. "Very well then," says she to her servants, "take him to his room, and see him safe to bed."

Off they all went together. One cat with a candlestick lighted him upstairs; one unlaced his shoes; one drew off his stockings; and a fourth, when he was snug in bed, blew out the candle. The next morning, when day was in the room again, they came to wake him and to help him to dress. One cat put on his stockings; one tied up his garters; one brought him his polished shoes; and another, with a bowl of well-water, washed his hands and face; and afterwards dried them with her tail.

"Well," thought Hans to himself; "that was all very pleasant." But although he was treated so graciously, and had cats to wait on him, he too had to serve his Mistress. Every day he went out to chop wood; and for this purpose she had given him an axe, its head of solid silver. The wedge he used to split the timber was also of fine solid silver; but the mallet with which he hammered home the silver wedge was made of copper. After that, he chopped up the wood into smaller sticks, and tied it in bundles all ready for use for the fires in his Mistress's enchanted castle.

And so the days, weeks and months went by, and the years began; and Hans still stayed on in the castle, serving his Mistress faithfully, according to the pledge and bargain made between them. He had good meat and good drink. But during the whole of this time, he never saw any trace of living creature in the castle except his Mistress, and her host of sleek and nimble servants, cats every one.

One fine morning when the suns of June had brought a host of flowers into bloom, and the grasses were beginning to seed, his Mistress called Hans to her. "Now Hans," says she, "you shall mow me my meadow, and make me my hay."

She gave him a scythe with a blade of silver, a whetstone for sharpening it of solid gold, and bade him bring them back to her when the day's work was finished. This Hans did. Hard, hot, yet pleasant work it was. In the cool of the evening he carried back the silver scythe and the golden whetstone into the castle. And being weary, and pining a little to be out in the world again, he asked his Mistress if the time was yet come for him to have his reward—that fine and noble horse she had promised him.

"Not quite yet, Hans," said his Mistress. "There is one other thing I wish you to do for me. Here are all the tools you will need: a carpenter's axe, a saw, and a hammer. All, you see, are of silver. No iron; but a plenty of silver. With these you shall build me a small beautiful house."

So Hans set to work. When at last he had finished the house, he told his Mistress. A fine and well-wrought job he had made of it. She praised him gladly. Then, said he, might he have his horse? Yet, although he was full of longing to see the horse, his seven long years had gone by for him as if they had been little more than as many moments, and even these as if in a dream. A little while afterwards his Mistress asked him if he would like to see her stables and horses. At this Hans marvelled, since, although he had lived so long in the enchanted moated castle and knew it through and through—courtyards, gardens, orchards, everywhere—he had never come across any stables, nor set eyes on a horse.

"Aye, Madam," said Hans to his Mistress, "I would *that*."

His Mistress then and there led him to the door of the house of silver which he himself had built for her. It stood wide open. And lo and behold, in the hall beyond, tossing their gentle heads and gazing out of their dark eyes stood twelve horses, horses as fine and comely and noble as man's eyes could wish to see.

"The Seven Years have passed away," said his Mistress to Hans. "The promised horse shall be yours. But not now. Return home to the Mill. In three days' time I will follow you, and bring it with me. Ask me no questions. You have served me well and faithfully. My secret shall soon be shared with you."

Having enquired his way back to his master's old mill,

Hans set out. Never throughout the seven years in
which he had served his Mistress had she given him a
new coat. So he had had only the old smock-frock which
he had brought with him, and this by now was not only
three parts patched and all but worn out, but was
everywhere—collar, arms, elbows—at least a size or two
too small for him.

When he reached the old mill, there, sure enough,
were the two other apprentices. Believing that Hans had
neither the gumption, craft nor mother wit to bring back
any horse at all, they had taken very little trouble. The
horse of the elder of the two was wall-eyed, and the
other was dead lame. At sight of Hans they burst out
laughing, and asked where *his* horse might be. Hans
stared at the two sad jades that were browsing nearby,
and replied that his horse would be following him in
three days' time. At this the pair of them only laughed
the louder.

"Three days! Aye, you stupid, numskull dumbledore,
we know all about that. A very fine horse *that* will be!"

But although for a moment his heart misgave him,
Hans believed in his Mistress, remembering all her kindness to him; and he went on into the mill, and into his
master's parlour. At very first glimpse of him, the miller
refused to let him sit down with them at table. His
old smock was so worn and patched and ragged, they
would have died for shame if any neighbour should
chance to come in. They gave him a platter of broken
meats, and sent him outside. When night came on, they
refused to let him sleep in the mill. Merely to get a roof
for shelter, Hans crept into the goose-house, and made

himself as comfortable as he could on a heap of mouldy straw.

He had taken two days on his journey. When, then, he awoke again, three had passed by; and sure enough, as his Mistress had promised him, when he peeped out of the little door of the goose-house, there stood in front of the mill a fine coach to which were harnessed six magnificent horses—a sight for sore eyes, and he had slept very little. With their trappings of silver, tossing their gentle heads, they were a rare delight to see; and apart from these six, there was a seventh—an even finer and more beautiful horse than the rest. And this horse was for Hans.

But instead of his Mistress, the Cat, whom he had expected to see, there came stepping down from out of the coach a young and lovely Princess. And at one glance his whole heart went out to her.

When this Princess was come into the parlour of the mill, she asked the miller why Hans was not there, and where he was. In fear and trembling the old man said that Hans had come back so ragged and woebegone that he was not fit to be in their company, and that he had spent the night, sleeping or waking, in the goose-house.

"Then," said this daughter of a king, "bring him in to me at once."

So, with little more than his old smock-frock to cover him, they brought Hans into the mill. Thereupon, the servants whom the Princess had brought with her unpacked from a coffer from out of the coach the most costly, splendid and beautiful garments. They washed Hans, and dressed him; and when this was done, and he

appeared in his raiment of cloth-of-gold, no son of a
Prince could have looked handsomer.

The Princess then said that she wished to see the horses
which the other two apprentices had brought home to
the old mill. One was wall-eyed; the other dead lame.
Then she ordered the servants to bring the seventh horse.
And when the miller saw this horse, he marvelled to his
very marrow; for never in his whole life long had the
likes of such a horse been seen in that countryside, let
alone pranced in the miller's yard.

"This horse is for Hans," said the Princess.

"Then," said the Miller, "Hans must have the mill."
And, despite the folly of the old man, the Princess spoke
kindly to the Miller, and told him he might keep the
horse and his mill as well. So saying, she bade her faithful Hans take his seat beside her in the coach, and they
drove away together.

When they came in sight of the enchanted castle,
there, before their eyes, stood the house which Hans
had built with the tools made of silver. Then it was
little, now it was a great house, and everything in it was
a marvel of beauty and made of silver or of gold. And
since she loved him and he loved her, the beautiful Princess and Hans, the miller's drudge, were married. And
he was so rich that he had enough and to spare for all
the rest of his life. Well and truly had he worked for it.
It seems that to be stupid and to be thought stupid are
not quite the same thing.

"IF"

If I had a donkey wot wouldn't go
D'ye think I'd wallop him?—no, no, no . . .
I'd give him some hay, and cry, Gee O!
        Come up, Neddy!

What makes me mention this, this morn
I seed that cruel chap, Bill Burn,
Whilst he was out a-crying his greens,
His donkey wallop with all his means:
He hit him over the head and thighs,
And brought the tears up on his eyes;
At last my blood began to rise
        And I said—
        If I had a donkey wot wouldn't go
        D'ye think I'd wallop him?—no, no, no . . .
        I'd give him some hay, and cry, Gee O!
                Come up, Neddy!

. . . Bill's donkey was ordered into court,
In which he caused a deal of sport;
He cock'd his ears and op'd his jaws;
As if he wished to plead his cause.
I proved I'd been uncommonly kind,
The ass got a verdict—Bill got fined;
For his worship and I were of one mind:
        And he said—
        If I had a donkey wot wouldn't go
        D'ye think I'd wallop him?—no, no, no . . .
        I'd give him some hay, and cry, Gee O!
                Come up, Neddy!

THE ASS, THE TABLE, AND
THE STICK

A lad named Jack was once so unhappy at home through his father's ill-treatment, that he made up his mind to run away and seek his fortune in the wide, wide world.

He ran, and he ran, till he could run no longer, and then he ran right up against a little old woman who was gathering sticks. He was too much out of breath to beg her pardon, but the woman was a good-natured old body, and as, she said, he seemed to be a likely lad, she would take him to be her servant, and would pay him well. He agreed, for he was very hungry, and she brought him to her house in the wood, where he served her for a twelvemonth and a day. When the year had passed, she called him to her, and said she had good wages for him, and she presented him with an ass out of the stable. He had but to pull Neddy's ears, she told him, to make him begin at once to hee-haw! And every time he brayed there dropped from his mouth silver sixpences, and half-crowns, and golden guineas.

The lad was well pleased with the wages he had received, and away he rode till he reached an inn. There he ordered the best of everything, and when the innkeeper refused to serve him unless he was paid beforehand, the boy went off to the stable, pulled the ass's ears and soon filled his pocket full of money. The innkeeper had watched all this through a crack in the door, and when night came on he put an ass of his own for the precious Neddy belonging to poor Jack. And Jack, next morning, without knowing that any change had been made, rode away home.

Now, I must tell you that near his father's house dwelt a poor widow with an only daughter. She and Jack were fast friends and trueloves; but when Jack asked his father's leave to marry the girl, "Never till you have the money to keep her," was the reply.

"But I have that already, father," said the lad, and going to the ass he pulled its long ears. Well, he pulled, and he pulled, till one of them came off in his hands; but as for this Neddy, though he opened his wide mouth and hee-hawed and hee-hawed to your heart's content, not a single sixpence dropped out of it. Thinking he had been tricked, Jack's father picked up a hayfork and drove his son out of the house. I promise you he ran.

Ah, yes! He ran and he ran until he came bang against a door, and burst it open, and there he was in a joiner's shop. "You're a likely-looking lad," said the joiner; "serve me for a twelvemonth and a day and I will pay you well."

So Jack agreed, and served the carpenter for a year and a day. "Now," said his master, "I will give you your wages," and he presented him with a table, telling him he had but to say, "Table, be covered," and at once it would be spread with lots of good things to eat and drink.

Jack hitched the table on to his back, and away he went with it till he came to the inn. "Host! Host!" he shouted, "give me my dinner, and let it be of the best."

The innkeeper said he was very sorry but that he had nothing in the house but ham and eggs.

"Ham and eggs!—for me!" exclaimed Jack. "I can do better than that." He put down his table, lifted his hand, and cried, "Table, be covered!"

At once the table was spread with turkey and sausages, roast mutton, potatoes, bacon and greens. The innkeeper opened his eyes and stared, but he said nothing, not he.

That night he fetched down from his attic a table very like Jack's, and exchanged the two. Jack, none the wiser, hitched the worthless table on to his back next morning, and carried it home.

"Now, father, may I marry the lass?" he said.

"Not unless you can keep her," replied the father.

THE ASS, THE TABLE, AND THE STICK

"See here, father!" exclaimed Jack. "That will be easy. I have a table which will do everything I ask of it."

"Let me see it," said the old man.

Jack set down the table from the inn in the middle of the room, and cried, "Table, be covered!" and again, "Table, be covered!" But whether he shouted or whispered, it was all in vain, the table remained bare.

In a rage, the father snatched the old warming-pan down from the wall and so warmed poor Jack's back with it that he fled howling from the house. And he ran and he ran till he came to a river and tumbled in.

Lucky for him, a man picked him out and, when he was dried a bit he told him to help him in making a bridge over the river. And how do you think he was doing it? Why, by casting a great growing tree across it. So Jack climbed up to the top of the tree and threw his weight on it, so that when the man had rooted the tree up, Jack and the tree-head dropped on to the further bank.

"That was well done," said the man; "and now I will pay you." So saying, he tore a branch from the tree, and fettled it up into a cudgel with his jack knife. "There," exclaimed he, "take this stick, and when you say to it, 'Up stick and bang him!' anyone who deserves it won't wait for a second dose."

Jack was overjoyed to get this stick—so away he went with it to the inn, and as soon as the innkeeper appeared, "Up stick and bang him!" was his cry. At the word the cudgel flew out of his hand, battered the old publican backside and front, rapped his head, bruised his arms, and tickled his ribs, until he fell groaning on the floor;

and still the stick went on belabouring the old cheat. Nor would Jack call it off till he had got back his stolen ass and table. Then he galloped home on the ass, with the table on his shoulders, and the stick in his hand. When he arrived, he found his father was dead; so he took his ass into the stable, and pulled its ears till he had filled the manger with money.

It was soon known through the town that Jack had returned rolling in wealth, and accordingly all the girls in the place set their caps at him. "See here," said Jack, "there's not much to choose between you. So I will marry the richest lass in the place. Come all of you to-morrow morning early down to my house with your money in your aprons."

Next morning the street was full of girls with aprons held out, jingling with gold and silver. And Jack's own sweetheart was among them, but she had neither gold nor silver: nothing but two copper pennies. They were all she had.

"Stand aside, lass," said Jack to her, speaking roughly. "Thou hast neither silver nor gold—stand away from the rest." She obeyed. And the tears ran down her cheeks, and filled her apron with diamonds.

"Up stick and at them!" cried Jack. In a flash away went his cudgel, and scampering along the line of girls, knocked them all on the head and left them senseless on the pavement. Jack helped himself to the money in their aprons, and poured it all into his truelove's lap. "Now, lass," he exclaimed, "thou are the richest, and I shall marry thee."

POOR OLD HORSE

My clothing was once of the linsey woolsey fine,
My tail it grew at length, my coat did likewise shine;
But now I'm growing old; my beauty does decay,
My master frowns upon me; one day I heard him
    say,
                    Poor old horse: poor old horse.

Once I was kept in the stable snug and warm,
To keep my tender limbs from any cold or harm;
But now, in open fields, I am forced for to go,
In all sorts of weather, let it be hail, rain, freeze, or
    snow.
                    Poor old horse: poor old horse.

Once I was fed on the very best corn and hay
That ever grew in yon fields, or in yon meadows gay;
But now there's no such doing can I find at all,
I'm glad to pick the green sprouts that grow behind yon
    wall.
                    Poor old horse: poor old horse.

"You are old, you are cold, you are deaf, dull, dumb and
    slow,
You are not fit for anything, or in my team to draw.
You have eaten all my hay, you have spoiled all my
    straw,
So hang him, whip, stick him, to the huntsman let him
    go."
                    Poor old horse: poor old horse.

POOR OLD HORSE

My hide unto the tanners then I would freely give,
My body to the hound dogs, I would rather die than
    live,
Likewise my poor old bones that have carried you many
    a mile,
Over hedges, ditches, brooks, bridges, likewise gates and
    stiles.

Poor old horse: poor old horse.

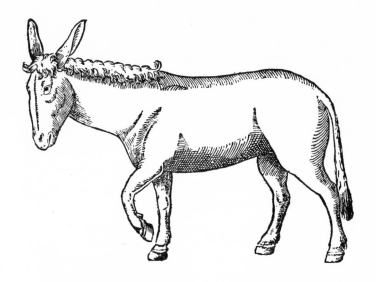

THE TRAVELLING MUSICIANS

An honest but miserly farmer once had an ass that had been a faithful servant to him for many years, but was now growing old and weary and worn, and every day less fit for work. His master was tired of keeping him, eyed him sourly, grudged him even a mouthful of hay, and began at last to think of putting an end to him altogether. The ass, who for some time past had seen that mischief was in the wind, decided to be gone. He managed one morning to push back the latch of the miserable tumbledown old stable he was kept in, took himself off, and set out for the famous city of Bremen. There, thought he to himself, as I at least have my voice left to me, I might turn musician, and do pretty well.

He had travelled not far on his way when he espied a dog stretched out on a patch of grass by the crossroads, his tongue hanging out of his head, and panting, poor wretch, as if his heart would burst through his body.

"What's wrong, my friend?" said the ass. "Has the sun dropped out of the sky?"

"Sun, indeed!" said the dog. "After twelve years of faithful service, my master only an hour gone was going to knock me over the head merely because I am getting old and weak, and can no longer be of much use to him. Such is life! So I ran away. But look at me; what can an old rattletrap body like mine do to get a livelihood. In fact, friend, I'm finished."

"Finished?" replied the ass. "Fiddlesticks! I am in much the same case myself; had just such a master as yours; and now I'm off to the famous city of Bremen to turn town musician. Suppose you come along with me, and see what we can do?"

The dog agreed, and they jogged on together.

They had gone but a few miles and were come to the last thatched house in a little village when they saw a cat. She sat hunched up on the old red-brick wall of an orchard in the sun, her woebegone face as long as a fiddle, with grief and chagrin.

"Pray, my good lady," said the ass, "what is amiss? You look sadly out of spirits!"

"Ay me!" said the cat. "It's not easy to be in good spirits when one's life is in danger. Because I'm no longer as young and frisky as I was, and had rather sit at my ease by the hearth than stay awake all night chasing the mice, my mistress laid hold of me this very morning, and was just about to drown me in the waterbutt with a brick tied round my neck, when I managed to shake free—claws and all. They are all alike. But what next? Where can I go? How am I going to make a living at my time of life?"

"A doleful tale, madam," said the ass; "but you've not yet come to the end of it. That voice of yours, for all its sorrow, sounds as sweet as a hive of bees. By all means come along with us. We are footing away to the famous city of Bremen. You can still pipe up a tuneful warbling on a moonshine night, I'll be bound. Musicians both, we are off to make our fortunes. We entreat you to join us."

The cat was mighty well pleased at this notion. She pricked up her whiskers, leapt down from the wall, and away they went together.

Not long afterwards, as they were passing a busy farm-yard—styes and barns and stables—they saw a cock perched on a five-barred gate, and screeching out his diddledido as if with the last breath in his body.

"Bravo!" cried the ass. "Upon my soul, Master Chanticleer, you are making a piercing song of it; but pray what is it all about?"

"About!" said the cock. "A few minutes ago I was telling my mistress, the farmer's wife, and her fat heartless cook that we should have fine weather for washing-day. Did I get a word of thanks? Not they! They threatened to chop off my weary old noddle in the morning, and make broth of me for their visitors on Sunday night!"

"Heaven forbid!" said the ass. "Broth! You come along with us, Master Chanticleer. You're welcome; and being alive and free is a long sight better than waiting for one's head to be chopped off! Besides—who

153

knows?—if we all take care to sing in tune and time to-gether, we might get up some kind of a concert. Hoosty-toosty! Let us be off to the great city, where fortunes are made."

"With all my heart," said the cock. So the four of them continued merrily on their way.

It was miles too far, however, for them to reach the city that evening. So when night began to come down, they went into a wood to sleep.

The ass and dog made themselves comfortable and cosy enough under the spreading branches of an oak. The cat climbed up into its branches. And the cock, thinking that the higher he roosted the safer he'd be, flew up to the topmost twigs of it, and there, according to his custom, before he went to sleep, he peered about and around on all sides of him to see that all was well.

And lo and behold, he spied afar off a little light brightly shining; and calling down to his companions, exclaimed, "I spy a light, my friends, with my round eye. There must be a house hereabouts."

"Ah!" cried the ass, "is that so, friend Chanticleer! Well said. Any roof is better than none. Come then, all of you, let us follow the light."

"What's more," added the dog, "I could myself do very well with a beef-bone with a juicy scrap of meat on it."

So up they got, and made their way softly through the wood towards the light which Chanticleer had seen gleaming and twinkling out of the darkness. As they drew near, it became larger and brighter, and at length they found themselves under the very walls of an old house which, although they were not aware of it, had long been the secret haunt of a wild and dangerous band of robbers.

The ass, being the tallest of the company, stepped quietly up to the window, lifted his great head, and peeped in.

"Well, friend Ass," muttered Chanticleer; "what do we see?"

"What do I *see*?" replied the ass. "Why, I see a long table spread with gold and silver plates and dishes and all manner of meats and drinks: a feast for a king! But I care less for the looks of the company—knaves and rascals every one. Take my word for it."

"It would make a noble lodging for *us*," said the cat, twitching her whiskers and gazing up at the lighted window. "And the smell's good."

"Aye," said the ass, "it would that, if the house were empty, and we could get in."

So they drew away a little and consulted together how they could contrive to get the robbers out of the house and themselves safely in. And at last they hit upon a plan. The ass reared himself up on his hindlegs, his forefeet resting against the window-sill; the dog leapt up on to his back; the cat scrambled up on to the dog's shoulders; and, with a scurry of wing, the cock flew up and perched on the cat's head.

When all were ready, the ass gave the signal, and with one accord the four friends set up suddenly such a squall of music as might have wakened the dead. The ass brayed, the dog barked, the cat squealed, the cock yelled; and the next moment they all came tumbling

155

and crashing through the window into the room beyond, cock, cat, dog, ass—helter-skelter, broken glass, crash-bang. A pretty din that was. The world might have come to an end. The feasting robbers, half-scared out of their wits already by the angelic concert they had heard, supposed that a frightful rabble of hobgoblin demons had broken in on them. They up from their chairs and without a look behind them rushed out of the room and into the night as fast as their legs could carry them.

The coast once clear, our happy travellers soon made themselves at home, and set to on the robbers' wines and viands and tasty dishes as if they meant to eat enough to last them a lifetime. When they had had enough and more than enough, they puffed out the candles, and each one sought out a resting-place to his own liking. The donkey stretched his bones on a heap of straw in the yard; the dog curled round, nose on paws, on a mat behind the door; the cat ensconced herself, tip to tail, on the warm ashes in the hearth; and the cock chose for his night-perch the very topmost chimney-pot of the house. He was heart and soul a watchman. And, since they were tired with their journey, and had supped heartily, they all four soon fell fast asleep.

About midnight, when the robbers perceived from afar that the lights had gone out in the house and that all was still and dark, they began to ask themselves why they had been in such haste to leave their plunder and run away. And presently, one of them, bolder than the rest, crept up under the window to see what might be going on. No spark of light; not a sound. Nothing stirring, except an owl in the woodland. He edged his way, noiseless as a shadow, to the back porch of the old house, and so, by way of a stone passage, into the kitchen. It was pitch dark; and groping about to find the wherewithal to light a candle, he espied the glittering fiery-green eyes of the cat, who had awoken at first tiptoe of his foot inside the door. He mistook them for live coals, and stooping down, held a splinter of wood to them for a light.

Grimalkin, the cat, having little taste for this poor joke, at once sprang into his face, spitting and swearing and, claws extended, scratched him cheek to chin. Blundering about in the dark, bruising his shins and elbows, the robber at last groped his way to the back door, where lay the dog, who leapt up with a growl and bit him in the leg to the very bone. Out he tumbled into the night, but as he came helter-skelter across the cobbled yard he fell headlong over the ass, who caught him a thumping kick with his hind leg to teach him manners; whereupon Chanticleer, who had been aroused by this din, lifted up his head, flapped his wings, and screeched as if to waken the dead.

Having had his bellyful of this welcome, the robber scuttled back as fast as his bruised bones could carry him to the band who were waiting in the wood.

"There's some evil and villainous old gally-trot come into that house," he told his Captain. "She screamed and spat at me and scotched me cheek to chin with the nine-inch talons on her long, lean, bony fingers. As soon as I had beaten her off, a demon with a long sharp knife in his hand, who was skulking behind the door, stabbed me in the leg; a huge black boggart stretched out in the yard felled me with his club; and the devil himself, squatting among the chimneypots, yelled, 'Hi! Hi! Cut the rascal into a million pieces!' "

What wonder that after this this band of robbers never dared to venture back to their old haunt in the woods. Indeed, they were never seen in them again. Our four musicians, moreover, were so pleased with their new quarters and the treasure heaped up in it that they decided to venture no further. A strange and jubilant music is heard there at times of an evening in the silence of the woods before night. And unless they have gone on to Bremen, there they remain to this day.

BINGO

The mill-dog lay at the mill-door,
    And his name was Little Bingo.
B with an I, I with an N, N with a G, G with an O,
    And his name was Little Bingo.

The miller he bought a cask of ale,
    And he called it right good Stingo.
S with a T, T with an I, I with an N, N with a G, G with
      an O,
    And he called it right good Stingo.

The miller he went to town one day,
    And he bought a wedding Ring-O!
R with an I, I with an N, N with a G, G with an O,
    And he bought a wedding Ring-O!

AWA'

    Awa', birds, awa',
    Take a peck
    And leave a seck,
    And come no more to day!

THE DOG AND THE SPARROW

There was once an old Sheepdog who in his early days had been well cared for, well fed, and well beloved. But by ill chance as age came over him he fell into the hands of a hard master who treated him shamelessly, beat, kicked and starved him, and begrudged him even a bone. For a time he patiently endured this hard lot, but at length despair began to creep in upon him; and at daybreak one morning, when the last bright stars were dwindling in the sky, he ran away, meaning to make a living as best he could; although he knew that any place for him, good master or bad, would be hard to come by. He was sick and famished. Besides, he was growing old. He ran on, fearing even to pause lest his cruel master should be at his heels, until he had little care left of what might become of him.

THE DOG AND THE SPARROW

As he turned aside for a moment's rest, there happened to be a sparrow there, perched on a thorn by the wayside. She too was no fledgeling and had had a good taste of the world—town-life and village-life, farm and field—and the sight of him, lean and haggard and in such distress, melted her heart within her.

"Why so miserable, my friend?" said she.

"Because," said the dog, "I am sick and old and homeless, and for two days and more have had nothing to eat."

"Glum news enough, my friend," said the sparrow. "But never say die. What you need first is a full stomach. Come along with me when you are rested, and I will soon find you plenty of food."

So on they went together, and came to a small fine country town. It was early afternoon, the weather sultry and hot, and there were few people in the streets. And as they passed by a butcher's shop, the sparrow said to the dog, "Stand close, my friend, in the shade there a while. This shop seems to be empty; I will see if I can peck you down a scrap of meat."

The sparrow flew into the shop, perched on a high shelf, and then upon the butcher's block beside his cleaver; and having first peeped heedfully about her, parlour and street, to be sure nobody was on the watch, she pecked and scratched and tugged at a juicy steak that lay on the edge of the block, until it fell down flat at last into the sawdust. In a trice the dog snapped it up and scrambled away with it into a safe corner, where he soon ate every morsel of it up.

"So far, so good," said the sparrow. "But farther would be better. I know another butcher round the corner, along Chamomile Street, and perhaps you shall have another steak even tastier."

When the dog had eaten this second steak, the sparrow said to him, "And now, my good friend, have you had enough? Enough is good, but a feast can be better."

"I have had plenty of meat," answered the dog, "but I could fancy a good hunch of bread."

"Come along with me then," said the sparrow, "and you shall have that too."

So she took him to a snug little baker's shop with bull's-eye windows, and pecked and pushed at a little loaf still warm from the oven that lay in the window till it fell down on the floor of the shop. And her friend gobbled it up.

As he still had room for more, she took him to another baker's shop, and pecked down a nice crisp roll for him there. When the last crumb of this was gone, the sparrow asked him whether he had had enough now.

"Plenty," said he. "Never can I tell you what your goodness and kindness have meant to me. But come, let us take a little walk together out of the town, and then we can talk in comfort."

This was all to the sparrow's liking. So, leaving the streets and the town behind them, they set out together into the country. But the day was warm, the sun beat down on the flinty dust, and they had not gone far before the dog sighed and said, "I am feeling very weary now, my good friend, and should like to have a little sleep."

"So be it," answered the sparrow. "And while you are enjoying your nap I will perch on that bushy willow

162

yonder and keep watch. What happy hours we will spend together, you and I.

So the dog stretched himself out on the road, and at once fell fast asleep. Whilst he lay sleeping, there came rumbling along the road a surly-looking waggoner in a tilted cart drawn by three fine glossy horses, and loaded with two great casks of wine. The sparrow watched; and seeing that the carter was making no attempt to turn aside, and that if he continued in the way he was going, he would assuredly drive over her friend the dog, she called out to warn him. He opened his eyes and stared, but twitched not a finger.

"Hi! Hi!" cheeped the sparrow again, in dread. "Stop, Master Carter. My friend! Stop, or it shall surely be the worse for thee!"

"Stop!" growled the carter. "Me! You! *That* lazy bag of bones! *You'll* make it the worse for me! What can *you* do? We'll soon see to that!" He cracked his brass-bound whip, urged on his horses, drove his cart clean over the sleeping dog, and its wide wheels crushed him to death.

"Ah!" wailed the sparrow. "*Ah!* Now see what thou hast done; and yet I warned thee! A curse on thee, thou cruel, heartless villain. Thou hast killed my poor, old, gentle, patient friend, the dog. Now hearken! This wicked deed of thine shalt cost thee every penny thou art worth."

The carter burst out laughing.

"Do your worst, and welcome," he jeered at her. "What mischief can the likes of you do to me, you saucy, draggle-tailed, goffeny, glass-eyed flibbertigib-bet!" He drove on. And soon all was quiet.

163

When he had gone, the sparrow fluttered down out of the pollard willow-tree, and took her last look at her friend the dog. She could help him no more. Then she rose again into the air and flew on until she had over-taken the wagon. Biding her time, she perched covertly on its tail-board, crept in under the tilt, and began peck-ing and pecking and pecking at the bung of one of the casks till at last she had loosened it. Presently there came a little oozing of the red wine out of the cask, then a jig-gling trickle, and then suddenly out came the bung and wine together in a continuous gush. The very air in the cart was sweet with grapes. When all but the last drop of the wine was dribbling out, the carter, fancying some-thing was amiss, chanced to look round, only to find that his cart was drenched inside with wine, and that the cask was all but empty. He stared at it in dismay.

What Satan's work is this, he thought, and for an in-stant fancied his eyes had cheated him. But it was no cheat; as far as he could see behind him the dust of the road was dark with the wine.

"Unlucky wretch that I am!" he cried aloud.

"Not wretched enough yet!" piped the sparrow, flit-ting up out of the cart and round its tilt. She then perched on the head of the leader of the carter's three horses, and pecked at him between the eyes until he reared up, plunging and kicking.

"Whoa, there! Hait now; km-over!" yelled the car-ter; and leaping down from the cart, he seized his hatchet and with all his might aimed a blow at the sparrow. But in a twink she was off and away, and, instead, the blow fell upon the horse's head with such force that without even a sigh or a groan it fell down stone dead.

"Luckless, luckless wretch that I am!" cried the carter, as he began to wheel his cart out of the way of the dead horse. "And gawmless-headed fool that you are!" he added, kicking its carcase.

"Not wretched enough yet!" said the sparrow, and away she flew.

At length the carter continued on his journey with the two horses that were left him. And again the sparrow crept in under the tilt of the cart, and pecked and pecked till out came the bung of the second cask, and soon away went all the wine to waste from that cask also.

When the carter discovered this, he cried in rage and despair, "Miserable, miserable wretch that I am!"

And yet again the sparrow answered him, "Not wretched enough yet!" And perching on the head of the second horse, she pecked at him too, making him rear up and all but overturn the wagon. The carter leapt down, ran up and struck at the sparrow again with his hatchet; but away she flew, and the blow fell upon the second horse and killed him on the spot.

"Wretch, wretch, wretch that I am!" cried he.

"Not wretched enough yet!" replied the sparrow; and perching between the ears of the third horse, she began to peck at him also. The carter was wild with fury. Yet again he struck at the sparrow—and killed his third fine horse as in his rage he had killed the other two.

"Third and last!" he cried. "Oh, wretch that I am!"

"Not wretched enough even yet!" piped the sparrow

as she flew away. "Now will I plague and punish thee at thine own house."

The carter was forced at last to leave his wagon behind him, and to trudge off home on foot, boiling with wrath and mortification.

"Wretched man that I am," said he to his wife, who stood watching for him. "Nowt but ill luck has befallen me! My wine is all spilt, and all my three horses are stone dead."

" 'Spilt!' 'Dead!' " she cried, and burst into tears. "Alas, we are ruined. What, what have you done, husband? And it's not only that! An evil bird has flown into the yard, and has brought with her all the birds in the world. They have fallen upon our corn in the loft, and are devouring it by the sackful!"

Away ran her husband, climbed up into his loft, and lo, there were thousands of birds hopping and pecking upon the floor, devouring his corn; and the sparrow in the midst of them.

"World's worst wretch that I am!" cried the carter, seeing that soon every grain of it would be gone, and ruin staring him in the face.

"Not wretched enough yet!" said the sparrow. "Not even wretched enough yet! Harkee, Master Carter, thy cruelty shall cost thee thy life!" And away she flew.

The carter, seeing that he had now lost all that he had, climbed down again from the loft and returned to his kitchen. Yet even now he felt no sorrow or regret for what he had done, but sat himself down, burning with anger and thoughts of revenge, in the chimney corner. And the sparrow sat watching him from the sill outside the casement window. Presently, in the silence, she lifted her bill and began gently tapping and tapping on the pane; and she called softly, "Harkee, harkee, Master Carter! Thy vile cruelty shall cost thee thy very life!"

With that the carter leapt up from his seat, seized his hatchet, and flung it with all his force at the sparrow. But it missed her, and merely crashed through the window. The sparrow hopped in, perched on the window-seat, and cried, "Murderer that thou art, Master Carter! thy cruelty shall cost thee thy life!"

At this the miserable carter became utterly mad and blind with rage, and struck at the window-seat with such force that he cleft it in two: and as the sparrow flew from place to place, the carter and his wife in their furious pursuit of her broke every stick of furniture they had: crockery, glass, chairs, benches, cupboard, table, and at last even the walls, without harming the bird at all.

In the end, however, the carter caught her and held her on high, clutched in his horny fist.

And his wife said, "Bide now, husband, and I will kill the vile varmint at once."

"Nay, nay," said the carter, trembling from head to foot, and clenching his teeth. "She shall die a blacker death than that. I will swallow her alive."

The sparrow pecked, clawed, struggled, stretching out her neck, and continuing to cry, even though it might be with her last breath, "Carter! Carter! It shall cost thee thy life; it shall cost thee thy life, Carter—even yet!"

With that, the carter could wait no longer. He gave

his wife the hatchet, and shouted, "Strike, wife, and strike hard! Kill! kill!"

Blinded with fury and terror, the woman lifted the hatchet, struck with might and main, and missed. Crash fell the hatchet on her husband's stooping head, killing him instantly. And, with a flutter of wing, the sparrow flew out of his hand, out of the window, and away.

"HUSH-A-BA"

Hush-a-ba, birdie, croon, croon,
    Hush-a-ba, birdie, croon.
The Sheep are gane to the Siller Wood,
    And the Cows are gane to the broom, **broom.**

And it's braw milking the Kye, Kye,
    It's braw milking the Kye,
The Birds are singing, the Bells are ringing,
    And the wild Deer come galloping by, by.

And hush-a-ba, birdie, croon, croon,
    Hush-a-ba, birdie, croon.
The Gaits are gane to the mountain hie,
    And they'll no be hame till noon, noon.

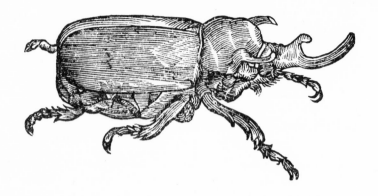

THE GRATEFUL BEASTS

There was once a man, who having lost almost all his money resolved to set off with the little he had left, and journey out of his troubles into the wide, wide world. While it was still early in the day, he came to a village, where the young people were running about like so many half-witted hoddy-doddies, bawling and squealing with joy.

"What has gone wrong? What is the matter?" he asked.

"Matter!" says one of them; "we have caught a mouse—a dancing mouse. Look at the little varmint! See, when we tickle her up, how she jumps and frisks about!"

But the man pitied the mouse, and said, "Let the little creature go, and here's a handful of money to pay for her." So he gave them the money, took the mouse, and set her free. In a trice, she had scampered off, jumped into a hole that was close by, and was soon safely out of their reach.

So the man continued on his way and came to another village. Here, on the green, he saw a host of children with an ass which, poor wretch, they were making stand up on its hind legs and jump about like a tumbler. At sight of its clumsy capers, they shouted with laughter, and thirsty and tired out though the poor beast was, they gave him not a moment's rest.

"See here," said the man, full of pity for the ass, "leave him alone, and I'll give you half the money left in my bundle." So the children shared the money between them; and with a bray of delight, away trotted the ass into the cool green fields out of their reach.

Towards evening, the man came to yet another village. Here the young people had got hold of an old brown bear, which they had muzzled and taught to dance. He could hardly grunt for weariness, but they left him not a moment's peace, still pestered and persecuted him. The man gave them all the money he had left to set the beast free. Rejoiced indeed was Bruin to get down on to his four paws again; and, not waiting even to look behind him, he at once shambled off into the darkening woods.

But the man, having now given away everything that he had in the world, hadn't even a ha'penny left for a crust for supper. He sat down by the wayside and began to think. The king, thought he, must have heaps upon heaps of gold in his treasury that is of no use to him. If I go on like this I shall die of hunger. Surely I shall be forgiven if I borrow just the little I need. And as soon as I have enough again, I can pay it all back. So on he went until he came to the palace of the king of that country.

By hook and by crook he crept his way into the king's treasury, and took three small pieces of gold out of one of the bags. But as he was stealing out again, the king's guards spied him out. Refusing to listen to a word he said, they charged him with being a thief and took him before the judge, who ordered that he should be shut up in a wooden chest and flung into the river. Now, whether to make his misery last the longer, or to give him a chance to keep alive, the lid of this chest had been pierced with a few small holes to give him air; and a loaf of bread and a jug of water had been put inside it.

So there he sat, knees to chin cramped up in the chest, bobbing sorrowfully along on the water and drifting down to the sea. The chest had floated on not more than a few miles when he fancied he heard something nibbling and gnawing at its lock. *Nibble-nibble-nibble.* And all of a sudden the lid sprang open, and who, with her round bead-bright eyes, should be sitting there but his friend the mouse. What's more, as soon as they saw that the lid of the chest was open, the ass and the bear, who had been watching from the banks of the river, swam out and lugged it ashore. And rejoiced indeed was the man to be safe on dry land again.

As the four friends sat consulting together by the waterside, not knowing what to do next, there came softly swimming along with the stream a stone white as snow and of the shape of an egg.

At sight of it, the bear cried out, "The luck is with us, friends! This is a wonder stone, and whosoever possesses it may have everything he wishes."

172

The man hastened down to the water, picked up the stone, and there and then wished for a palace, a fine garden, and a stable full of horses. No sooner said than done —there before his very eyes was a palace, a bountiful garden of trees and fountains, stables and horses all complete; and all so full of beauty that he could but gaze and marvel.

Now it came to pass after some little time that certain merchants with their servants and mules and horses passed that way. They stayed in wonder, whispering one to the other. "See now that princely palace! The last time we were here, this place was nothing but a desert. What mystery is this?"

Very curious they were to know how this had happened. So they went in through the gates of the palace, and knocked at the great door. And the man himself, out of the little barred window in the door, looked out at them.

The merchants questioned him. "How comes it about," they said, "that this beautiful palace is here and this fine garden? It's a palace fit for a king; yet when last we came this way, there was nought here but a wilderness."

And the man told the merchants of the stone. They looked covertly one at another, and then again at the rare and splendid things around them.

"A stone," they said. "It must in sooth be a powerful and marvellous stone."

He invited them in and showed them the stone. They asked the man if he would sell it, offering in exchange for it the whole of their rich merchandise. So rare and fine and costly was this merchandise that the man, in envy of it, clean forgot that the stone itself would bring him in an instant things a thousand times more beautiful and valuable; and he agreed to the bargain.

Scarcely, however, was the stone out of his fingers before his magical palace, his fine garden and stables, and all his possessions had vanished away; and the very next moment he found himself squatting shut up in the chest again at the waterside, his jug and loaf of bread beside him just as he had left them.

But his three friends, the mouse, the ass, and the bear, had by no means forgotten him, and came at once to his help. This time, however, the mouse, gnaw as she might with her small sharp teeth, could not loosen the lock. It stayed fast.

Then said the bear, "My friends, there is only one thing to do; and we must do it. Let us seek for the stone again. Else all our endeavours will be in vain." So off they went.

The merchants, in the meantime, had taken up their abode in the magical palace. Away went the three friends, and when they approached the palace, they hid themselves in a grove of trees, and the bear said, "Mouse, do you creep you in, peep through every key-hole, and spy out where the stone is kept. You are quick and small and secret; nobody will see you."

The mouse did as she was told, but presently after came scampering back and said, "Bad news, my friends. Bad news, I fear. I looked into the great chamber, and the stone dangles down from its high ceiling before a great shining looking-glass by a red silk string; and on either side of it sits an immense cat with fiery flaming eyes to watch and guard it."

Then all three took council together again, and at last the bear said to the mouse, "Creep once more back again, Mistress Mouse, wait till the master of the palace is in bed asleep, then nip his nose with those sharp teeth of yours, and tug smartly at his hair."

Away went the mouse, and did just as the bear had said. This way she peeped and that way she peeped, until she came to the best bedroom in the magical palace. There, silent as a shadow, she crept up the silken hangings of the great four-poster bed in which snored the chief of the merchants, and tip-a-tapped over his huge pillow. One tug at his lanky hair, and one sharp nip of his long thin nose were enough. He woke, leapt up in his bed, clutching his nose in a fury, and shouted, "Villainous, rascally cats that you are, and good-for-nothing; without stirring a whisker you have let the mice gnaw the very nose off my face, and the hair off my head!" He leapt out of his great bed, and drove the two cats which with their flaming eyes still sat in watch over the stone out of the room.

The next night, as soon as the chief merchant was sound asleep, the mouse crept into his silent bedchamber again, and, perched on her hind legs, tail dangling, nibbled and nibbled at the red silken string at the end of which hung the magic stone, until it fell on to the thick silken carpet beneath. Little by little, this way and that, she managed to trundle it out of the room and down the wide staircase until at last she came to the little round hole in the door through which she had entered the palace. Nibbling and nibbling, she made the hole large enough to push the stone through; and there stood the ass, awaiting her on the other side.

To keep it safe, he put the stone into his mouth under his long tongue; and away they went to the river. To make sure of reaching the chest in which their friend still sat grieving, the bear, who was a very good swimmer, scrambled down into the water, and bade the ass put his forefeet on his shoulders. "Hold fast there!" says he to the ass, "and never stir." The mouse, meanwhile, had seated herself in the bear's right ear. And away they went.

They hadn't swum very far before the bear, lifting his mouth out of the water, began boasting. "What think you of my swimming?" he bragged. "Were there ever three such bold brave fellows! What say you, Master Ass?"

But the ass held his tongue, and answered never a word.

This angered the bear. "Why don't you answer?" he growled. "Haven't you a word in that empty old noddle of yours? Were you never taught to speak when you were spoken to?"

At this the ass could hold his peace no longer; he opened his mouth to reply and out from under his tongue and between his great teeth dropped the marvellous stone, which immediately sank and vanished.

"How could I speak?" he brayed. "Didn't you know I had the stone in my mouth? Now it is gone for ever. And you alone are to blame."

"Hold that silly tongue of yours, do; you do nothing

but talk," said the bear. "Let us land, and talk over what is to be done."

So the three of them held yet another council, and at last they went to the King of the Frogs, and asked him to call together all his subjects: their wives and children, brothers and sisters, aunts and uncles, all their relations and friends. When they were assembled together, the King of the Frogs cried, "My people, an enemy is approaching, who is intent on devouring you one and all. But have courage; let us prepare for him. Bring in every stone large and small you can find, and a fortress shall be built to guard us against him."

Filled with alarm at these tidings, the frogs instantly set to work, bringing up a myriad stones from out of the river and piling them up into heaps ready for the building.

And at last there came swimming along a slow, fat, bull frog, dragging behind him by the end of its silken string the magic stone which he had found sunken in the very midst of the river. When the bear saw it, he jumped for joy. He thanked the King of the Frogs for his courtesy and kindness. The King announced that all danger was now over, and his subjects were very well pleased. Besides, if any such enemy should appear, here were stones in plenty in readiness for him.

The three friends without delay set off down the river. They reached the chest in the nick of time. Every crumb of the loaf of bread had been eaten; not a drop of water remained in the jug. The good man inside the box, almost with his last breath, wished himself safe and sound in his palace again. All in a moment, as swiftly as a dream comes and goes, in his palace he was. Another wish, and the merchants found themselves, their merchandise restored, outside the palace gates once more, and unlikely ever to enter it again! There, in his magical palace, with its fine gardens, its orchards of fruit-trees, its birds and flowers and fountains and pleasant streams, the man and his three faithful friends dwelt together. And merry and happy were they their whole lives long.

TONY O

Over the bleak and barren snow
A voice there came a-calling;
"Where are you going to, Tony O!
Where are you going this morning?"

"I am going where there are rivers of wine,
The mountains bread and honey;
There Kings and Queens do mind the swine,
And the poor have all the money."

COLIN FRANCIS

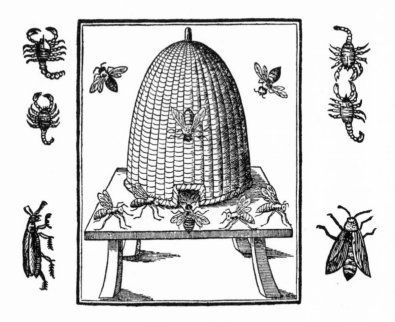

THE QUEEN BEE

The two elder sons of a king once upon a time went out into the world to seek their fortunes; but they fell into a wild and foolish way of living, and could not go back. Time went by; and their younger brother, who was little in stature but of a stout heart and whom they had nicknamed Dummling or Silly Silly, set out to seek them, and his own fortune too.

When at last he had found them and told them that he too was going to try his luck, they only laughed and jeered at him—to suppose that anyone so young and simple as he should dare such a venture after having heard that they had failed! However, they all set out together.

They came at length to a wood. And beside the path that meandered through this wood were many mounds of fir-needles, the nests of myriads of wood-ants, a host of which were creeping about their business in the grass and moss around them. The two elder brothers wanted to stir up one of these great nests and destroy it, so that they could watch its little people in their alarm and terror rushing this way and that in the attempt to carry off their eggs and young ones out of danger. But Dummling said, "No. Leave the poor harmless little creatures in peace; or I warrant it will be the worse for you." They mocked at his stupidity, but he said no more. And they went on together.

By and by they came to a lake where a quacking multitude of ducks were swimming on the water, or preening their wings and basking in the sunshine on its banks.

The two elder brothers wanted to catch and roast a brace of them for supper. But Dummling said, "Let the happy creatures live and enjoy themselves. You shall *not* kill them." They eyed him sullenly, but he said no more. And they went on together.

A day or two afterwards, they came to a hollow tree in whose bole a legion of bees had built their hive. So many of these bees were flying to and fro about the sunny entrance to their hive that the air resounded with their droning; and there was so vast and rich a hoard of golden honeycomb in the tree that some of it was trickling down the trunk.

The two elder brothers began to gather sticks to make a fire, and smoke the bees out, so that they could rob them of their honey. And again Dummling refused to let them have their way. "Let the pretty insects enjoy themselves as they please. You shall *not* burn them." They reviled and scoffed at him, but he said no more. And they went on.

Time passed, and the three brothers came at length to a castle. Its vast walls and turrets towered against the evening sky. But all was still and silent. Not a bird sang; not a soul was stirring. As they passed by its stables they espied horses, standing motionlessly at their mangers; but when they came near they found they were horses of stone. No living creature was to be seen.

They made their way into the castle, and through its great vacant hall, and on from echoing room to room until they came to a door which was locked with three locks of gold. In the middle of this door was a little grill or wicket, through which they could see into the room beyond. And they saw through this narrow grill a little grey old man seated at a table, motionless and alone. They called him; and then again; but he seemed not to have heard them. At their third call he rose from his chair, turned with the keys that hung at his girdle the wards of the three locks of the door, opened it, and came out to them.

But he said never a word, only beckoned them on, and led them into the banqueting-hall of the castle, where a table was already spread with all manner of wines and dainties. When they had eaten and drunk, he showed each one of them to a separate bedchamber. There they slept. Next morning, unknown to the others, he came early to the eldest brother's bedchamber, and beckoned him down to a room below, in which stood a table made of stone. On this table there lay three tablets of marble, and on the first of these tablets were written the following words: "Beneath the moss of the woods that skirt this castle lie scattered a thousand pearls, the dowry of the youngest daughter of the king. He who would free her and this abode from enchantment must find every pearl; and if by set of sun even no more than one of them is missing, he shall be turned into stone."

The eldest brother went out secretly into the woods and sought for the pearls. But the day latened; and when evening came he had found scarcely a hundred of the hidden thousand. At set of sun he rose up to go back to the castle, but remained motionless. As the tablet had foretold, he had been turned into stone.

Next day, having read the tablet, the second brother began his search. The woods were still. Not a live thing— bird nor fly nor insect showed itself. When the sun sank slowly behind the trees, he had found fewer than another hundred of the pearls. At first stroke of the coming dark he too was turned into stone.

Only Dummling now was left. On the third day the little grey old man led him into the room where lay the marble tablets. And he too went out into the woods, sought high and low throughout the morning, found many of the pearls; but at noonday sat down to rest, wearied out and all but in despair. The air was heavy and close in those tangled thickets, and as he sat in a narrow glade on a fallen tree not far distant from a hollow where stood an image in stone, green with rain and weather, he sighed.

"I would," he said to himself, "there were anyone, even the least of creatures, who would come and help me."

As he spoke, the faintest of echoes stole back to him in the silence, and presently after, in the winter's withered beechleaves behind him, he heard a low continuous rustling; and behold, the Queen of the Ants whose people he had saved from destruction had sent her princes with five thousand of her winged soldiers to bring him aid; and before the sun had set, the thousand pearls lay in a glimmering heap together.

Next day, he was taken down to the room again by the little grey old man, and was shown the second tablet of marble. On this was inscribed: "The key of the casket of the youngest of the king's three daughters lies in the moat of the castle. He who would free this castle from enchantment must find it before set of sun, or woe betide him."

He had been for some hours wading among the water-lilies at the margin of the moat, and ever and again diving head foremost to search among their thick writhen roots deep in the water, when he heard a noise of wings from over the castle, and there alighted on the moat a bevy of wild ducks that had flown from the lake which the three brothers had passed on their travels. The ducks looked hard at Dummling out of their round black eyes, and then in a trice set to work, one this way, one that, swimming and diving and scuppering among the oozy weeds and water-lily roots. About two hours before sunset, the lost rusty key was found and laid at his feet. Whereupon, with a sudden loud clatter of wing, the ducks rose into the air, and flew away over the castle.

Next morning, the little grey old man, having shown Dummling the third marble tablet, led him up into a vaulted room in which, mute and motionless, sat the three enchanted daughters of the king; one at her spinning-wheel, another stooping her head over a piece of embroidery that had long fallen into decay, the third gazing out of the window. There they sat, just as when the spell that had been laid over the castle had overtaken them and they had been turned into stone.

Now the third marble tablet had decreed that he must choose out the youngest, the most beautiful, the best, and most lovable of the three daughters of the king—or at sunset suffer the same enchantment as theirs. But all three of them were young, all three were beautiful: how then, by mere looking could he decide which of them was the best? The only guidance the little grey old man had given him was that the eldest, in the hour before the spell had fallen, had eaten a lump of sugar, the next a spoonful of sweet syrup, and the youngest a scrap of honeycomb.

"Alas," thought Dummling, as he stood gazing at her, lost in delight at her beauty and sure of her in his heart, "if only there were anyone to help me." And presently there sounded a faint droning at the window; and there came winging into the room through a crevice the Queen of the Bees whose hive he had saved from being burnt.

Having made a circuit of the room, she first flew to the lips of the princess who had eaten the lump of sugar, and paused; then to the lips of the princess who had swallowed the spoonful of syrup, and paused again; and last she alighted on the honeyed lips of the youngest, and there awhile she stayed.

Thus, at last, the spell was broken; all creatures in the castle that had been turned into stone awoke and lived again. The two elder brothers married the two elder of the king's daughters; and Dummling, the youngest, the most beautiful, the most lovable, and the best. And after the king's death, he reigned in his stead.

THE TREE IN THE VALLEY

There was a tree, and a very fine tree,
As fine a tree as ever you did see;
And the tree was away down in the valley, oh!

There was a branch, and a very fine branch,
As fine a branch as ever you did see;
And the branch was on the tree,
And the tree was away down in the valley, oh!

There was a twig, and a very fine twig,
As fine a twig as ever you did see;
And the twig was on the branch,
And the branch was on the tree,
And the tree was away down in the valley, oh!

There was a nest, and a very fine nest,
As fine a nest as ever you did see;
And the nest was on the twig,
And the twig was on the branch,
And the branch was on the the tree,
And the tree was away down in the valley, oh!

There was an egg, and a very fine egg,
As fine an egg as ever you did see;
And the egg was in the nest,
And the nest was on the twig,
And the twig was on the branch,
And the branch was on the tree,
And the tree was away down in the valley, oh!

There was a chick, and a very fine chick,
As fine a chick as ever you did see;

THE TREE IN THE VALLEY

And the chick was in the egg,
And the egg was in the nest,
And the nest was on the twig,
And the twig was on the branch,
And the branch was on the tree,
And the tree was away down in the valley, oh!

There was a leg, and a very fine leg,
As fine a leg as ever you did see;
And the leg was on the chick,
And the chick was in the egg,
And the egg was in the nest,
And the nest was on the twig,
And the twig was on the branch,
And the branch was on the tree,
And the tree was away down in the valley, oh!

There was a claw, and a very fine claw,
As fine a claw as ever you did see;
And the claw was on the leg,
And the leg was on the chick,
And the chick was in the egg,
And the egg was in the nest,
And the nest was on the twig,
And the twig was on the branch,
And the branch was on the tree,
And the tree was away down in the valley, oh!

THE GOLDEN BIRD

A certain king of old had a beautiful pleasure-garden in which was a tree that bore golden apples. When the apples were ripening, they were counted every morning, and it was found that night after night one of them had been stolen. When the king heard this he was wroth, and ordered that a close watch should be kept on the tree from dusk until daybreak.

Now the king's chief gardener had three sons. The following evening he set the eldest of them to keep watch, telling him on no account to close his eyes. But when midnight was nearly come, he could keep awake no longer. He fell asleep at the foot of the tree; and when he awoke, another of the golden apples was gone.

Next night this gardener's second son was set to keep watch, and it fared no better with him. A little before the palace clock struck twelve, he also fell asleep, and next morning another apple was gone. The king was furious.

On the following day the third son entreated his father to let him keep watch. He feared for him, but at last consented. So as soon as it was beginning to be dark, this young man sat himself down beneath the tree, his bow and quiver beside him on the grass. The hours went by, a full moon rose over the garden, but he refused to let sleep master him. And as the strokes of midnight died away, he heard a faint far rustling in the air. He seized his bow and leapt to his feet; and behold, there came a bird flying over the garden whose feathers in the moonlight seemed to be of the palest gold. He watched the bird alight on the tree, and as it was snapping at one of the apples with its beak, he let fly an arrow. Unharmed, it flew away, leaving only a golden feather from its tail behind it.

Next morning the feather was taken to the king and he was told what had passed during the night. The king called his council together, and it was agreed that a feather of so rare and fine a gold as this was of more value than all the wealth in the king's realm. Then said the king, "If this be true, one feather only is not enough for me. I must have the whole bird!"

Forthwith, the eldest son set out to seek and find the Golden Bird, which, having a good conceit of himself, he thought would be easy. He had not gone far when he came to a wood; and at the edge of this wood there sat a Fox. It made no stir at his approach but steadily regarded him. He stayed still, drew his bow and took aim at the Fox. The Fox gazed on.

"Shoot me not," it called out to him. "I know who you are and what your business is and can give you good counsel. You are seeking the Golden Bird, and this evening you will come to a village in which are two inns facing each other across the street. One of them is a fine handsome place, and all goes merrily inside it. But enter it not. Rest for the night in the other inn, however mean and poverty-stricken it may look."

The young man heard the Fox out. "What!" thought he to himself. "Give advice to *me*! What can a crack-brained animal like this know about the matter!" And he let fly his arrow. It whizzed through the air and pierced the root of a tree about a hand's breadth above the Fox's head. The Fox looked steadily at him yet again; then cocking its bushy tail, it ran off into the wood.

As the Fox had foretold, a little before nightfall the young man came to a village in which were two inns, facing each other across the highway. One of them was a fine bright place; lights were in the windows; and there came out of them a noise of music and singing and dancing. The other inn was small and dark and silent. "A pretty fool I should be," he thought to himself, "to sleep in a hovel like that." So he went into the other inn, calling for the landlord, and supped at his ease. There he stayed, idling and carousing; and forgot the Bird, the Fox, the king, and his country too.

Time passed, and as nothing had been heard of the eldest son, the second at length set out to seek the Golden Bird. Everything happened as before. There sat the Fox at the edge of the wood, and gave him the same counsel as he had given his brother concerning the two inns. Not a whit cared he. He flung a stone at the Fox, journeyed on, and came in the evening to the two inns. And there at an open window sat his elder brother, eating and drinking, while from beyond came a fine noise of fiddles and shouting and dancing. He did not even turn his head to look at the other inn, dingy, dark, and silent; but joined those who were making merry with his brother, stayed on, and forgot father, Bird, Fox, king, and his own country.

Time passed; nothing had been heard of either of them. And at length the third and youngest son asked his father if he too might try his luck and set out into the wide world to seek the Golden Bird. For a long while his father refused to listen to him. He loved his youngest son, whatever he might think of his wits; and he feared that, once gone, some misfortune would overtake him, and that he would never come back. But the young man gave him no peace; and, sad at heart, he let him go.

Off then he went first thing in the morning, came early to the wood, and there sat the Fox, steadily regarding him. His fingers went to his bow, but there they stayed. When he had heard all that the Fox had to tell him, far from letting fly an arrow, he thanked him with all his heart. "Let us away, then," said the Fox. "Seat yourself on my tail and we shall get along faster." So the young man seated himself on the Fox's tail, his feet together in front of him on its narrow back, and off they went over stock and stone so swiftly that the hair on his head fairly whistled in the wind.

When they came to the village, the young man followed the Fox's advice, went into the dark and dreary little inn, and there slept in peace.

Next morning, the Fox sat awaiting him by the wayside. "Follow this road," said he, "turn not aside until you come to a castle. Under its great walls will be lying an armed troop of soldiers still fast asleep and snoring. Take no notice of them, tread softly by, go into the castle, pass on from room to room until you come to one wherein the Golden Bird sits in an old wicker cage. Close beside it stands a cage of gold. But beware. Make no attempt to take the Bird out of the worn-out wicker cage and to put it into the golden cage. If you do, you will repent it."

The Fox stretched out his bushy tail, the young man sat himself down, and away they went again, over stock and stone, and so swiftly that his hair fairly whistled in the wind.

When he came to the castle, all was as the Fox had foretold. The troop of soldiers, still fast asleep and snoring, were camped before its gates. He passed them by, went on into the castle, and came at length to the chamber wherein the Golden Bird hung in the wicker cage. Beneath it stood the cage of gold, and beside it lay three golden apples. The young man gazed at the Bird in wonder, and then at the cage. "It would be a stupid thing, forsooth," he thought to h.mself, "to carry away a Bird so marvellous in that old cage." He drew open the little wicker door, thrust in his hand, seized the Bird, and put it into the cage of gold. But at this the Bird uttered so shrill and wild a scream that it awakened the soldiers, who forthwith took him captive and brought him before the king.

Next morning he was taken before a court of justice, and when all had been heard, he was sentenced to death.

The king, however, decreed that his life should be spared
on one condition—that he should bring him the Golden
Horse which could outpace the wind. If he succeeded in
this, he should have the Golden Bird for his reward.

He set out once more on his journey, sighing his heart
out with regret; but his faithful friend the Fox was
awaiting him. "Listen," said the Fox, "see what has
come upon you because you refused to heed my counsel.
Nevertheless, be of good courage. You shall find the
Golden Horse if you do exactly as I bid you. Go straight
on until you come to a castle. In its stables stands the
Golden Horse in his stall. Beside him in the straw his
groom will be lying lost in sleep. Enter softly. Lead the
Horse out of the stable with all caution, and be sure to
saddle him with the old leather saddle that hangs over
his stall and not with the golden saddle you will see near
by. Beware!"

Again the young man seated himself on the Fox's tail,
and away they went over stock and stone, his hair
fairly whistling in the wind.

All went well. The groom lay snoring in the straw,
one hand still resting in his sleep on the golden saddle.
The young man looked at the old leather saddle. "Surely, surely," he thought to himself, "it would be a mortal
pity to shame so noble an animal with a saddle as mean
as that."

"But scarcely had he so much as touched the saddle of
gold when the horse whinnied, the groom awoke, the
guards ran up, seized the young man, and flung him into
prison. Next morning he was again sentenced to death.
And yet again the king of the country promised him his

life if he should bring back a beautiful Princess whom he had striven in vain to decoy away, and who lived in a castle some seven leagues off.

Heavy in heart and filled with shame, the young man set out once more. He had trudged on for many a weary mile when yet again he found his trusty Fox awaiting him at the wayside.

The Fox upbraided him. "Why did you refuse to listen to me?" he said. "The Bird and Horse were yours if only you had followed my advice. And now for a second time your very head is in danger. Nevertheless, be of good courage. The road on which you are travelling leads straight to the Golden Castle of the Princess. You will reach it by the evening. Hide yourself as best you can. At midnight the beautiful Princess goes down to the bathing-house by the river to bathe. Steal softly up as she enters it, and give her a kiss. She will consent to come away with you; but of a surety, however much she may try to persuade and entreat you, suffer her not to leave you for a moment to bid farewell to her father and her mother. Beware!"

The Fox stretched out his tail, and away they went again, the two of them together, over stock and stone, the young man's hair fairly whistling in the wind.

Come to the Golden Castle at evening, the young man hid himself in the woods beside the river. When midnight struck, and it seemed the whole world was asleep, the beautiful young Princess came down alone to the bathing-house. He stole softly to her side in the darkness, and kissed her cheek. And as the Fox had foretold, she agreed to go away with him, but pleaded pitifully that she might first take leave of her father and mother. Again and again the young man refused to listen; but when she continued to weep and at last fell at his feet entreating only this, he relented. But no sooner had she and the young man set foot on the castle drawbridge than the guards were aroused. They seized him and threw him into a dungeon.

Next morning he was brought before the king of the castle. "Your head," said the king, "shall pay forfeit for this. One thing alone can save you. Unless in the space of eight days you remove yonder wooded hill that stands before my castle, darkens my windows, and prevents my seeing beyond it, you shall die. Do this, and you shall have my daughter for reward." And well might he say it. So huge was the wooded hill which faced the castle that not even the world's armies could have removed it in the time. Six days the young man toiled on and on, digging and shovelling without rest, and with scarcely a bite of food to keep body and soul together. All hope in him was all but gone. On the seventh day, about nightfall, the Fox stole up to him. "Say nothing," he said. "I have kept watch on you. Be still of good courage. Leave everything to me. Lie down, and stir not until the morning." The young man did as he was told; and, behold, when he awoke in the morning, the hill had vanished. Not a trace of it remained. The king marvelled. But he loved his daughter, and much against his will, kept his word. So the young man and the Princess set out forthwith. They had gone but a little distance when they met the Fox; and merrily he greeted them. "The best of what we want," he said to the young man, "is ours already; but there is more to come and we shall soon have all three—the Princess, the Horse, and the Golden Bird."

"Ah," said the young man, "nothing could be better than that; but how can it be done?"

"Only listen to me," replied the Fox, "and all will be well. When you come back to the castle, go alone into the presence of the king, leaving the Princess outside the door. He will at once ask for her, and his joy and astonishment will be the greater when you answer, 'Here she is!' So greatly will he rejoice that he will command that the Golden Horse shall at once be given to you. Mount it immediately, put out your hand to take leave of all who are there, but proffer it last of all to the Princess. Lift her swiftly into the saddle behind you, clap spurs to the horse, and gallop away."

Everything fell out as the Fox had predicted. When they met again, he bade the young man continue on his way to the castle where he had left the Golden Bird.

"Ride up into the courtyard of the castle," he said, "while I keep guard over the Princess, and demand to see the king. But by no means dismount. When he sees the Horse, he will be filled with joy and will bid his servants bring out the Golden Bird. The instant the cage is in your hand, gallop away. No-one can overtake you."

All went well; cage in hand, the beautiful Princess behind him, he rode on until they came to a great forest. And there, under a cedar tree, sat the Fox. "How can I ever repay you," said the young man, "for all you have done for me? My heart is full, but I can find no words."

"Do me only one favour," said the Fox, regarding

197

him earnestly. "Kill me here and now in this forest, and chop off my head and my feet."

"Alas," said the young man. "Ask me anything in the world but that I should do you an injury. Fine thanks that would be!"

Then said the Fox, "Even if you cannot grant me this favour, great though my need is, I can at least continue to give you good counsel. Beware, then, of two things only. Buy no gallows'-meat, and rest not a moment beside running water." That said, he ran off into the forest.

"Well," thought the young man as he rode on with the Princess, "friend indeed the Fox has been to me; but he has strange fancies! What should I want with gallows'-meat, or, in the haste I am in, how should I have any wish to rest beside a river?"

They came at length to the village of the two inns. There, not far distant from the inns, was assembled a great concourse of people shouting and bawling; a scaffold had been set up in the midst; and the whole place was filled with noise and hubbub and uproar. He was told that two murderous robbers were about to be hanged—vile creatures that deserved no mercy. When he came near and looked into their faces, he saw that these two men were his brothers. He took pity on them. "Is there no way in which they can be saved?" he asked of them that stood near. "None," was the reply, "unless any friend can be found to ransom them with all the money he possesses." He stayed not a moment to consider this; paid the ransom demanded; and set off home with his two brothers.

When they were come to the wood where they had all three of them encountered the Fox, it looked so green and cool and pleasant that it was agreed they should enter it and rest awhile; and they came to a precipitous gorge that was the bed of a stream now run almost dry by reason of the heat of the summer. The young man, who was leading his horse, paused to look down into this gorge; and his brothers, seizing their opportunity, crept close behind him and flung him over the edge. There they left him, supposing him dead, and made all haste to return home, bringing the Princess, the Golden Horse and the Bird with them. The king made a feast, and all who cared might come to see these wonders. There was great rejoicing. But the Horse would not eat, the Bird would not sing, and the Princess wept. And his father continued to mourn for his youngest son, and wished he had never let him go.

But his son was not dead. By good fortune only a shallow runlet of water coursed between the boulders of the river bed. But although he could quench his thirst, and none of his bones had been broken, he was bruised from head to foot, and too weak to climb up out of the ravine. Even yet the faithful Fox had not abandoned him. He came at evening, softly stepping down from stone to stone to where he lay.

"Alas," he said, "if you had listened to me, no evil would have befallen you. But be of good comfort and have courage; lay hold of my tail, and hold fast, and I will help you out of this sorry place into safety." So he hauled and he tugged and at length the young man was got up out of the ravine.

When he was rested, the Fox told him that he was still in great danger, since his brothers had set a watch about the wood lest he should still be alive, and he was to be killed at sight. "Disguise yourself, then," said the Fox, "put on beggar's rags; go in secret to the court of the king, and mingle with the serving-men and any other strangers or vagrants who may be there."

This the young man did; and although no eye recognised him, as soon as he entered the king's palace the Golden Bird began to sing, the Horse began to eat, and the Princess left off weeping. The king was astonished, and asked her the cause of this change and what had restored her spirits.

"I cannot tell," she said, fearing what revenge the two brothers would wreak on her if she revealed their wickedness. "These many days I have been lost in grief and despair; now I am happy and could out-sing the Golden Bird itself. It is as though he whom I love and grieve for were come near."

The king commanded that every stranger in the palace should at once be brought before him. When the youngest son appeared, disguised in his beggar's rags, the Princess instantly knew him, ran to him, fell upon his neck, and wept for joy. No mercy was shown to the two elder brothers. They were hanged by the neck from a high turret of the palace until they were dead. Thus the young man won his Princess, and the childless king made him the heir to his kingdom.

Years passed. But he had not forgotten the faithful friend to whom he owed nearly every joy he had. And one still evening, as he was once again walking in the wood thinking of these things, behold there sat the Fox, as of old, and glad he was at sight of him. And in a while, yet again, the Fox besought him, tears trickling from his eyelids, to doubt no longer, but to kill him, and then to chop off his head and his feet.

"I am in misery as I am," he said; "you alone can set me free."

At last the young man was persuaded. Instantly the enchantment that had so long oppressed the Fox fell away, and he stood up in his true shape and image—the brother of the beautiful Princess, who had been absent from her for many many years.

A DIS, A DIS

A dis, a dis, a green grass,
A dis, a dis, a dis;
Come all you pretty fair maids
And dance along with us.

For we are going roving,
A roving in this land;
We take this pretty fair maid,
We take her by the hand.

She shall get a duke, my dear,
As duck do get a drake;
And she shall have a young prince,
For her own fair sake.

And if this young prince chance to die,
She shall get another;
The bells will ring, and the birds will sing,
And we clap hands together.

THE DONKEY

Once upon a time there was a king and a queen who had everything in the world that heart could desire—except children. The queen grieved over this day in, day out. She would sigh in the darkness of the night, "I am like a field wherein nothing grows." And she gave God no peace with her prayers.

At last her wish was given her. But when the child which she had so long pined for came into the world, it was quite unlike other new-born humans. It was lean and lank and hairy, and it had four long spindly legs. It was a little Ass. When the queen looked upon this infant Ass, she fell into bitter grief and refused to be comforted. She would rather have been given no child at all. In her woe, she told her women to take the sprawling little creature away and throw it into the river, that the fishes might devour it.

But, "No," said the king. "If it is God's will that this shall be my son and heir, so be it. He shall be brought up

203

as a prince should be. And after my death, he shall sit on my throne, and wear my crown."

This little Ass, then, was cared for and nurtured like any other human child, and as befitted a prince. Never was Ass more gentle or more lively. His two round eyes were clear and bright and luminous, his coat was soft and silky, his two hairy ears stood up peaked and straight above his long flat-cheeked head. Not only was he a handsome and sprightly little Ass, but of a gay and merry disposition. He leapt about, enjoyed his daily hay and corn and water, played and diverted himself to his heart's content. Music in particular was his constant joy. He took so much pleasure in it that he went to the king's chief musician, and said, "Teach me thine art, I pray thee; so that I may at last learn to play the lute even comparably to thyself."

"Ah, but my dear and honoured little master," replied the king's musician, "such learning would come all too hard to thee. Thy—thy hand is not well suited to the lyre but to other skill, and would fare far better with the cymbals, or, perchance, the drum. There is nothing too dainty about thee. Thou would'st soon wear out the strings."

Nevertheless, the little Ass could not be dissuaded. He had set his heart upon the lute, and spent every hour he could spare from his other tasks of learning on his music. Morning and evening found him strumming at the strings until at last he became all but as fine and skilful a player as was the king's master-musician himself.

Up to this time, he had no notion what he looked like.

As soon as he had been born, all looking-glasses and mirrors had been forbidden in the king's palace. But as he grew up to full age, he began to be thoughtful and reflective, and would sit for minutes together silent, his lyre forgotten, and aware deep within him that something was amiss.

At length one day he went out walking alone, and came to a well. It was cool and pleasant at the well-side, under the trees, after the glare and heat of the sun. Presently he leaned over and peered down into the well, and there, in the dim round of still clear water far beneath him, he saw for the first time what he looked like—long, flat, hairy face; wide mouth; a lank pair of hairy twitching ears—an Ass. For a while he could not believe his eyes. Then he moved his great head—now this way, now that; cocked one ear, then the other; looked sidelong, and tried to smile. But this only showed his long flat teeth. No: whatever he might be in himself, the face he was looking at was the visage of an ass, and that visage was his own. So sharp was his pain and grief at this discovery that he knew not where to turn, where to hide himself, whither to flee away. Only of one thing was he certain. He could not go back to his father's court. With little but his beloved lute and only one faithful friend and companion, he set out into the wide world, where no-one would recognise him or know him for what he was.

They travelled up, they travelled down, and at last came into a region where reigned an old king who had only one child, a daughter. And she was marvellously beautiful.

THE DONKEY

When, in the heat of the afternoon, the two travellers came in sight of this old king's castle, the Ass, who knew nothing of this, said to his servant, "Here we will stay. We will venture no further." He bade him go knock on the great gate of the castle. His servant cried, "Ho, there! A noble stranger waits without. Open, that he may enter."

There came no answer. No face looked down from the watch-tower. The gate remained shut. Butterflies fluttered from flower to flower in the weeds on the castle wall, but not a bird called.

Then the prince sat himself down on a green grass bank a little beyond the great gate, took out his lute, and began to play upon it with such skill and sweetness that the summer air rang with the strains of his music. Roused out of his dreams at last by the sound of the strings, the watchman stirred in his sleep, opened his eyes, listened, rose and looked out. And, at sight of the Ass sitting there with his lute, he instantly ran off in haste to the king, his master.

"A marvel, my lord king," said he. "Not nine paces from my watch-tower there sits on his hinders by the gate of the castle what seems nought but a young and lusty four-legged Ass. Yet he can play on the lute as if he would steal the heart out of a man's body."

"Let him be brought forthwith into my presence," said the king.

So the Ass came in and stood before the king, and the king commanded him to discourse upon his lute. In spite of his gentle bearing and his enchanting skill in music, at sight of the Ass solemnly bowing before the king, everyone present began to laugh. And its being the hour when the Court supped in the great hall, the king's chamberlain bade the Ass take his place among the serving-men and eat with them.

"Nay," said the Ass, "that shall never be. Seem what I may, I am no common stable-ass, but of noble birth and lineage."

At this, those who heard him laughed the more.

"Hail, Prince of Asses!" they mocked him; "if that is so, go up higher and seat thyself with the king's chief officers and men of war!"

"Not even that," said the Ass. "If I sup at all, I will sit by the king."

Hearing these words, the king looked long again at this strange visitor, smiled softly to himself, and said in all good humour, "Well, well, Master Ass, let it be as thou wilt. Seat thyself here by me." So the Ass came nearer and stood at the high table.

Again smiling softly to himself, the king said, "Tell me, Master Ass, and there never was sweeter lute-player, how doth my daughter please thee?"

The Ass turned slowly his great head towards the princess, gazed at her, solemnly nodded, and replied, "She delights me past words to tell, O King. I have never before set eyes on any face so lovely."

"Well said," answered the king. "Then shalt thou sit betwixt us twain."

"That, my Lord King," said the Ass, "was what it was in my heart to desire."

So he made his way on, and seated himself between the king and the princess at the table, and ate and drank as nicely and daintily as any one else there who was of noble blood.

Time went by. The Ass was now a welcome guest in the king's court, and yet he was not happy. "What good can come of all this?" he would think to himself when he was alone. "No-one knows who I am; my secret may be discovered; and the day must come when I shall have to go home again." At thought of it, deep grief stole over him. None the less, he went at length and besought the king to give him leave for his dismissal.

But the king was very loth to give him leave. He had grown fond of the Ass and delighted in his company.

"Why, now," he said, "what ails thee, gentle Ass? Thy countenance is as sad and sour as a jug of vinegar. Anything thou wantest is thine for the asking. Is it gold, perchance?"

"Nay," said the Ass, shaking his head. "Not gold."

"Is it jewels and fine raiment, then?"

"Nay, none of these."

"Soothly," said the king, "would'st thou be content with half my kingdom?"

"Nay, not even that," replied the Ass.

Then said the king, "I would that I knew what would restore thee to thine old happiness again. Would'st have my lovely daughter to wife?"

"Ah, your majesty," cried the Ass; "that has long been my one and only desire."

This said, every trace of sorrow and pining left him. All in a moment he became as merry and joyful as the day is long. It was as if at knowledge of the love burning in his heart, a sure and certain hope had sprung up within him.

So a great and splendid banquet was prepared, and guests from near and far were bidden to the wedding. When night was come, and the princess and her bridegroom were led up with music and jollity to the chamber that had been prepared for them, the king, anxious to know how an Ass of so gentle a nature and understanding would behave himself, bade one of his servants hide himself in the room and watch all that passed.

When the two of them, the Ass and his bride, were within the chamber and alone, the Ass, after bolting the door behind him, gazed steadfastly around him, and, believing that none was near to look or listen, immediately and as if by magic threw off the ass's skin that had so long disguised him, and stood before her in his true shape—as noble and handsome a prince as you could wish to see. "See, Sweetheart," he cried; "here now I am *as* I am. And I beseech thee not to think me unworthy of thee."

The princess marvelled indeed; her joy knew no bounds. She kissed him and loved him dearly.

When morning was come, he leapt out of bed and, easily as hand into glove, slipped back into his ass's skin. Only a Wizard could have guessed what shape and being was hidden beneath it.

Soon came the old king to wish them both good-morrow.

"Ah," cried he, "my gentle and beloved Ass is merry, I see. And thyself," he said to his daughter, "art thou not a little sad that God hath not given thee a prince for a husband?"

" 'A prince,' dear father," said she. "I love the husband I have been given no less than if he were the noblest
and handsomest prince in the world. Indeed, there is
none to compare with him. And my love shall be true to
him as long as I live."

The king was astonished. But in a while the servant,
who had hidden himself in the bedchamber, came to the
king and revealed everything that he had seen and heard.
But the king was angry and refused to believe him.
"Then, my lord king," said the servant, "I entreat thee
to keep watch thyself during the night that is coming;
and witness what I myself saw with mine own eyes. And
if what I have told thee proves false, then let my head be
the forfeit. Moreover, my lord king, if thou wert to
steal this ass's skin away from him and fling it into a fire
and burn it to ashes, then the prince would be compelled
to reveal himself in his true shape."

"Thy counsel is good," said the king.

That night then, when the princess and her bridegroom were happily asleep again, the king himself stole
into their bedchamber, and saw clear as crystal by the
light of the moon a noble-looking youth lying there
asleep beside his daughter; and the ass's skin, which he
had flung off him, lying empty on the floor. So he took
the skin away; and before morning broke, a great fire
was lighted beneath the palace walls and the king himself threw the skin into the flames, and stayed until it was
consumed in the fire and burnt to ashes. Then he returned again into hiding in the bridal chamber to watch
the night out. When the prince had slept out his first
sleep, he rose from his bed at daybreak and searched in

vain for his ass's skin. It was nowhere to be found. Smitten sorely with alarm and dread at the thought of his secret being discovered, and what might come of it, he cried to himself, "Alas, alas, my loved one! What shall I do? How shall we escape from the trap that has been laid for us?" Inch by inch he drew open the door of the room; and there stood the king.

"My son," said he, smiling, "whither away in such haste? What troubles thee? Even in thy strange disguise, I learned to love thee. And now, never shalt thou leave us. Half my kingdom shall be thine; and when death overtakes me, then thou shalt have the whole of it."

At this glad ending to what had begun in grief, the prince rejoiced indeed. The old king gave him half his kingdom, and when he died, the whole of it was his. After the death of his own father, yet another kingdom was his also. He lived in magnificence, his queen was his dearest treasure, and they were beloved by all their subjects.

SLEEPEST OR WAKEST THOU?

Sleepest or wakest thou, jolly shepherd?
 Thy sheep be in the corn;
And for one blast of thy minikin mouth,
 Thy sheep shall take no harm.

WILLIAM SHAKESPEARE.

THE GOOSE-GIRL

An old queen, whose husband had been dead some years, had a beautiful daughter. When she grew up, she was betrothed to a prince who lived a great way off; and as the time drew near for her to be married, she made ready to set off on her long journey. Her mother, the queen, packed up for her journey many costly things: gold and silver, jewels and trinkets—everything indeed that befitted a royal bride; for she loved her daughter very dearly. To ride with her, and be her companion, and to take care of her, she gave her one of her waiting-maids, charging this woman to bring her in safety into her bridegroom's hands. Now the princess's horse was called Falada, and it could speak.

When the time came for them to set out, the old queen went into her bed-chamber, took a little knife, and cut her finger until the blood came. Three drops only of the blood she let fall upon a handkerchief. This she gave to her daughter, saying, "My child, keep and preserve this with the utmost care; it is a charm that will be of service to you on your way." The princess kissed her mother, and put the precious handkerchief into her bosom.

Early next morning they took a sorrowful leave of one another. The princess mounted her horse and, with her waiting-maid, set off on her journey to her bridegroom's kingdom.

Next day, as they were riding together in the heat and stillness, they came to a little brook; and the princess, being parched with thirst, turned to her maid and said, "I pray thee dismount and fetch me some water in my golden cup out of yonder brook, for I am thirsty and would drink."

"Nay," said the maid insolently, "if you are thirsty, get down yourself and drink as best you can; I don't choose to wait on you any longer."

So thirsty was the princess that she dismounted from her horse, and hastening to the bank of the little brook, knelt down and drank. Frightened at the sullen and angry looks of her waiting-maid, she had not dared to bring with her her golden cup. She was weary, and she wept. "Alas!" she thought to herself, "what will become of me?" And the drops of blood made answer to her and said—

> "If this your loving mother knew,
> Her gentle heart would break in two."

But the princess was by nature meek and gentle. She made no complaint, but in silence mounted her horse again.

Thus they continued on their journey; and the sun continued to beat down so scorchingly out of the heavens that the princess began to feel very thirsty again. At last, when after noonday they came to a river, she had forgotten her maid's insolence, and said, "I pray thee dismount, take my golden cup, and fetch me some water from yonder river to drink."

But the maid answered her more rudely and haughtily than before. "Drink if you want to! But fetch your cup yourself. From this time on you get no more of me."

So great was her need that the princess once more dismounted from her horse. She stooped her head over the stream and, having drunken of the running water, sighed deeply and said, "Alas, alas! What will become of me?" And again the three drops of blood made answer and said—

> "If this your loving mother knew,
> Her gentle heart would break in two."

Her eyes dim with tears, she stooped lower, and her mother's handkerchief slipped from out of her bosom and floated away with the water. This she had not seen; but her waiting-maid, who sat watching and knew well of this charm, rejoiced. She hated and envied her mistress; and from henceforth she would be in her power.

When, then, the princess arose from her knees and would have mounted her horse again, the maid angrily prevented her. There and then, she compelled her to strip off her bride's apparel and put on her own clothes. Then she mounted Falada, and bade the princess follow her on the jaded nag which she herself had been riding.

When, moreover, they were nearing the end of their journey, she drew rein and made the princess swear solemnly by the skies above her that no word of what had passed should ever be uttered to living soul.

"Swear!" she cried, "or you shall pay for it with your life."

In fear and trembling, the princess did as she was bidden; but Falada had seen and heard all this, and had marked it well.

Thus, then, they went on their way until at length they came to the palace of the king. The whole Court rejoiced at their coming. The prince sprang forward to greet them, and lifting the waiting-maid from her horse, supposing her to be the princess who was to be his bride, he led her up the great staircase to the royal chamber. But the princess was bidden stay in the courtyard below.

Now the old king happened to be looking out of a window, and saw her standing there, and how beautiful she was, and gentle and delicate. And he himself went immediately to the royal guest-chamber, and asked the false princess who it was that she had brought with her and had been left forlornly waiting in the courtyard.

And she lied to the king. "I picked her up on the road," she said, "and brought her with me for company on the long journey. I pray you give the jade some work to do, that she may not be idle."

The old king for some time could not think of any work for the maid to do; but he said at last, "I have a boy who takes care of my geese. She shall help him." Now the name of this boy, who was little more than a child, was Curdken.

That evening the false princess said to the prince, "I beseech you, dear husband, do me one small kindness?"

"That will I," said the prince.

"It is only," she said, "that you send for a slaughterer and tell him to cut off the head of the horse I rode on my journey hither. It is a stubborn and unruly beast, and plagued me sadly on the way." This she did because she knew that Falada could speak, and she feared what secrets he might tell.

The prince listened and said nothing; but a little before dark set in, the slaughterer did as he had been told. He killed the princess's horse, Falada, and cut off its head. When the true princess heard of this, she grieved bitterly and wept; and she went privily to the slaughterer and promised him a piece of gold if he would nail up the head of her faithful Falada over the arch of a great gloomy gateway that led out of the city. There she would be able to see it every day when she and Curdken went out in the morning with their geese into the meadows, and came back at evening. And the slaughterer agreed. He took Falada's head and that night nailed it fast on the arch above the gloomy gateway.

Early the next morning, as with their geese she and Curdken went out through the gate, she looked up at the head nailed over the dark arch, and said sorrowfully:—

"Alas, poor Falada, hanging there!"

And the head made answer:—

"Alas, poor princess! Ill we fare.
If this your loving mother knew,
Her tender heart would break in two."

The two of them then went on together out of the city, driving their geese before them. And when they were come to the meadows, she sat down upon a green bank and unbound her hair, which was of pure gold. When Curdken saw it shining and glittering in the sun, he coveted a lock for himself and wanted to pull one out. But she cried:—

"Blow, blow, blow, sweet wind, I say,
And carry Curdken's hat away;
Let him chase it everywhere—
Hill and dale—and chase in vain,
Till I have combed my golden hair,
And bound its tresses up again."

And there came a little wind out of the heavens across the meadows. It blew off Curdken's hat, and away it floated and trundled, hill and dale; and away he ran after it. By the time he came back she had finished combing and braiding her golden hair. He was angry and sulked, and refused to speak to her. But they watched and tended

their geese until the evening came on, and they drove
their flock homeward again.

Next morning, as, with sorrow in her heart, they were
passing again under the dark gate, she looked up at the
head of her horse, Falada, nailed above the arch, and
cried:—

"Alas, poor Falada, hanging there!"

And the head answered her:—

"Alas, poor princess! Ill we fare.
If this your loving mother knew,
Her gentle heart would break in two."

Then she followed after the geese and so into the meadows; and again began to comb out the tresses of her
golden hair. Again Curdken ran up to her, pining to
touch it with his hand, and to steal a lock. Again she
cried out:—

"Blow, blow, blow, sweet wind, I say,
And carry Curdken's hat away;
Let him chase it everywhere—
Hill and dale—and chase in vain,
Till I have combed my golden hair,
And bound its tresses up again."

Whereupon a gust of wind came out of the cloudless
sky; off flew his hat—hill and dale, and far away; and he
himself went chasing after it. When he came back, she
had done up her hair again, all was safe, and he could
steal none of it. In silence they watched and tended their
geese until it began to grow dark.

That evening, when they were come back to the palace, Curdken went to the old king, and said, "I refuse to tend the geese with that goose-girl any longer."

"And why?" said the old king.

"She teases and vexes me the whole day long. Besides, she is bewitched."

The old king bade him tell him all that had passed. And Curdken said, "When, in the early morning, we go with our geese under the dark gateway out of the city, she begins to weep and wail as we pass a dried-up horse's head that is nailed upon the wall; and, she says to it:—

'Alas, poor Falada, hanging there!'

And the head answers:—

'Alas, my Princess! Ill we fare.
If this your loving mother knew,
Her tender heart would break in two'."

He then told the king what happened in the meadows where they kept their geese; how his hat had been blown away, and he had been compelled to chase after it and leave his flock with only the goose-girl to watch over it.

Then the old king bade him drive out his flock of geese as usual the next day. When morning was come, he had concealed himself behind the dark gateway. He watched all that took place, listened closely when the goose-girl spoke to Falada, and marvelled as he heard the head of the dead horse make reply. He then went on himself secretly into the meadows, concealed himself behind the willows at the waterside, and saw with his own eyes how, as soon as she had sat down on the green bank, she unplaited her golden hair, shining and glittering in the sun, and how when Curdken kept on pestering her she cried:—

> "Blow, blow, blow, sweet wind, I say,
> And carry Curdken's hat away;
> Let him chase it everywhere—
> Hill and dale—and chase in vain,
> Till I have combed my golden hair,
> And bound its tresses up again."

Yet again the wind blew, and away went the hat and Curdken after it. All this the old king secretly observed. Unseen, he went his way. And when the goose-girl had come home in the evening, he sent for her as he sat alone, and asked her the meaning of these things. And she told the king that she could not reveal her secret, or declare her sorrows to any human being since she had made a vow by the heavens above her never to do so; and that, if she had refused to obey, she would have paid for it with her life. The old king still continued to urge her to share her secret with him, but in vain.

Then said he, "If thou can'st not confide in me, whisper thy sorrows up into the chimney there. It will be well with thee." And he went away. When he had gone, she went to the hearth, as he had counselled her, and began to weep, confessing everything that was in her heart, and saying:—"Here am I, utterly alone in the world, and yet the daughter of a king. I have been betrayed by the treachery of a false waiting-maid who has brought me to this woeful pass, and compelled me to put off my royal apparel, and has taken my place with the prince who was to be my bridegroom. Alas, if my mother could see me in these rags, tending the geese, verily her heart would break."

The old king, however, had been listening, and had heard everything that she had said. He returned to her, took her by the hand and kissed her, and bade his servants attire her in raiment befitting a princess. He gazed at her in wonder, marvelling at her beauty. He then sent for his son and told him all that had passed.

The prince rejoiced. No love had sprung up in his heart for the woman who had lied and deceived him. Here at last was the princess, as good as she was beautiful, to whom he had been betrothed.

A great feast was prepared, which was attended by a multitude of the old king's people and many guests. The prince sat at the head of the table, the true princess on the one side of him and the false waiting-maid on the other. But the waiting-maid was so blinded with pride and vanity that she failed to recognise the princess.

When all present had eaten and drunk their fill and were merry, the old king related the whole story. Then he turned to the waiting-maid and put this riddle to her: "What punishment dost thou think should be meted out to any human being guilty of such treachery and wickedness?"

The waiting-maid answered him and said, "She deserves nothing better than to be stripped naked and put into a barrel stuck round with pointed nails. Two white horses should be harnessed to it, to drag her from thy palace through every street of the city, until she is dead."

"Thou art that evil thing," said the king. "As thou hast said, so shall it be done unto thee."

The people rejoiced at the marriage of the prince to his lovely bride; and after the old king's death, they reigned over his kingdom in peace and happiness their whole lives long.

WHAT'S IN THERE?

Faht's in there?
Gold and money.
Fahr's[1] my share o't?
The moosie ran awa' wi't.
Fahr's the moosie?
In her hoosie.
Fahr's her hoosie?
In the wood.
Fahr's the wood?
The fire burnt it.
Fahr's the fire?
The water quencht it.
Fahr's the water?
The broon bull drank it.
Fahr's the broon bull?
Back a Burnie's hill.
Fahr's Burnie's hill?
A' claid wi' snaw.[2]
Fahr's the snaw?
The sun meltit it.
Fahr's the sun?
Heigh, heigh up i' the air!

[1] Where's.   [2] Deep, deep in snow.

THE BLACK BULL OF NORROWAY

And many a hunting song they sung,
 And song of game and glee;
Then tuned to plaintive strains their tongue,
 'Of Scotland's luve and lee'.
To wilder measures next they turn
 'The Black, Black Bull of Norroway!'
Sudden the tapers cease to burn,
 The minstrels cease to play.

In Norroway, langsyne, there lived a certain lady, and she had three dochters[1]. The auldest o' them said to her mither: "Mither, bake me a bannock, and roast me a collop[2], for I'm gaun awa' to seek my fortune." Her mither did sae; and the dochter gaed awa' to an auld witch washerwife and telled her purpose. The auld wife bade her stay that day, and gang and look out o' her

  [1] Daughters.   [2] Minced meat.

back door, and see what she could see. She saw nocht the first day. The second day she did the same, and saw nocht. On the third day she looked again, and saw a coach-and-six coming alang the road. She ran in and telled the auld wife what she saw. "Aweel," quo' the auld wife, "yon's for you." Sae they took her into the coach, and galloped aff.

The second dochter next says to her mither: "Mither, bake me a bannock, and roast me a collop, for I'm awa' to seek my fortune." Her mither did sae; and awa' she gaed to the auld wife, as her sister had dune. On the third day she looked out o' the back door, and saw a coach-and-four coming alang the road. "Aweel," quo' the auld wife, "yon's for you." Sae they took her in, and aff they set.

The third dochter says to her mither: "Mither, bake me a bannock, and roast me a collop, for I'm awa' to seek my fortune." Her mither did sae; and awa' she gaed to the auld witch-wife. She bade her look out o' her back door, and see what she could see. She did sae; and when she came back said she saw nocht. The second day she did the same, and saw nocht. The third day she looked again, and on coming back said to the auld wife she saw nocht but a muckle Black Bull coming roaring alang the road. "Awell," quo' the auld wife, "yon's for you." On hearing this she was next to distracted wi' grief and terror; but she was lifted up and set on his back, and awa' they went.

Aye they travelled, and on they travelled, till the lady grew faint wi' hunger. "Eat out o' my right lug[1]," says the

[1] Ear.

Black Bull, "and drink out o' my left lug, and set by your leavings." Sae she did as he said, and was wonderfully refreshed. And lang they gaed, and sair they rade, till they came in sight o' a very big and bonny castle. "Yonder we maun be this night," quo' the bull; "for my auld brither lives yonder;" and presently they were at the place. They lifted her aff his back, and took her in, and sent him away to a park for the night. In the morning, when they brought the bull hame, they took the lady into a fine shining parlour, and gave her a beautiful apple, telling her no to break it till she was in the greatest strait ever mortal was in in the world, and that wad bring her out o't. Again she was lifted on the bull's back, and after she had ridden far, and farer than I can tell, they came in sight o' a far bonnier castle, and far farther awa' than the last. Says the bull till her: "Yonder we maun be the night, for my second brither lives yonder;" and they were at the place directly. They lifted her down and took her in, and sent the bull to the field for the night. In the morning they took the lady into a fine and rich room, and gave her the finest pear she had ever seen, bidding her no to break it till she was in the greatest strait ever mortal could be in, and that wad get her out o't. Again she was lifted and set on his back, and awa' they went. And lang they gaed, and sair they rade, till they came in sight o' the far biggest castle, and far farthest aff, they had yet seen. "We maun be yonder the night," says the bull, "for my young brither lives yonder;" and they were there directly. They lifted her down, took her in, and sent the bull to the field for the night. In the morning they took her into a room, the finest of a', and gied her a plum, telling her no to break it till she was in the greatest strait mortal could be in, and that wad get her out o't. Presently they brought hame the bull, set the lady on his back, and awa' they went.

And aye they gaed, and on they rade, till they came to a dark and ugsome glen, where they stopped, and the lady lighted down. Says the bull to her: "Here ye maun stay till I gang and fight the deil. Ye maun seat yoursel' on that stane, and move neither hand nor fit[1] till I come back, else I'll never find ye again. And if everything round about ye turns blue I hae beaten the deil; but should a' things turn red he'll hae conquered me." She set hersel' down on the stane, and by and by a' round her turned blue. O'ercome wi' joy, she lifted the ae fit and crossed it owre the ither, sae glad was she that her companion was victorious. The bull returned and sought for but never could find her.

Lang she sat, and aye she grat, till she wearied. At last she rase and gaed awa', she kendna whaur till[2]. On she wandered till she came to a great hill o' glass, that she tried a' she could to climb, but wasna able. Round the bottom o' the hill she gaed, sabbing and seeking a passage owre, till at last she came to a smith's house; and the smith promised, if she wad serve him seven years, he wad make her iron shoon, wherewi' she could climb owre the glassy hill. At seven years' end she got her iron shoon, clamb the glassy hill, and chanced to come to the auld washerwife's habitation. There she was telled of a gallant young knight that had given in some bluidy sarks[3] to wash, and whaever washed thae sarks was to be his wife.

[1] Foot.   [2] She didn't know where to.   [3] Shirts.

THE BLACK BULL OF NORROWAY

The auld wife had washed till she was tired, and then she set to her dochter, and baith washed, and they washed, and they better washed, in hopes of getting the young knight; but a' they could do they couldna bring out a stain. At length they set the stranger damosel to wark; and whenever she began the stains came out pure and clean, but the auld wife made the knight believe it was her dochter had washed the sarks. So the knight and the eldest dochter were to be married, and the stranger damosel was distracted at the thought of it, for she was deeply in love wi' him. So she bethought her of her apple, and breaking it, found it filled with gold and precious jewellery, the richest she had ever seen. "All these," she said to the eldest dochter, "I will give you, on condition that you put off your marriage for ae day, and allow me to go into his room alone at night." So the lady consented; but meanwhile the auld wife had prepared a sleeping-drink, and given it to the knight, wha drank it, and never wakened till next morning. The leelang night the damosel sabbed and sang:

> "Seven lang years I served for thee,
> The glassy hill I clamb for thee,
> The bluidy shirt I wrang for thee;
> And wilt thou no wauken and turn to me?"

Next day she kentna what to do for grief. She then brak the pear, and found it filled wi' jewellery far richer than the contents o' the apple. Wi' thae jewels she bargained for permission to be a second night in the young knight's chamber; but the auld wife gied him anither sleeping-drink, and he again sleepit till morning. A' night she kept sighing and singing as before:

> "Seven lang years I served for thee,
> The glassy hill I clamb for thee,
> The bluidy shirt I wrang for thee;
> And wilt thou no wauken and turn to me?"

Still he sleepit, and she nearly lost hope a' thegeither. But that day when he was out at the hunting, somebody asked him what noise and moaning was yon they heard all last night in his bedchamber. He said he heardna ony noise. But they assured him there was sae; and he resolved to keep waking that night to try what he could hear. That being the third night, and the damosel being between hope and despair, she brak her plum, and it held far the richest jewellery of the three. She bargained as before; and the auld wife, as before, took in the sleeping-drink to the young knight's chamber; but he telled her he couldna drink it that night without sweetening. And when she gaed awa' for some honey to sweeten it wi', he poured out the drink, and sae made the auld wife think he had drunk it. They a' went to bed again, and the damosel began, as before, singing:

> "Seven lang years I served for thee,
> The glassy hill I clamb for thee,
> The bluidy shirt I wrang for thee;
> And wilt thou no wauken and turn to me?"

He heard, and turned to her. And she telled him a'

230

that had befa'en her, and he telled her a' that had happened to him. And he caused the auld washerwife and her dochter to be burnt. And they were married, and he and she are living happy till this day, for aught I ken.

CRRKK—CRRKK

A muttering and a muttering from the marshes;
    A creaking and a croaking from the fen:
Crrkk—Crrkk—Crrkk—Crrkk—
    Again and again and again.

A myriad eyes in the pitch darkness;
    A myriad mouths agog:
And *Crrkk—Crrkk—Crrkk* in the slimy ooze,
    From frog to frog to frog.

CHERRY, OR THE FROG-BRIDE

There was once a king who had three sons. A little beyond the outskirts of his realm there lived an old woman who had an only daughter, called Cherry. Cherry was her name and cherry was her nature. Of all fruits, she liked these clear sweet dangling red-cheeked berries far the best; and pined for them in season and out. And what wonder? Her lips were as sweet and she as lovely as they. Now the day came when this king sent his three sons away to see the world, to learn the ways and customs of foreign lands, and so to gain wisdom and skill in ruling the kingdom that they would in time to come have for their own.

Meanwhile this old woman was living in peace and quiet at home with her daughter, Cherry. There was but one thing wanting. She had no garden, and little money either. So in season or out of season, she often found it hard to get cherries for her daughter, whom she loved dearly. At last she could think of nothing else but to go, day by day, to a neighbouring nunnery-garden and beg the finest cherries she could get from the nuns; for she dared not let her daughter go out by herself, fearing that some mischance might befall her.

Now it so happened that the abbess of this nunnery was fully as fond of cherries as Cherry was herself, though she little resembled one; and she soon discovered where all the ripe fruit was going to. This holy mother became angrier and angrier not only at there often not being a dish of cherries for her to eat, but on discovering who had them instead.

Now the three princes, who had set out on their travels, came one day to the quiet narrow street where Cherry lived with her mother; and as they passed along it, they looked up, and saw at the window the beautiful maiden who stood there, combing the long fair strands of her flaxen hair. In that same moment all three of them fell in love with her, and each began to sing her praises and to vow he would take her for his wife. Scarcely had the wish been uttered, when they began to quarrel. Their rage and jealousy waxed hotter and hotter. From quarrelling they set to fighting, a fight which would soon have made blood begin to flow, if at last the abbess, hearing the uproar, had not come to the gate of the nunnery and looked out at them through its grill. On hearing that her neighbour was the cause of the dispute, her spite against her broke out afresh, and in her fury she cried to herself: "O that this vile Cherry should be changed into a hideous frog, squatting in the water under the bridge at the world's end!"

No sooner were the words uttered than her wish was fulfilled. One moment Cherry had been sitting in her loveliness at the window, the next she was gone.

The three princes having now nothing left to fight for, and only a memory whereon to grieve, sheathed their swords, made friends, and, desiring nothing else in the world but Cherry, turned home.

Their father, the old king, was now growing old and feeble; and was weary of his throne. He desired to be at peace, and to put off the burden and cares off his kingdom. But which of his three sons should he choose to succeed him? This was a riddle which his heart found hard to answer. He loved them all alike. He called them before him.

"My sons," said he, "I am old and weary, and desire to give up my kingdom. But one matter sorely perplexes me. Seeing that I love you all so dearly, I cannot decide which of you should follow me and reign in my stead. Besides, I wish with all my heart that my people shall have the best and wisest and subtlest of you to reign over them. For this cause alone, I have decided to make trial of your wits, skill and courage, and to set you three tests. Whichever one of you surmounts them all and wins the prize shall have my kingdom. The first test is to go out into the world and bring me back a hundred ells of fine linen. But it must be a linen so fine that I shall be able to draw it without creasing through this, my golden ring."

The three princes vowed that they would do their utmost, and set out forthwith.

The two eldest brothers took with them many servants and followers, horsemen and coaches and wagons wherein to bring back with them the finest and most beautiful linens they could find. But the youngest of them took nothing but himself. All three soon came to where the high road branched off into three byways. Two ran through green and pleasant meadows, set about with woods and shady groves. The third, dismal and drear, straggled out of sight over a waste of barren and boggy moorland.

The elder princes chose the wide and pleasant way. The youngest took his leave of them and whistling to himself to keep up his courage set out over the moor.

Wherever, shop or mill or market-place, fine linen was to be had for money, the two elder brothers bought it. They bought so much that their coaches and waggons groaned beneath the burden.

The youngest prince trudged on alone many and many a weary day, and found no place where he could buy so much as a single length of cloth fine and beautiful enough to please him. His spirits sank. Every mile he went left him only the more weary and sorrowful. At length he came to an old old bridge, green and grey with moss and lichen, that spanned a deep dark sluggish stream. There he sat himself down to rest his bones and to bemoan his bad luck. He had however sat there but a little while when a squat and ugly frog softly popped up its flat green head out of the water, and asked him what his trouble was.

"Alas!" he answered. "How, gentle creature, could it be in the power of a frog to help me?"

"That we shall see," replied the frog. "Share thy secret with me; tell me what ails thee."

It was cool and peaceful by the stream, and though he knew not why, it eased the prince's sorrow to tell the frog his story.

"Grieve no more," croaked the frog at the end of it. "Trust in me. I will help you."

This said, it sank beneath the softly bubbling water of the stream and vanished. But not for long. When it appeared again, it had brought up out of the depths of the water a ragged scrap of linen no wider than the palm of a man's hand, and soiled with mire and mud. This the frog bade the prince carry away with him, and keep with the utmost care. The prince had little liking for this scrap of wet and filthy rag. Nevertheless, he remembered his kindness and courtesy, and there was something in the speech and aspect of the frog that turned his heart to put his trust in it.

"Well," he thought to himself, "it can do no harm, even if it does no good. A little is better than nothing."

So he took the scrap of cloth, put it safely in his pocket, and thanked the frog. Whereupon, puffing out its sides as if weary, the frog sank once more beneath the water and vanished from his sight. And the prince turned home again.

The further he went on his journey, the heavier, he found to his surprise and delight, his pocket grew, and he rejoiced. He reached home about the same time as his brothers, who, with their servants and horsemen, their coaches and wagons heavily laden, were come into the courtyard of their father's palace.

CHERRY, OR THE FROG-BRIDE

The old king was full of gladness to see his three sons again. He embraced them each in turn, eldest to youngest, and when they had refreshed themselves after the journey, he bade them bring before him what they had found on their travels. And he began with the two elder brothers. Bale after bale of linen of every colour and texture was carried into the palace and shown to the king. But none was anything near fine enough to pass without creasing through his ring; nor would even a strip of any, even if its whole width of linen had been divided into ten.

The two princes stood abashed, their only consolation being that their younger brother, whom they despised, seemed to have come back empty-handed.

"And now, my son," said the old king, turning to him; "how did *you* fare on your travels?"

The courtiers that stood watching smiled in derision. But they smiled too soon. The youngest prince said not a word, but thrusting his hand into his pocket drew out of it, ell after ell up to a hundred, a strip of linen of full width which for fineness, softness and whiteness had never been excelled or matched in the world before. It passed with ease and without the least creasing, every ell of it, through the king's ring and would so have done had it been folded in two. The old king kissed his youngest son, and having perceived the contempt and envy on the faces of the two elder princes, he commanded his servants to take out their bales of linen and to fling them into the sea.

"And now, my sons," he said, "pay heed to my second test. And be all of you of good heart. To fail once is not to fail always; fortune smiles on whom she loves, and perchance not without reason. What I now have in mind is a little lapdog: a lapdog so minute and of a shape so delicate that it can crouch in comfort in a nutshell. This shall be my second test."

The two elder princes heard him in dismay, having a poor stomach for anything so foolish. But they both of them coveted and envied him the crown, and each had decided what to do with the other when their father was dead and gone. So all three brothers set out once more on their travels, and as before parted at the cross-roads, the two elder princes scoffing at the youngest for choosing again the dismal track over the moor—bright-green with bog, and stretching on as if to the world's edge. Nor had they even the wits to send a servant to follow him.

What was in his heart was to ask counsel of the frog that had already befriended him. And while he was as eager as ever to achieve what his father had set him to do, he pined also for the peace and solitude of the stream in the shade of the bridge. Sure enough, as soon as he had come to it, his friend the frog came leaping out of the water, settled itself beside him where he sat on the bank, and as before, opening its wide slit of a mouth, croaked, "Greeting, Prince; what brings thee here again?"

This time the prince doubted nothing. Happy and at ease, he told the frog why he had come and what he was seeking.

"Wait, then, in patience," said the frog, "and I will be back anon."

Leaping into the dark deep waters of the stream, it

vanished as before, and in a while returned, carrying in its mouth a hazel-nut, which it laid at his feet, bidding him return to his father, crack the shell gently, and see what would follow. The prince went on his way very well pleased, and the frog, wearied out, scrambled back into the water.

Again his brothers had reached home before him, and the walls of the palace re-echoed with the barking and yapping of a host of little dogs of every kind and breed. The old king, anxious to help them all he could, sent for the largest walnut shell that could be found. And although many of the dogs were all but small enough to couch within it, not one could quite succeed. Of this one everything went in but the hind legs; of another, all but its head; of a third, all but one forefoot; of a fourth, everything except its tail. One way or another, not a single little lapdog among them could lie at ease in so small a kennel.

When all had been tried and had failed, the youngest, bowing low before the king, presented him with the hazel-nut he had brought back from the river, beseeching him to crack its shell with the utmost care. And lo, out leapt a little lapdog so minute that it could couch with ease upon the king's little-finger-nail. It wagged its tail, it fondled its new master, then lifted its head and barked furiously at the other small beasts it saw around it. This it did with all the grace and naturalness in the world, and to the delight of the whole Court. The old king, laughing and rejoicing, embraced his youngest son; then turned and ordered his servants to fling all the other dogs into the sea.

Then said he to his three sons: "Two of the difficult tests I set you are now finished with. This is the third and the last: whichever one of you brings back the loveliest lady he can persuade to come with him shall inherit my crown and ascend my throne."

Yet again, away went the three princes on their journey; and, as before, parted at the cross-roads. This time, however, the youngest despaired of what might come. My friend the frog, he thought sadly to himself, squat and ugly though it is, has been a friend in need and in deed; but how is it possible that it can seek me out a lady of any grace and beauty, still less a lovelier than ever was seen before at my father's Court, Why, the boggy swamp wherein it lives is inhabited only by newts and voles and toads and snakes and suchlike creatures; nothing human or of good liking. None the less, he continued on his way, heavy-hearted; and with a deep sigh which shook him all over, sat down once more beside the cold old bridge.

"Alas, my friend," said he, at sight of the frog squatting there on the margin of the stream as if in wait for him; "alas, all thy kindness was in vain. This time what I would ask of thee is far beyond thy doing."

The frog gawped back at him, and for a few moments said never a word, the water the while babbling on beneath the bridge. At last it spoke.

"Thou lookest grieved and weary, prince; but have no fear. Tell me what thy need may be."

So the prince told his faithful friend the trouble that had now overtaken him. Yet again the frog gazed at the prince without speech.

"Go thy way home," it croaked at last; "and what thou hast in mind will follow hard after thee. But have a care: be sure not to laugh nor even to smile at whatever may befall."

That said, it leapt into the deep murky water again, and was at once out of sight.

Still heavily sighing, since this time he had little trust in the frog's promise, the prince set out on his return journey. He had gone but a little way when he heard a strange noise behind him. Glancing over his shoulder along the path by which he had come, he saw six plump water-rats dragging along an immense pumpkin as if it were a coach, full trot and with all speed. On high on the box of the coach sat a huge toad, reins and whip in his paws; and behind the coach stood two small green frogs for footmen; and two brisk field-mice with prinked-up whiskers scampered beside it at either door. Inside the coach, who should be sitting but his old friend, the frog, as misshapen as ever and of no beauty in his eyes, yet with something of a graceful air and bearing as, leaning towards the window of the coach, it bowed to the prince in passing.

Still wrapped sadly in his thoughts, and in despair of his chance of finding any fair lady whom he could persuade to go back with him to his father the king, the prince paid little heed to the coach, and had less mind to laugh or even so much as to smile at it. In a trice, it had turned the corner of the woodland and was out of sight.

He stood still in wonder and astonishment, then, when, on turning the corner himself, he found standing in the way a coach of ivory and ebony, gold and silver, and harnessed to it, six jet-black horses. The coachman on its box was in a splendid scarlet livery, postilions no less gay bestrode the two foremost horses; and inside the coach, at the window, sat the most beautiful lady he had ever seen —she indeed to whom at very first glimpse of her he had long ago given his heart—the lovely Cherry. His heart all but leapt into his mouth for joy at seeing her again.

When he came up to the coach, one of the footmen opened the door. He climbed in and seated himself beside his loved one.

When the coach rattled in over the drawbridge into the courtyard of his father's palace, a multitude of fair ladies were already assembled there; but as soon as Cherry was to be seen descending from the coach, a *huzza* went up to rend the heavens. With one voice, the onlookers bestowed on her the crown of beauty—and this even before the king himself had set eyes on her. But he too was of the same mind. In pride and delight he embraced and kissed his son, set his crown upon his head, and there and then appointed him heir to his throne. This done, alas, alackaday, he commanded that all the other beautiful ladies should be drowned in the deep blue sea. And the wicked old abbess went in after them.

There was a fine great wedding, and the old woman, Cherry's mother, in a gown of spangled satin, was chief guest. The new king and his bride lived long and happily together; and never had such cherry orchards been seen in the world before—with their snow-white flowers in springtime, and in summer red and dangling with their fruits.

BUCKEE, BUCKEE

Buckee, Buckee, biddy Bene,
Is the way now fair and clean?
Is the goose ygone to nest,
And the fox ygone to rest?
Shall I come away?

MR. FOX

Lady Mary was young, and Lady Mary was fair.
She had two brothers, and more lovers than she
could count. But of them all, the bravest and
most gallant, was a Mr. Fox, whom she met when she
was down at her father's country-house. No one knew
who Mr. Fox was; but he was certainly brave, and surely
rich, and of all her lovers, Lady Mary cared for him
alone. At last it was agreed upon between them that they
should be married. Lady Mary asked Mr. Fox where
they should live, and he described to her his castle, and
where it was; but, strange to say, did not ask her, or her
brothers, to come and see it.

So one day, near the wedding-day, when her brothers
were out, and Mr. Fox was away for a day or two on
business, as he said, Lady Mary set out for Mr. Fox's
castle. And after many searchings, she came at last to it,
and a fine strong house it was, with high walls and a deep
moat. And when she came up to the gateway she saw
written on it:

Be bold, be bold.

And as the gate was open, she went through it, and found
no one there. So she went up to the doorway, and over
it she found written:

MR. FOX

Be bold, be bold, but not too bold.

Still she went on, till she came into the hall, and went up the broad stairs till she came to a door in the gallery, over which was written:

> *Be bold, be bold, but not too bold,*
> *Lest that your heart's blood should run cold.*

But Lady Mary was a brave one, she was, and she opened the door, and what do you think she saw? Why, bodies and skeletons of beautiful young ladies all stained with blood. So Lady Mary thought it was high time to get out of that horrid place, and she closed the door, went through the gallery, and was just going down the stairs, and out of the hall, when who should she see through the window, but Mr. Fox dragging a beautiful young lady along from the gateway to the door. Lady Mary rushed downstairs, and hid herself behind a cask, just in time, as Mr. Fox came in with the poor young lady who seemed to have fainted. Just as he got near Lady Mary, Mr. Fox saw a diamond ring glittering on the finger of the young lady he was dragging, and he tried to pull it off. But it was tightly fixed, and would not come off, so Mr. Fox cursed and swore, and drew his sword, raised it, and brought it down upon the hand of the poor lady. The sword cut off the hand, which jumped up into the air, and fell of all places in the world into Lady Mary's lap. Mr. Fox looked about a bit, but did not think of looking behind the cask, so at last he went on dragging the young lady up the stairs into the Bloody Chamber.

As soon as she heard him pass through the gallery,

Lady Mary crept out of the door, down through the gateway, and ran home as fast as she could.

Now it happened that the very next day the marriage contract of Lady Mary and Mr. Fox was to be signed, and there was a splendid breakfast before that. And when Mr. Fox was seated at table opposite Lady Mary, he looked at her. "How pale you are this morning, my dear." "Yes," said she, "I had a bad night's rest last night. I had horrible dreams." "Dreams go by contraries," said Mr. Fox; "but tell us your dream, and your sweet voice will make the time pass till the happy hour comes."

"I dreamed," said Lady Mary, "that I went yestermorn to your castle, and I found it in the woods, with high walls, and a deep moat, and over the gateway was written:

Be bold, be bold.

"But it is not so, nor it was not so," said Mr. Fox.

"And when I came to the doorway over it was written:

Be bold, be bold, but not too bold.

"It is not so, nor it was not so," said Mr. Fox.

"And then I went upstairs, and came to a gallery, at the end of which was a door, on which was written:

Be bold, be bold, but not too bold,
Lest that your heart's blood should run cold.

"It is not so, nor it was not so," said Mr. Fox.

"And then—and then I opened the door, and the room was filled with bodies and skeletons of poor dead women, all stained with their blood."

"It is not so, nor it was not so. And God forbid it should be so," said Mr. Fox.

"I then dreamed that I rushed down the gallery, and just as I was going down the stairs, I saw you, Mr. Fox, coming up to the hall door, dragging after you a poor young lady, rich and beautiful."

"It is not so, nor it was not so. And God forbid it should be so," said Mr. Fox.

"I rushed downstairs, just in time to hide myself behind a cask, when you, Mr. Fox, came in dragging the young lady by the arm. And, as you passed me, Mr. Fox, I thought I saw you try and get off her diamond ring, and when you could not, Mr. Fox, it seemed to me in my dream, that you out with your sword and hacked off the poor lady's hand to get the ring."

"It is not so, nor it was not so. And God forbid it should be so," said Mr. Fox, and was going to say something else as he rose from his seat, when Lady Mary cried out:

"But it is so, and it was so. Here's hand and ring I have to show," and pulled out the lady's hand from her dress, and pointed it straight at Mr. Fox.

At once her brothers and her friends drew their swords and cut Mr. Fox into a thousand pieces.

THE LAILY WORM AND THE
MACHREL OF THE SEA

A very old ballad which "has never been retouched by a pen"—but a few words have here been Anglicized.

"I was but seven year auld
    When my moder she did dee,
My father married the ae[1] warst woman
    The world did ever see.

"For she has made me the laily[2] worm
    That lays att the foot of the tree,
An o my sister Maisry
    The machrel of the sea.

"An every Saterday att noon
    The machrel comes to me,
An she takes my laily head
    An lays it on her knee,
An kames it wi a silver kame
    An washes it in the sea.

"Seven knights ha I slain
    Since I lay att the foot of the tree;
If ye war na my ain father,
    The eight one ye sud be."

"Sing on your song, ye laily worm,
    That ye sung to me;"
"I never sung that song
    But what I wad sing to ye.

[1] One.   [2] Loathly.

THE LAILY WORM AND THE MACHREL

"I was but seven year auld
  When my moder she did dee,
My father married the ae warst woman
  The world did ever see.

"She changed me to the laily worm
  That lays att the foot of the tree,
An my sister Maisry
  [To] the machrel of the sea.

"And every Saterday att noon
  The machrel comes to me,
An she takes my laily head,
  An layes it on her knee,
An kames it weth a siller kame,
  An washes it in the sea.

"Seven knights ha I slain
  Since I lay att the foot of the tree;
If ye war na my ain father,
  The eight ye sud be."

He sent for his lady
  As fast as sen could he:
"Where is my son,
  That ye sent fra me,
And my daughter,
  Lady Maisry?"

"Yer son is att our king's court,
  Sarving for meat an fee,

THE LAILY WORM AND THE MACHREL

And yer daughter is att our queen's court,
  A mary[1] sweet an free."

"Ye lee,[2] ye ill woman,
  Sa loud as I hear ye lee,
For my son is the laily worm
  That lays at the foot of the tree,
An my daughter Maisry
  The machrel of the sea."

She has ta'en a silver wand
  An gine him strokes three,
An he started up the bravest knight
  Your eyes did ever see.

She has ta'en a small horn
  An loud an shrill blew she,
An a' the fish came her tell but the proud machrel,
  An she stood by the sea:
"Ye shaped me ance an unshemly shape,
  An ye's never more shape me."

He has sent to the wood
  For hawthorn an fun.[3]
An he has ta'en that gay lady,
  And ther he did her burne.

[1] A lady-in-waiting. [2] Lie. [3] Whin or furze.

THE BAD MOTHER

[A Gypsy Folk-Tale]

There was an emperor. He had been married ten years, but had no children. And God granted that his empress conceived and bore a son. Now that son was heroic; there was none other found like him. And the father lived half a year longer, and died. Then what is the lad to do? He took and departed in quest of heroic achievements. And he journeyed a long while, and took no heed, and came into a great forest. In that forest there was a certain house, and in that house were twelve dragons. Then the lad went straight thither, and saw that there was no one. He opened the door and went in, and he saw a sabre on a nail and took it, and posted himself behind the door, and waited for

252

the coming of the dragons. They, when they came, did not go in all at once, but went in one by one. The lad waited, sabre in hand; and as each one went in, he cut off his head, flung it on the floor. So the lad killed eleven dragons, and the youngest dragon remained. And the lad went out to him, and took and fought with him, and fought half a day. And the lad vanquished the dragon, and took him and put him in a jar, and fastened it securely.

And the lad went to walk, and came on another house, where there was only a maiden. And when he saw the maiden, how did she please his heart. As for the maiden, the lad pleased her just as well. And the maiden was yet more heroic than the lad. And they formed a strong love. And the lad told the maiden how he had killed eleven dragons, and one he had left alive and put in a jar.

The maiden said, "You did ill not to kill it; but now let it be."

And the lad said to the maiden, "I will go and fetch my mother, for she is alone at home."

Then the maiden said, "Fetch her, but you will rue it. But go and fetch her, and dwell with her."

So the lad departed to fetch his mother. He took his mother, and brought her into the house of the dragons whom he had slain. And he said to his mother, "Go into every room; only into this chamber do not go."

His mother said, "I will not, darling."

And the lad departed into the forest to hunt.

And his mother went into the room where he had told her not to go. And when she opened the door, the dragon saw her and said to her, "Empress, give me a little water, and I will do you much good."

She went and gave him water and he said to her, "Dost love me, then will I take thee, and thou shalt be mine empress."

"I love thee," she said.

Then the dragon said to her, "What will you do, to get rid of your son, that we may be left to ourselves? Make yourself ill,[1] and say you have seen a dream, that he must bring you a porker of the sow in the other world; that, if he does not bring it you, you will die; but that, if he brings it you, you will recover."

Then she went into the house; and tied up her head, and made herself ill. And when the lad came home and saw her head tied up, he asked her, "What's the matter, mother?"

She said, "I am ill, darling. I shall die. But I have seen a dream, to eat a porker of the sow in the other world."

Then the lad began to weep, for his mother will die. And he took[2] and departed. Then he went to his sweetheart, and told her. "Maiden, my mother will die. And she has seen a dream, that I must bring her a porker from the other world."

The maiden said, "Go, and be prudent; and come to me as you return. Take my horse with the twelve wings, and mind the sow does not seize you, else she'll eat both you and the horse."

So the lad took the horse and departed. He came there, and when the sun was midway in his course he went to the little pigs, and took one, and fled. Then the sow heard him, and hurried after him to devour him. And

[1] Pretend to be ill.　　　[2] Took himself off.

at the very brink (of the other world), just as he was leaping out, the sow bit off half of the horse's tail. So the lad went to the maiden. And the maiden came out, and took the little pig, and hid it, and put another in its stead. Then he went home to his mother, and gave her *that* little pig, and she dressed it and ate, and said that she was well.

Three or four days later she made herself ill again, as the dragon had shown her.

When the lad came, he asked her, "What's the matter now, mother?"

"I am ill again, darling, and I have seen a dream that you must bring me an apple from the golden apple-tree in the other world."

So the lad took and departed to the maiden; and when the maiden saw him so troubled, she asked him, "What's the matter, lad?"

"What's the matter! my mother is ill again. And she has seen a dream that I am to bring her an apple from the apple-tree in the other world."

Then the maiden knew that his mother was plotting to bring him to his death, and she said to the lad, "Take my horse and go, but be careful the apple-tree does not seize you there. Come to me, as you return."

And the lad took and departed, and came to the brink of the world. And he let himself in, and went to the apple-tree at mid-day when the apples were resting. And he took an apple and ran away. Then the leaves perceived it and began to scream; and the apple-tree took itself after him to lay its leafy hand on him and kill him. And the lad came out from the brink, and arrived in our world, and went to the maiden. Then the maiden took the apple, stole it from him, and hid it, and put another in its stead. And the lad stayed a little longer with her, and departed to his mother. Then his mother, when she saw him, asked him, "Have you brought it, darling?"

"I've brought it, mother."

So she took the apple and ate, and said there was nothing more the matter with her.

In a week's time the dragon told her to make herself ill again, and to ask for water from the great mountains. So she made herself ill.

When the lad saw her ill, he began to weep and said, "My mother will die, God. She's always ill." Then he went to her and asked her, "What's the matter, mother?"

"I am like to die, darling. But I shall recover if you will bring me water from the great mountains."

Then the lad tarried no longer. He went to the maiden and said to her, "My mother is ill again; and she has seen a dream that I must fetch her water from the great mountains."

The maiden said, "Go, lad; but I fear the clouds will catch you, and the mountains there, and will kill you. But do you take my horse with twenty-and-four wings; and when you get there, wait afar off till mid-day, for at mid-day the mountains and the clouds set themselves at table and eat. Then do you go with the pitcher, and draw water quickly, and fly."

Then the lad took the pitcher, and departed thither to the mountains, and waited till the sun had reached the middle of his course. And he went and drew water and fled. And the clouds and the mountains perceived him, and took themselves after him, but they could not catch

256

him. And the lad came to the maiden. Then the maiden went and took the pitcher with the water, and put another in its stead without his knowing it. And the lad arose and went home, and gave water to his mother, and she recovered.

Then the lad departed into the forest to hunt. His mother went to the dragon and told him, "He has brought me the water. What am I to do now with him?"

"What are you to do! why, take and play cards with him. You must say, 'For a wager, as I used to play with your father. And the wager shall be a wish.'"

So the lad came home and found his mother merry: it pleased him well. And she said to him at table, as they were eating, "Darling, when your father was alive, what did we do? When we had eaten and risen up, we took and played cards for a wager. And the wager was a wish."

Then the lad: "If you like, play with me, mother."

So they took and played cards; and his mother beat him and won her wish. And she took silken cords, and bound his two hands so tight that the cord cut into his hands.

And the lad began to weep, and said to his mother, "Mother, release me or I die."

She said, "That is my wish and just what I was wanting to do to you." And she called the dragon, "Come forth, dragon, come and kill him."

Then the dragon came forth, and took him, and cut him in pieces, and put him in the saddle-bags, and placed him on his horse, and let him go, and said to the horse,

"Carry him, horse, dead, whence thou didst carry him alive."

Then the horse hurried to the lad's sweetheart, and went straight to her there. Then, when the maiden saw him, she began to weep, and she took him and put piece to piece; where one was missing, she cut the porker of the sow in the other world, and supplied flesh from the porker. So she put all the pieces of him in their place. And she took the water from the great mountains and poured it on him, and he became whole. And she squeezed the apple in his mouth from the apple-tree in the other world, and brought him to life.

So when the lad arose, he went home to his mother, and drove a stake into the earth, and placed both her and the dragon on one great pile of straw. And he set it a-light, and they were consumed. And he departed thence, and took the maiden, and made a marriage, and kept up the marriage three months day and night. And I came away and told the story.

WHO ? WHO ?

"Who—Who—the bride will be?"
"The owl she the bride shall be."
    The owl quoth,
    Again to them both,
"I am sure a grim ladye;
    Not I the bride can be,
    I not the bride can be!"

TROPSYN

[*A Gypsy Folk-Tale*]

There was a poor man, and he had four sons. And they went out to service, and went to a gentleman to thrash wheat. And they received so much wheat for a wage, and brought it to their father. "Here, father, eat; we will go out to service again."

And they went again to a gentleman, who was to give them each a horse at the year's end. And the youngest son was called Tropsyn; and the gentleman made him his groom. And a mare brought forth a colt; and that colt said, "Tropsyn, take me. Your year is up now."

The gentleman said, "Choose your horses."

So the three elder brothers chose good horses; but Tropsyn said, "Give me this colt, master."

"What will you do with it? it's so little."

"So it may be."

Tropsyn took it and departed; and the colt said, "Let me go, Tropsyn, to my dam to suck."

And he let it go, and it went to its dam, and came back a horse to terrify the world.

"Now mount me."

He mounted, and the horse flew. He caught up his brothers, and his brothers asked him, "Where did you get that horse from?"

"I killed a gentleman, and took his horse."

"Let's push on, and escape."

Night fell upon them as they were passing a meadow, and in that meadow they saw the light of a fire. They made for the light. It was an old woman's, and she was a witch, and had four daughters. And they went there, and went into the house; and Tropsyn said, "Good-night.[1]"

"Thank you."

"Can you give us a night's lodging?"

"I'm not sure; my mother is not at home. When she comes you had better ask her."

The mother came home. "What are you wanting, young fellows?"

"We've come to demand your daughters in marriage."

"Good."

She made them a bed on the ground with its head to the threshold, and her daughters' beds with head to the wall. And the old woman sharpened her sword to cut off their heads. And Tropsyn took his brothers' caps, and put them on the girls' heads. And the old woman arose, and kept feeling the caps, and kept cutting off the heads, and killed her daughters.

[1] Good-evening.

Tropsyn arose, and led his brothers outside. "Come, be off." And he arose, Tropsyn; and the old woman had a golden bird in a cage; and Tropsyn said to the horse, "I will take a feather of the bird."

And the horse said, "Don't."

"Bah! I will." And he took a feather, and put it in his pocket.

And they mounted their horses and rode away, and went to a city. There was a great lord, a count; and he asked them, "Where are you going?"

"We are going to service."

"Take service with me, then."

And that lord was still unmarried. And they went to him, and he gave them each a place. One he set over the horses, and one he set over the oxen, and one he set over the swine; and Tropsyn he made coachman. Of a night Tropsyn stuck the feather in the wall, and it shone like a candle. And his brothers were angry, and went to their master. "Master, Tropsyn has a feather, such that one needs no candle—of gold."

The master called: "Tropsyn, come here, bring me the feather."

Tropsyn brought it, and gave it to his master. The master liked him better than ever, and the brothers went to the master, and said to him, "Master, Tropsyn has said that he'll bring the bird alive."

The master called Tropsyn. "Tropsyn, bring me the bird. If you don't, I shall cut off your head."

He went to his horse. "What am I to do, horse, for the master has told me to bring the bird?"

"Fear not, Tropsyn; jump on my back."

So he mounted the horse, and rode to the old woman's. And the horse said to him, "Turn a somersault,
and you'll become a flea, and creep into her breast and
bite her. And she'll fling off her smock, and do you go
and take the bird."

And he took the bird, and departed to his master; the
master made him a lackey.

And there was in the Danube a lady, a virgin; and of
a Sunday she would come up and go out on the water in
a boat. And his brothers came to their master and said,
"Master, Tropsyn boasts that he'll bring the lady from
the bottom of the Danube."

"Tropsyn, come here. What is this you've been boasting, that you'll bring me the lady?"

"I didn't."

"You've got to, else I shall cut off your head."

He went to his horse. "What am I to do, horse, for
how shall I bring her?"

And the horse said, "Fear not, let him give you twelve
hides and a jar of pitch, and put them on me, and let him
make you a small ship, not big, and let him put various
drinks in the ship. And do you hide yourself behind the
door. And she will come, and drink brandy, and get
drunk, and sleep. And do you seize her, and jump on my
back with her, and I will run off home."

The horse ran home to the master, and Tropsyn gave
her to his master in the castle. The count shut the doors,
and set a watch at the window to prevent her escape, for
she was wild. The count wanted to marry her; she will
not.

"Let them bring my herd of horses, then I will marry

you. He who brought me, let him bring also my horses."

The count said, "Tropsyn, bring the horses."

Tropsyn went to his horse. "What am I to do, horse? How shall I bring the horses from the Danube?"

"Come with me, fear not."

When he came to the Danube, the horse leapt into the Danube, and caught the mother of the horses by the mane, and led her out. And Tropsyn caught her, and mounted her, and galloped off. And the whole herd came forth, and ran after their dam home to the count's palace. The lady cried "Halt!" to the horses.

The count wants to marry her. She says, "Let him milk my mares, and when you have bathed in their milk, then I will marry you."

The count cried, "Tropsyn, milk the mares."

And Tropsyn went to his horse. "What shall I do, horse? How shall I milk the mares?"

"Fear not, for I will catch her by the mane, and do you milk, and fear not."

And he milked a whole caldron full.

And the lady said, "Make a fire, and boil the milk."

And they made a fire, and the milk boils.

"Now," said the lady, "let him who milked the mares bathe in the milk."

And the count said, "Tropsyn, go and bathe in the milk."

He went to the horse. "What shall I do, horse? for if I bathe, then I shall die."

The horse said, "Fear not, lead me to the caldron; I will snort through my nostrils, and breathe out frost."

He led the horse; the horse snorted through his nostrils; then the milk became lukewarm. Then Tropsyn leapt into the caldron, and fair as he was before, he came out fairer still. When he came out, the horse snorted through his nostrils, and breathed fire into the caldron, and the milk boiled again.

And the lady said to the count, "Go thou too and bathe in the milk, then will I live with thee."

The count went to the caldron and said, "Tropsyn, bring me my horse."

Tropsyn brought him his horse; the horse trembled from afar. The count mounted him and leapt into the boiling caldron; only bones were to be seen at the bottom of the caldron.

Then cried the lady, "Come hither, Tropsyn; thou art my lord, and I am thy lady."

A SUNNY SHAFT

A sunny shaft did I behold,
    From sky to earth it slanted:
And poised therein a bird so bold—
    Sweet bird, thou wert enchanted!

He sunk, he rose, he twinkled, he trolled
    Within that shaft of sunny mist;
His eyes of fire, his beak of gold,
    All else of amethyst! . . .

SAMUEL TAYLOR COLERIDGE

THE JUNIPER TREE

Along while ago, at least two thousand years, there lived a rich man who had a good and beautiful wife. They loved one another very dearly; but they had no children; and she prayed and longed for a child with a great longing.

Now in the courtyard that lay beneath the windows of the house in which they lived there stood a juniper tree which, however long the night or sharp the frost, was never without its dark-green, needle-pointed leaves. And one sunlit winter's day as she was standing beneath it, paring an apple, she cut her finger, and the drops of blood trickled down from her finger on to the snow.

"Ah!" said she, with a sigh as she gazed at it, "how happy should I be if only I had a child, as white as that snow, as red as that blood!"

As she uttered these words, her heart lightened, a wild joy sprang up in her, and she knew that her wish would come true. The happy days went by. When winter was

gone and its snows had melted away, the meadows began
to grow green again. April came; the woods and fields
were sweet with the flowers of spring; the trees put
forth their green leaves; the wild cherries shed their
petals upon the ground; and the birds poured out their
songs, daybreak to evening, in the woods and groves.
Then followed summer. The small spicy flowers of the
juniper began to unfold, her heart leapt within her at
their fragrance, and she fell on her knees, beside herself
for joy. When autumn drew near, ripening fruit hung
thick upon the trees; and one still and lovely evening
she ate greedily of the juniper berries. But after that she
began to be sick and sad and sorrowful. And when the
eighth month was passed, she called her husband to her,
wept, and said, "If I should die, then I pray thee bury
me under this juniper tree."

Not long after this, her child was born—the child of
her desire, and lovely; as red as blood, as white as snow;
but she herself was weak and wearied out. As soon as she
had looked upon it, an exceeding great joy overcame
her, and she fainted away and died.

Her husband buried her under the juniper tree, and
wept and mourned over her. But in time his grief began
to abate, and he to forget. And at length he dried his
tears, and took to himself another wife.

Time passed on, and a daughter was born to her; but
the child of his first wife was a boy. The mother loved
and doted on her daughter, but she hated her stepson.
She knew that he would inherit her husband's possessions, and the very sight and thought of him cut her to
the heart. And she began to think how she might get

everything for her daughter only. So she treated him very harshly, half starved him, never let him rest, and would beat and punish him for no fault and without reason, so that he went continually in fear of her and could find no place in the house to play in, or be at peace. And as time went by her cruelty increased, and she hated him more and more.

Now it happened one day, when the mother was in her store-room, that her little girl ran up to her, and said, "Mother, may I have an apple?"

"Why, yes, my pretty dear," she said; and gave her a ripe rosy apple out of her apple-chest. Now this chest had a heavy and cumbersome lid, and was fitted with a broad sharp lock of iron.

"Mother," said the little girl, "may I have an apple for my little brother too?"

A pang of envy and jealousy went through the woman's breast, but she showed no sign of it. "Yes, indeed, my child," she said. "When he comes in from school, he too shall have an apple."

As she was speaking, she happened to look out of the window and saw the little boy in the distance coming home from school. At sight of him the Evil One entered into her heart. She took back the apple she had given her daughter, threw it into the apple-chest and shut down the lid, telling her that she should have an even sweeter one before she went to bed.

When the little boy came in at the door, she was lying in wait for him, and alone; and she said to him in a small wheedling voice, her face cold and grey with wickedness, "Come in, my dear, and I will give you an apple."

269

The little boy gazed at her. "Thank you, Mother," he said. "I should like to have an apple. But how strange and dreadful you look!"

It seemed to her that she was compelled to listen to a voice within her. "Look!" she said. "Come with me." And she took him in secret into her store-room, lifted the heavy lid of the chest, and said, "There, you shall choose one for yourself."

So he came near, and as he stooped himself over the edge of the apple-chest to do as she had bidden him, of a sudden and with all her force she let fall the lid with its iron lock upon his neck, and his head fell off among the apples.

When she lifted the lid and saw what she had done, she was stricken with terror, not knowing—when her husband came home—how she should explain this dreadful thing and free herself from it. She sat down to think. And presently she stole upstairs into an upper room, took a white linen handkerchief out of a drawer, and having returned to the chest, set the little boy's head upon his narrow shoulders again, tied the handkerchief round his neck, and carrying him out, seated him on a stool in the yard and put an apple in his hand.

Not long after this her little daughter came running into the kitchen to her mother, who was standing bent double by the fire, stirring the soup in a great caldron that had been prepared for her husband's supper.

"Mother," said she, "little brother is sitting in the garden with an apple in his hand. I asked him to give me a taste, but he didn't answer me. And his face looked so pale and still that I was frightened."

"Nonsense, child!" said her mother. "Go back to him. Speak to him again, and if he refuses to answer you, give him a sound box on the ear. That will call him to his senses."

The child went back, and said, "Brother, please, please give me a taste of your apple." But the mouth answered never a word; so she hit him lightly on the cheek; and immediately his head fell off. At sight of it she was terrified and ran screaming back to her mother, and hid her eyes in her lap. She wept and wept and would not be comforted.

"My dear, my own pretty dear!" cried her mother; "what have you done! Alas, what dreadful thing is this! But hold your tongue. Let nobody hear of it. Leave all to me." And she took the body of the little boy, cut it into pieces, and put them into the caldron.

When her husband came home and sat down to supper, he asked her, "Where is my son?"

She made no answer, as if she had not heard; and served up a great bowl of black soup upon the table. And the girl sat silently weeping.

"I asked," said the man again, "where is my son?"

"Your son?" said the woman. "A friend of his mother's came and has taken him away to stay with his great-uncle."

"Taken him away!" said her husband. "But he did not even stay to bid goodbye to me."

"He begged me to let him go," said the woman. "He cried to go. Again and again I said, 'No; your father will miss you.' He would not listen. He is a stubborn child. But, why trouble? He will be well taken care of."

"Ay," said her husband; "but I am grieved to think of it. He should not have gone away without wishing me goodbye." He turned away from her. "Weep no more, child," he said to his daughter. "Your brother will come back again."

With that he began to eat. But he stayed sad and sorrowful, and as he ate, his misery increased with his hunger and it seemed he could never be satisfied. His supper done, he went out alone, his mind tormented with dread and horror. And his wife took the great caldron and in the dusk of the evening emptied out what was in it on the stones of the yard—soup, bones and all.

But her little daughter had been watching all that she did; and on seeing this, went softly upstairs and fetched a brightly coloured silk handkerchief, which her father had given her, from out of a drawer. With this she crept downstairs again and out into the garden. There she wrapped up the bones in her handkerchief, as if in a shroud, and, weeping bitterly, carried them out into the yard and laid them under the juniper tree.

And in the quiet of the evening the juniper tree began to bestir itself, and its branches to sway gently to and fro, to open out their bushy-green leaves, and as gently bring them together again, like a child softly clapping its hands for gladness. At the same time a little cloud, as it were, seemed to arise from out of the midst of the tree, and within the cloud there burned a radiance as of a fire. And there fluttered up from out of the fire a bird marvellous in beauty, which mounted into the air and, singing wildly and sweetly, flew away. When the bird had vanished into the evening, the branches of the juniper tree became still and dark again; and the bones that had lain at the foot of the tree were there no longer. At this the little girl was comforted, and her heart leapt for joy. It was as if she knew that her brother who had been dead was now alive again. She went merrily into the house, sat down to her supper, and ate.

The night went by; and early the next morning the bird that had soared up from out of the tree came flying over the village and alighted on the roof of the house of a goldsmith. And there it began to warble and sing.

> "My mother slew her little son;
> My father thought me lost and gone:
> Out in the dusk on the darkening stones
> She flung in hatred my poor bones.
> My gentle sister pitied me,
> And laid me under the juniper tree;
> Now, now I wander merrily,
> Over hill and dale I fly.
>   *Soo-eet, soo-eet—*
>   *Ki-weet, ki-weet:*
> Oh, what a happy bird am I!"

Now the goldsmith in his apron was sitting in his workshop fitting together the last links of a slender gold chain. When he heard the strange bird singing on the housetop he rose from his stool so suddenly that one of his slippers fell off. Without staying to put it on again, his chain in one hand, his pincers in the other, he ran out into the street and gazed up at the bird, its bright feathers burnished with the shining of the sun. And he said to the bird, "A marvellous sweet song that was, my pretty bird. Pray sing it to me again and I shall hear every single note of it."

"Nay," answered the bird. "I may not sing twice for nothing. But give me that chain of gold, and I will sing again gladly."

It swooped down from the roof, and perching on the goldsmith's shoulder sang its song again, took the slender chain of gold in its claw, and flew away, until it came to the house of a cobbler who was sitting within mending a shoe.

At sound of its first few notes, the cobbler was spell-bound; he called his wife and his children, boys and girls, to come and listen; and there they all stood in the sunny street, their eyes fixed on this strange bird, that had now fallen silent. "A marvellous sweet song, that was," he said. "Pray, pretty bird, sing it all over again."

"Nay," answered the bird; "I may not sing twice for nothing."

At this the cobbler bade his wife run upstairs to the garret. "On the topmost shelf of the cupboard," he told her, "you will find a pair of small red shoes of the finest leather ever made. Bring them down to me."

At sight of the shoes, the bird came near, took them dangling in its other claw, returned to the gable of the cobbler's house, and repeated its song.

And when the song was over, with the golden chain in its one claw, the red shoes in the other, it flew away, far away, until it came to a mill, where on a green bank beside the mill-dam sat a miller with his men hicking and hacking at a new mill-stone. *Hick-hack, hick-hack* went their mallets and chisels: *Klippity-klop, klippity-klop* went the old mill-wheel. And the bird, having perched on the branch of a linden tree that stood near at hand, began to sing.

"My mother slew her little son . . ."

The miller stopped working to listen:

"My father thought me lost and gone . . ."

One of his men began listening:

"Out in the dusk on the darkening stones
She flung in hatred my poor bones . . ."

And another:

"My gentle sister pitied me,
And laid me under the juniper tree . . ."

And yet another:

"Now, now I wander merrily,
Over hill and dale I fly.
Soo-eet, soo-eet—
Ki-weet, ki-weet:
Oh, what a happy bird am I!"

Now all had stopped working and were listening. And the miller—beside himself with delight at the song and at the bird itself, with its sunlit shimmering feathers, red and emerald, the bright golden ring about its neck, and eyes which glittered like dark clear waterdrops as it gazed down on them—besought it with tears in his own to sing again.

"Nay," answered the bird; "I may not sing twice for nothing. Give me that nether mill-stone and I will most gladly."

To the amazement of the miller, the bird flew down among them, and when he and his men had heaved up the heavy mill-stone upon its edge, it thrust its gentle head through the hole which they had pierced in the middle of the stone, and flew back again into the linden tree. There it repeated its song.

When its last note had died away and the dull *klippity-klop*, *klippity-klop* of the mill-wheel was heard again, it spread its wings, and—the mill-stone about its neck, the chain of gold in one claw, the red shoes in the other—it flew and flew until it came and alighted on the roof of the house in the courtyard of which stood the juniper tree from whence it had sprung. There it stayed silent a while.

And the three of them—the man and his wife and the little girl—were sitting within the house at meat.

"I know not why," said the father; "but I feel lighter in spirit than for many hours past. It may be because the sun is shining; it may be a friend is coming, bringing good news."

At this moment, the bird flew down from the roof of the house and perched above its porch.

"Good news, forsooth!" cried the woman. "Or *evil*. You must be mad, husband. There is thunder in the air; it's growing dark. I am in a fever; my teeth keep chattering; my heart is like lead in my body."

She tore open her bodice with a shuddering sigh.

But the little girl sat listening, the tears from her eyes

dropping slowly down upon her plate, half for joy and half for sadness; for the bird above the porch had begun to sing—although the words of its song came but faintly to the ears of those who were sitting within the house.

At its close, the man rose from his chair. "Never in all the days of my life," he said, "have I heard bird sing a song so strange and so marvellous sweet as that. I must go out and see. It may be, if we do not scare it away, it can be enticed to sing again."

"Go out! No!" said the woman. "I entreat you not to leave me. There is dread and danger in the air. The blood in my veins runs like fire. I am sick, and must die."

But he was gone, and the bird had begun to sing again:

> "My mother slew her little son;
> My father thought me lost and gone . . ."

With these words, the bird so let fall the golden chain dangling from its claw that it encircled his neck. Filled with delight, he hastened back into the house.

"See," he said, "what this magical and marvellous bird has given me, a necklet of the finest gold!"

At this, the little girl also got up from her stool and ran out. And the bird had been singing on:

> "Out in the dusk on the darkening stones
> She flung in hatred my poor bones.
> My gentle sister pitied me,
> And laid me under the juniper tree. . . ."

At this, the bird let fall the bright red-leather shoes at her feet. She ran back, wild with joy.

277

"Look, look, dear father," she cried; "see what the bird has brought for me!"

> "Now, now I wander merrily,
> Over hill and dale I fly.
> *Soo-eet, soo-eet*—
> *Ki-weet, ki-weet:*
> Oh, what a happy bird am I!"

The song had come to an end, and again there was silence both in the house and out. At this, the woman could endure herself no longer. Her face was grey and drawn with misery.

"I cannot breathe," she said. "It is as though the world were coming to an end. O, where to hide myself! I must be gone."

But as she stepped beyond the threshold of the house and out from the porch, the bird let fall the mill-stone upon her, and without sigh or sound, she fell dead in the shadow of the juniper tree.

At noise of her fall, the father and the little girl ran out of the house; and lo, there, under the juniper tree, stood the little boy, come back from his enchantment. He leapt into his father's arms. They wept together for joy, the man and his two children, and returned into the house.

THE GAY GOSHAWK

The lover in this old ballad, who is in "fair Scotland", bids his gay goshawk take a message and a letter to his love. She is "the fairest flower in fair England". The hawk answers him in his own tongue, as do most living creatures in these old tales and ballads. In stanza 7 the hawk perches on a birch tree beyond her shot-window—a window that opens on a hinge at its top. In stanza 13 she sends her message back. She then asks a boon of her father; but he, knowing what is in her heart, refuses it before she can put it into words. She then pleads only that if she should die in southern lands, her body should be borne away to Scotland, there to be buried. She takes a "sleepy", or sleeping, draught, and thus feigns death. Her body, in an embroidered sark or shroud, is laid on a bier of gold and silver, and the long slow journey to Scotland is begun. The lovely last two lines of the last stanza but two tell how, after her sleep, she awakens; the last but one, how hungry she is; and the last of all, how she has out-played not only her father but her seven brothers. As for the gay goshawk, swift of wing, keen in speech, sharp of understanding, and with a voice to charm the angels—Hawk in excelsis he is; and, with Coleridge's "Sweet Bird", Skelton's sparrow and Keats's nightingale, one of the rarest and most heart-enticing birds in English and Scottish verse.

"O well's me o my gay goss-hawk,
        That he can speak and flee;
    He'll carry a letter to my love,
        Bring back another to me."

"O how can I your true-love ken,
        Or how can I her know?
    Whan frae her mouth I never heard couth,[1]
        Nor wi my eyes her saw."

"O well sal ye my true-love ken,
        As soon as you her see;

[1] Whisper.

THE GAY GOSHAWK

For, of a' the flowrs in fair Englan,
    The fairest flowr is she.

"At even at my love's bowr-door
    There grows a bowing birk[1],
An sit ye down and sing thereon,
    As she gangs to the kirk.

"An four-and-twenty ladies fair
    Will wash and go to kirk,
But well shall ye my true-love ken,
    For she wears goud[2] on her skirt.

"An four-and-twenty gay ladies
    Will to the mass repair,
But well sal ye my true-love ken
    For she wears goud on her hair."

O even at that lady's bowr-door
    There grows a bowin birk,
An he set down and sang thereon,
    As she ged to the kirk.

"O eet and drink, my marys a'[3],
    The wine flows you among,
Till I gang to my shot-window,
    An hear yon bonny bird's song.

"Sing on, sing on, my bonny bird,
    The song ye sang the streen,[4]

[1] Birch-tree.   [2] Gold.   [3] Maidens all.   [4] Yester-night.

For I ken by your sweet singin
      You're frae my true-love sen."

O first he sang a merry song,
      An then he sang a grave,
An then he peckd his feathers gray,
      To her the letter gave.

"Ha, there's a letter frae your love,
      He says he sent you three;
He canna wait your love langer,
      Bot for your sake he'll die.

"He bids you write a letter to him;
      He says he's sent you five;
He canna wait your love langer,
      Tho you're the fairest woman alive."

"Ye bid him bake his bridal-bread,
      And brew his bridal-ale,
An I'll meet him in fair Scotlan
      Lang, lang or it be stale."

She's doen her to her father dear,
      Fa'n low down on her knee:
"A boon, a boon, my father dear,
      I pray you, grant it me."

"Ask on, ask on, my daughter,
      An granted it sal be;
Except ae squire in fair Scotlan,
      An him you sall never see."

THE GAY GOSHAWK

"The only boon, my father dear,
    That I do crave of thee,
Is, gin[1] I die in southin lands,
    In Scotland to bury me.

"An the firstin kirk that ye come till,
    Ye gar the bells be rung,
An the nextin kirk that ye come till,
    Ye gar the mess[2] be sung.

"An the thirdin kirk that ye come till,
    You deal gold for my sake,
An the fourthin kirk that ye come till,
    You tarry there till night."

She is doen her to her bigly[3] bowr,
    As fast as she coud fare,
An she has tane a sleepy draught,
    That she had mixed wi care.

She's laid her down upon her bed,
    An soon she's fa'n asleep,
And soon oer every tender limb
    Cauld death began to creep.

When night was flown, an day was come,
    Nae ane that did her see
But thought she was as surely dead
    As ony lady coud be.

[1] If.   [2] Bid that the Mass.   [3] Pleasant.

THE GAY GOSHAWK

Her father an her brothers dear
 Gard[1] make to her a bier;
The tae[2] half was o gude red gold,
 The tither[3] o silver clear.

Her mither an her sisters fair
 Gard work for her a sark[4];
The tae half was o cambrick fine,
 The tither o needle wark.

The firstin kirk that they came till,
 They gard the bells be rung,
An the nextin kirk that they came till,
 They gard the mess be sung.

The thirdin kirk that they came till,
 They dealt gold for her sake,
An the fourthin kirk that they came till,
 Lo, there they met her make[5]!

"Lay down, lay down the bigly[6] bier,
 Lat me the dead look on;"
Wi cherry cheeks and ruby lips
 She lay an smil'd on him.

"O ae sheave o your bread, true-love,
 An ae glass o your wine,
For I hae fasted for your sake
 These fully days is nine.

[1] Did.   [2] One.   [3] Other.
[4] Shift.   [5] Mate, lover.   [6] Richly-wrought

THE GAY GOSHAWK

"Gang hame, gang hame, my seven bold
    brothers,
Gang hame and sound your horn;
An ye may boast in southin lans
Your sister's playd you scorn."

ASHPUTTEL

The wife of a rich man fell sick: and when she felt that her end drew nigh, she called her only daughter to her bedside, and said, "Always be a good girl; I love you dearly and I will look down from heaven and watch over you." Soon afterwards she shut her eyes and died, and was buried not in the churchyard but in a wilderness of wild flowers at the far end of the garden. The little girl went every day to her grave and wept, and was always good and kind to all about her. Winter came; the snow spread its shining white coverlet over the grave; but by the time the sun had melted the snow away, her father had taken another wife.

This new wife had two daughters of her own, whom she brought with her: they were fair in face, but foul at heart, and it was now a sad and sorry time for the motherless little girl. "What is this good-for-nothing doing in the parlour?" they said. "They who would eat bread should first earn it; away with her to the kitchen!" They took away the pretty clothes her mother had made for her, gave her an ugly old frock to wear, laughed at her, and turned her into the kitchen.

There she was forced to do all the hard work; to rise before it was day, to fetch in water from the well, to lay the fire, to cook and to wash the clothes. Besides that, the two sisters plagued her in every way they could think of, teased, beat, and mocked at her. At night, when she was tired out, they gave her no bed to lie on, and she must needs sleep in the hearth among the ashes; and, as she was always dusty and dirty, they called her Ashputtel.

It happened one day that her father was going to the fair. Before he set out he asked his wife's daughters what he should bring them.

"Fine clothes," said the first.

"Pearls and diamonds," said the second.

"And you, child," said he to his own daughter, "what will you have?"

"The first sprig of any tree, dear father, that rubs against your hat on your way home," said she.

At the fair he bought for the two first the fine clothes and pearls and diamonds they had asked for: and on his way home, as he came riding through a green copse, a sprig of hazel brushed against his shoulder and almost pushed off his hat. It reminded him of his promise.

He broke off this hazel-sprig and brought it away with him; and when he came home he gave it to his daughter. She took it, went down to her mother's grave, and planted it there; and cried so much that it was watered with her tears. There it grew and flourished and became at length a tall leafy tree. Three times every day she visited it and wept; and one morning, in the spring, there came a small bird and built its nest in the tree, and talked with her, and watched over her, and brought her whatever she wished for.

286

Now some time afterwards it happened that the king
of this country held a feast which was to last three days,
and, out of those who were invited to come, his son was
to choose a bride for himself. And Ashputtel's two sisters
were bidden to the feast. On the first day they called her
up from the kitchen and said, "Now, comb and dress
our hair, polish our shoes, and tie our sashes for us, for
we are going to dance at the king's feast." Ashputtel did
as she was told, but when all was done and she was alone
she could not help grieving; she was filled with such a
longing to go to the dance too. At last she entreated her
step-mother to let her go.

"You! Ashputtel?" she jeered. "You, who have nothing fit to wear, and cannot even dance—*you* want to go
to the king's ball?"

And when Ashputtel kept on begging, her step-
mother, merely to get rid of her, said at last, "Look,
then; I will throw this basin-full of peas on the ash-heap;
if you have picked every one of them out of it in an
hour's time, you shall go to the feast." So she threw the
basin of peas on to the ashes and left her. Then Ashputtel
ran out into the garden, and cried out:

> "Hither, hither, through the sky,
> Turtle-dove and linnet, fly!
> Blackbird, thrush, and chaffinch gay,
> Hither, hither, haste away!
> All sweet birds, come help me quick,
> Hasten, hasten—*pick, pick, pick!*"

And in a little while, first there came two wood-
pigeons flying in at the kitchen window; next there came

two turtle-doves; and after these all the little birds under heaven came chirping and fluttering in, and flew down among the ashes. First the wood-pigeons stooped their heads and set to work, *pick, pick, pick*; and then the turtle-doves, and then all the other birds of every kind began to *pick, pick, pick*. Presently they had picked out every single pea, and had dropped them into the basin; there was not one pea left in the ashes. Their work done, all the birds flew out at the kitchen window. Then Ashputtel brought the basin up to her step-mother, over-joyed at the thought that now she could go to the feast.

"What, you slut!" cried her step-mother. "You, who have nothing but filthy rags to wear, and cannot even dance; *you* go to the ball! Away with you to your work!" And she drove her down to the kitchen.

Nevertheless, Ashputtel went on begging so hard to go, that, in order to be rid of her, her step-mother seized the basin and flung two whole basin-fulls of peas on the ashes. "See here, then," she cried in a rage, "gather those up again, every one, in half an hour, and you shall go to the ball."

As soon as she was gone, Ashputtel ran out into the long garden, now full of the evening sun, and cried out as before:

> "Hither, hither, through the sky,
> Turtle-dove and linnet, fly!
> Blackbird, thrush, and chaffinch gay
> Hither, hither, haste away!
> All sweet birds, come help me quick,
> Hasten, hasten—*pick, pick, pick!*"

In less than twice as many minutes as before, their work was done, and all the birds flew out at the kitchen window. And Ashputtel took up the two basins full to the brim with peas to her step-mother, rejoicing at the thought that now she should be able to go to the ball. But her step-mother only flew into a passion. "What!" she shouted, "shall I never be rid of you! Off to your cinders again, and dance with the rats!" With that, she flung the basin of peas in her face and drove her out of the room; and she herself went off to the ball.

Now all were gone, and the house was empty. Weeping bitterly, Ashputtel crept out into the garden and sat herself down under the nut-tree over her mother's grave. She fancied she heard a little stirring in its leaves. And, "Oh," she cried in her heart,

"Green and shadowy hazel-tree,
Shed gold and silver over me!"

Instantly, with a song of joy, the bird flew up out of the tree, to return in a while, first with a dress of gold and silver, and presently after with slippers of spangled silk. Ashputtel lost not a moment. She washed herself in the cold well-water, put on the dress of gold and silver and the slippers of spangled silk, and followed her sisters to the feast at the king's palace.

When she came into the ballroom, her step-mother and sisters did not recognise her. They thought this must be some strange princess from a far country, she looked so lovely. Never once did they give a thought to Ashputtel, supposing only she was long ago fast asleep in her kitchen among the ashes.

At first sight of her, the king's son came up to her, took her by the hand, and danced with her. He never left her side, and danced with no-one else the whole long evening through.

When midnight struck, Ashputtel told the prince that she must go home.

"Come, then," he said, "we will go together, and I will take care of you." For his one desire was to see where she lived. But she slipped away from him unawares, and ran off as fast as she could, the prince following after her. When she came back at last to the garden, she ran up the steps in the moonlight into the pigeon-house, and shut the door behind her, answering never a word. There the prince stayed until her father came home. He then told him what had happened—how he had pursued an unknown and beautiful maiden who had danced with him at the feast; and that she had hidden herself in the pigeon-house.

They broke open the door of the pigeon-house, but found only the doves there, awoken from sleep. Else, it was empty. On their return, they passed through the kitchen; and there, among the ashes and in her old ragged clothes, her dim little lamp still burning in the chimney, lay Ashputtel, seemingly fast asleep. As quickly as she could, she had climbed out through a hole in the roof of the pigeon-house, and on to the hazel-tree, whose branches reached its upper wall. Having stripped off her dress of gold and silver, and taken off her slippers of spangled silk, she had put them under the hazel tree so that the bird might carry them away. Then she had put on her old gray frock, and had lain down among the ashes.

On the second day of the feast, when her father and mother and sisters had gone, and the long day's work was over, Ashputtel went again to the hazel-tree, and cried:

"Shake, shake, hazel-tree,
Gold and silver over me!"

The bird came at once to her call, bringing with it a dress even rarer and finer than the one she had worn the night before. When Ashputtel came into the ballroom, everyone there marvelled at her beauty, and the king's son, who had been awaiting her, took her by the hand and danced with her, refusing to give her up, no matter who might plead to dance with her.

When midnight came, she entreated him to let her go home, and she sped away. But he followed her swiftly, burning to see from whence she had come. As fast as she could run, she came in the moonlight to the wall of the garden of her father's house, scrambled over it, and having nowhere else to hide, climbed up breathlessly into the branches of a great pear-tree, already dangling with its ripening fruit. There she hid herself among the leaves.

The king's son sought in vain for her; watched until her father came home from the feast; and then said to him, "The lovely stranger who danced with me all the evening has slipped away again, and I think she must have hidden herself in yonder pear-tree."

For an instant her father thought within himself, "Can this stranger be my daughter Ashputtel?" But he put it out of his mind and said nothing. He gave orders that an axe should be brought, and the pear-tree cut down; but, apart from its fruit, there was nothing to be seen in its branches. When they returned to the kitchen, there lay Ashputtel in the ashes as usual; for the moment the prince had turned away, she had slipped down on the other side of the pear-tree, and having hidden her clothes at the foot of the hazel-tree, had hastened back to her kitchen.

The next evening she again whispered to her hazel-tree:

"Shake, shake, hazel-tree,
Gold and silver over me!"

and the bird brought her a dress even richer and rarer and finer than the last; and slippers of gold.

When for the third time she came into the great room in the king's palace, no one could find words to express their wonder at her beauty. The king's son danced with her the whole evening, and would allow no-one else a minute of her company. When midnight struck once more, he vowed to himself, "Not this time, not *this* time shall she escape me."

None the less, Ashputtel contrived to slip away from him, though in her haste she left behind her one of her golden slippers on the stairs. The prince himself found the slipper; went the next day to the king, his father, and said, "I will take to wife the lady whose left foot fits this golden slipper, and her alone." So the king made a pro-clamation.

Ashputtel's step-sisters rejoiced to hear it. They flattered themselves they had slim and beautiful feet, and had no doubt they could wear the golden slipper. The elder went first into the room to try on the slipper; and her mother stood by watching. But try as she would, her great toe refused to go into it. By the length and breadth of her great toe the slipper was too small for her. Then the mother gave her a knife, and said, "What, one toe in the way! Cut it off, daughter. When you are queen, you will never need to fret yourself about one toe more or less, since you will never go out on foot."

So the silly girl cut off her great toe, squeezed on the slipper, and limped downstairs and out to where the king's son was waiting. He gazed at her in dismay, but the golden slipper fitted, he kept his word, set her up behind him on his horse, and rode away.

In a little while he came riding along beside the garden wall and not far from where on the other side of it grew the hazel-tree that Ashputtel had planted. And in the silence of the morning there sat a bird on the branches of the tree, and this is what it sang:

> "Turn again! Turn again! Look to your shoe!
> It's a toe's length too small, and was not made for you!
> Turn again, Prince! Look elsewhere for thy bride,
> A cheat and deceiver sits there at thy side."

On hearing this, the prince immediately dismounted, and examined the slipper that hung beside his stirrup. It was dripping wet with blood. And he saw the trick that had been played on him. He turned his horse about, brought the false creature back to her father's house, and said, "This is not the lady I am seeking. Let her sister try on the slipper."

So the younger sister went into the room with her mother to put it on. The five toes slipped in easily, every one; but not her heel. By her heel's length and breadth the slipper was too small for her. Her mother, watching her, fell into a rage. By hook and by crook, she pushed and squeezed her daughter's heel into the slipper until the blood came; then she took her down to the king's son. He set her behind him on his horse, and rode away.

In a little while, they came again to the hazel-tree. The bird was still perched among its branches; and again it sang out:

"Turn again! Turn again! Look to your shoe!
It's a heel's length too small, and was not made for you!
Turn again, Prince! Look elsewhere for thy bride,
A cheat and deceiver sits there at thy side."

Again he dismounted, and so much blood had come oozing from the heel of the sister that now sat behind his saddle that her white stocking was dyed red with it. So he turned his horse about again and brought her back. "Neither is this the lady I am seeking," he said to her father; "have you no other daughter?"

"None," said he, "except only a poor drudge who works in the kitchen and whom we call Ashputtel. She is the child of my first wife, and lay asleep in the kitchen when I returned after the feast."

None the less, the prince bade him send for her. At this her stepmother cried out, "No, no, she is a slattern; and much too dirty to show herself. She will not dare to appear."

But the prince insisted on seeing her, and she was brought up from the kitchen.

Just as she was, she came into the room, and curtsied to the prince. He knelt before her, took off the clumsy

294

wooden shoe from her left foot, and put on the golden slipper. Heel to toe, it fitted perfectly. He looked closely into her face, and his heart went out to her.

"This is the lady," he said, "whom these many days I have been seeking—and seeking in vain."

On hearing this, the step-mother and her daughters turned ashen pale with fear and rage, but dared utter never a word. They watched from the window as the prince lifted Ashputtel on to his horse, and rode away with her.

When the two of them came to the hazel-tree, the bird perched among its leaves sang out:

"Home, now! Home, again! Look at the shoe!
Princess! 'twas I who brought it to you.
Prince! hie away with thy beautiful bride,
She alone is thy loved one and sits at thy side!"

Its song finished, it fluttered down from the hazel-tree and alighted on Ashputtel's shoulder. And so they went on together.

ONCE

Once I was a monarch's daughter,
    And sat on a lady's knee;
But am now a nightly rover,
    Banished to the ivy tree.

Crying *hoo, hoo, hoo, hoo, hoo, hoo,*
    Hoo, hoo, hoo, my feet are cold.
Pity me, for here you see me
    Persecuted, poor, and old.

CAT-SKIN

There was once a king whose queen had hair of the purest clearest gold, and who was so beautiful that there was no-one to rival her on the whole face of the earth. There came a day when she fell ill. When she felt in her heart that her end was drawing near, she called the king to her bedside and said, "Vow to me, beloved one, that you will never marry again, unless you meet with one who is as beautiful as I am, and whose hair is of as clear and pure a gold as mine." When the king in his grief had vowed all that she asked of him, she closed her eyes and died.

The king was not to be comforted, and for a long time never thought of taking another wife. At last, however, his counsellors said, "This will not do. The people are complaining. This foolish mourning must cease. The king must marry again, that we may have a queen."

So messengers were sent far and wide, to seek for a bride as beautiful as the queen for whom the king

297

continued to grieve. But there was no princess in the world to be compared to her, and none assuredly who had hair of a gold resembling hers. So the messengers came home. Their travail, their journeyings, had been in vain.

Now the king had a daughter who was not only as beautiful as her mother but whose hair was of the purest clearest gold. When she was grown up, the king looked up at her out of his thoughts one day and marvelled at this similitude. It was as though his queen herself in her first beauty was there before him. He summoned his counsellors and said, "You tell me my people are discontented, that there must be a queen. Let me then marry my daughter. Assuredly there can be none so like my dead wife in the whole world. As for her hair it is of thrice-refined gold. How else can I keep the vow I made?"

When his counsellors heard this, they were dismayed, supposing that the old king's wits were leaving him.

"Heaven forbid," said they, "that a father should marry his own daughter! No good could come of so great a sin as that."

The princess herself was no less grieved and shamed, and hoped that he would soon banish such wild fancies from his mind. But as he continued to brood on this, she came and said to him, "Before I marry any one, whoever it may be, I must have three dresses: one of a gold like the sun's, one of a silver like the moon's, and a third as bright and dazzling as the stars. Besides this, a mantle must be made for me of a thousand kinds of fur, to which every beast in the kingdom must give an inch-width of its skin." By this means she thought to drive her father's madness out of his mind.

But the king at once set the most skilful weavers in his kingdom to work, commanding them to make him three dresses: one of a gold like the sun's, one of a silver like the moon's, and the third as bright and dazzling as the stars. Moreover, his huntsmen were told to hunt down a single beast of every kind that roved his kingdom—forest, mountain, desert—and to cut an inch-wide patch of their finest fur from out of their skins. Of these, at length, the mantle of a thousand furs was made.

When all was ready, the king sent the three dresses and the mantle to his daughter. Her hope had proved vain. In her grief at this, she rose up in the night, when all were asleep, hid in the hem of her dress three of her trinkets, a gold ring, a gold necklace, and a gold brooch; packed the three dresses of the sun, moon, and stars in a nutshell; wrapped herself up in the mantle of a thousand kinds of fur, and, to conceal her beauty, besmeared her face and hands with soot and ashes. Entreating heaven to help her, she stole out of her father's palace into the darkness, and journeyed on the whole night through. At last she came to a wide wild wood. Weary and footsore, she sat herself down in the hollow of a great tree, and soon fell fast asleep. Here she slept the sun up, and until noonday.

Now it chanced that the king to whom the wood belonged had gone hunting that very morning. But even his far-off huntsmen's horns did not awaken her. His dogs came streaming on before him through the wood, and so to the tree. There they began to sniff and snuff and whimper, to run about and about, and then to bark. The forest re-echoed with their din.

"Away!" cried the king to his huntsmen, "and see what sort of game lies couching there."

The huntsmen, calling off their dogs, went up to the hollow tree, peered in, and stood in wonder.

"In the hollow of the tree," they told the king, "there lies the strangest beast we have any of us ever set eyes on. The like of it was never in the world before. Its skin is of a thousand kinds of fur; and there, its head in shadow, it lies fast asleep."

"Look you," said the king, "catch this monster alive, keep it safe, and carry it back with you." And the king rode away home.

So the huntsmen returned to the tree. But when they set about capturing the creature they had found there in their nets, the princess awoke out of her sleep, and gazed at them in terror. She pleaded with them to take pity on her. "I am motherless and alone in the world," she told them. "Spare my life and take me with you." But at sight of her soot-stained face, they jeered and mocked at her, and called her *Cat-skin*. Nevertheless, fearing the king's displeasure, they did her no harm, and took her back in safety to the king's palace.

That night she was given for bed a heap of musty straw in a corner under a staircase, where never light of day peeped in. "There, my lady Cat-skin," they scoffed, "sleep sound, and happy deams to you! But beware of the Walk-by-Nights!"

Next morning, she was set to work in the great kitchen. She was made to fetch wood and water, blow

up the fire, pluck the poultry, pick the herbs, sift the
ashes; and, indeed, not only to do all the dirtiest work,
but to be at everyone's bidding, from the king's chief
cook to the lowest of his scullions.

In this way she lived for a long time, toiling the long day
through, sorrowing in the night. And although she tried
to keep a cheerful face, she was grieved to her inmost
heart. "Ah! my pretty princess," she would scoff at herself; "once so beautiful! *Now* what will become of you?"

Now it happened one day that a feast was to be held
in the king's castle, and Cat-skin said to the chief cook,
"May I go up a little while, peep in at the door and
watch a little what is going on? If I stay in hiding no-one
shall see me." The cook grudgingly gave his consent, but
bade her be back again within half an hour to rake
out the ashes of the grate in the kitchen and finish her
long day's work.

She took a little lamp, hastened away into the dark
little closet where she slept under the stairs, stripped off
her skin of fur, and washed the soot and ashes from her
face and hands. Her beauty shone out like the sun from
behind clouds. She then opened her nutshell, took out
the dress that in its gold and splendour resembled the
shining sun itself, and went up to the feast. Every one
made way for her, none knew who she was. Seeing her in
her loveliness, they thought she could be no less than the
daughter of a king. Indeed the king himself came up to
her, gave her his hand, and entreated her to dance with
him, musing the while as he gazed at her: "Never so long
as I have been alone in this world have I seen anyone half
so beautiful."

When the dance was over, she curtsied to the king, vanished out of his sight, and was gone; no-one knew whither. He summoned the guards who kept the castle gates; but they had seen no stranger. The truth was, that she had instantly run back to her little closet, had taken off her golden dress, blackened her face and hands with soot and ashes, put on her cloak, and become Cat-skin again. When she went back into the kitchen and knelt down to rake out the smouldering ashes, the cook bade her leave this dirty work awhile, and, instead, to heat the king's soup.

"I myself," he said, "am going up to watch the feast. Beware that not a hair of your head fall into the soup. If it does, you shall never have bite or sup again."

As soon as the cook had gone, Cat-skin stirred and heated the king's soup, and toasted a slice of bread as daintily as she could. When it was ready, she fetched her treasured golden ring, and dropped it into the soup-bowl. When the feasting and dancing were over, the king commanded that his supper should be brought up. The soup pleased him well; he had never tasted better. And at the last spoonful, he looked and perceived to his astonishment a gold ring lying at the bottom of the bowl. He sent at once for the cook. At this sudden summons, the cook was frightened half out of his wits.

"The king," he said angrily to Cat-skin, "*must* have found a hair in his soup. If that be so, you shall have a sounder beating than ever lazy slut had yet."

When he came before the king, he was asked who had prepared the soup.

"'Twas I, my Lord King," he replied; "I cooked the king's soup."

But the king refused to believe him. "You lie," he said. "No soup you ever made could be compared with it."

At this the chief cook confessed that it was not his soup, but that a drab of a wench called Cat-skin had made it.

"Send this wench to me at once," said the king.

"Who are you?" said the king to Cat-skin, when she stood before him.

"I am young but alone in the world," she answered him, "having neither father nor mother."

"How came you into my palace?" the king asked her, scanning closely her sooty face.

"I am good for nothing," said she, "but to be the lowest drudge in the kitchen, and to wait on the scullions, who, if I do anything wrong, throw their shoes at my head."

"But how came the gold ring into my soup?" enquired the king. "Whose ring was that?"

But Cat-skin stood silent and would answer never a word about the ring. And doubting somewhat in his mind, the king sent her away.

Time went by; there was another feast, and again Cat-skin asked the chief cook to let her go up and peep at it from behind the door. "Be off," said the cook, "but on your life be back again in half an hour, and make the king some of that soup he fancies."

So Cat-skin ran off to her little closet, washed herself hastily, took from its nutshell the dress that was of silver

like the moon, and put it on. When she appeared again
in her beauty, the king rejoiced to see her. Again they
danced together; but, the dance at an end, she managed
as before to slip away out of his sight so swiftly and
stealthily that the king failed to follow her even with his
eyes. In but a few minutes she was Cat-skin again, back
in the kitchen and stirring the king's soup.

When it was ready, the chief cook being away, she
fetched her golden necklace, and dropped that into the
soup. Come to the last spoonful and no less pleased with
the soup than before, the king found the golden necklace
in the bowl. Again Cat-skin was brought into his presence, but not a word would she utter concerning the
necklace, repeating only that she was no more than a
kitchen drudge, the least of his servants, and fit only,
when she did anything wrong, to have the shoes of the
scullions flung at her head.

When for the third time the king commanded that a
feast should be made ready, everything happened as before. But this time the chief cook stared long at Cat-skin.

"There must be devil's witchcraft in your soup," he
said to her at last, "if it so mightily pleases the king." Still,
in spite of his envy and jealousy, he let her go as before.

She ran off, opened her nutshell, and took out the
dress that was as bright and dazzling as the stars.

As they danced together, the king gazed at her in
wonder and admiration of her beauty. Never had he
seen a face so enchanting. He commanded that the
dance should be continued, and, without her being
aware of it, slipped a ring upon the third finger of the
hand that lay at rest upon his arm.

When the dance at length was over, he would have held her fast; but she contrived to slip away, and vanished so quickly in the multitude of dancers that he yet again lost sight of her. Cheeks scarlet, her heart beating its wings like a bird in a cage, she sped away; but this time she had outstayed the half hour given her by the cook, and there was not time enough to take off her starry dress. She flung her fur mantle over it, and, in her haste, failed to soot her face and hands all over, leaving one of her fingers white.

And so she came back to the kitchen and cooked the king's soup, and when it was ready she dropped her golden brooch into the bowl. There the king found it, at the bottom of the bowl. This time he wasted no time upon the cook, but instantly sent for Cat-skin.

When he spied out the one white finger and the ring that he had secretly slipped over it whilst they were dancing, he seized her hand, and kept fast hold of it; and when, in dismay, she tried to withdraw herself and spring away, the cloak of a thousand furs fell a little to one side off her shoulder, and the starry dress showed sparkling beneath it.

So Cat-skin could no longer hide herself from the king. He drew off the cloak of a thousand furs; and as she stood before him—her hair falling in pure clear golden tresses upon her shoulders—there could be no question that, in spite of her soot-grimed cheeks, she was the most beautiful thing in the whole world; until, that is, she had washed off the soot and ashes. And then she was still more so.

Then said the king, "Here at last is the beloved bride

my heart has long been seeking, and we will never more be parted one from another."

The poor old king, her father, being now gone to his rest, the wedding feast was held, as splendid as ever was seen in a king's palace before. When it was over, Cat-skin herself brought up the king's supper bowl of soup; and a merry day that was.

THE BROOMFIELD HILL

Brome, brome on hill,
The gentle brome on hill, hill,
Brome, brome on Hive hill,
The gentle brome on Hive hill,
The brome stands on Hive hill-a. . . .

. . . "O where were ye, my milk-white steed,
    That I hae coft sae dear[1],
That wadna watch and waken me
    When there was maiden here?"

"I stampèd wi' my foot, master,
    And gard[2] my bridle ring,
But na kin thing wald waken ye,
    Till she was past and gane."

"And wae betide ye, my gay goss-hawk,
    That I did love sae dear,
That wadna watch and waken me
    When there was maiden here."

"I clappèd wi' my wings, master,
    And aye my bells I rang,
And aye cryed, Waken, waken, master,
    Before the ladye gang."

"But haste and haste, my gude white steed,
    To come the maiden till[3],
Or a' the birds of gude green wood
    Of your flesh shall have their fill."

[1]Paid so much money for.   [2]Made.   [3] To.

THE BROOMFIELD HILL

"Ye need na burst your gude white steed
Wi' racing o'er the howm[1];
Nae bird flies faster through the wood,
Than she fled through the broom."

[1]The green margin of a river.

THE SIX SWANS

Once upon a time, a certain king went hunting in a great forest, and chased a wild beast so hotly and eagerly that none of his huntsmen could keep up with him. At set of sun he drew rein, stayed, looked around him, and discovered that he had lost himself. He sought this way and that, but in vain. All but wearied out at length he perceived an old, old woman, whose head nid-nodded perpetually on her shrunken shoulders, approaching him in the gathering gloom of the night. And she was a witch. "Good woman," said he to her, "can you show me the way out of this forest? I am lost."

"Ay, my lord king," she replied, "that I can. But on

one condition. If that is not fulfilled, you will never get out of the forest, but will wander on and on, and perish of hunger."

"What condition is that," asked the king, eyeing her from his milk-white horse.

"I have a daughter," said the witch. "She is as beautiful as any princess in the world, and will never shame you. Swear to make her your queen and I will show you the way out of the forest."

The king stared long at this old beldame, but at last consented. The old woman then led the king to her wattled cabin in the midst of the forest. There was her daughter sitting by the fire. She received the king as if she had been expecting him. But although her beauty was beyond denial, the king found no pleasure in it. He could not look at her without a secret horror. But he had made his vow. He set her behind him on his horse. The old woman told him the way out of the forest; and at length, in dead of darkness, and sick at heart, he reached his palace again. There the wedding was celebrated.

Now this king had already been married once, and by his first wife had had seven children—six boys and a girl. He loved them better than anything else in the world. Fearful that their new step-mother might not treat them well and kindly but might even do them some injury, he took them to a solitary castle which stood in the midst of a forest. This castle lay so closely concealed, and the way thither was so difficult to follow, that he himself would have failed to find it if a certain wise woman had not given him a ball of yarn of a strange magic. When he threw the ball of yarn in front of him, it swiftly unwound itself and showed him his way through the forest.

Time went by. The king set out so often to visit his seven children that the queen at last noticed his absence and kept watch on him. She pined to discover the reason for these journeys and what he did when he was alone and absent. So she bribed his servants to spy, and reveal where he went. They not only betrayed the king's secret, but told her also of the magic ball of yarn which alone could show her the way to the solitary castle in the forest. There was no peace in her mind until she had discovered where the king kept hidden the ball of yarn. She then made some little shirts of white silk, and, as she had been taught the art of witchcraft by her mother, in every one she stitched a charm.

When one day the king had gone hunting, she disguised herself, took the little shirts, and set out alone into the forest. And the ball, obeying its magic, showed her the way. The six young sons of the king, who had seen from a distance a traveller approaching the castle, supposed that their father was come again to visit them, and, wild with joy, ran out to meet him.

But, when, one after another, they came up to this stranger who stood awaiting them in the shade of a great tree, over each in turn she threw one of the little white silken shirts which she had made. No sooner had the shirts touched their bodies than one and all they were instantly changed into swans—their eyes dark as well-water, their plumage white as snow. Mounting on their wings, they fled away over the forest.

The queen, overjoyed that she had now rid herself

once and for all of her step-children, made her way back
to the palace as secretly as she had set out. One of them,
however, the king's youngest child, his only daughter,
had not run out with her brothers. But of her the queen
knew nothing.

Next day, the king went to visit his children. He found
no-one in the castle to greet him but the little girl.

He embraced and kissed her. Then, "Where are thy
brothers?" asked the king.

"Alas, alas, dear father," she answered; "they have
gone away and left me alone!" And she told him how,
as she stood looking out of her little window, she had
watched her six brothers run out as they thought to meet
him; how, as she watched, she had seen them changed
into swans, then rise one by one and fly away over the
forest. And she showed him some wisps of down from
the feathers of their wings which had drifted through
the still air into the courtyard of the castle, and which
she had picked up after her brothers had flown away.
The king was stricken with grief to hear it, unwitting that
the queen herself had done this wicked deed. He feared
that his only loved and loving daughter would also be
stolen away from him, and was of a mind to carry her off
at once to a place of safety. But the hour was now late,
and afraid that the queen might by then have noticed
his absence, he decided to let her sleep but one night
more in the solitary castle.

When he was gone, the child thought to herself, "I
can stay here no longer without my brothers. I will go
at once and seek until I find them." Not even waiting
until the day broke, she ran away into the forest, and

walked the whole night through and most of the following day, until she could scarcely go a step further for
weariness. She came to a woodman's hut, in the midst of
the forest, went in, and found a room upstairs wherein
stood six little beds. She did not venture to lie down on
one of the beds, but crept in under the last and lay down
on the floor, hoping to pass the night there in safety. A
little before sunset, she heard in the silence the sound of
the rustling of many wings, and one by one there came
flying in at the window six wild swans, their feathers
white as snow. Having alighted in the room, they thrust
out their long necks and breathed gently through their
bills one upon another. Their feathers vanished and the
swan's skin fell off them as if it were a shirt. Full of gladness at seeing her brothers again, she crept out from
under the bed. They were no less delighted to see their
sister; but in a little while they fell silent and were sad.

"Here thou can'st not stay," they told her. "This
place is the resort of robbers. If they should find thee,
they would kill thee without mercy."

"But are *you* not here?" she asked them. "What harm,
dear brothers, could come to me with you?"

"Alas," they replied, "only for one fleeting quarter of
an hour every evening are we free from this evil enchantment, and can be together in human form. After that,
we become wild, winged, homeless swans again; and
must fly away over the forest."

At this she began to weep, and said, "Is there no way
to set you free?"

"None, dearest sister," they answered her, "except only
what would be much too hard for thee! For six whole

years thou would'st be forbidden either to speak or to laugh: and in those six years thou would'st have to spend thy time making six little shirts for us out of the petals of the flowers of the starwort. But if a single word, meantime, should pass thy lips, all thy labour would be lost." This said, the time appointed by the charm was over. Her six brothers before her eyes were changed into swans again, and they flew out of the window over the wide forest.

But their sister had already resolved to deliver her brothers from this enchantment even if it should cost her her life. She left the woodman's hut, ran away into the midst of the forest, hid herself in the branches of a tree, and there passed the night.

Next morning she woke early and went out to gather flowers of the starwort, and began to sew. If by chance any stranger came her way, or she met a woodman or a charcoal-burner, she refused even to lift her head, pretending to be dumb. Nor had she any wish to laugh. She worked on and on, intent only on the shirts she was stitching together.

When she had thus spent a very long time, it came to pass that the king of that country went hunting in the forest; and his huntsmen came to the tree in the leafy branches of which she was sitting half-hidden. They called up to her, and said, "Who art thou?"

She made no answer.

"Come down to us," they cried; "no harm shall befall thee."

She only shook her head.

When they continued to urge her to come down, and

to ask her questions, she threw down to them her golden necklace, hoping they would be content with it and would leave her in peace. But still they pestered her. She then threw her girdle down to them; and when this too proved to be of no purpose, her garters, and one by one every garment she had on, until she was all but naked, and sat only in her shift. Even this failed to persuade them to leave her. They climbed the tree, compelled her to come down, and led her before the king.

When she stood before him, the king asked her, "Who art thou? And why wert thou hiding in the tree?"

She made no answer.

Supposing her to be a stranger in his country, he put these questions to her in every language that he knew. But she answered never a word, and remained as mute as a fish. The king's heart was touched by her beauty and simplicity, and he was suddenly smitten with a great love for her. He covered her with his own mantle, placed her before him on his horse, and carried her away to his castle. There he caused her to be dressed in rich raiment. She shone in her beauty like the day; but no word could she be persuaded to utter. She sat beside him at the table when they were at meat, and her gentle bearing and courtesy pleased him so greatly that he vowed within himself, "This is the one woman in the wide world whom I wish to make my wife." And so it was. After some days had passed, they were united.

This king, however, had a wicked mother who hated his marriage and spoke ill of the young queen.

"Who knows," said she, "from whence this dumb creature has come? She is not worthy of a king."

When a year has passed by, the queen brought her
first child into the world. The old woman who waited
on her, at the bidding of the king's mother, took the
child away from her and, as it lay asleep, smeared its
face with blood. And the king saw the blood on the face
of the child. The old woman then had the child sent
away into hiding; went to the king, and accused the
queen of having devoured it. Although to his great
sorrow the child was gone, the king refused to believe
the old woman's story, and would suffer no-one to do
its mother any injury. Meanwhile, the queen sat continually stitching away at the shirts made of the flowers
+ of the starwort, and heeded nothing else.

Time went by. A second child was born to her, a
son; and her false-hearted mother-in-law used the
same treachery as before. Yet again the king refused
to give any credence to what was told him. She was,
he knew well, of a gentle tender nature, and incapable
of any evil.

But when for the third time the old woman stole
away her newly born child, and for the third time her
wicked mother-in-law made her evil accusation against
the queen, and again the queen refused to utter a word
in her defence; then the king—grieved to the heart—
consented to deliver her over to justice; and she was
sentenced to suffer death by fire.

When the day came for this judgment to be executed,
it chanced to be the last day of the six years during
which she had vowed that she would neither speak nor
laugh, so that she could deliver her dear brothers from
the power of the enchantment that had been cast over

them. The six shirts were now ready, except only that the left sleeve of the sixth was still wanting.

When, then, she was led to the stake, she took with her the shirts upon her arm. Silent and forsaken, she stood on high before the multitude assembled in the market-place. And the hangman came with his torch. For the last time she lifted her eyes to look into the sky. And lo, far, far in its blue showed specks that might be birds flying, and they drew nearer. And behold, as she gazed, six wild swans came arrowing swiftly through the air towards her. Then she knew that her deliverance was near, and her heart leapt within her in rapture and delight.

One by one the swans swept lower and lower until each in turn drew so near that she could cast the shirts over them as they sped by. As soon as the shirts touched their plumage, their disguise fell off, and her six brothers in their natural bodily shape stood before her, vigorous and handsome young men; except that the fairest and youngest of them lacked his left arm, and in place of it the snow-white wing of a swan was upon that shoulder. They embraced and kissed one another. Then went she to the king, and for the first time since they had begun to love one another he heard her voice.

"Most dear of husbands," she said, laughing and weeping all for joy, "I have kept my vow. I now say and declare unto thee that I love thee heart and soul beyond words to tell; that I am innocent of the charges that have been brought against me, and that I have been falsely accused."

She then told him of the treachery of the old woman

who, one by one, had taken away her three children and left them in hiding. To the unutterable joy of the king, the three children were restored him. As for his envious and wicked mother, she was bound to the stake and burnt to ashes, while the king and queen, with her six brothers now freed from their enchantment, lived for many years in happiness and peace.

I SAW A PEACOCK

I saw a Peacock with a fiery tail
I saw a blazing Comet drop down hail
I saw a Cloud wrapped with ivy round
I saw an Oak creep on along the ground
I saw a Pismire swallow up a Whale
I saw the Sea brim full of Ale
I saw a Venice Glass five fathoms deep
I saw a Well full of men's tears that weep
I saw red Eyes all of a flaming Fire
I saw a House bigger than the Moon and higher
I saw the Sun at twelve o'clock at night
I saw the Man that saw this wondrous sight.

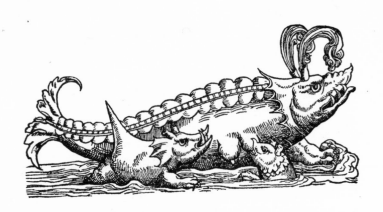

HOW THE MANX CAT LOST
ITS TAIL

Far, far away in the Irish Sea there is a tiny island called the Isle of Man where the cats have no tails. They are called Manx cats and the people who live on this little island are called Manx, too.

Although Manx cats are just as pretty as other cats, they look different because they have no tails and because their hind legs are longer than ordinary cats' legs. With these long hind legs they can hop like a rabbit and this they always do when they are in a hurry. Their silky fur may be black, white, gray or striped, but the realest-real Manx cat has stripes of three colours, black, white and amber.

No one knows the true story about the Manx tailless cats. They lost their tails many hundreds of years ago when people were not paying much attention to such trifles. But the Manx people who know most about it, say that this is the way it happened.

At the time when Noah was calling all the animals

into the Ark made of gopher wood, there was one Manx cat that was out mousing. Sure enough, it had a striped coat of three colours, black, white and a lovely amber. Noah was eager to have this cat on board his Ark because a cat of three colours always brings good luck. To lose this cat now would mean bad luck to the Ark and all that was in it.

It had taken Noah, his wife and three sons many years to get all the animals together in the Ark. They had worked hard arranging the animals in their places and keeping them friendly. Shem, the first son, had complete charge of all the birds of the air. Ham, the second son, had complete charge of all the fishes of the sea. And Japhet, the third son, had complete charge of all the animals of the forest and jungle. Then, since Noah's wife was such a good housewife and knew so well how to take care of children's pets, Noah gave her complete charge of all the pet dogs, cats, ponies, birds, goldfish and every other kind of pet animal you could imagine. For, you remember, there were two of every living creature in this Ark made of gopher wood.

After Noah discovered that the Manx cat was the only animal not in the Ark, he took upon himself the task of calling it in. He stood at the door of the Ark all of ten years calling "kitty, kitty, kitty, kitty", and he was just about worn out. Who would not be worn out if he was six hundred years old and had been calling "kitty" for ten years?

One day, Noah was about to give up. His thin legs would not hold him up any longer, so his creaking old body slid down by the door of the Ark. There he sat stroking his long white whiskers. He must have been there a month or more when up came Shem, his first son, greatly excited. The birds had heard Noah calling the cat and they were all perched out on the roof ready to fly away. So Shem came to Noah to ask him what to do. But when he saw him, what he said was, "Why, Father Noah, whatever is the matter with you? In all these three hundred years I have never seen you so tired and nervous."

"Quite so," said Noah to his first son, "the Manx cat does not come when I call her. The sky is getting darker and darker. I am afraid the rain will begin to fall any minute and I will have to close the door before the cat gets in."

"Well, I'll try," said Shem and he called "kitty, kitty, kitty, kitty," for a month or so. But no cat appeared.

By this time some of the fish had heard about the cat, so all the little fish hid behind the whales and seals. This worried Ham, the second son, so he came running to Noah to find out what to do. But when he saw him, what he said was, "Why, Father Noah, whatever is the matter with you? In all these two hundred and fifty years I have never seen you so tired and nervous."

"Quite so," said Noah to his second son, "the Manx cat does not come when I call her. The sky is getting darker and darker. I am afraid the rain will begin to fall any minute and I will have to close the door before the cat gets in."

"Well, I'll try," said Ham, and he called "kitty, kitty, kitty, kitty", as loud as his two-hundred-and-fifty-year-old voice would permit. But no cat came.

HOW THE MANX CAT LOST ITS TAIL

It does not take rats and mice very long to get the news that there is a cat anywhere near, so they all locked themselves up in the elephant's trunk. This worried Japhet, the third son, so he ran to Noah to find out what to do. But when he saw him, what he said was, "Why, Father Noah, whatever is the matter with you? In all these two hundred years I have never seen you so tired and nervous."

"Quite so," said Noah to his third son, "the Manx cat does not come when I call her. The sky is getting darker and darker. I am afraid the rain will begin to fall any minute and I will have to close the door before the cat gets in."

"Well, I'll try," said Japhet, and he called "kitty, kitty, kitty, kitty", as loud as his two-hundred-year-old voice would permit. Still there was no sight of the cat.

While Japhet was calling the cat, the mice had wiggled around in the elephant's trunk and tickled it so that the elephant was running wild all over the Ark. When it got to the side where the hippopotamus was, the Ark almost tipped over.

Noah's wife could not stand to have things all out of order and when the Ark almost tipped, she ran to Noah to learn what to do. When she saw him, what she said was, "Why, Father Noah, whatever is the matter? In all these four hundred years I have never seen you so tired and nervous."

"Quite so, dear wife," said Noah, "the Manx cat does not come when I call her. The sky is getting darker and darker. I am afraid the rain will begin to fall any minute and I will have to close the door before the cat gets in."

"Well, I'll try," said his wife, and this is the way she called the Manx cat. "Spss, pss, pss, pss." She must have been a Manx housewife for she knew how they call the cats in the Isle of Man.

No sooner had she finished than the rain began to fall. Noah called his sons to help him close the heavy door of the Ark. He called out sharply, "Who's out, is out, and who's in, is in," and slam went the door.

As soon as the cat had heard Noah's wife call "spss" it came running as fast as it could. Half drowned, it just squeezed in as the heavy door closed, but not in time to save its tail, which was sadly cut off.

For a long time, no one on the Ark noticed the cat. It had sneaked off into a corner feeling very sad over losing its tail. This was the most painful experience it had ever had and it hardly knew what to do or where to go. But it had learned this lesson—that it never pays to wait till the last minute.

Then one happy day for the cat, Noah's wife found it. She took it to the fire to dry and, with many bandages and good care, the place where its tail had been soon healed up.

The first time the cat walked about to see how well it could balance itself without any tail, it met Father Noah.

"What a queer look Father Noah is giving me," thought the cat, "I guess he does not know how I sneaked in and he cut off my tail with that heavy door. I'll just speak to him.

HOW THE MANX CAT LOST ITS TAIL

> "Bee-bo, bend-it
> My tail's ended;
> I'll go back to Man
> As soon as I can
> And get copper nails
> To mend it."

After forty long days and forty long nights of the flood had ended, the cat found its way back to the Isle of Man. It hunted everywhere for its tail.

> Up to the top of Snaefel Mountain,
> Down to the bottom of the deepest glen;
> All along the rocky shore,
> And then all over again.

Of course, by this time, the tail had probably been washed away in the flood. Or it may be that, if the cat found its tail, there were no copper nails to mend it. Hundreds of years have passed since then but to-day you will find hundreds of cats without any tails living their nine lives on the Isle of Man.

BLANCHE COWLEY YOUNG

THE CROCODILE

Now listen, you landsmen, unto me, to tell you the truth
      I'm bound,
What happened to me by going to sea, and the wonders
      that I found;
Shipwrecked I was once off Perouse and cast upon the
      shore,
So then I did resolve to roam, the country to explore.
    Tomy rit fal lal li bollem tit! tomy rit fal lal li dee!
    Tomy rit fal lal li bollem tit! tomy rit fal lal li dee!

'Twas far I had not scouted out when close alongside the
      ocean
I saw something move which at first I thought was all
      the world in motion;
But steering up close alongside I found 'twas a croco-
      dile,
And from his nose to the top of his tail he measured five
      hundred mile.
    Chorus.

While up aloft the wind was high, it blew a gale from
      the south,
I lost my hold and away did fly right into the crocodile's
      mouth.
He quickly closed his jaws on me, and thought he'd got
      a victim,
But I ran down his throat, d'ye see? and that's the way I
      tricked him.
    Chorus.

326

I travelled on for a month or two, till I got into his maw,
Where I found of rum-kegs not a few, and a thousand
  fat bullocks in store.
Of life I banished all my care, for of grub I was not
  stinted,
And in this crocodile I lived ten years and very well
  contented.
  Chorus.

This crocodile being very old, one day, alas, he died,
He was ten long years a-getting cold, he was so long and
  wide.
His skin was eight miles thick, I'm sure, or very near
  about,
For I was full ten years or more a-cutting my way out.
  Chorus.

And now I am once more got on earth, I've vow'd no
  more to roam,
In a ship that passed I got a berth, and now I'm safe at
  home.
And if my story you should doubt, should you ever
  travel the Nile,
It's ten to one you'll find the shell of the wonderful croco-
  dile.
  Tomy rit fal lal li bollem tit! tomy rit fal lal li dee!
  Tomy rit fal lal li bollem tit! tomy rit fal lal li dee!

A SAILOR'S YARN

"Once upon a time there was a clipper ship called the *Mary*, and she was lying in Panama waiting for a freight. It was hot, and it was calm, and it was hazy, and the men aboard her were dead sick of the sight of her. They had been lying there all the summer, having nothing to do but to wash her down, and scrape the royal masts with glass, and make the chain cables bright. And aboard of her was a big A.B. from Liverpool, with a tatooed chest on him and an arm like a spar. And this man's name was Bill.

"Now, one day, while the captain of this clipper was sunning in the club, there came a merchant to him offering him a fine freight home and 'despatch' in loading.

So the old man went aboard that evening in a merry temper, and bade the mates rastle the hands aft. He told them that they could go ashore the next morning for a 'liberty-day' of four-and-twenty hours, with twenty dollars pay to blue, and no questions asked if they came aboard drunk. So forward goes all hands merrily, to rout out their go-ashore things, their red handkerchiefs, and 'sombre-airers', for to astonish the Dons. And ashore they goes the next morning, after breakfast, with their silver dollars in their fists, and the jolly-boat to take them. And ashore they steps, and 'So long' they says to the young fellows in the boat, and so up the Mole to the beautiful town of Panama.

"Now the next morning that fellow Bill I told you of was tacking down the city to the boat, singing some song or another. And when he got near to the jetty he went fumbling in his pocket for his pipe, and what should he find but a silver dollar that had slipped away and been saved. So he thinks, 'If I go aboard with this dollar, why the hands'll laugh at me; besides, it's a wasting of it not to spend it.' So he casts about for some place where he could blue it in.

"Now close by where he stood there was a sort of a great store, kept by a Johnny Dago. And if I were to tell you of the things they had in it, I would need nine tongues and an oiled hinge to each of them. But Billy walked into this store, into the space inside, into like the 'tween decks, for to have a look about him before buying. And there were great bunches of bananas a-ripening against the wall. And sacks of dried raisins, and bags of dried figs, and melon seeds, and pomegranates enough to sink you. Then there were cotton bales, and calico, and silk of Persia. And rum in puncheons, and bottled ale. And all manner of sweets, and a power of a lot of chemicals. And anchors gone rusty, fished up from the bay after the ships were gone. And spare cables, all ranged for letting go. And ropes, and sails, and balls of marline stuff. Then there was blocks of all kinds, wood and iron. Dunnage there was, and scantling, likewise sea-chests with pictures on them. And casks of beef and pork, and paint, and peas, and peterolium. But for not one of these things did Billy care a handful of bilge.

"Then there were medical comforts, such as ginger and calavances. And plug tobacco, and coil tobacco, and tobacco leaf, and tobacco clippings. And such a power of a lot of bulls' hides as you never saw. Likewise there was tinned things like cocoa, and boxed things like China tea. And any quantity of blankets, and rugs, and donkeys' breakfasts. And oilskins there was, and rubber sea-boots, shore-shoes, and Crimee shirts. Also dungarees, and soap, and matches, so many as you never heard tell. But no, not for one of these things was Bill going for to bargain.

"Then there were lamps and candles, and knives and nutmeg-graters, and things made of bright tin and saucers of red clay; and rolls of coloured cloth, made in the hills by the Indians. Bowls there were, painted with twisty-twirls by the folk of old time. And flutes from the tombs (of the Incas), and whistles that looked like flower-pots. Also fiddles and beautiful melodeons. Then there were paper roses for ornament, and false white flowers for graves; also paint-brushes and coir-brooms.

There were cages full of parrots, both green and grey; and white cockatoos on perches a-nodding their red crests; and Java love-birds a-billing, and parrakeets a-screaming, and little kittens for the ships with rats. And at the last of all there was a little monkey, chained to a sack of jib-hanks, who sat upon his tail a-grinning.

"Now Bill he sees this monkey, and he thinks he never see a cuter little beast, not never. And then he thinks of something, and he pipes up to the old Johnny Dago, and he says, pointing to the monkey:

" 'Hey-a Johnny! How much-a-take-a little munk?'

"So the old Johnny Dago looks at Bill a spell, and then says:

" 'I take-a five-a doll' that-a little munk.'

"So Billy planks down his silver dollar, and says:

" 'I give-a one doll,' you cross-eyed Dago.'

"Then the old man unchained the monkey, and handed him to Bill without another word. And away the pair of them went, down the Mole to where the boats lay, where a lanchero took them off to the *Mary*.

"Now when they got aboard all hands came around Bill, saying: 'Why, Bill, whatever are you going to do with that there little monkey?' And Bill he said: 'You shut your heads about that there little monkey. I'm going to teach that little monkey how to speak. And when he can speak I'm going to sell him to a museum. And then I'll buy a farm. I won't come to sea any more.' So they just laugh at Bill, and by and by the *Mary* loaded, and got her hatches on, and sailed south-away, on the road home to Liverpool.

"Well, every evening, in the dog-watch, after supper,

while the decks were drying from the washing-down, Bill used to take the monkey on the fo'c's'le head, and set him on the capstan. 'Well, ye little divvle,' he used to say, 'will ye speak? Are ye going to speak, hey?' and the monkey would just grin and chatter back at Billy, but never no Christian speech came in front of them teeth of his. And this game went on until they were up with the Horn, in bitter cold weather, running east like a stag, with a great sea piling up astern. And then one night, at eight bells, Billy came on deck for the first watch, bringing the monkey with him. It was blowing like sin, stiff and cold, and the *Mary* was butting through, and dipping her fo'c's'le under. So Bill takes the monkey, and lashes him down good and snug on the drum of the capstan, on the fo'c's'le head. 'Now, ye little divvle,' he said, 'will ye speak? Will ye speak, eh?' But the monkey just grinned at him.

"At the end of the first hour he came again. 'Are ye going to speak, ye little beggar?' he says, and the monkey sits and shivers, but never a word does the little beggar say. And it was the same at four bells, when the lookout man was relieved. But at six bells Billy came again, and the monkey looked mighty cold, and it was a wet perch where he was roosting, and his teeth chattered; yet he didn't speak, not so much as a cat. So just before eight bells, when the watch was nearly out, Billy went forward for the last time. 'If he don't speak now,' says Billy, 'overboard he goes for a dumb animal.'

"Well, the cold green seas had pretty nearly drowned that little monkey, and the spray had frozen him over like a jacket of ice, and right blue his lips were, and an icicle was a-dangling from his chin, and he was shivering like he had an ague. 'Well, ye little divvle,' says Billy, 'for the last time, will ye speak? Are ye going to speak, hey?' And the monkey spoke. '*Speak* is it? *Speak* is it?' he says. 'It's so cold it's enough to make a little fellow *swear.*'

"It's the solemn gospel truth that story is."

JOHN MASEFIELD

THE GREAT SILKIE OF SULE SKERRY*

This old ballad was "written down from the dictation of a venerable lady of Snarra Voe, Shetland"

An eartly nourris¹ sits and sings,
 And aye she sings, Ba, lily wean!
Little ken I my bairnis father,
 Far less the land that he staps in.

Then ane arose at her bed-fit²,
 An a grumly guest I'm sure was he:
"Here am I, thy bairnis father,
 Although that I be not comelie.

"I am a man, upon the lan,
 An I am a silkie³ in the sea;
And when I'm far and far frae lan,
 My dwelling is in Sule Skerrie."

"It was na weel," quo the maiden fair,
 "It was na weel, indeed," quo she,
"That the Great Silkie of Sule Skerrie
 Suld hae come and aught a bairn to me⁴."

* " 'Finns', as they are for the most part called, denizens of a region below the depths of the ocean, are able to ascend to the land above by donning a seal-skin, which then they are wont to lay off, and, having divested themselves of it, they 'act just like men and women'."

¹ Nurse.   ² Bed-foot.   ³ Seal.
⁴ Given me a child.

THE GREAT SILKIE OF SULE SKERRY

Now he has taen a purse of goud[1],
    And he has pat it upo her knee,
Sayin, "Gie to me my little young son,
    An tak thee up thy nourris-fee.

"An it sall come to pass on a simmer's day,
    When the sin shines het on evera stane,
That I will tak my little young son,
    An teach him for to swim the faem.

"An thu sall marry a proud gunner[2],
    An a proud gunner I'm sure he'll be,
An the very first schot that ere he schoots,
    He'll schoot baith my young son and me."

[1] Gold.   [2] Perhaps one who hunts wild fowl.

THE SEAL MAN

"The seals is pretty when they do be playing," said the old woman. "Ah, I seen them frisking their tails till you'd think it was rocks with the seas beating on them, the time the storm's on. I seen the merrows of the sea sitting yonder on the dark stone, and they had crowns on them, and they were laughing. The merrows is not good; it's not good to see too many of them. They are beautiful like young men in their shirts playing hurley. They're as beautiful as anything you would be seeing in Amerikey or Australeyey, or any place. The seals is beautiful too, going through the water in the young of the day; but they're not so beautiful as them. The seals is no good either. It's a great curse keeps them the way they are, not able to live either in the sea or on the land.

"One time there was a man of the O'Donnells came here, and he was a bad man. A saint in Heaven would have been bothered to find good in him. He died of the fever that came before the Famine. I was a girl then; and if you'd seen the people in them times; there wasn't enough to bury them. The pigs used to eat them in the loanings. And their mouths would be all green where they'd eaten grass from want of food. If you'd seen the house there was then, indeed, you'd think the place bewitched. But the cabins is all fell in, like yonder, and there's no dancing or fiddling, or anything at all, and all of my friends is gone to Amerikey or Australeyey; I've no one at all to bury me, unless it's that humpy one who comes here, and she's as proud as a Jew. She's no cause to be proud, with a hump on her; her father was just a poor man, the same as any.

"This O'Donnell I was telling you. My father was at his wake. And they'd the candles lit, and they were drinking putcheen. My father was nearest the door, and a fear took him, and he got up, with his glass in his hand, and he cried out: 'There's something here is not good.' And another of them said: 'There's something wants to get out.' And another said: 'It's himself wants to go out into the dark night.' And another said: 'For the love of God, open the door.' So my father flung the door open; and, outside, the moon shone down to the sea. And the corpse of the O'Donnell was all blue, and it got up with the sheet knotted on it, and walked out without leaving a track. So they followed it, saying their prayers to Almighty God, and it walked on down to the sea. And when it came to the edge of the sea, the sea was like a flame before it. And it bowed there, three times; and each time it rose up it screamed. And all the seals, and all the merrows, and all them that's under the tides, they came up to welcome it. They called out to the corpse and laughed; and the corpse laughed back, and fell on to the sand. My father and the other men saw the wraith pass from it, into the water, as it fell. It was like a little black boy, laughing, with great long arms on him. It was all bald and black; and its hands moved like he was tickling someone.

"And after that the priest had him buried, like they buried the Old Ones; but the wraith passed into a bull seal. You would be feared to see the like of the bull seal. There was a man of the O'Kanes fired a blessed shilling at him, and the seal roared up at him and tore his arm across. There was marks like black stars on him after till he died. And the bull seal walked like a man at the change of the moon, like a big, tall, handsome man stepping the roads. You'd be feared, sir, if you saw the like. He set his eyes on young Norah O'Hara. Lovely she was. She'd little ways, sir, would draw the heart out of an old bachelor. Wasn't it a great curse he should take her when there was old hags the like of Mary that has no more beauty than a withered broom that you wouldn't be bothered to mend or a done-out old gather-up of a duck that a hungry dog would blush to be biting? Still, he took Norah.

"She had a little son, and the little son was a seal-man; the priest wouldn't sign him with the cross. When Norah died he used always to be going to the sea; he would always be swimming. He'd little soft brown hair, like a seal's, the prettiest you would be seeing. He used to talk to the seals. My father was coming home one night from Carnmore, and he saw the little seal-man in the sea; and the seals were playing with him, singing songs. But my father was feared to hear; he ran away. They

stoned the seal-man, whiles, after that; but, whiles they
didn't stone it. They had a kindness for it, although it
had no holy water on it. It was a very young thing to be
walking the world, and it was a beautiful wee thing,
with its eyes so pretty; so it grew up to be a man.

"Them that live in the water, they have ways of calling people. Them who passed this seal-man, they felt
the call in their hearts. Indeed, if you passed the seal-
man, stepping the roads, you would get a queer twist
from the way he looked at you. And he set his love on a
young girl of the O'Keefe's, a little young girl with no
more in her than the flower on its stalk. You would see
them in the loanings coming home, or in the bright of
the day going. There was a strong love was on them two
young things; it was like the love of the Old Ones that
took nine deaths to kill. They would be telling Kate it
was not right she should set her love on one who
wasn't like ourselves; but there's few indeed is the
young'll listen. They are all for pleasure, all for pleasure,
before they are withered old hags, the like of my sister
Mary. And at last they shut her up at home, to keep her
from seeing him. And he came by her cabin to the west
of the road, calling. There was a strong love came up in
her at that, and she put down her sewing on the table,
and 'Mother,' she says, 'there's no lock, and no key, and
no bolt, and no door. There's no iron, nor no stone, nor
anything at all will keep me this night from the man I
love.' And she went out into the moonlight to him,
there by the bush where the flowers is pretty, beyond
the river. And he says to her: 'You are all of the beauty
of the world, will you come where I go, over the waves

of the sea?' And she says to him: 'My treasure and my strength,' she says, 'I would follow you on the frozen hills, my feet bleeding.'

"Then they went down into the sea together, and the moon made a track upon the sea, and they walked down it, it was like a flame before them. There was no fear at all on her; only a great love like the love of the Old Ones, that was stronger than the touch of the fool. She had a little white throat, and little cheeks like flowers, and she went down into the sea with her man, who wasn't a man at all. She was drowned, of course. It's like he never thought she wouldn't bear the sea like himself. She was drowned, drowned.

"When it come light they saw the seal-man sitting yonder on the rock, and she lying by him, dead, with her face as white as a flower. He was crying and beating her hands to bring life to her. It would have drawn pity from a priest to hear him, though he wasn't Christian. And at last, when he saw that she was drowned, he took her in his arms and slipped into the sea like a seal. And he swam, carrying her, with his head up, laughing and laughing and laughing, and no one ever saw him again at all."

JOHN MASEFIELD

AY ME, ALAS, HEIGH HO!

Ay me, alas, heigh ho, heigh ho!
Thus doth Messalina go
Up and down the house a-crying,
For her monkey lies a-dying.
Death, thou art too cruel
To bereave her of her jewel,
Or to make a seizure
Of her only treasure.
If her monkey die,
She will sit and cry,
Fie fie fie fie fie!

THE LORD FISH

O nce upon a time there lived in the village of
Tussock in Wiltshire a young man called John
Cobbler. Cobbler being his name, there must
have been shoe-making in his family. But there had been
none in John's lifetime; nor within living memory either.
And John cobbled nothing but his own old shoes and his
mother's. Still, he was a handy young man. He could
have kept them both with ease, and with plenty of butter
to their bread, if only he had been a little different from
what he was. He was lazy.

Lazy or not, his mother loved him dearly. She had
loved him ever since he was a baby, when his chief joy
was to suck his thumb and stare out of his saucer blue
eyes at nothing in particular except what he had no
words to tell about. Nor had John lost this habit, even
when he was being a handy young man. He could make

baskets—of sorts; he was a wonder with bees; he could mend pots and pans, if he were given the solder and could find his iron; he could grow cabbages, hoe potatoes, patch up a hen-house or lime-wash a sty. But he was only à jack of such trades, and master of none. He could seldom finish off anything; not at any rate as his namesake the Giant Killer could finish off his giants. He began well; he went on worse; and he ended, yawning. And unless his mother had managed to get a little washing and ironing and mending and sweeping and cooking and stitching from the gentry in the village, there would often have been less in the pot for them both than would keep their bodies and souls—and the two of them—together.

Yet even though John was by nature idle and a day-dreamer, he might have made his mother far easier about his future if only he could have given up but one small pleasure and pastime; he might have made not only good wages, but also his fortune—even though he would have had to leave Tussock to do it quick. It was his love of water that might some day be his ruin. Or rather, not so much his love of water as his passion for fishing in it. Let him but catch sight of a puddle, or of rain gushing from a waterspout, or hear in the middle of the night a leaky tap singing its queer *ding-dong-bell* as drop followed drop into a basin in the sink, let the wind but creep an inch or two out of the east and into the south; and every other thought would instantly vanish out of his head. All he wanted then was a rod and a line and a hook and a worm and a cork; a pond or a stream or a river—or the deep blue sea. And it wasn't even fish he pined for, merely fishing.

343

There would have been little harm in this craving of his if only he had been able to keep it within bounds. But he couldn't. He fished morning, noon, and even night. Through continually staring at a float, his eyes had come to be almost as round as one, and his elbows stood out like fins when he walked. The wonder was his blood had not turned to water. And though there are many kinds of tasty English fish, his mother at last grew very tired of having *any* kind at every meal. As the old rhyme goes:

> A Friday of fish
> Is all man could wish.
> Of vittles the chief
> Is mustard and beef.
> It's only a glutton
> Could live on cold mutton;
> And bacon when green
> Is too fat or too lean.
> But all three are sweeter
> To see in a dish
> By any wise eater
> Than *nothing* but FISH!

Quite a little fish, too, even a roach, may take as many hours to catch and almost as many minutes to cook as a full-sized one; and they both have the same number of bones. Still in spite of his fish *and* his fishing, his mother went on loving her son John. She hoped in time he might weary of them himself. Or was there some secret in his passion for water of which she knew nothing? Might he some day fish up something really worth having—something to keep? a keg perhaps of rubies and diamonds, or a coffer full of amber and gold? Then all their troubles would be over.

Meanwhile, John showed no sign at all of becoming less lazy or of growing tired of fishing, though he was no longer content to fish in the same places. He would walk miles and miles in hope to find pond, pool or lake that he had never seen before, or a stream strange to him. Wherever he heard there was water within reach between dawn and dark, off he would go to look for it. Sometimes in his journeyings he would do a job of work, and bring home to his mother not only a few pence but a little present for herself—a ribbon, or a needle-case, a bag of jumbles or bull's-eyes, or a duck's egg for her tea; any little thing that might take her fancy. Sometimes the fish he caught in far-off waters tasted fresher, sweeter, richer, juicier than those from nearer home; sometimes they tasted worse—dry, poor, rank and muddy. It depended partly on the sort of fish, partly on how long he had taken to carry them home, and partly on how his mother felt at the moment.

Now there was a stream John Cobbler came to hear about which for a long time he could never find. For whenever he went to look for it—and he knew that it lay a good fourteen miles and more from Tussock—he was always baulked by a high flintstone wall. It was the highest wall he had ever seen. And, like the Great Wall of China, it went on for miles. What was more curious, although he had followed the wall on and on for hours at a stretch, he had never yet been able to find a gate or door to it, or any way in.

When he asked any stranger whom he happened to

meet at such times if he knew what lay on the other side of this mysterious wall, and whether there were any good fish in the stream which he had been told ran there, and if so, of what kind, shape, size and flavour they might be—every single one of them told him a different tale. Some said there was a castle inside the wall, a good league or so away from it, and that a sorcerer lived in it who had mirrors on a tower in which he could detect any stranger that neared his walls. Others said an old, old Man of the Sea had built himself a great land mansion there in the middle of a Maze—of water and yew trees; an old Man of the Sea who had turned cannibal, and always drowned anybody who trespassed over his wall before devouring him. Others said water-witches dwelt there, in a wide lake made by the stream beside the ruinous walls of a palace which had been the abode of princes in old times. All agreed that it was a dangerous place, and that they would not venture over the wall, dark or daylight, for a pocketful of guineas. On summer nights, they said, you could hear voices coming from away over it, very strange voices, too; and would see lights in the sky. And some avowed they had heard hunting-horns at the rise of the moon. As for the fish, all agreed they must be monsters.

There was no end to the tales told John of what lay beyond the wall. And he, being a simple young man, believed each one of them in turn. But none made any difference to the longing that had come over him to get to the other side of this wall and to fish in the stream there. Walls that keep out so much, he thought, must keep something well worth having *in*. All other fishing

346

now seemed tame and dull. His only hope was to find out the secret of what lay beyond this high, grey, massive, mossy, weed-tufted, endless wall. And he stopped setting out in its direction only for the sake of his mother.

But though for this reason he might stay at home two or three days together, the next would see him off again, hungering for the unknown waters.

John not only thought of the wall all day, he dreamed of it and of what might be beyond it by night. If the wind sighed at his window he saw wide moonlit lakes of water in his sleep; if a wild duck cried overhead under the stars, there would be thousands of wild duck and wild swans too and many another water-bird haunting his mind, his head on his pillow. Sometimes great whales would come swimming into his dreams. And he would hear mermaids blowing in their hollow shells and singing as they combed their hair.

With all this longing he began to pine away a little. His eye grew less clear and lively. His rib-bones began to show. And though his mother saw a good deal more of her son John since he had given up his fishing, at last she began to miss more and more and more what she had become accustomed to. Fish, that is:—boiled, broiled, baked, fried or Dutch-ovened. And her longing came to such a pass at last that she laid down her knife and fork one supper-time beside a half-eaten slice of salt pork and said, "My! John, how I would enjoy a morsel of tench again! Do you remember those tench you used to catch up at Abbot's Pool? Or a small juicy trout, John! Or some stewed eels! Or even a few roach out of the moat of the old Grange, even though they *are* mostly mud!

347

It's funny, John, but sea-fish never did satisfy me even
when we could get it; and I haven't scarcely any fancy
left for meat. What's more, I notice cheese now gives
you nightmares. But fish?—never!"

This was enough for John. For weeks past he had been
sitting on the see-saw of his mind, so that just the least
little tilt like that bumped him clean into a decision. It
was not fear or dread indeed, all this talk of giants and
wizardry and old bygone princes that had kept him from
scaling the great wall long ago, and daring the dangers
beyond it. It was not this at all. But only a half-hidden
feeling in his mind that if once he found himself on the
other side of it he might never be quite the same creature
again. You may get out of your bed in the morning, the
day's usual sunshine at the window and the birds singing
as they always sing, and yet know for certain that in the
hours to come something is going to happen—something that hasn't happened before. So it was with John
Cobbler. At the very moment his mother put down her
knife and fork on either side of her half-eaten slice of salt
pork and said, "My! John, how I would enjoy a morsel
of tench again!...Or a small juicy trout, John!" his mind
was made up.

"Why, of course, mother dear," he said to her, in a
voice that he tried in vain to keep from trembling. "I'll
see what I can do for you to-morrow." He lit his candle
there and then, and scarcely able to breathe for joy at
thought of it, clumped up the wooden stairs to his attic
to look out his best rod and get ready his tackle.

While yet next morning the eastern sky was pale blue
with the early light of dawn, wherein tiny clouds like a

shoal of silver fishes were quietly drifting on—before, that is, the flaming sun had risen, John was posting along out of Tussock with his rod and tackle and battered old creel, and a hunk of bread and cheese tied up in a red-spotted handkerchief. There was not a soul to be seen. Every blind was down; the chimneys were empty of smoke; the whole village was still snoring. He whistled as he walked, and every now and again took a look at the weather. That vanishing fleecy drift of silver fishes might mean wind, and from the south, he thought. He plodded along to such good purpose, and without meeting a soul except a shepherd with his sheep and dog and an urchin driving a handful of cows—for these were solitary parts —that he came to the wall while it was still morning, and a morning as fresh and green as even England can show.

Now John wasn't making merely for the wall, but for a certain place in it. It was where, one darkening evening some little time before, he had noticed the still-sprouting upper branches of a tree that had been blown down in a great wind over the edge of the wall and into the narrow grassy lane that skirted it. Few humans seemed ever to come this way, but there were hosts of rabbits, whose burrows were in the sandy hedgerow, and, at evening, nightjars, croodling in the dusk. It was, too, John had noticed, a favourite resort of bats.

After a quick look up and down the lane to see that the coast was clear, John stood himself under the dangling branches—like the fox in the fable that was after the grapes—and he jumped, and jumped. But no matter how high he jumped, the lowermost twigs remained out of his reach. He rested awhile looking about him, and spied a large stone half-buried in the sandy hedgerow. He trundled it over until it was under the tree, and after a third attempt succeeded in swinging himself up into its branches, and had scrambled along and dropped quietly in on the other side almost before news of his coming had spread among the wild things that lived on the other side of it. Then blackbird to blackbird sounded the alarm. There was a scurry and scamper among the leaves and bracken. A host of rooks rose cawing into the sky. Then all was still. John peered about him; he had never felt so lonely in his life. Never even in his dreams had he been in a place so strange to him as this. The foxgloves and bracken of its low hills and hollows showed bright green where the sunshine struck through the great forest trees. Else, so dense with leaves were their branches that for the most part there was only an emerald twilight beneath their boughs. And a deep silence dwelt there.

For some little time John walked steadily on, keeping his eyes open as he went. Near and far he heard jays screaming one to the other, and wood-pigeons went clattering up out of the leaves into the sun. Ever and again, too, the hollow tapping of a woodpecker sounded out in the silence, or its wild echoing laughter, and once he edged along a glade just in time to see a herd of deer fleeting in a multitude before him at sight and scent of man. They sped soundlessly out of view across the open glade into covert. And still John kept steadily on, lifting his nose every now and again to sniff the air; for his fisherman's wits had hinted that water was near.

And he came at length to a gentle slope waist-high

with spicy bracken, and at its crest found himself looking down on the waters of a deep and gentle stream flowing between its hollow mossy banks in the dingle below him. "Aha!" cried John out loud to himself; and the sound of his voice rang so oddly in the air that he whipped round and stared about him as if somebody else had spoken. But there was sign neither of man nor bird nor beast. All was still again. So he cautiously made his way down to the bank of the stream and began to fish.

For an hour or more he fished in vain. The trees grew thicker on the further bank, and the water was deep and dark and slow. None the less, though he could see none, he knew in his bones that it was fairly alive with fish. Yet not a single one of them had as yet cheated him even with a nibble. Still, John had often fished half a day through without getting so much as a bite, and so long as the water stole soundlessly on beneath him and he could watch the reflection of the tree boughs and of the drifts of blue sky between them in this dark looking-glass, he was happy and at ease. And then suddenly, as if to mock him, a fish with a dappled green back and silver belly and of a kind he never remembered to have seen before, leapt clean out of the water about three yards from his green and white float, seemed to stare at him a moment with fishy lidless eyes, and at once plunged back into the water again. Whether it was the mere noise of its water-splash, or whether the words had actually sounded from out of its gaping jaws he could not say, but it certainly seemed as if before it vanished he had heard a strange voice cry, "Ho, there! John! . . . Try lower down!"

He laughed to himself; then listened. Biding a bit, he clutched his rod a little tighter, and keeping a more cautious look-out than ever on all sides of him, he followed the flow of the water, pausing every now and again to make a cast. And still not a single fish seemed so much as to have seen, sniffed or even sneered at his bait, while yet the gaping mouths of those leaping up out of the water beyond his reach seemed to utter the same hollow and watery-sounding summons he had heard before: "Ho, John! Ho! Ho, you, John Cobbler, there! Try lower down!" So much indeed were these fish like fish enchanted that John began to wish he had kept to his old haunts and had not ventured over the wall; or that he had at least told his mother where he meant to be. Supposing he never came back? Where would she be looking for him? Where? Where? And all she had asked for, and perhaps for his own sake only, was a fish supper!

The water was now flowing more rapidly in a glass-green heavy flood, and before he was ready for it John suddenly found himself staring up at the walls of a high dark house with but two narrow windows in the stone surface that steeped up into the sky above. And the very sight of the house set his heart beating faster. He was afraid. Beyond this wall to the right showed the old grey stones of lesser buildings, and moss-clotted fruit trees gone to leaf. Busying to and fro above the roof were scores of choughs and jackdaws, their jangled cries sounding out even above the roaring of the water, for now close beneath them the stream narrowed to gush in beneath a low-rounded arch in the wall, and so into the silence and darkness beyond it.

Two thoughts had instantly sprung up in John's mind as he stared up at this strange solitary house. One that it must be bewitched, and the other that except for its birds and the fish in its stream it was forsaken and empty. He laid his rod down on the green bank and stole from one tree trunk to another to get a better view, making up his mind that if he had time he would skirt his way round the walled garden that he could see, but would not yet venture into the open on the other side of the house.

It was marvellously quiet in this dappled sunshine, and John decided to rest awhile before venturing further. Seating himself under a tree he opened his handkerchief, and found not only the hunch of bread and cheese he had packed in it, but a fat sausage and some cockled apples which his mother must have put in afterwards. He was ravenously hungry, and keeping a wary eye on the two dark windows from under the leaves over his head, he continued to munch. And as he munched, the jack-daws, their black wings silvered by the sun, continued to jangle, and the fish silently to leap up out of their watery haunts and back again, their eyes glassily fixed on him as they did so, and the gathering water continued to gush steadily in under the dark rounded tunnel beneath the walls of the house.

But now as John listened and watched he fancied that above all these sounds interweaving themselves into a gentle chorus of the morning, he caught the faint strains as of a voice singing in the distance—and a sweet voice too. But water, as he knew of old, is a curious deceiver of the ear. At times as you listen to it, it will sound as if drums and dulcimers are ringing in its depths; at times as if fingers are plucking on the strings of a harp, or invisible mouths calling. John stopped eating to listen more intently.

And soon there was no doubt left in his mind, that this was no mere water noise, but the singing of a human voice, and that not far away. It came as if from within the walls of the house itself, but he could not detect any words to the song. It glided on from note to note as though it were an unknown bird piping in the first cold winds of April after its sea-journey from Africa to English shores; and though he did not know it, his face, as he listened, puckered up almost as if he were a child again and was going to cry.

He had heard tell of the pitiless sirens, and of sea-wandering mermaids, and of how they sing among their island rocks, or couched on the oceanic strands of their sunny islands, where huge sea-fish disport themselves in the salt waters: porpoise and dolphin, through billows clear as glass, and green and blue as precious stones. His mother too had told him as a child—and like Simple Simon himself he had started fishing in her pail!—what danger there may be in listening to such voices; how even sailors have stopped up their ears with wax lest they should be enticed by this music to the isles of the sirens and never sail home again. But though John remembered this warning, he continued to listen, and an intense desire came over him to discover who this secret singer was, and where she lay hid. He might peep perhaps, he thought to himself, through some lattice or cranny in the dark walls and not be seen.

But although he stole on, now in shadow, now in sun, pushing his way through the tangled brambles and briars, the bracken and bryony that grew close in even under the walls of the house, he found—at least on this side of it—no doorway or window or even slit in the masonry through which to look in. And he came back at last, hot, tired and thirsty to the bank of the stream where he had left his rod.

And even as he knelt down to drink by the waterside, the voice, which had been silent awhile, began to sing again, as sad as it was sweet; and not more than an arm's length from his stooping face a great fish leapt out of the water, its tail bent almost double, its goggling eyes fixed on him, and out of its hook-toothed mouth it cried, "*A-whoof! Oo-ougoolkawott!*" That at least to John was what it seemed to say. And having delivered its message, it fell back again into the dark water and in a wild eddy was gone. Startled by this sudden noise John drew quickly back, and in so doing dislodged a large moss-greened stone on the bank, which rolled clattering down to its plunge into the stream; and the singing again instantly ceased. He glanced back over his shoulder at the high wall and vacant windows, and out of the silence that had again descended he heard in mid-day a mournful hooting as of an owl, and a cold terror swept over him. He leapt to his feet, seized his rod and creel, hastily tied up what was left of his lunch in his red-spotted handkerchief, and instantly set out for home. Nor did he once look back until the house was hidden from view. Then his fear vanished, and he began to be heartily ashamed of himself.

And since he had by now come into sight of another loop of the stream, he decided, however long it took him, to fish there until he had at least caught *something*—if only a stickleback—so that he should not disappoint his mother of the supper she longed for. The minnow smeared with pork marrow which he had been using for bait on his hook was already dry. None the less he flung it into the stream, and almost before the float touched the water a swirl of ripples came sweeping from the further bank, and a greedy pike, grey and silver, at least two feet long if he was an inch, had instantly gobbled down bait and hook. John could hardly believe his own eyes. It was as if it had been actually lying in wait to be caught. He stooped to look into its strange motionless eye as it lay on the grass at his feet. Sullenly it stared back at him as though, even if it had only a minute or two left to live in, it were trying to give him a message, yet one that he could not understand.

Happy at heart, he stayed no longer. Yet with every mile of his journey home the desire grew in him to return to the house, if only to hear again that doleful voice singing from out of the darkness within its walls. But he told his mother nothing about his adventures, and the two of them sat down to as handsome a dish of fish for supper as they had ever tasted.

"What's strange to me, John," said his mother at last, for they had talked very little, being so hungry, "is that though this fish here is a pike, and cooked as usual, with a picking of thyme and marjoram, a bit of butter, a squeeze of lemon and some chopped shallots, there's a good deal more to him than just that. There's a sort of savour and sweetness to him, as if he had been daintily fed. Where did you catch him, John?"

But at this question John was seized by such a fit of coughing—as if a bone had stuck in his throat—that it seemed at any moment he might choke. And when his mother had stopped thumping him on his back she had forgotten what she had asked him. With her next mouthful, too, she had something else to think about; and it was fortunate that she had such a neat strong row of teeth, else the crunch she gave to it would certainly have broken two or three of them in half.

"Excusing me, John," she said, and drew out of her mouth not a bone, but something tiny, hard and shiny, which after being washed under the kitchen tap proved to be a key. It was etched over with figures of birds and beasts and fishes, that might be all ornament or might, thought John, his cheeks red as beetroot, be a secret writing.

"Well I never! Brass!" said his mother, staring at the key in the palm of her hand.

"Nor didn't I," said John. "I'll take if off to the blacksmith's at once, mother, and see what he makes of it."

Before she could say Yes or No to this, John was gone. In half an hour he was back again.

"He says, mother," said he, "it's a key, mother; and not brass but solid gold. A gold key! Whoever? And in a fish!"

"Well, John," said his mother, who was a little sleepy after so hearty a supper, "I never—mind you—did see much good in fishing except the fish, but if there are any more gold keys where that pike came from, let's both get up early, and we'll soon be as rich as Old Creatures."

John needed no telling. He was off next morning long before the sun had begun to gild the dewdrops in the meadows, and he found himself, rod, creel and bait, under the magician's wall a good three hours before noon. There was not a cloud in the sky. The stream flowed quiet as molten glass, reflecting the towering forest trees, the dark stone walls, and the motionless flowers and grass-blades at its brim. John stood there gazing awhile into the water, just as if to-day were yesterday over again, then sat himself down on the bank and fell into a kind of daydream, his rod idle at his side. Neither fish nor key nor the freshness of the morning nor any wish or thought was in his mind, but only a longing to hear again the voice of the secret one. And the shadows around him had crept less even than an inch on their daily round, and a cuckoo under the hollow sky had but thrice cuckoo'd in some green dell of the forest, when there slid up into the air the very notes that had haunted him, waking and sleeping, ever since they had first fallen on his ear. They rang gently on and on, in the hush, clear as a cherub in some quiet gallery of paradise, and John knew in his heart that she who sang was no longer in fear of his company, but out of her solitude was beseeching his aid.

He rose to his feet, and once more searched the vast frowning walls above his head. Nothing there but the croaking choughs and jackdaws among the chimneys, and a sulphur-coloured butterfly wavering in flight along the darkness of their stones. They filled him with

dread, these echoing walls; and still the voice pined on.
And at last he fixed his eyes on the dark arch beneath
which coursed in heavy leaden flow the heaped-up
volume of the stream. No way in, indeed! Surely, where
water could go, mightn't *he*?

Without waiting a moment to consider the dangers
that might lie in wait for him in the dark flood beneath
the walls, he had slipped out of his coat and shoes and had
plunged in. He swam on with the stream until he was
within a little way of the yawning arch; then took a deep
breath and dived down and down. When he could hold
it no longer he slipped up out of the water—and in the
nick of time. He had clutched something as he came to
the surface, and found himself in a dusky twilight, looking up from the foot of a narrow flight of stone steps—
with a rusty chain dangling down the middle of it. He
hauled himself up out of the water and sat down a
moment to recover his breath, then made his way up the
steps. At the top he came to a low stone corridor. There
he stayed again.

But here the voice was more clearly to be heard. He
hastened down the corridor and came at last to a high
narrow room full of sunlight from the window in its
walls looking out over the forest. And, reclining there
by the window, the wan green light shining in on her
pale face and plaited copper-coloured hair, was what
John took at first to be a mermaid; and for the very good
reason that she had a human head and body, but a fish's
tail. He stayed quite still, gazing at her, and she at him,
but he could think of nothing to say. He merely kept his
mouth open in case any words should come, while the

water-drops dripped from his clothes and hair on to the
stone flags around him. And when the lips in the fair
small face of this strange creature began to speak to him,
he could hardly make head or tail of the words. Indeed
she had been long shut up alone in this old mansion from
which the magician who had given her her fish's tail, so
that she should not be able to stray from the house, had
some years gone his way, never to come back. She had
now almost forgotten her natural language. But there is
a music in the voice that tells more to those who understand it than can any words in a dictionary. And it didn't
take John very long to discover that this poor fish-tailed
creature, with nothing but the sound of her own sad
voice to comfort her, was mortally unhappy; that all she
longed for was to rid herself of her cold fish's tail, and so
win out into the light and sunshine again, freed from the
spell of the sorcerer who had shut her up in these stone
walls.

John sat down on an old wooden stool that stood beside the table, and listened. And now and then he himself
sighed deep and nodded. He learned—though he learned
it very slowly—that the only company she had was a deaf
old steward who twice every day, morning and evening,
brought her food and water, and for the rest of the time
shut himself up in a tower on the further side of the house
looking out over the deserted gardens and orchards that
once had flourished with peach and quince and apricot
and all the roses of Damascus. Else, she said, sighing, she
was always alone. And John, as best he could, told her in
turn about himself and about his mother. "She'd help
you all she could to escape away from here—I know *that*,

if so be she *could*. The only question is, How? Since, you
see, first it's a good long step for mother to come and
there's no proper way over the wall, and next if she managed it, it wouldn't be easy with nothing but a tail to
walk on. I mean, lady, for *you* to walk on." At this he
left his mouth open, and looked away, afraid that he
might have hurt her feelings. And in the same moment
he bethought himself of the key, which if he had not
been on the verge of choking, his mother might have
swallowed in mistake for a mouthful of fish. He took it
out of his breeches' pocket and held it up towards the
window, so that the light should shine on it. And at
sight of it it seemed that something between grief and
gladness had suddenly overcome the poor creature with
the fish's tail, for she hid her face in her fingers and wept
aloud.

This was not much help to poor John. With his idle
ways and love of fishing, he had been a sad trial at times
to his mother. But she, though little to look at, was as
brave as a lion, and if ever she shed tears at all, it was in
secret. This perhaps was a pity, for if John had but once
seen her cry he might have known what to do now. All
that he actually did do was to look very glum himself
and turn his eyes away. And as they roved slowly round
the bare walls he perceived what looked like the crack of
a little door in the stones and beside it a tiny keyhole.
The one thing in the world he craved was to comfort
this poor damsel with the fish's tail, to persuade her to
dry her eyes and smile at him. But as nothing he could
think to say could be of any help, he tiptoed across and
examined the wall more closely. And cut into the stone

above the keyhole he read the four letters—*C.A.V.E.!*
What they meant John had no notion, except that a cave
is something hollow—and usually empty. Still, since
here was a lock and John had a key, he naturally put
the key into the lock with his clumsy fingers to see
if it would fit. He gave the key a gentle twist. And
lo and behold, there came a faint click. He tugged,
drew the stone out upon its iron hinges, and looked
inside.

What he had expected to see he did not know. All that
was actually within this narrow stone cupboard was a
little green pot, and beside it a scrap of what looked like
parchment, but was actually monkey skin. John had
never been much of a scholar at his books. He was a
dunce. When he was small he had liked watching the
clouds and butterflies and birds flitting to and fro and the
green leaves twinkling in the sun, and found frogs and
newts and sticklebacks and minnows better company
than anything he could read in print on paper. Still he
had managed at last to learn all his letters and even to
read, though he read so slowly that he sometimes forgot
the first letters of a long word before he had spelled out
the last. He took the piece of parchment into the light,
held it tight between his fingers, and, syllable by syllable,
muttered over to himself what it said—leaving the
longer words until he had more time.

And now the pale-cheeked creature reclining by the
window had stopped weeping, and between the long
strands of her copper hair was watching him through
her tears. And this is what John read:

THE LORD FISH

Thou who wouldst dare
To free this Fair
From fish's shape,
And yet escape
O'er sea and land
My vengeful hand:—
Smear this fish-fat on thy heart,
And prove thyself the jack thou art!

With tail and fin
Then plunge thou in!
And thou shalt surely have thy wish
To see the great, the good Lord Fish!

Swallow his bait in haste, for he
Is master of all wizardry.
And if he gentle be inclined,
He'll show thee where to seek and find
The Magic Unguent that did make
This human maid a fish-tail take.

But have a care
To make short stay
Where wields his sway,
The great Lord Fish;
'Twill be too late
To moan your fate
When served with sauce
Upon his dish!

John read this doggerel once, he read it twice, and
though he couldn't understand it all even when he read

it a third time, he understood a good deal of it. The one thing he could not discover, though it seemed the most important, was what would happen to him if he did as the rhyme itself bade him do—smear the fish-fat over his heart. But this he meant to find out.

And why not at once, thought John, though, except when he hooked a fish, he was seldom as prompt as that. He folded up the parchment very small, and slipped it into his breeches' pocket. Then imitating as best he could the motion of descending the steps and diving into the water, he promised the maid he would return to her the first moment he could, and entreated her not to sing again until he came back. "Because . . ." he began, but could get no further. At which, poor mortal, she began to weep again, making John, for very sadness to see her, only the more anxious to be gone. So he took the little pot out of the stone cupboard, and giving her for farewell as smiling and consoling a bob of his head as he knew how, hurried off along the long narrow corridor, and so down the steep stone steps to the water.

There, having first very carefully felt with his fingertips exactly where his heart lay beating, he dipped his finger into the green ointment and rubbed it over his ribs. And with that, at once, a dreadful darkness and giddiness swept over him. He felt his body narrowing and shortening and shrinking and dwindling. His bones were drawing themselves together inside his skin; his arms and legs ceased at last to wave and scuffle, his eyes seemed to be settling into his head. The next moment, with one convulsive twist of his whole body, he had fallen plump into the water. There he lay awhile in a motionless horror. Then he began to stir again, and after a few black dreadful moments found himself coursing along so swiftly that in a trice he was out from under the arch and into the green gloaming of the stream beyond it. Never before had he slipped through the water with such ease. And no wonder!

For when he twisted himself about to see what had happened to him, a sight indeed met his eye. Where once had been arms were now small blunt fins. A gristly little blunted beard hung on either side of his mouth. His short dumpy body was of a greeny brown, and for human legs he could boast of nothing now but a fluted wavering tail. If he had been less idle in his young days he might have found himself a fine mottled trout, a barbel, a mullet, or a lively eel, or being a John he might well have become a jack. But no, he was fisherman enough to recognise himself at sight—a common tench, and not a very handsome one either! A mere middling fish, John judged. At this horrifying discovery, though the rhyme should have warned him of it, shudder after shudder ran along his backbone and he dashed blindly through the water as if he were out of his senses. Where could he hide himself? How flee away? What would his mother say to him? And alackaday, what had become of the pot of ointment? "Oh mercy me, oh misery me!" he moaned within himself, though not the faintest whisper sounded from his bony jaws.

He plunged on deeper and deeper, and at length, nuzzling softly the sandy bed of the stream with his blunt fish's snout, he hid his head between two boulders at the bottom. There, under a net of bright green water-weed, he lay for a while utterly still, brooding again on his mother and on what her feelings would be if she should see him no more—or in the shape he was! Would that he had listened to her counsel, and had never so much as set eyes on rod or hook or line or float or water. He had wasted his young days in fishing, and now was fish for evermore.

But as the watery moments sped by, this grief and despondency began to thin away and remembrance of the crafty and cruel magician came back to mind. Whatever he might look like from outside, John began to be himself again within. Courage, even a faint gleam of hope, welled back into his dull fish's brains. With a flick of his tail he had drawn back out of the gloomy cranny between the boulders, and was soon disporting himself but a few inches below the surface of the stream, the sunlight gleaming golden on his scales, the cold blood coursing through his body, and but one desire in his heart.

These high spirits indeed almost proved the end of him. For at this moment a prowling and hungry pike having from its hiding-place spied this plump young tench, came flashing through the water like an arrow from a bow, and John escaped the snap of its sharp-toothed jaws by less than half an inch. And when on land he had always supposed that the tench who is the fishes' doctor was safe from any glutton! After this dizzying experience he swam on more heedfully, playing a kind of hide-and-seek among the stones and weeds, and nibbling every now and again at anything he found to his taste. And the world of trees and sky in which but a few hours before he had walked about on his two human

legs was a very strange thing to see from out of the
rippling and distorting wavelets of the water.

When evening began to darken overhead he sought
out what seemed to be a safe lair for the night, and must
soon have fallen into a long and peaceful fish's sleep—a
queer sleep too, for having no lids to his eyes they both
remained open, whereas even a hare when he is asleep
shuts only one!

Next morning very early John was about again. A
south wind must be blowing, he fancied, for there was a
peculiar mildness and liveliness in the water, and he
snapped at every passing tit-bit carried along by the
stream with a zest and hunger that nothing could satisfy.
Poor John, he had never dreamed a drowned fly or bee
or a grub or caterpillar, or even water-weed, could taste
so sweet. But then he had never tried to find out. And
presently, dangling only a foot or two above his head, he
espied a particularly juicy-looking and wriggling red
worm.

Now though, as has been said already, John as a child,
or even as a small boy, had refrained from tasting cater-
pillars or beetles or snails or woodlice, he had once—
when making mud pies in his mother's garden—nibbled
at a little earth-worm. But he had not nibbled much. For
this reason only perhaps, he stayed eyeing this wriggling
coral-coloured morsel above his head. Memory too had
told him that it is not a habit of worms to float wriggling
in the water like this. And though at sight of it he grew
hungrier and hungrier as he finned softly on, he had the
good sense to cast a glance up out of the water. And there
—lank and lean upon the bank above—he perceived the

strangest shape in human kind he had ever set eyes on. This bony old being had scarcely any shoulders. His grey glassy eyes bulged out of his head above his flat nose. A tuft of beard hung from his cod-like chin, and the hand that clutched his fishing-rod was little else but skin and bone.

"Now," thought John to himself, as he watched him steadily from out of the water, "if that old rascal there ain't the Lord Fish in the rhyme, I'll eat my buttons." Which was an easy thing to promise, since at this moment John hadn't any buttons to eat. It was by no means so easy to make up his hungry fishy mind to snap at the worm and chance what might come after. He longed beyond words to be home again; he longed be-yond words to get back into his own body again—but only (and John seemed to be even stubborner as a fish than he had been as a human), *only* if the beautiful lady could be relieved of her tail. And how could there be hope of any of these things if he gave up this chance of meeting the Lord Fish and of finding the pot of "un-guent" he had read of in the rhyme? The other had done its work with him quick enough!

If nothing had come to interrupt these cogitations, John might have cogitated too long. But a quick-eyed perch had at this moment finned into John's pool and had caught sight of the savoury morsel wiggling and waggling in the glass-clear water. At very first glimpse of him John paused no longer. With gaping jaws and one mad swirl of his fish-tail he sprang at the worm. A dart of pain flashed through his body. He was whirled out of the water and into the air. He seemed on the point of suffocation. And the next instant found him gasping and floundering in the lush green grass that grew beside the water's brink. But the old angler who had caught him was even more skilful in the craft of fishing than John Cobbler was himself. Almost before John could sob twice, the hook had been extracted from his mouth, he had been swathed up from head to tail in cool green moss, a noose had been slipped around that tail, and poor John, dangling head downwards from the fisherman's long skinny fingers, was being lugged away he knew not where. Few, fogged and solemn were the thoughts that passed through his gaping, gasping head on this dismal journey.

Now the Lord Fish who had caught him lived in a low stone house which was surrounded on three sides by a lake of water, and was not far distant from his master's— the Sorcerer. Fountains jetted in its hollow echoing chambers, and water lapped its walls on every side. Not even the barking of a fox or the scream of a peacock or any sound of birds could be heard in it; it was so full of the suffling and sighing, the music and murmuration of water, all day, all night long. But poor John being upside down had little opportunity to view or heed its marvels. And still muffled up in his thick green overcoat of moss he presently found himself suspended by his tail from a hook in the Lord Fish's larder, a long cool dusky room or vault with but one window to it, and that only a hole in the upper part of the wall. This larder too was of stone, and apart from other fish as luckless as John who hung there gaping from their hooks, many more, plumper and heavier than he, lay still and cold on the slate-slab shelves around him. Indeed if he could have done so, he might have hung his head a little lower at being so poor a fish by comparison.

Now there was a little maid who was in the service of this Lord Fish. She was the guardian of his larder. And early next morning she came in and set about her day's work. John watched her without ceasing. So fish-like was the narrow face that looked out from between the grey-green plaits of her hair that he could not even guess how old she was. She might, he thought, be twelve; she *might*, if age had not changed her much, be sixty. But he guessed she must be about seventeen. She was not of much beauty to human eyes—so abrupt was the slope of her narrow shoulders, so skinny were her hands and feet.

First she swept out the larder with a besom and flushed it out with buckets of water. Then, with an earthenware watering pot, and each in turn, she sprinkled the moss and weed and grasses in which John and his fellows were enwrapped. For the Lord Fish, John soon discovered, devoured his fish raw, and liked them fresh. When one of them, especially of those on the shelves, looked more solemn and motionless than was good for him, she dipped him into a shallow trough of running water that lay outside the door of the larder. John indeed heard running water all day long—while he himself could scarcely flick a fin. And when all this was done, and it was done twice a day, the larder-maid each morning chose out one or two or even three of her handsomest fish and carried them off with her, John knew—to his horror—to what end.

But there were two things that gave him heart and

courage in this gruesome abode. The first was that after her second visit the larder-maid treated him with uncommon kindness. Perhaps there was a look on his face not quite like that of her other charges. For John with his goggling ogling eyes would try to twist up his poor fish face into something of a smile when she came near him, and—though very faintly—to waggle his tail tips, as if in greeting. However that might be, there was no doubt she had taken a liking to him. She not only gave him more of her fish-pap then she gave the rest, to fatten him up, but picked him out special dainties. She sprinkled him more slowly than the others with her water-pot so that he could enjoy the refreshment the more. And, after a quick, sly glance over her shoulder one morning she changed his place in the larder, and hung him up in a darker corner all to himself. Surely, surely, this must mean, John thought, that she wished to keep him as long as she could from sharing her master's table. John did his best to croak his thanks, but was uncertain if the larder-maid had heard.

This was one happy thing. His other joy was this. Almost as soon as he found himself safe in his corner, he had discovered that on a level with his head there stood on a shelf a number of jars and gallipots and jorams of glass and earthenware. In some were dried roots, in some what seemed to be hanks of grass, in others black-veined lily bulbs, or scraps of twig, or dried-up buds and leaves, like tea. John guessed they must be savourings his cook-maid kept for the Fish Lord to soak his fish in, and wondered sadly which, when his own turn came, would be his. But a little apart from the rest and not above eighteen inches from his nose, there stood yet another small glass jar, with greenish stuff inside it. And after many attempts and often with eyes too dry to read, John spelled out at last from the label of this jar these outlandish words: UNGUENTUM AD PISCES HOMINIBUS TRANSMOGRIFICANDOS. And he went over them again and again until he knew them by heart.

Now John had left school very early. He had taken up crow-scaring at seven, pig-keeping at nine, turnip-hoeing at twelve—though he had kept up none of them for very long. But even if John had stayed at school until he was grown up, he would never have learned any Latin —none at all, not even dog Latin—since the old dame who kept the village school at Tussock didn't know any herself. She could cut and come again as easily as you please with the cane she kept in her cupboard, but this had never done John much good, and she didn't know any Latin.

John's only certainty then, even when he had learned these words by heart, was that they were not good honest English words. Still, he had his wits about him. He remembered that there had been words like these written in red on the parchment over the top of the rhyme that now must be where his breeches were, since he had tucked it into his pocket—though where *that* was he hadn't the least notion. But *unguent* was a word he now knew as well as his own name; and it meant ointment. Not many months before this, too, he had mended a chair for a great lady that lived in a high house on the village green—a queer lady too though she was the youngest daughter of a marquis of those parts. It was

a job that had not taken John very long, and she was
mightily pleased with it. "Sakes, John," she had said,
when he had taken the chair back and put it down in the
light of a window, "sakes, John, what a *transmogrification!*" And John had blushed all over as he grinned back
at the lady, guessing that she meant that the chair
showed a change for the better.

Then, too, when he was a little boy, his mother had
often told him tales of the *piskies*. "Piskies", PISCES, muttered John to himself on his hook. It sounded even to *his*
ear poor spelling, but it would do. Then too, HOMINES.
If you make a full round O of the first syllable it sounds
uncommonly like *home*. So what the Lord Fish, John
thought at last, had meant by this lingo on his glass pot
must be that it contained an UNGUENT to which some
secret PISKY stuff or what is known as wizardry had been
added, and that it was useful for "changing" for the
better anything or anybody on which it was rubbed
when away from HOME. And nobody could call the
chamber in which the enchanted maid with the fish-tail
was kept shut up a *home*; even John himself at this
moment was a good many miles from his mother!

Besides the stuff in the glass pot was uncommonly like
the ointment which he had taken from the other pot and
had smeared on his ribs. After all this thinking John was
just clever enough to come to the conclusion that the one
unguent had been meant for turning humans into fish,
and that this in the pot beside him was for turning fish
into humans again. At this his flat eyes bulged indeed in
his head, and in spite of the moss around them his fins
stood out stiff as knitting needles. He gasped to himself,

like a tench out of water. And while he was still brooding on his discovery, the larder-maid opened the door of the larder with her iron key to set about her morning duties.

"*Ackh*," she called softly, hastening towards him, for now she never failed to visit him first of all her charges, "*ackh*, what's wrong with 'ee? What's amiss with 'ee?" and with her lean finger she gently stroked the top of his head, her narrow bony face crooked up with care at seeing this sudden change in his looks. She did not realise that it was not merely a change but a transmogrification! She sprinkled him twice, and yet a third time, with her ice-cold water, and with the tips of her small fingers pushed tiny gobbet after gobbet of milk-pap out of her basin into his mouth until John could swallow no more. Then with gaspings and gapings he fixed his nearer eye on the jar of unguent or ointment, gazed back rapidly at the little larder-maid, then once again upon the jar.

Now this larder-maid was a great-grandniece of the Lord Fish, and had learned a little magic. "Aha," she whispered, smiling softly and wagging her finger at him. "So that's what you are after, Master Tench? That's what you are after, you crafty Master Sobersides. Oh, what a scare you gave me!"

Her words rang out shrill as a whistle, and John's fellow fish, trussed up around him in their moss and grass and rushes on their dishes, or dangling from their hooks, trembled at sound of it. A faint chuffling, a lisping and quiet gaggling, tiny squeaks and groans filled the larder. John had heard these small noises before, and had supposed them to be fish talk, but though he had tried to imitate them he had never been sure of an answer. All he could do, then, was what he had done before—he fixed again his round glassy eye first on the jar and then on the little larder-maid, and this with as much gentle flattery and affection as he could manage. Just as when he was a child at his mother's knee he would coax her to give him a slice of bread pudding or a spoonful of jam.

"Now I wonder," muttered the larder-maid as if to herself, "if you, my dear, are the one kind or the other. And if you are the *other*, *shall* I, my gold-green Tinker, take the top off the jar?"

At this John wriggled might and main, chapping with his jaws as wide and loud as he could, looking indeed as if at any moment he might burst into song.

"Ah," cried the maid, watching him with delight, "he understands! That he does! But if I did, precious, what would my lord the Lord Fish say to me? What would happen to *me*, eh? You, Master Tench, I am afraid, are thinking only of your own comfort."

At this John sighed and hung limp as if in sadness and dudgeon and remorse. The larder-maid eyed him a few moments longer, then set about her morning work so quickly and with so intense a look on her lean narrow face, with its lank dangling tresses of green-grey hair, that between hope and fear John hardly knew how to contain himself. And while she worked on, sprinkling, feeding, scouring, dipping, she spoke to her charges in much the same way that a groom talks to his horses, a nurse to a baby, or a man to his dogs. At last, her work over, she hastened out of the larder and shut the door.

Now it was the habit of the Lord Fish on the Tuesdays, Thursdays and Saturdays of every week, to make the round of his larder, eyeing all it held, plump fish or puny, old or new, ailing or active; sometimes gently pushing his finger in under the moss to see how they were prospering for his table. This was a Thursday. And sure enough the larder-maid presently hastened back, and coming close whispered up at John, "Hst, he comes! The Lord Fish! Angry and hungry. Beware! Stay mum as mum can be, you precious thing. Flat and limp and sulky, look 'ee, for if the Lord Fish makes his choice of 'ee now, it is too late and all is over. And above all things, don't so much as goggle for a moment at that jar!"

She was out again like a swallow at nesting-time, and presently there came the sound of slow scraping foot-steps on the flagstones, and there entered the Lord Fish into the larder, the maid at his heels. He was no lord to look at, thought John; no marquis, anyhow. He looked as glum and sullen as some old Lenten cod in a fish-monger's, in his stiff drab-coloured overclothes. And John hardly dared to breathe, but hung—mouth open and eyes fixed—as limp and lifeless from his hook in the ceiling as he knew how.

"*Hoy, hoy, hoy,*" grumbled the Lord Fish, when at last he came into John's corner. "Here's a dullard. Here's a rack of bones. Here's a sandy gristle-trap. Here's a good-as-dead-and-gone-and-useless! Ay, now, my dear, you can't have seen him. Not this one. You must have let him go by, up there in the shadows. A quick eye, my dear, a quick watchful eye! He's nought but muddy sluggard tench 'tis true. But, oh yes, we can better him! He wants life, he wants exercise, he wants cossetting and feeding and *fattening*. And then—why then, there's the makings in him of as comely a platter of fish as would satisfy my Lord Bishop of the Seven Sturgeons himself." And the little larder-maid, her one hand clutching a swab of moss and the other demurely knuckled over her mouth, sedately nodded.

"Ay, master," said she, "he's hung up there in the shadows, he is. In the dark. He's a mumper, that one, he's a moper. He takes his pap but poorly. He shall have a washabout and a dose of sunshine in the trough. Trust me, master, I'll soon put a little life into him. Come next Saturday, now!"

"So, so, so," said the Lord Fish. And having made the round of John's companions he retired at last from out of his larder, well content with his morning's visit. And with but one quick reassuring nod at John over her narrow shoulder, his nimble larder-maid followed after him. John was safe until Saturday.

Hardly had the Lord Fish's scuffling footsteps died away when back came the little maid, wringing her hands in glee, and scarcely able to speak for laughing. "Ay, Master Tench, did you hear that? 'Up there in the shadows. Here's a dullard; here's a rack of bones; here's a gristle-trap. He wants cossetting and feeding and fattening.' Did he not now? Was I sly, was I cunning? Did the old Lord nibble my bait, Master Tench? Did he *not* now? Oho, my poor beautiful; fatten, indeed!" And she lightly stroked John's snout again. "What's wrong with the old Lord Fish is that he eats too much and sleeps too long. Come 'ee now, let's make no more ado about it."

She dragged up a wooden stool that stood close by, and, holding her breath, with both hands she carefully lifted down the jar of green fat or grease or unguent. Then she unlatched John from his hook, and laid him gently on the stone slab beside her, bidding him meanwhile have no fear at all of what might happen. She stripped off his verdant coat of moss, and, dipping her finger in the ointment, smeared it on him, from the nape of his neck clean down his spine to the very tip of his tail.

For a few moments John felt like a cork that, after bobbing softly along down a softly-flowing river, is suddenly drawn into a roaring whirlpool. He felt like a firework squib when the gushing sparks are nearly all out of it and it is about to burst. Then gradually the fog in his eyes and the clamour in his ears faded and waned away, and lo and behold, he found himself returned safe and sound into his own skin, shape and appearance again. There he stood in the Lord Fish's fish larder, grinning down out of his cheerful face at the maid who in stature reached not much above his elbow.

"Ah," she cried, peering up at him out of her small water-clear eyes, and a little dazed and dazzled herself at this transmogrification. "So you *were* the other kind, Master Tench!" And the larder-maid looked at him so sorrowfully and fondly that poor John could only blush and turn away. "And now," she continued, "all you will be wanting, I suppose, is to be gone. I beseech you then make haste and be off, or my own skin will pay for it."

John had always been a dullard with words. But he thanked the larder-maid for all she had done for him as best he could. And he slipped from off his little finger a silver ring which had belonged to his father, and put it into the palm of the larder-maid's hand; for just as when he had been changed into a fish, all his clothes and everything about him had become fish itself, so now when he was transformed into human shape again, all that had then been his returned into its own place, even to the parchment in his breeches' pocket. Such it seems is the law of enchantment. And he entreated the maid, if ever she should find herself on the other side of the great wall, to ask for the village of Tussock, and when she came to Tussock to ask for Mrs. Cobbler.

"That's my mother," said John, "is Mrs. Cobbler. And she'll be mighty pleased to see you, I promise you. And so will I."

The larder-maid looked at John. Then she took the ring between finger and thumb, and with a sigh pushed it into a cranny between the slabs of stone for a hiding-place. "Stay there," she whispered to the ring, "and I'll come back to 'ee anon."

Then John, having nothing else handy, and knowing that for the larder-maid's sake he must leave the pot behind him, took out of the fob in his breeches' pocket a great silver watch that had belonged to his grandfather. It was nothing now but a watch *case*, since he had one day taken out the works in hopes to make it go better, and had been too lazy to put them back again. Into this case he smeared as much of the grease out of the pot as it would hold.

"And now, Master Tench, this way," said the larder-maid, twisting round on him. "You must be going, and you must be going for good. Follow that wall as far as it leads you, and then cross the garden where the Lord Fish grows his herbs. You will know it by the scent of them in the air. Climb the wall and go on until you come to the river. Swim across that, and turn sunwards while it is morning, The Lord Fish has the nose of a she-wolf. He'd smell 'ee out across a bean field. Get you gone at once then, and meddle with him no more. Ay, and I know it is not on *me* your thoughts will be thinking when you get to safety again."

John, knowing no other, stooped down and kissed this little wiseacre's lean cold fingers, and casting one helpless and doleful look all about the larder at the fish on hook and slab, and seeing none, he fancied, that could possibly be in the same state as himself, hastened out.

There was no missing his way. The Lord Fish's walls and water conduits were all of stone so solid that they might have been built by the Romans, though, truly, they were chiefly of magic, which has nothing to do with time. John hurried along in the morning sunshine, and came at length to the stream. With his silver watch between his teeth for safety he swam to the other side. Here grew very tall rough spiny reeds and grasses, some seven to nine feet high. He pushed his way through them, heedless of their clawing and rasping, and only just in time. For as soon as he was safely hidden in the low bushes beyond them, whom did he now see approaching on the other side of the stream, rod in hand, and creel at his elbow, but the Lord Fish himself—his lank face erected up into the air and his nose sniffing the morning as if it were laden with the spices of Arabia. The larder-maid had told the truth indeed. For at least an hour the Lord Fish stood there motionless on the other side of the stream immediately opposite John's hiding-place. For at least an hour he pried and peeped about him, gently sniffing on. And, though teased by flies and stung with nettles, John dared not stir a finger. At last even the Lord Fish grew weary of watching and waiting, and John, having seen him well out of sight, continued on his way. . . .

What more is there to tell? Sad and sorrowful had been the maid's waiting for him, sad beyond anything else in the fish-tailed damsel's memory even, for since she had so promised him, she had not even been able to sing to keep herself company. But when seventeen days after he had vanished, John plunged in again under the stone arch and climbed the steep stone steps to her chamber, he spent no time in trying to find words and speeches that would not come. Having opened the glass of his watch, he just knelt down beside her, and said, "*Now*, if you please, lady. If you can keep quite still, I will be quick. If only *I* could bear the pain I'd do it three times over, but I promise 'ee it's soon gone." And with his finger he gently smeared the magic unguent on the maid's tail down at last to the very tip.

Life is full of curiosities, and curious indeed it was that though at one moment John's talk to the enchanted creature had seemed to her little better than Double Dutch, and she could do his bidding only by the signs he had made to her, at the next they were chattering together as

381

merrily as if they had done nothing else all their lives. But they did not talk for long, since of a sudden there came the clatter of oars, and presently a skinny hand was thrust over the window-sill, and her daily portion of bread and fruit and water was laid out on the sill. The sound of the Lord Fish's "Halloo!" when he had lowered his basket into the boat made the blood run cold again in John's body. He waited only until the rap and griding of the oars had died away. Then he took the maid by the hand, and they went down the stone steps together. There they plunged into the dark water, and presently found themselves breathless but happy beyond words seated together on the green grass bank in the afternoon sunshine. And there came such a chattering and cawing from the rooks and jackdaws over their heads that it seemed as if they were giving thanks to see them there. And when John had shaken out the coat he had left under the tree seventeen days before, brushed off the mildew, and dried it in the sun, he put it over the maid's shoulders.

It was long after dark when they came to Tussock, and not a soul was to be seen in the village street or on the green. John looked in through the window at his mother. She sat alone by the hearthside, staring into the fire, and it seemed to her that she would never get warm again. When John came in and she was clasped in his arms, first she thought she was going to faint, then she began to cry a little, and then to scold him as she had never scolded him before. John dried her tears and hushed her scoldings. And when he had told her a little of his story, he brought the maid in. And John's mother first bobbed her a curtsey, then kissed her and made her welcome. And she listened to John's story all over again from the beginning to the end before they went to bed—though John's bed that night was an old armchair.

Now before the bells of Tussock church—which was a small one and old—rang out a peal for John's and the fish-maid's wedding, he set off as early as ever one morning to climb the wall again. In their haste to be gone from the Sorcerer's mansion she had left her belongings behind her, and particularly, she told John, a leaden box or casket, stamped with a great A—for Almanara; that being her name.

Very warily John stripped again, and, diving quietly, swam in under the stone arch. And lo, safe and sound, in the far corner of the room of all her grief and captivity, stood the leaden casket. But when he stooped to lift it, his troubles began. It was of lead and it was heavy, and to swim with it on his shoulders would be to swim to the bottom! He sat awhile and pondered, and at last climbed up to the stone window, carved curiously with flowers and birds and fish, and looked out. Water lay beneath him in a moat afloat with lilies, though he couldn't tell how deep. But by good fortune a knotted rope hung from a hook in the window sill—for the use, no doubt, of the Lord Fish in his boat. John hauled the rope in, tied one end of it to the ring in the leaden casket and one to a small wooden stool. At last after long heaving and hoisting he managed to haul the casket on to the sill. He pushed it over, and—as lively as a small pig—away went the stool after it. John clambered up to the window again and again looked out. The stool, still bobbing, floated on the water beneath him. Only a deeper quiet had followed the splash of the casket. So, after he had dragged it out of the moat and on to the bank, John ventured on beyond the walls of the great house in search of the Lord Fish's larder. He dearly wanted to thank the larder-maid again. When at last he found it, it was all shut up and deserted. He climbed up to the window and looked in, but quickly jumped down again, for every fish that hung inside it hung dead as mutton. The little larder-maid was gone. But whether she had first used the magic unguent on the Lord Fish himself and then in dismay of what followed had run away, or whether she had tried it on them both and now was what John couldn't guess, he never knew and could never discover. He grieved—not to see her again, and always thought of her with kindness.

Walking and resting, walking and resting, it took him three days, even though he managed to borrow a wheel-barrow for the last two miles, to get the casket home. But it was worth the trouble. When he managed at last to prize the lid open, it was as though lumps of a frozen rainbow had suddenly spilled over in the kitchen, the casket was crammed so full of precious stones. And after the wedding Almanara had a great J punched into the lead of the box immediately after her great A—since now what it held belonged to them both.

But though John was now married, and not only less idle, but as happy as a kingfisher, *still* when the sweet south wind was blowing, and the leaves were green on the trees, and the birds in song, he could not keep his thoughts from hankering after water. So sometimes he made himself a little paste or dug up a few worms, and went off fishing. But he made two rules, which he *kept*. First, whenever he hooked anything—and especially a tench—he would always smear a speck or two of the unguent out of his grandfather's silver watch-case on the top of its head; and next, having made sure that his fish was fish, wholly fish, and nothing but fish, he would put it back into the water again. As for the ruinous mansion of the Sorcerer and the Lord Fish, he had made a vow to Almanara and to his mother that he would never never go fishing *there*. And he never did.

WALTER DE LA MARE

THE STRANGE VISITOR

A wife was sitting at her reel[1] ae[2] night;
    And aye she sat, and aye she reeled, and aye she
      wished for company.

In came a pair o' braid braid soles, and sat down at the
      fireside;
    And aye she sat, and aye she reeled, and aye she
      wished for company.

In came a pair o' sma' sma' legs, and sat down on the
      braid braid soles;
    And aye she sat, and aye she reeled, and aye she
      wished for company.

In came a pair o' muckle muckle knees, and sat down on
      the sma' sma' legs;
    And aye she sat, and aye she reeled, and aye she
      wished for company.

In came a pair o' sma' sma' thees[3], and sat down on the
      muckle muckle knees;
    And aye she sat, and aye she reeled, and aye she
      wished for company.

In came a pair o' muckle muckle hips, and sat down on
      the sma' sma' thees;
    And aye she sat, and aye she reeled, and aye she
      wished for company.

[1]Spooling off the yarn she was spinning.
[2]One.   [3]Thigh bones.

THE STRANGE VISITOR

In came a sma' sma' waist, and sat down on the muckle
  muckle hips;
  And aye she sat, and aye she reeled, and aye she
  wished for company.

In came a pair o' braid braid shouthers, and sat down
  on the sma' sma' waist;
  And aye she sat, and aye she reeled, and aye she
  wished for company.

In came a pair o' sma' sma' arms, and sat down on the
  braid braid shouthers;
  And aye she sat, and aye she reeled, and aye she
  wished for company.

In came a pair o' muckle muckle hands, and sat down on
  the sma' sma' arms;
  And aye she sat, and aye she reeled, and aye she
  wished for company.

In came a sma' sma' neck, and sat down on the braid
  braid shouthers;
  And aye she sat, and aye she reeled, and aye she
  wished for company.

In came a great big head, and sat down on the sma' sma'
  neck;
  And aye she sat, and aye she reeled, and aye she
  wished for company.

"What way[1] hae ye sic braid braid feet?" quo' the wife.
"Muckle ganging, muckle ganging."

[1]Why?

"What way hae ye sic sma' sma' legs?"
"*Aih-h-h!*—late—and *wee-e-e* moul."
"What way hae ye sic muckle muckle knees?"
"Muckle praying, muckle praying."
"What way hae ye sic sma' sma' thees?"
"*Aih-h-h!*—late—and *wee-e-e* moul."
"What way hae ye sic muckle, muckle hips?"
"Muckle sitting, muckle sitting."
"What way hae ye sic a sma' sma' waist?"
"*Aih-h-h!*—late—and *wee-e-e* moul."
"What way hae ye sic braid braid shouthers?"
"Wi' carrying broom, wi' carrying broom."
"What way hae ye sic sma' sma' arms?"
"*Aih-h-h!*—late—and *wee-e-e* moul."
"What way hae ye sic muckle muckle hands?"
"Threshing wi' an iron flail, threshing wi' an iron flail."
"What way hae ye sic a sma' sma' neck?"
"*Aih-h-h!*—late—and *wee-e-e* moul."
"What way hae ye sic a muckle muckle head?"
"Muckle wit, muckle wit."
"What do you come for?"
"For YOU!"

THE FATAL MERMAID

One Friday morn when we set sail,
    Not very far from land,
We there did espy a fair pretty maid
    With a comb and a glass in her hand,
        her hand, her hand,
    With a comb and a glass in her hand.
      While the raging seas did roar,
        And the stormy winds did blow,
      While we jolly sailor-boys were up into the top,
        And the land-lubbers lying down
          below, below, below,
        And the land-lubbers lying down
          below.

Then up starts the captain of our gallant ship,
    And a brave young man was he:
"I've a wife and a child in fair Bristol town,
    But a widow I fear she will be."
      While the raging seas, *etc.*

Then up starts the mate of our gallant ship,
    And a bold young man was he:
"Oh! I have a wife in fair Portsmouth town,
    But a widow I fear she will be."
      While the raging seas, *etc.*

Then up starts the cook of our gallant ship,
    And a gruff old soul was he:
"Oh! I have a wife in fair Plymouth town,
    But a widow I fear she will be."
      While the raging seas, *etc.*

THE FATAL MERMAID

And then up spoke the little cabin-boy,
    And a pretty little boy was he;
"Oh! I am more grieved for my daddy and my mammy
    Than you for your wives all three."
        While the raging seas, *etc.*

Then three times round went our gallant ship,
    And three times round went she;
For the want of a life-boat they all went down,
    And she sank to the bottom of the sea, the sea, the
      sea,
    And she sank to the bottom of the sea.
        While the raging seas did roar,
           And the stormy winds did blow,
        While we jolly sailor-boys were up into the
           top,
           And the land-lubbers lying down below,
           below, below,
           And the land-lubbers lying down below.

RUNNING WOLF

The man who enjoys an adventure outside the general experience of the race, and imparts it to others, must not be surprised if he is taken for either a liar or a fool, as Malcolm Hyde, hotel clerk on a holiday, discovered in due course. Nor is "enjoy" the right word to use in describing his emotions; the word he chose was probably "survive".

When he first set eyes on Medicine Lake he was struck by its still, sparkling beauty, lying there in the vast Canadian backwoods; next, by its extreme loneliness; and, lastly—a good deal later, this—by its combination of beauty, loneliness, and singular atmosphere, due to the fact that it was the scene of his adventure.

"It's fairly stiff with big fish," said Morton of the Montreal Sporting Club. "Spend your holiday there— up Mattawa way, some fifteen miles west of Stony Creek. You'll have it all to yourself except for an old Indian who's got a shack there. Camp on the east side—

if you'll take a tip from me." He then talked for half an hour about the wonderful sport; yet he was not otherwise very communicative, and did not suffer questions gladly, Hyde noticed. Nor had he stayed there very long himself. If it was such a paradise as Morton, its discoverer and the most experienced rod in the province, claimed, why had he himself spent only three days there?

"Ran short of grub," was the explanation offered; but to another friend he had mentioned briefly, "flies," and to a third, so Hyde learned later, he gave the excuse that his half-breed "took sick," necessitating a quick return to civilization.

Hyde, however, cared little for the explanations; his interest in these came later. "Stiff with fish" was the phrase he liked. He took the Canadian Pacific train to Mattawa, laid in his outfit at Stony Creek, and set off thence for the fifteen-mile canoe trip without a care in the world.

Travelling light, the portages did not trouble him; the water was swift and easy, the rapids negotiable; everything came his way, as the saying is. Occasionally he saw fish making for the deeper pools, and was sorely tempted to stop; but he resisted. He pushed on between the immense world of forests that stretched for hundreds of miles, known to deer, bear, moose, and wolf, but strange to any echo of human tread, a deserted and primeval wilderness. The autumn day was calm, the water sang and sparkled, the blue sky hung cloudless over all, ablaze with light. Toward evening he passed an old beaver-dam, rounded a little point, and had his first sight of Medicine Lake. He lifted his dripping paddle; the canoe shot with silent glide into calm water. He gave an exclamation of delight, for the loveliness caught his breath away.

Though primarily a sportsman, he was not insensible to beauty. The lake formed a crescent, perhaps four miles long, its width between a mile and half a mile. The slanting gold of sunset flooded it. No wind stirred its crystal surface. Here it had lain since the Redskin's god first made it; here it would lie until he dried it up again. Towering spruce and hemlock trooped to its very edge, majestic cedars leaned down as if to drink, crimson sumachs shone in fiery patches, and maples gleamed orange and red beyond belief. The air was like wine, with the silence of a dream.

It was here the Red man formerly "made medicine", with all the wild ritual and tribal ceremony of an ancient day. But it was of Morton, rather than of Indians, that Hyde thought. If this lonely, hidden paradise was really stiff with big fish, he owed a lot to Morton for the information. Peace invaded him, but the excitement of the hunter lay below.

He looked about him with quick, practised eye for a camping-place before the sun sank below the forests and the half-lights came. The Indian's shack, lying in full sunshine on the eastern shore, he found at once; but the trees lay too thick about it for comfort, nor did he wish to be so close to its inhabitant. Upon the opposite side, however, an ideal clearing offered. This lay already in shadow, the huge forest darkening it toward evening; but the open space attracted. He paddled over quickly and examined it. The ground was hard and dry, he found, and a little brook ran tinkling down on one side of it into the lake. This outfall, too, would be a good fishing spot. Also it was sheltered. A few low willows marked the mouth.

An experienced camper soon makes up his mind. It was a perfect site, and some charred logs, with traces of former fires, proved that he was not the first to think so. Hyde was delighted. Then, suddenly, disappointment came to tinge his pleasure. His kit was landed, and preparations for putting up the tent were begun, when he recalled a detail that excitement had so far kept in the background of his mind—Morton's advice. But not Morton's only, for the storekeeper at Stony Creek had reinforced it. The big fellow with straggling moustache and stooping shoulders, dressed in shirt and trousers, had handed him out a final sentence with the bacon, flour, condensed milk, and sugar. He had repeated Morton's half-forgotten words :

"Put yer tent on the east shore. I should," he had said at parting.

He remembered Morton, too, apparently. "A shortish fellow, brown as an Indian and fairly smelling of the woods. Travelling with Jake, the half-breed." That assuredly was Morton. "Didn't stay long, now, did he?" he added in a reflective tone.

"Going Windy Lake way, are yer? Or Ten Mile Water, maybe?" he had first inquired of Hyde.

"Medicine Lake."

"Is that so?" the man said, as though he doubted it for some obscure reason. He pulled at his ragged moustache a moment. "Is that so, now?" he repeated. And the final words followed him downstream after a considerable pause—the advice about the best shore on which to put his tent.

All this now suddenly flashed back upon Hyde's mind with a tinge of disappointment and annoyance, for when two experienced men agreed, their opinion was not to be lightly disregarded. He wished he had asked the storekeeper for more details. He looked about him, he reflected, he hesitated. His ideal camping-ground lay certainly on the forbidden shore. What in the world, he wondered, could be the objection to it?

But the light was fading; he must decide quickly one way or the other. After staring at his unpacked dunnage and the tent, already half erected, he made up his mind with a muttered expression that consigned both Morton and the storekeeper to less pleasant places. "They must have had *some* reason," he growled to himself; "fellows like that usually know what they're talking about. I guess I'd better shift over to the other side—for to-night, at any rate."

He glanced across the water before actually reloading. No smoke rose from the Indian's shack. He had seen no sign of a canoe. The man, he decided, was away. Reluctantly, then, he left the good camping-ground and paddled across the lake, and half an hour later his tent was up, firewood collected, and two small trout were already caught for supper. But the bigger fish, he knew, lay waiting for him on the other side by the little outfall, and he fell asleep at length on his bed of balsam boughs, annoyed and disappointed, yet wondering how a mere sentence could have persuaded him so easily against his own better judgment. He slept like the dead; the sun was well up before he stirred.

But his morning mood was a very different one. The brilliant light, the peace, the intoxicating air, all this was too exhilarating for the mind to harbour foolish fancies, and he marvelled that he could have been so weak the night before. No hesitation lay in him anywhere. He struck camp immediately after breakfast, paddled back across the strip of shining water, and quickly settled in upon the forbidden shore, as he now called it, with a contemptuous grin. And the more he saw of the spot, the better he liked it. There was plenty of wood, running water to drink, an open space about the tent, and there were no flies. The fishing, moreover, was magnificent. Morton's description was fully justified, and "stiff with big fish" for once was not an exaggeration.

The useless hours of the early afternoon he passed dozing in the sun, or wandering through the underbrush beyond the camp. He found no sign of anything unusual. He bathed in a cool, deep pool; he revelled in the lonely little paradise. Lonely it certainly was, but the loneliness was part of its charm; the stillness, the peace, the isolation of this beautiful backwoods lake delighted him. The silence was divine. He was entirely satisfied.

After a brew of tea, he strolled toward evening along the shore, looking for the first sign of a rising fish. A faint ripple on the water, with the lengthening shadows, made good conditions. *Plop* followed *plop*, as the big fellows rose, snatched at their food, and vanished into the depths. He hurried back. Ten minutes later he had taken his rods and was gliding cautiously in the canoe through the quiet water.

So good was the sport, indeed, and so quickly did the big trout pile up in the bottom of the canoe that, despite the growing lateness, he found it hard to tear himself away. "One more," he said, "and then I really will go." He landed that "one more," and was in the act of taking it off the hook, when the deep silence of the evening was curiously disturbed. He became abruptly aware that someone watched him. A pair of eyes, it seemed, were fixed upon him from some point in the surrounding shadows.

Thus, at least, he interpreted the odd disturbance in his happy mood; for thus he felt it. The feeling stole over him without the slightest warning. He was not alone. The slippery big trout dropped from his fingers. He sat motionless, and stared about him.

Nothing stirred; the ripple on the lake had died away; there was no wind; the forest lay a single purple mass of shadow; the yellow sky, fast fading, threw reflections that troubled the eye and made distances uncertain. But there was no sound, no movement; he saw no figure anywhere. Yet he knew that someone watched him, and a wave of quite unreasoning terror gripped him. The nose of the canoe was against the bank. In a moment, and instinctively, he shoved it off and paddled into deeper water. The watcher, it came to him also instinctively, was quite close to him upon that bank. But where? And who? Was it the Indian?

Here, in deeper water, and some twenty yards from the shore, he paused and strained both sight and hearing to find some possible clue. He felt half ashamed, now that the first strange feeling passed a little. But the certainty remained. Absurd as it was, he felt positive that someone watched him with concentrated and intent regard. Every fibre in his being told him so; and though he could discover no figure, no new outline on the shore, he could even have sworn in which clump of willow bushes the hidden person crouched and stared. His attention seemed drawn to that particular clump.

The water dripped slowly from his paddle, now lying across the thwarts. There was no other sound. The canvas of his tent gleamed dimly. A star or two were out. He waited. Nothing happened.

Then, as suddenly as it had come, the feeling passed, and he knew that the person who had been watching him intently had gone. It was as if a current had been turned off; the normal world flowed back; the landscape emptied as if someone had left a room. The disagreeable feeling left him at the same time, so that he instantly turned the canoe in to the shore again, landed, and, paddle in hand, went over to examine the clump of willows he had singled out as the place of concealment. There was no one there, of course, nor any trace of recent human occupancy. No leaves, no branches stirred, nor was a single twig displaced; his keen and practised sight detected no sign of tracks upon the ground. Yet for all that, he felt positive that a little time ago someone had crouched among these very leaves and watched him. He remained absolutely convinced of it. The watcher, whether Indian, hunter, stray lumberman, or wandering half-breed, had now withdrawn, a search was useless, and dusk was falling. He returned to his little camp, more disturbed perhaps than he cared to acknowledge. He cooked his supper, hung up his catch on a string, so that no prowling animal could get at it during the night, and prepared to make himself comfortable until bedtime. Unconsciously, he built a bigger fire than usual, and found himself peering over his pipe into the deep shadows beyond the firelight, straining his ears to catch the slightest sound. He remained generally on the alert in a way that was new to him.

A man under such conditions and in such a place need not know discomfort until the sense of loneliness strikes him as too vivid a reality. Loneliness in a backwoods camp brings charm, pleasure, and a happy sense of calm until, and unless, it comes too near. It should remain an ingredient only among other conditions; it should not be directly, vividly noticed. Once it has crept within short range, however, it may easily cross the narrow line between comfort and discomfort, and darkness is an undesirable time for the transition. A curious dread may easily follow—the dread lest the loneliness suddenly be disturbed, and the solitary human feel himself open to attack.

For Hyde, now, this transition had been already accomplished; the too intimate sense of his loneliness had shifted abruptly into the worse condition of no longer being quite alone. It was an awkward moment, and the hotel clerk realized his position exactly. He did not quite like it. He sat there, with his back to the blazing logs, a very visible object in the light, while all about him the darkness of the forest lay like an impenetrable wall. He could not see a foot beyond the small circle of his camp-fire; the silence about him was like the silence of the dead. No leaf rustled, no wave lapped; he himself sat motion-less as a log.

Then again he became suddenly aware that the person who watched him had returned, and that same intent and concentrated gaze as before was fixed upon him where he lay. There was no warning; he heard no steal-thy tread or snapping of dry twigs, yet the owner of those steady eyes was very close to him, probably not a dozen feet away. This sense of proximity was over-whelming.

It is unquestionable that a shiver ran down his spine. This time, moreover, he felt positive that the man crouched just beyond the firelight, the distance he him-self could see being nicely calculated, and straight in front of him. For some minutes he sat without stirring a single muscle, yet with each muscle ready and alert, straining his eyes in vain to pierce the darkness, but only succeeding in dazzling his sight with the reflected light. Then, as he shifted his position slowly, cautiously, to ob-tain another angle of vision, his heart gave two big thumps against his ribs and the hair seemed to rise on his scalp with the sense of cold that shot horribly up his spine. In the darkness facing him he saw two small and greenish circles that were certainly a pair of eyes, yet not the eyes of Indian, hunter, or of any human being. It was a pair of animal eyes that stared so fixedly at him out of the night. And this certainty had an immediate and natural effect upon him.

For, at the menace of those eyes, the fears of millions

of long dead hunters since the dawn of time woke in him. Hotel clerk though he was, heredity surged through him in an automatic wave of instinct. His hand groped for a weapon. His fingers fell on the iron head of his small camp axe, and at once he was himself again. Confidence returned; the vague, superstitious dread was gone. This was a bear or wolf that smelt his catch and came to steal it. With beings of that sort he knew instinctively how to deal, yet admitting, by this very instinct, that his original dread had been of quite another kind.

"I'll damned quick find out what it is," he exclaimed aloud, and snatching a burning brand from the fire, he hurled it with good aim straight at the eyes of the beast before him.

The bit of pitch-pine fell in a shower of sparks that lit the dry grass this side of the animal, flared up a moment, then died quickly down again. But in that instant of bright illumination he saw clearly what his unwelcome visitor was. A big timber wolf sat on its hind quarters, staring steadily at him through the firelight. He saw its legs and shoulders, he saw its hair, he saw also the big hemlock trunks lit up behind it, and the willow scrub on each side. It formed a vivid, clear-cut picture shown in clear detail by the momentary blaze. To his amazement, however, the wolf did not turn and bolt away from the burning log, but withdrew a few yards only, and sat there again on its haunches, staring, staring as before. Heavens, how it stared! He "shooe-d" it, but without effect; it did not budge. He did not waste another good log on it, for his fear was dissipated now; a timber wolf was a timber wolf, and it might sit there as long as it pleased, provided it did not try to steal his catch. No alarm was in him any more. He knew that wolves were harmless in the summer and autumn, and even when "packed" in the winter, they would attack a man only when suffering desperate hunger. So he lay and watched the beast, threw bits of stick in its direction, even talked to it, wondering only that it never moved. "You can stay there for ever, if you like," he remarked to it aloud, "for you cannot get at my fish, and the rest of the grub I shall take into the tent with me!"

The creature blinked its bright green eyes, but made no move.

Why, then, if his fear was gone, did he think of certain things as he rolled himself in the Hudson Bay blankets before going to sleep? The immobility of the animal was strange, its refusal to turn and bolt was still stranger. Never before had he known a wild creature that was not afraid of fire. Why did it sit and watch him, as with purpose in its dreadful eyes? How had he felt its presence earlier and instantly? A timber wolf, especially a solitary timber wolf, was a timid thing, yet this one feared neither man nor fire. Now, as he lay there wrapped in his blankets inside the cosy tent, it sat outside beneath the stars, beside the fading embers, the wind chilly in its fur, the ground cooling beneath its planted paws, watching him, steadily watching him, perhaps until the dawn.

It was unusual, it was strange. Having neither imagination nor tradition, he called upon no store of racial visions. Matter-of-fact, a hotel clerk on a fishing holiday, he lay there in his blankets, merely wondering and puzzled. A timber wolf was a timber wolf and nothing more. Yet this timber wolf—the idea haunted him—was different. In a word, the deeper part of his original uneasiness remained. He tossed about, he shivered sometimes in his broken sleep; he did not go out to see, but he woke early and unrefreshed.

Again, with the sunshine and the morning wind, however, the incident of the night before was forgotten, almost unreal. His hunting zeal was uppermost. The tea and fish were delicious, his pipe had never tasted so good, the glory of this lonely little lake amid the primeval forests went to his head a little; he was a hunter before the Lord, and nothing else. He tried the edge of the lake, and in the excitement of playing a big fish, knew suddenly that *it*, the wolf, was there. He paused with the rod, exactly as if struck. He looked about him, he looked in a definite direction. The brilliant sunshine made every smallest detail clear and sharp—boulders of granite, burned stems, crimson sumach, pebbles along the shore in neat, separate detail—without revealing where the watcher hid. Then, his sight wandering farther inshore among the tangled undergrowth, he suddenly picked up the familiar, half-expected outline. The wolf was lying behind a granite boulder, so that only the head, the muzzle, and the eyes were visible. It merged in its background. Had he not known it was a wolf, he could never have separated it from the landscape. The eyes shone in the sunlight.

There it lay. He looked straight at it. Their eyes, in fact, actually met full and square. "Great Scott!" he exclaimed aloud, "why, it's like looking at a human being!" From that moment, unwittingly, he established a singular personal relation with the beast. And what followed confirmed this undesirable impression, for the animal rose instantly and came down in leisurely fashion to the shore, where it stood looking back at him. It stood and stared into his eyes like some great wild dog, so that he was aware of a new and almost incredible sensation—that it courted recognition.

"Well! well!" he exclaimed again, relieving his feelings by addressing it aloud, "if this doesn't beat everything I ever saw! What d'you want, anyway?"

He examined it now more carefully. He had never seen a wolf so big before; it was a tremendous beast, a nasty customer to tackle, he reflected, if it ever came to that. It stood there absolutely fearless and full of confidence. In the clear sunlight he took in every detail of it—a huge, shaggy, lean-flanked timber wolf, its wicked eyes staring straight into his own, almost with a kind of purpose in them. He saw its great jaws, its teeth, and its tongue, hung out, dropping saliva a little. And yet the idea of its savagery, its fierceness, was very little in him.

He was amazed and puzzled beyond belief. He wished the Indian would come back. He did not understand this strange behaviour in an animal. Its eyes, the odd expression in them, gave him a queer, unusual, difficult feeling. Had his nerves gone wrong? he almost wondered.

The beast stood on the shore and looked at him. He wished for the first time that he had brought a rifle. With a resounding smack he brought his paddle down flat upon the water, using all his strength, till the echoes rang as from a pistol-shot that was audible from one end of the lake to the other. The wolf never stirred. He shouted, but the beast remained unmoved. He blinked his eyes, speaking as to a dog, a domestic animal, a creature accustomed to human ways. It blinked its eyes in return.

At length, increasing his distance from the shore, he continued fishing, and the excitement of the marvellous sport held his attention—his surface attention, at any rate. At times he almost forgot the attendant beast; yet whenever he looked up, he saw it there. And worse; when he slowly paddled home again, he observed it trotting along the shore as though to keep him company. Crossing a little bay, he spurted, hoping to reach the other point before his undesired and undesirable attendant. Instantly the brute broke into that rapid, tireless lope that, except on ice, can run down anything on four legs in the woods. When he reached the distant point, the wolf was waiting for him. He raised his paddle from the water, pausing a moment for reflection; for this very close attention—there were dusk and night yet to come—he certainly did not relish. His camp was near; he had to land; he felt uncomfortable even in the sunshine of broad day, when, to his keen relief, about half a mile from the tent, he saw the creature suddenly stop and sit down in the open. He waited a moment, then paddled on. It did not follow. There was no attempt to move; it merely sat and watched him. After a few hundred yards, he looked back. It was still sitting where he had left it. And the absurd, yet significant, feeling came to him that the beast divined his thought, his anxiety, his dread, and was now showing him, as well as it could, that it entertained no hostile feeling and did not meditate attack.

He turned the canoe toward the shore; he landed; he cooked his supper in the dusk; the animal made no sign. Not far away it certainly lay and watched, but it did not advance. And to Hyde, observant now in a new way, came one sharp, vivid reminder of the strange atmosphere into which his commonplace personality had strayed: he suddenly recalled that his relations with the beast, already established, had progressed distinctly a stage further. This startled him, yet without the accompanying alarm he must certainly have felt twenty-four hours before. He had an understanding with the wolf. He was aware of friendly thoughts towards it. He even went so far as to set out a few big fish on the spot where he had first seen it sitting the previous night. "If he comes," he thought, "he is welcome to them. I've got plenty, anyway." He thought of it now as "he".

Yet the wolf made no appearance until he was in the act of entering his tent a good deal later. It was close on ten o'clock, whereas nine was his hour, and late at that, for turning in. He had, therefore, unconsciously been waiting for him. Then, as he was closing the flap, he saw the eyes close to where he had placed the fish. He waited, hiding himself, and expecting to hear sounds of munching jaws; but all was silence. Only the eyes glowed steadily out of the background of pitch darkness. He closed the flap. He had no slightest fear. In ten minutes he was sound asleep.

He could not have slept very long, for when he woke up he could see the shine of a faint red light through the canvas, and the fire had not died down completely. He rose and cautiously peeped out. The air was very cold;

he saw his breath. But he also saw the wolf, for it had
come in, and was sitting by the dying embers, not two
yards away from where he crouched behind the flap.
And this time, at these very close quarters, there was
something in the attitude of the big wild thing that
caught his attention with a vivid thrill of startled surprise
and a sudden shock of cold that held him spellbound. He
stared, unable to believe his eyes; for the wolf's attitude
conveyed to him something familiar that at first he was
unable to explain. Its pose reached him in the terms of
another thing with which he was entirely at home. What
was it? Did his senses betray him? Was he still asleep and
dreaming?

Then, suddenly, with a start of uncanny recognition,
he knew. Its attitude was that of a dog. Having found the
clue, his mind then made an awful leap. For it was, after
all, no dog its appearance aped, but something nearer to
himself, and more familiar still. Good heavens! It sat
there with the pose, the attitude, the gesture in repose of
something almost human. And then, with a second
shock of biting wonder, it came to him like a revelation.
The wolf sat beside that camp-fire as a man might sit.

Before he could weigh his extraordinary discovery,
before he could examine it in detail or with care, the
animal, sitting in this ghastly fashion, seemed to feel his
eyes fixed on it. It slowly turned and looked him in the
face, and for the first time Hyde felt a full-blooded,
superstitious fear flood through his entire being. He
seemed transfixed with that nameless terror that is said to
attack human beings who suddenly face the dead, finding themselves bereft of speech and movement. This

moment of paralysis certainly occurred. Its passing, however, was as singular as its advent. For almost at once he was aware of something beyond and above this mockery of human attitude and pose, something that ran along unaccustomed nerves and reached his feeling, even perhaps his heart. The revulsion was extraordinary, its result still more extraordinary and unexpected. Yet the fact remains. He was aware of another thing that had the effect of stilling his terror as soon as it was born. He was aware of appeal, silent, half expressed, yet vastly pathetic. He saw in the savage eyes a beseeching, even a yearning, expression that changed his mood as by magic from dread to natural sympathy. The great grey brute, symbol of cruel ferocity, sat there beside his dying fire and appealed for help.

This gulf betwixt animal and human seemed in that instant bridged. It was, of course, incredible. Hyde, sleep still possibly clinging to his inner being with the shades and half shapes of dream yet about his soul, acknowledged, how he knew not, the amazing fact. He found himself nodding to the brute in half consent, and instantly, without more ado, the lean shape rose like a wraith and trotted off swiftly, but with stealthy tread, into the background of the night.

When Hyde woke in the morning his first impression was that he must have dreamed the entire incident. His practical nature asserted itself. There was a bite in the fresh autumn air; the bright sun allowed no half lights anywhere; he felt brisk in mind and body. Reviewing what had happened, he came to the conclusion that it was utterly vain to speculate; no possible explanation of the animal's behaviour occurred to him: he was dealing with something entirely outside his experience. His fear, however, had completely left him. The odd sense of friendliness remained. The beast had a definite purpose, and he himself was included in that purpose. His sympathy held good.

But with the sympathy there was also an intense curiosity. "If it shows itself again," he told himself, "I'll go up close and find out what it wants." The fish laid out the night before had not been touched.

It must have been a full hour after breakfast when he next saw the brute; it was standing on the edge of the clearing, looking at him in a way now become familiar. Hyde immediately picked up his axe and advanced toward it boldly, keeping his eyes fixed straight upon its own. There was nervousness in him, but kept well under; nothing betrayed it; step by step he drew nearer until some ten yards separated them. The wolf had not stirred a muscle as yet. Its jaws hung open, its eyes observed him intently; it allowed him to approach without a sign of what its mood might be. Then, with these ten yards between them it turned abruptly and moved slowly off, looking back first over one shoulder and then over the other, exactly as a dog might do, to see if he was following.

A singular journey it was they then made together, animal and man. The trees surrounded them at once, for they left the lake behind them, entering the tangled bush beyond. The beast, Hyde noticed, obviously picked the easiest track for him to follow; for obstacles that meant nothing to the four-legged expert, yet were difficult for a man, were carefully avoided with an almost uncanny skill, while yet the general direction was accurately kept. Occasionally there were windfalls to be surmounted; but though the wolf bounded over these with ease, it was always waiting for the man on the other side after he had laboriously climbed over. Deeper and deeper into the heart of the lonely forest they penetrated in this singular fashion, cutting across the arc of the lake's crescent, it seemed to Hyde; for after two miles or so, he recognized the big rocky bluff that overhung the water at its northern end. This outstanding bluff he had seen from his camp, one side of it falling sheer into the water; it was probably the spot, he imagined, where the Indians held their medicine-making ceremonies, for it stood out in isolated fashion, and its top formed a private plateau not easy of access. And it was here, close to a big spruce at the foot of the bluff upon the forest side, that the wolf stopped suddenly and for the first time since its appearance gave audible expression to its feelings. It sat down on its haunches, lifted its muzzle with open jaws, and gave vent to a subdued and long-drawn howl that was more like the wail of a dog then the fierce barking cry associated with a wolf.

By this time Hyde had lost not only fear, but caution too; nor, oddly enough, did this warning howl revive a sign of unwelcome emotion in him. In that curious sound he detected the same message that the eyes conveyed—appeal for help. He paused, nevertheless, a little startled, and while the wolf sat waiting for him, he looked about him quickly. There was young timber here; it had once been a small clearing, evidently. Axe and fire had done their work, but there was evidence to an experienced eye that it was Indians and not white men who had once been busy here. Some part of the medicine ritual, doubtless, took place in the little clearing, thought the man, as he advanced again towards his patient leader. The end of their queer journey, he felt, was close at hand.

He had not taken two steps before the animal got up and moved very slowly in the direction of some low bushes that formed a clump just beyond. It entered these, first looking back to make sure that its companion watched. The bushes hid it: a moment later it emerged again. Twice it performed this pantomine, each time, as it reappeared, standing still and staring at the man with as distinct an expression of appeal in the eyes as an animal may compass, probably. Its excitement, meanwhile, certainly increased, and this excitement was, with equal certaintly, communicated to the man. Hyde made up his mind quickly. Gripping his axe tightly, and ready to use it at the first hint of malice, he moved slowly nearer to the bushes, wondering with something of a tremor what would happen.

If he expected to be startled, his expectation was at once fulfilled; but it was the behaviour of the beast that made him jump. It positively frisked about him like a happy dog. It frisked for joy. Its excitement was intense, yet from its open mouth no sound was audible. With a sudden leap, then, it bounded past him into the clump of bushes, against whose very edge he stood, and began scraping vigorously at the ground. Hyde stood and stared, amazement and interest now banishing all his nervous-

411

ness, even when the beast, in its violent scraping, actually touched his body with his own. He had, perhaps, the feeling that he was in a dream, one of those fantastic dreams in which things may happen without involving an adequate surprise; for otherwise the manner of scraping and scratching at the ground must have seemed an impossible phenomenon. No wolf, no dog certainly, used its paws in the way those paws were working. Hyde had the odd, distressing sensation that it was hands, not paws, he watched. And yet, somehow, the natural, adequate surprise he should have felt was absent. The strange action seemed not entirely unnatural. In his heart some deep hidden spring of sympathy and pity stirred instead. He was aware of pathos.

The wolf stopped in its task and looked up into his face. Hyde acted without hesitation then. Afterwards he was wholly at a loss to explain his own conduct. It seemed he knew what to do, divined what was asked, expected, of him. Between his mind and the dumb desire yearning through the savage animal there was intelligent and intelligible communication. He cut a stake and sharpened it, for the stones would blunt his axe-edge. He entered the clump of bushes to complete the digging his four-legged companion had begun. And while he worked, though he did not forget the close proximity of the wolf, he paid no attention to it; often his back was turned as he stooped over the laborious clearing away of the hard earth; no uneasiness or sense of danger was in him any more. The wolf sat outside the clump and watched the operations. Its concentrated attention, its patience, its intense eagerness, the gentleness and docility of the grey, fierce, and probably hungry brute, its obvious pleasure and satisfaction too, at having won the human to its mysterious purpose—these were colours in the strange picture that Hyde thought of later when dealing with the human herd in his hotel again. At the moment he was aware chiefly of pathos and affection. The whole business was, of course, not to be believed, but that discovery came later, too, when telling it to others.

The digging continued for fully half an hour before his labour was rewarded by the discovery of a small whitish object. He picked it up and examined it—the finger-bone of a man. Other discoveries then followed quickly and in quantity. The *cache* was laid bare. He collected nearly the complete skeleton. The skull, however, he found last, and might not have found at all but for the guidance of his strangely alert companion. It lay some few yards away from the central hole now dug, and the wolf stood nuzzling the ground with its nose before Hyde understood that he was meant to dig exactly in that spot for it. Between the beast's very paws his stake struck hard upon it. He scraped the earth from the bone and examined it carefully. It was perfect, save for the fact that some wild animal had gnawed it, the teeth-marks being still plainly visible. Close beside it lay the rusty iron head of a tomahawk. This and the smallness of the bones confirmed him in his judgment that it was the skeleton not of a white man, but of an Indian.

During the excitement of the discovery of the bones one by one, and finally of the skull, but, more especially, during the period of intense interest while Hyde was examining them, he had paid little, if any, attention to the wolf. He was aware that it sat and watched him, never moving its keen eyes for a single moment from the actual operations, but of sign or movement it made none at all. He knew that it was pleased and satisfied, he knew also that he had now fulfilled its purpose in a great measure. The further intuition that now came to him, derived, he felt positive, from his companion's dumb desire, was perhaps the cream of the entire experience to him. Gathering the bones together in his coat, he carried them, together with the tomahawk, to the foot of the big spruce where the animal had first stopped. His leg actually touched the creature's muzzle as he passed. It turned its head to watch, but did not follow, nor did it move a muscle while he prepared the platform of boughs upon which he then laid the poor worn bones of an Indian who had been killed, doubtless, in sudden attack or ambush, and to whose remains had been denied the last grace of proper tribal burial. He wrapped the bones in bark; he laid the tomahawk beside the skull; he lit the circular fire round the pyre, and the blue smoke rose upward into the clear bright sunshine of the Canadian autumn morning till it was lost among the mighty trees far overhead.

In the moment before actually lighting the little fire he had turned to note what his companion did. It sat five yards away, he saw, gazing intently, and one of its front paws was raised a little from the ground. It made no sign of any kind. He finished the work, becoming so absorbed in it that he had eyes for nothing but the tending and

414

guarding of his careful ceremonial fire. It was only when the platform of boughs collapsed, laying their charred burden gently on the fragant earth among the soft wood ashes, that he turned again, as though to show the wolf what he had done, and seek, perhaps, some look of satisfaction in its curiously expressive eyes. But the place he searched was empty. The wolf had gone.

He did not see it again; it gave no sign of its presence anywhere; he was not watched. He fished as before, wandered through the bush about his camp, sat smoking round his fire after dark, and slept peacefully in his cosy little tent. He was not disturbed. No howl was ever audible in the distant forest, no twig snapped beneath a stealthy tread, he saw no eyes. The wolf that behaved like a man had gone for ever.

It was the day before he left that Hyde, noticing smoke rising from the shack across the lake, paddled over to exchange a word or two with the Indian, who had evidently now returned. The Redskin came down to meet him as he landed, but it was soon plain that he spoke very little English. He emitted the familiar grunts at first; then bit by bit Hyde stirred his limited vocabulary into action. The net result, however, was slight enough, though it was certainly direct.

"You camp there?" the man asked, pointing to the other side.

"Yes."

"Wolf come?"

"Yes."

"You see wolf?"

"Yes."

The Indian stared at him fixedly a moment, a keen, wondering look upon his coppery, creased face.

"You 'fraid wolf?" he asked after a moment's pause.

"No," replied Hyde, truthfully. He knew it was useless to ask questions of his own, though he was eager for information. The other would have told him nothing. It was sheer luck that the man had touched on the subject at all, and Hyde realized that his own best role was merely to answer, but to ask no questions. Then, suddenly, the Indian became comparatively voluble. There was awe in his voice and manner.

"Him no wolf. Him big medicine wolf. Him spirit wolf."

Whereupon he drank the tea the other had brewed for him, closed his lips tightly, and said no more. His outline was discernible on the shore, rigid and motionless, an hour later, when Hyde's canoe turned the corner of the lake three miles away, and he landed to make the portages up the first rapid of his homeward stream.

It was Morton who, after some persuasion, supplied further details of what he called the legend. Some hundred years before, the tribe that lived in the territory beyond the lake began their annual medicine-making ceremonies on the big rocky bluff at the northern end; but no medicine could be made. The spirits, declared the chief medicine man, would not answer. They were offended. An investigation followed. It was discovered that a young brave had recently killed a wolf, a thing strictly forbidden since the wolf was the totem animal of the tribe. To make matters worse, the name of the guilty man was Running Wolf. The offence being unpardonable, the man was cursed and driven from the tribe.

"Go out. Wander alone among the woods, and if we see you we slay you. Your bones shall be scattered in the forest, and your spirit shall not enter the Happy Hunting Grounds till one of another race shall find and bury them."

"Which meant," explained Morton laconically, his only comment on the story, "probably for ever."

ALGERNON BLACKWOOD

ACKNOWLEDGMENTS

For very kind permission to include in this Collection the following stories and rhymes, I am most grateful:

To Mr. S. R. Littlewood for his translation of "Puss in Boots" from Charles Perrault's *Fairy Tales*;

To Mr. John Masefield (and Messrs. Ivor Nicholson & Watson Ltd.) for "A Sailor's Yarn" and "The Seal Man" from *A Mainsail Haul*;

To Mr. Algernon Blackwood for "Running Wolf" from *Wolves of God*;

To Mr. W. H. Auden and Mr. John Garrett for two old nursery rhymes and a folk song from *The Poet's Tongue*;

To Miss Blanche Cowley Young for "How the Manx Cat Lost its Tail", a story published in an American magazine, *Story Parade*;

To Mr. Colin Francis for his poem, "Tony O";

To Messrs. Longmans, Green & Co Ltd. for a rhyme, entitled "The Hare", from *Songs of Childhood*;

To Messrs. Faber & Faber Ltd. for "The Lord Fish" from a Collection of stories of the same title;

To Mr. Basil Blackwell for my versions, since revised, of "The Hare and the Hedgehog" and "The Wolf and the Fox" from *Told Again*; also for "All Gone" from *Readings*, and there entitled "The Pot of Fat";

And last to Mr. Arthur I. Ellis and to Messrs. Maggs for their very kind help in connection with the illustrations in this volume.

ACKNOWLEDGMENTS

Five of the following stories, marked with an asterisk in the Table of Contents—of which "The Ass, the Table, and the Stick" has been to some extent revised—have been taken from an admirable volume entitled *English Fairy Tales*, collected and adapted by Joseph Jacobs and published in 1890. I owe my first acquaintance with this to a friend.

"The Bad Mother" and "Tropsyn" are from a volume entitled *Gypsy Folk-Tales,* edited by Francis Hindes Groome, and published in 1899. I much regret that I have been unable to obtain any information in respect to the present ownership of the copyright of this Collection.

"The Derby Ram", "The Tree in the Valley" and "The Crocodile" are traditional songs which have been taken from a Collection with musical settings, compiled by Miss Lucy Broadwood and by Mr. Fuller Maitland, and published by the Leadenhall Press in 1893.

If, through inadvertence, I have omitted to make acknowledgment where it is due, I beg to offer my sincere apologies to those concerned.